MARK TWAIN'S
TALES
OF THE
MACABRE &
MYSTERIOUS

T0268193

MARK TWAIN'S TALES OF THE MACABRE & MYSTERIOUS

Edited by

R. KENT RASMUSSEN

LYONS
PRESS

ESSEX, CONNECTICUT

An imprint of The Globe Pequot Publishing Group, Inc.
64 South Main Street
Essex, CT 06426
www.globepequot.com

Distributed by NATIONAL BOOK NETWORK

British Library Cataloguing in Publication Information Available

Library of Congress Cataloging-in-Publication Data

Names: Twain, Mark, 1835–1910, author. | Rasmussen, R. Kent, editor.
Title: Mark Twain's tales of the macabre & mysterious / edited by R. Kent
  Rasmussen.
Description: Essex, Connecticut : Lyons Press, [2024]
Identifiers: LCCN 2024015200 (print) | LCCN 2024015201 (ebook) | ISBN
  9781493086139 (paperback) | ISBN 9781493086146 (epub)
Subjects: LCSH: Short stories, American—19th century. | Short stories,
  American—20th century.
Classification: LCC PS1303 .R37 2024 (print) | LCC PS1303 (ebook) | DDC
  813/.4—dc23/eng/20240508
LC record available at https://lccn.loc.gov/2024015200
LC ebook record available at https://lccn.loc.gov/2024015201

For my pals

MARK DAWIDZIAK—

imaginative film scholar, clever writer, talented actor,

and master of the macabre in his own unique way

and

TIM CHAMPLIN—

clever novelist and dialogue expert who has written almost as much about

Tom Sawyer and Huck Finn as Mark Twain did

CONTENTS

NOTE ON THE TEXTS AND ILLUSTRATIONS

Texts of the stories in this book are mostly exactly as they appeared in their original publications. In addition to silently correcting obvious typographical errors, I have occasionally changed Mark Twain's eccentric spellings and punctuation and have replaced a small number of words now considered offensive with italicized words enclosed in square brackets. Most of the text selections are complete, but some are excerpts from longer works, such as Mark Twain's travel books, and I have indicated deleted portions with ellipses. Mark Twain often wrote some painfully long paragraphs, some of which I have broken up to make reading them easier.

To help focus attention on macabre and mysterious themes, I have given most of the tales fresh titles. In all cases, however, the original titles are also supplied at the end of each text.

This volume may be considered unusual in that *every* image in its stories is entirely original. I have created all the pictures with the aid of Microsoft Bing's online Image Creator program, which uses artificial intelligence (AI) to construct images from an immense databank of digitized pictures. Some pictures in the present volume illustrate stories that have never—to my knowledge—been illustrated before, such as "The Facts Concerning the Recent Carnival of Crime in Connecticut," which appears below as "Facing One's Most Pitiless Enemy." The photo-realistic details in many of the pictures and their relevance to the texts are a tribute to the incredible advances in AI technology.

—The Editor

INTRODUCTION

An outstanding characteristic of the immense body of works that Mark Twain wrote is their diversity. His writings include novels, short stories, news articles, sketches, letters, travel books, essays, and more. He was an insatiable reader whose broad interests moved him to write about almost every imaginable subject—from ordinary domestic life to world politics, science, technology, geography, religion, philosophy, and much more. He was no respecter of genre boundaries, so another characteristic of many of his writings is the difficulty one has labeling them with specific genres. His travel books, for example, are marvelously chaotic blends of sober reportage, autobiographical reminiscences, and pure invention. Should those books be regarded as fiction or nonfiction? Few readers agree. Some even classify the travel books as "novels." In fact, some of his autobiographic writings have been called fiction. His official biographer, Albert Bigelow Paine, who knew him well and worked closely with him when he was dictating his autobiography to a stenographer over a long period, wrote that after listening to Mark Twain's "marvelous reminiscences," he came to realize they "bore only an atmospheric relation to history . . ." In reading anything that Mark Twain wrote about his own life, therefore, we need not be overly punctilious about distinctions between fact and fiction.

The term "macabre" is usually understood as pertaining to death or gruesome things and is sometimes used as a synonym for "horror." Mark Twain clearly wrote a lot about death and sometimes about things that are gruesome, but "horror" doesn't quite seem right to describe any of his writings. It thus makes sense that of the many different genre terms assigned to his writings, one term that is almost never used is "horror." In a way, that is ironic, as the vampire novel *Dracula* (1897), written by his Irish friend Bram Stoker, actually alludes to him directly! In chapter 14 of that classic horror story, Professor Van Helsing tells a group of vampire hunters, "I heard once of an American who so defined faith: 'that faculty which enables us to believe things which we know to be untrue.' For one, I follow that man." "That man" was, in fact, Mark Twain himself. However, aside from Mark Twain's own offhand mention of an imaginary novel titled *Gonderil the Vampire*,

Or, the Dance of Death in chapter 34 of his co-authored novel, *The Gilded Age* (1874), *Dracula*'s allusion to him is as close as Mark Twain himself ever got to vampires in any book during his lifetime. Although he owned a personally inscribed copy of Stoker's novel, he is not known for certain to have read it. (According to Alan Gribben's monumental *Mark Twain's Literary Resources*, vol. 2, 2022, physical signs on his copy of the novel suggest that he may have started reading the book but didn't get very far.) When it comes to horror fiction, Mark Twain was such an innocent that another pervasive genre term, "zombie," seems never to have appeared in any of his writings, and it's not clear he was even aware of the word. (Readers of his sketch "A Literary Nightmare" in the present volume may, however, object that Mark Twain was at least aware of the concept of zombiism.)

While it's fair to say that Mark Twain wrote macabre stories, it would be a stretch to say he wrote horror fiction. He wrote a great many stories, and even some autobiographical reminiscences, containing horrific elements, but he wrote few of such stories with the conscious intent to shock, startle, or repulse his readers. Nevertheless, some of his works have that effect. For example, a respected literary scholar once famously called Mark Twain's novel *The Adventures of Tom Sawyer* (1876) "a nightmare vision of American boyhood" and suggested it was an inappropriate book for children (or perhaps anyone else) to read. Happily, that scholar's view has been persuasively debunked, but the novel really does have disturbing undertones. After all, Tom Sawyer goes through most of its narrative fearing that the murderous Injun Joe is going to kill him after he testifies against Joe in Muff Potter's murder trial. (Never mind the fact that Joe never actually makes a move against Tom.)

The present volume collects thirty-two stories and extracts from longer works that have macabre or mysterious elements. It is designed primarily as a fun book to read, but part of its purpose is serious—to call attention to some of Mark Twain's least-known and unjustly overlooked writings. For that reason, readers will not find here any passages from Mark Twain's most famous works, such as *The Adventures of Tom Sawyer*, in which Tom has frightening encounters with Injun Joe in a midnight graveyard scene and inside a pitch-black labyrinthine cavern, or *Adventures of Huckleberry Finn* (1885), among whose chilling adventures are Huck's near-encounter with a band of ruthless murderers inside a wrecked steamboat minutes away from total destruction. Readers will instead find such underappreciated tales as "Politically Correct Cannibals" (originally known as "Cannibalism in the Cars"), whose very title suggests macabre happenings on a passenger train stalled by a prairie blizzard, and "Joy Cometh in the Mourning" (a.k.a. "The Undertaker's Tale"), which explores the gruesomely inverted relationship between the health of a community and the health of a mortuary business.

About a third of the tales in this book are extracted from four of Mark Twain's travel books—*The Innocents Abroad* (1869), *Roughing It* (1872), *A Tramp Abroad* (1880), and *Life on the Mississippi* (1883). None of these books is exactly obscure, but given the length and complexity of the volumes, it is easy for readers not to fully savor the delights of the macabre and mysterious tales they contain. It is hoped that by extracting some of those tales and enhancing them with provocative original illustrations, readers will appreciate them more fully. The first such tale in this volume, for example, "The Dead-House," from *Life on the Mississippi*, is a macabre and richly complex story of gory revenge with a powerful Gothic feel.

Mark Twain wrote a great deal about death, murder, and funerals in his various works, but nowhere more so, perhaps, than in *Roughing It*. That partly fictionalized and often hilarious account of his time in the Far West during the early 1860s contains more than its share of murder and frontier violence. It also has some almost sweetly macabre passages about funerals. The best of these, appearing below as "That Mysterious Country from Whose Bourne No Traveler Returns," revolves around the difficult struggle of a stalwart ruffian named Scotty Briggs to make funeral arrangements for a friend with a refined young pastor from the East who is new to western Nevada. This passage is one of Mark Twain's most delicious examples of an extended dialogue. What makes Scotty and the pastor's conversation so much fun is the bewildering variety of ways each of them speaks of death—a mysterious country, indeed!

In addition to its extracts from travel books, this volume contains several extracts from Mark Twain's novels. The first of these is from *The Prince and the Pauper* (1881), his novel about sixteenth-century England in which a lowly pauper boy named Tom Canty accidentally changes places with Prince Edward VI, who happens to look exactly like him. Edward was a real historical figure who became king when his father, Henry VIII, died in 1547. In the context of the novel, as the royal prince's accidental replacement, Tom Canty himself becomes king and, not surprisingly, finds himself in some strange situations, such as his encounter with an accused witch in "The Witch & the Pauper," below. *The Prince and the Pauper* is not one of Mark Twain's obscure works, but the spookiness of the passage about a witch is easily overlooked.

Another of Mark Twain's novels extracted here is *A Connecticut Yankee in King Arthur's Court* (1889), his story about a late-nineteenth-century man, the Yankee, who is inexplicably sent back to sixth-century England, which he tries to modernize, drawing on his deep technical knowledge, skills, and inventiveness. Any story mixing an agent of modern science and democratic values with technologically primitive and superstitious beliefs is bound to send sparks flying, and Mark Twain's novel doesn't disappoint. The novel is full of violent and macabre elements, not to mention myriad mysteries. Extracted here are two passages of special interest. The first—"Welcome to the Sixth Century!"— describes the superstitious nonsense the Yankee must cut through to survive. The second, "The Fragility of Fame," is an example of Mark Twain's use of simple logic to expose a fraudulent magician.

Although it has been in print in many editions for well over one hundred years, *Christian Science* has always been one of Mark Twain's least-read books. Most of it, frankly, is a tedious denunciation of Mary Baker Eddy, the founder of the Church of Christ, Scientist, whose writings on religion he found incomprehensible. The book opens, however, with an entertaining burlesque in which Mark Twain describes being treated by a Christian Science "doctor" after he sustains terrible injuries from falling off a cliff. Presented below as "Nothing Exists but Mind," the passage is another excellent example of a dialogue between two people incapable of a meeting of the minds.

The tales in this collection are informally arranged under these six broad subject headings: "Tales Spooky & Grisly," "Unpleasant Places," "Remarkable Characters," "Curious Talk & Strange Obsessions," "Worlds Remote in Time & Space," and "Ironic Twists & Clever Deceptions." Many of the tales would easily fit under more than one category, but that shouldn't get in the way of readers enjoying them!

The volume concludes, appropriately, with an unusual obituary summarizing Mark Twain's incredible life.

PART I.

—————•—————

Tales Spooky & Grisly

Although Mark Twain has never been known for writing horror stories, spooky and grisly elements pervade his writings, especially his earliest works, such as his novel *The Adventures of Tom Sawyer* (1876). In that famous story, many bad things happen to Tom and his friends. Throughout much of the book, Tom is beset by horrific nightmares of being killed by the murderous Injun Joe. Tom's nightmares may have set the stage for the frightening dreams characters have in many of Mark Twain's later writings. This section, however, presents some of his more straightforwardly spooky and grisly tales, beginning with "A Bloody Massacre," a gory hoax that helped make him famous—or perhaps infamous—during his early writing career when he was a Nevada journalist. Next is one of his earliest dream stories, about a ghost he encounters in a lonely New York hotel. Mark Twain didn't write a lot about witches, but the next story is about the pauper boy Tom Canty, of *The Prince and the Pauper*, encountering an accused witch during the brief period when he accidentally finds himself accepted as the true king of England. Next, in "Out of Focus Imaginations," a young man is accompanying the recently deceased body of a friend in a long-distance train's baggage car. His sad journey starts out fine but starts to go bad when he and the baggage expressman are gradually overwhelmed by a fetid stench that their overcharged imaginations make unbearable. The "Dead-House" chapter from *Life on the Mississippi* is full of grisly scenes, including a dramatically macabre moment in the German dead-house itself. Finally, "The Cross of the Mysterious Avenger," also from *Life on the Mississippi*, is about one of Mark Twain's boyhood heroes—a bloodthirsty carpenter who has dedicated his own life to cruelly ending the life of every person he meets named Lynch.

1.

"A BLOODY MASSACRE"

Mark Twain wrote this brief sketch for Virginia City's Territorial Enterprise *when he was a news reporter in Nevada in 1863; it may be his most macabre story. It's certainly one of his bloodiest pieces of writing, and it's definitely not for the squeamish!*

From Abram Curry, who arrived here yesterday afternoon from Carson [City], we have learned the following particulars concerning the bloody massacre which was committed in Ormsby county night before last. It seems that during the past six months a man named P. Hopkins, or Philip Hopkins, has been residing with his family in the old log house just at the edge of the great pine forest, which lies between Empire City and Dutch Nick's. The family consisted of nine children—five girls and four boys—the oldest of the group, Mary, being nineteen years old, and the youngest, Tommy, about a year and a half. Twice in the past two months Mrs. Hopkins, while visiting in Carson, expressed fears concerning the sanity of her husband, remarking that of late he had been subject to fits of violence, and that during the prevalence of one of these he had threatened to take her life. It was Mrs. Hopkins' misfortune to be given to exaggeration, however, and but little attention was paid to what she said.

About ten o'clock on Monday evening Hopkins dashed into Carson on horseback, with his throat cut from ear to ear, and bearing in his hand a reeking scalp from which the warm, smoking blood was still dripping, and fell in a dying condition in front of the Magnolia saloon. Hopkins expired in the course of five minutes, without speaking. The long red hair of the scalp he bore marked it as that of Mrs. Hopkins. A number of citizens, headed by Sheriff Gasherie, mounted at once and rode down to Hopkins' house, where a ghastly scene met their gaze. The scalpless corpse of Mrs. Hopkins lay across the threshold, with her head split open and her right hand almost severed from the wrist. Near her lay the ax with which the murderous deed had been committed. In one of the bedrooms six of the children were found, one in bed, and the others scattered about the floor. They were all dead. Their brains had evidently been dashed out with a club, and every mark about them seemed to have been made with a blunt instrument. The children must have struggled hard for their lives, as articles of clothing and broken furniture were strewn about the room in the upmost confusion. Julia and Emma, aged respectively, fourteen and seventeen, were found in the kitchen, bruised and insensible, but it is thought their recovery is possible. The eldest girl, Mary, must have taken refuge, in her terror, in the garret, as her body was found there, frightfully, mutilated, and the knife with which her wounds had been inflicted still sticking in her side. The two girls, Julia and Emma, who had recovered sufficiently to be able to talk yesterday morning, state that their father knocked them down with a billet of wood and stamped on them. They think they were the first attacked. They further state that Hopkins had shown evidence of derangement all day, but had exhibited no violence. He flew into a passion and attempted to murder them because they advised him to go to bed and compose his mind.

His throat slashed from ear to ear, Hopkins starts to collapse after riding four miles from his home to the town's Magnolia Saloon.

Curry says Hopkins was about forty-two years of age, and a native of Western Pennsylvania; he was always affable and polite, and until very recently we had never heard of his ill treating his family. He had been a heavy owner in the best mines of Virginia [City] and Gold Hill, but when the San Francisco newspapers exposed the game of cooking dividends in order to bolster up our stocks he grew afraid and sold out, and invested to an immense amount in the Spring Valley Water Company of San Francisco. He was advised to do this by a relative of his, one of the editors of the San Francisco *Bulletin*, who had suffered pecuniarily by the dividend-cooking scheme as applied to Daney Mining Company recently. Hopkins had not long ceased to own in the various claims on the Comstock lead, however, when several dividends were cooked on his newly acquired property, their water totally dried up, and Spring Valley stock went down to nothing. It is presumed that this misfortune drove him mad and resulted in his killing himself and the greater portion of his family. The newspapers of San Francisco permitted this water company to go on borrowing money and cooking dividends, under cover of which cunning financiers crept out of the tottering concern, leaving the crash to come upon poor and unsuspecting stockholders, without offering to expose the villainy at work. We hope the fearful massacre detailed above may prove the saddest result of their silence.

—"A Bloody Massacre Near Carson" (1863)

Readers of this grisly tale may be pleased to learn that it is a complete hoax, even though the Territorial Enterprise *originally published it as a legitimate news story. Mark Twain wrote it to call attention to shady dealings in a San Francisco water company by claiming that one of its investors was driven mad by its stock-cooking schemes. Other West Coast newspapers reprinted the story, accepting it as authentic news, and Mark Twain's reputation as a serious journalist took a dive, despite his quickly issuing an apologetic explanation. Seven years later, he published a fuller explanation, which called attention to such details as the story's geographical absurdities and the fact that Hopkins—the man who murdered his family—was a well-known bachelor who had no family. And for those unfamiliar with western Nevada's residents and geography, he pointed out the most obvious absurdity of all: that any man who slashed his throat—a wound that "would kill an elephant in the twinkling of an eye"—could not jump on a horse and ride four miles before dropping dead.*

2.

"THE GHOST WHO MADE
AN ASS OF HIMSELF"

———••·•——

Around the year 1870, America was abuzz with excitement about the discovery in upstate New York of a petrified human body that came to be known as the "Cardiff Giant." Confronting the ten-and-one-half-foot tall ghost of that giant in a dark unfamiliar room would unnerve anyone, even if the "giant" proved to be a hoax—and Mark Twain, as we've seen, loved hoaxes. Here he describes meeting that ghost in a spooky hotel in New York City, not far from the museum in which showman P. T. Barnum housed the giant itself.

———••·•——

I took a large room, far up Broadway, in a huge old building whose upper stories had been wholly unoccupied for years, until I came. The place had long been given up to dust and cobwebs, to solitude and silence. I seemed groping among the tombs and invading the privacy of the dead, that first night I climbed up to my quarters. For the first time in my life a superstitious dread came over me; and as I turned a dark angle of the stairway and an invisible cobweb swung its lazy woof in my face and clung there, I shuddered as one who had encountered a phantom.

I was glad enough when I reached my room and locked out the mould and the darkness. A cheery fire was burning in the grate, and I sat down before it with a comforting sense of relief. For two hours I sat there, thinking of bygone times; recalling old scenes, and summoning half-forgotten faces out of the mists of the past; listening, in fancy, to voices that long ago grew silent for all time, and to once familiar songs that nobody sings now. And as my reverie softened down to a sadder and sadder pathos, the shrieking of the winds outside softened to a wail, the angry beating of the rain against the panes diminished to a tranquil patter, and one by one the noises in the street subsided, until the hurrying footsteps of the last belated straggler died away in the distance and left no sound behind.

The fire had burned low. A sense of loneliness crept over me. I arose and undressed, moving on tip-toe about the room, doing stealthily what I had to do, as if I were environed by sleeping enemies whose slumbers it would be fatal to break. I covered up in bed, and lay listening to the rain and wind and the faint creaking of distant shutters, till they lulled me to sleep.

I slept profoundly, but how long I do not know. All at once I found myself awake, and filled with a shuddering expectancy. All was still. All but my own heart—I could hear it beat. Presently the bed clothes began to slip away slowly toward the foot of the bed, as if some one were pulling them! I could not stir; I could not speak. Still the blankets slipped deliberately away, till my breast was uncovered. Then with a great effort I seized them and drew them over my head. I waited, listened, waited. Once more that steady pull began, and once more I lay torpid a century of dragging seconds till my breast was naked again. At last I roused my energies and snatched the covers back to their place and held them with a strong grip. I waited. By and by I felt a faint tug, and took a fresh grip. The tug strengthened to a steady strain—it grew stronger and stronger. My hold parted, and for the third time the blankets slid away. I groaned. An answering groan came from the foot of the bed! Beaded drops of sweat stood upon my forehead. I was more dead than alive. Presently I heard a heavy footstep in my room—the step of an elephant, it seemed to me—it was not like anything human. But it was moving *from* me—there was relief in that. I heard it approach the door—pass out without moving bolt or lock—and wander away among the dismal corridors, straining the floors and joists till they creaked again as it passed—and then silence reigned once more.

When my excitement had calmed, I said to myself, "This is a dream—simply a hideous dream." And so I lay thinking it over until I convinced myself that it *was* a dream, and then a comforting laugh relaxed my lips and I was happy again. I got up and struck a light; and when I found that the locks and bolts were just as I had left them, another soothing laugh welled in my heart and rippled from my lips. I took my pipe and lit it, and was just sitting down before the fire, when—down went the pipe out of my nerveless fingers, the blood forsook my cheeks, and my placid breathing was cut short with a gasp! In the ashes on the hearth, side by side with my own bare footprint, was another, so vast that in comparison mine was but an infant's! Then I *had* had a visitor, and the elephant tread was explained.

I put out the light and returned to bed, palsied with fear. I lay a long time, peering into the darkness, and listening. Then I heard a grating noise overhead, like the dragging of a heavy body across the floor; then the throwing down of the body, and the shaking of my windows in response to the concussion. In distant parts of the building I heard the muffled slamming of doors. I heard, at intervals, stealthy footsteps creeping in and out among the corridors, and up and down the stairs. Sometimes these noises approached my door, hesitated, and went away again. I heard the clanking of chains faintly, in remote passages, and listened while the clanking grew nearer—while it wearily climbed the stairways, marking each move by the loose surplus of chain that fell with an accented rattle upon each succeeding step as the goblin that bore it advanced. I heard muttered sentences; half-uttered screams that seemed smothered violently; and the swish of invisible garments, the rush of invisible wings. Then I became conscious that my chamber was invaded—that I was not alone. I heard sighs and breathings about my bed, and mysterious whisperings. Three little spheres of soft phosphorescent light appeared on the ceiling directly over my head, clung and glowed there a moment, and then dropped—two of them upon my face and one upon the pillow. They spattered, liquidly, and felt warm. Intuition told me they had turned to gouts of blood as they fell—I needed no light to satisfy myself of that. Then I saw pallid faces, dimly luminous, and white uplifted hands, floating bodiless in the air— floating a moment and then disappearing. The whispering ceased, and the voices and the sounds, and a solemn stillness followed. I waited and listened. I felt that I must have light or die. I was weak with fear. I slowly raised myself toward a sitting posture, and my face came in contact with a clammy hand! All strength went from me apparently, and I fell back like a stricken invalid. Then I heard the rustle of a garment—it seemed to pass to the door and go out.

When everything was still once more, I crept out of bed, sick and feeble, and lit the gas with a hand that trembled as if it were aged with a hundred years. The light brought some little cheer to my spirits. I sat down and fell into a dreamy contemplation of that great footprint in the ashes. By and by its outlines began to waver and grow dim. I glanced up and the broad gas flame was slowly wilting away. In the same moment I heard that elephantine tread again. I noted its approach, nearer and nearer, along the musty halls, and dimmer and dimmer the light waned. The tread reached my very door and paused—the light had dwindled to a sickly blue, and all things about me lay in a spectral twilight. The door did not open, and yet I felt a faint gust of air fan my cheek, and presently was conscious of a huge, cloudy presence before me. I watched it with fascinated eyes. A pale glow stole over the Thing; gradually its cloudy folds took shape—an arm appeared, then legs, then a body, and last a great sad face looked out of the vapor. Stripped of its filmy housings, naked, muscular and comely, the majestic Cardiff Giant loomed above me!

All my misery vanished—for a child might know that no harm could come with that benignant countenance. My cheerful spirits returned at once, and in sympathy with them the gas flamed up brightly again. Never a lonely outcast was so glad to welcome company as I was to greet the friendly giant. I said:

"Why, is it nobody but you? Do you know, I have been scared to death for the last two or three hours? I am most honestly glad to see you. I wish I had a chair— Here, here, don't try to sit down in that thing!"

Wrapping himself in a blanket, the Cardiff Giant makes himself comfortable.

But it was too late. He was in it before I could stop him, and down he went—I never saw a chair shivered so in my life.

"Stop, stop, you'll ruin ev—"

Too late again. There was another crash, and another chair was resolved into its original elements.

"Confound it, haven't you got any judgment at all? Do you want to ruin all the furniture on the place? Here, here, you petrified foo—"

But it was no use. Before I could arrest him he had sat down on the bed, and it was a melancholy ruin.

"Now what sort of a way is that to do? First you come lumbering about the place bringing a legion of vagabond goblins along with you to worry me to death, and then when I overlook an indelicacy of costume which would not be tolerated anywhere by cultivated people except in a respectable theater, and not even there if the nudity were of *your* sex, you repay me by wrecking all the furniture you can find to sit down on. And why will you? You damage yourself as much as you do me. You have broken off the end of your spinal column, and littered up the floor with chips of your hams till the place looks like a marble yard. You ought to be ashamed of yourself—you are big enough to know better."

"Well, I will not break any more furniture. But what am I to do? I have not had a chance to sit down for a century." And the tears came into his eyes.

"Poor devil," I said, "I should not have been so harsh with you. And you are an orphan, too, no doubt. But sit down on the floor here—nothing else can stand your weight—and besides, we cannot be sociable with you away up there above me; I want you down where I can perch on this high counting-house stool and gossip with you face to face."

So he sat down on the floor, and lit a pipe which I gave him, threw one of my red blankets over his shoulders, inverted my sitz-bath on his head, helmet fashion, and made himself picturesque and comfortable. Then he crossed his ankles, while I renewed the fire, and exposed the flat, honey-combed bottoms of his prodigious feet to the grateful warmth.

"What is the matter with the bottom of your feet and the back of your legs, that they are gouged up so?"

"Infernal chilblains—I caught them clear up to the back of my head, roosting out there under Newell's farm. But I love the place; I love it as one loves his old home. There is no peace for me like the peace I feel when I am there."

We talked along for half an hour, and then I noticed that he looked tired, and spoke of it.

"Tired?" he said. "Well, I should think so. And now I will tell you all about it, since you have treated me so well. I am the spirit of the Petrified Man that lies across the street there in the Museum. I am the ghost of the Cardiff Giant. I can have no rest, no peace, till they have given that poor body burial again. Now what was the most natural thing for me to do, to make men satisfy this wish? Terrify them into it!—haunt the place where the body lay! So I haunted the museum night after night. I even got other spirits to help me. But it did no good, for nobody ever came to the museum at midnight. Then it occurred to me to come over the way and haunt this place a little. I felt that if I ever got a hearing I must succeed, for I had the most efficient company that perdition could furnish. Night after night we have shivered around through these mildewed halls, dragging chains, groaning, whispering, tramping up and down stairs, till, to tell you the truth, I am almost worn out. But when I saw a light in your room to-night I roused my energies again and went at it with a deal of the old freshness. But I am tired out—entirely fagged out. Give me, I beseech you, give me some hope!"

I lit off my perch in a burst of excitement, and exclaimed:

"This transcends everything—everything that ever did occur! Why you poor blundering old fossil, you have had all your trouble for nothing—you have been haunting a *plaster cast* of yourself—the real Cardiff Giant is in Albany! Confound it, don't you know your own remains?"

I never saw such an eloquent look of shame, of pitiable humiliation, overspread a countenance before.

The Petrified Man rose slowly to his feet, and said:

"Honestly, *is* that true?"

"As true as I am sitting here."

He took the pipe from his mouth and laid it on the mantel, then stood irresolute a moment (unconsciously, from old habit, thrusting his hands where his pantaloons pockets should have been, and meditatively dropping his chin on his breast), and finally said:

"Well—I *never* felt so absurd before. The Petrified Man has sold everybody else, and now the mean fraud has ended by selling its own ghost! My son, if there is any charity left in your heart for a poor friendless phantom like me, don't let this get out. Think how *you* would feel if you had made such an ass of yourself."

I heard his stately tramp die away, step by step down the stairs and out into the deserted street, and felt sorry that he was gone, poor fellow—and sorrier still that he had carried off my red blanket and my bath tub.

—"A Ghost Story" (1870)

———————

As Mark Twain himself points out in a footnote to this story, the Cardiff Giant was, indeed, a giant hoax. Being the ghost of a hoax is bad enough, but when the ghost realizes that the giant it has been haunting in P. T. Barnum's New York City museum isn't even the "genuine" giant, its mortification is complete. It is, incidentally, true that when the ghost left, he took the narrator's blanket and sitz-bath with him.

———————

3.

"THE WITCH & THE PAUPER"

———••••———

The time is the mid-sixteenth century, and the place is the royal court in London, England. The pauper boy Tom Canty and his exact lookalike, the Prince of Wales, have playfully switched clothes. Thanks to a series of accidents, they have also switched roles, and now King Henry's death has placed the pauper boy on the throne of England! After four days as king, Tom is beginning to find his way, and he uses his new powers to investigate cases of witchcraft.

———••••———

The next day the foreign ambassadors came, with their gorgeous trains; and Tom, throned in awful state, received them. The splendors of the scene delighted his eye and fired his imagination at first, but the audience was long and dreary, and so were most of the addresses—wherefore, what began as a pleasure, grew into weariness and homesickness by and by. Tom said the words which Hertford put into his mouth from time to time, and tried hard to acquit himself satisfactorily, but he was too new to such things, and too ill at ease to accomplish more than a tolerable success. He looked sufficiently like a king, but he was ill able to feel like one. He was cordially glad when the ceremony was ended.

The larger part of his day was "wasted"—as he termed it, in his own mind—in labors pertaining to his royal office. Even the two hours devoted to certain princely pastimes and recreations were rather a burden to him than otherwise, they were so fettered by restrictions and ceremonious observances. However, he had a private hour with his whipping-boy which he counted clear gain, since he got both entertainment and needful information out of it.

The third day of Tom Canty's kingship came and went much as the others had done, but there was a lifting of his cloud in one way—he felt less uncomfortable than at first; he was getting a little used to his circumstances and surroundings; his chains still galled, but not all the time; he found that the presence and homage of the great afflicted and embarrassed him less and less sharply with every hour that drifted over his head.

But for one single dread, he could have seen the fourth day approach without serious distress—the dining in public; it was to begin that day. There were greater matters in the program—for on that day he would have to preside at a Council which would take his views and commands concerning the policy to be pursued toward various foreign nations scattered far and near over the great globe; on that day, too, Hertford would be formally chosen to the grand office of Lord Protector; other things of note were appointed for that fourth day also, but to Tom they were all insignificant compared with the ordeal of dining all by himself with a multitude of curious eyes fastened upon him and a multitude of mouths whispering comments upon his performance—and upon his mistakes, if he should be so unlucky as to make any.

Still, nothing could stop that fourth day, and so it came. It found poor Tom low-spirited and absent-minded, and this mood continued; he could not shake it off. The ordinary duties of the morning dragged upon his hands, and wearied him. Once more he felt the sense of captivity heavy upon him.

Late in the forenoon he was in a large audience chamber, conversing with the Earl of Hertford and duly awaiting the striking of the hour appointed for a visit of ceremony from a considerable number of great officials and courtiers.

After a little while Tom, who had wandered to a window and become interested in the life and movement of the great highway beyond the palace gates—

Excited by a commotion he sees in the street below a palace window, the young pretend king wants to know what is going on.

and not idly interested, but longing with all his heart to take part in person in its stir and freedom—saw the van of a hooting and shouting mob of disorderly men, women, and children of the lowest and poorest degree approaching from up the road.

"I would I knew what 'tis about!" he exclaimed, with all a boy's curiosity in such happenings.

"Thou art the king!" solemnly responded the earl, with a reverence. "Have I your grace's leave to act?"

"Oh, blithely, yes! Oh, gladly, yes!" exclaimed Tom, excitedly, adding to himself with a lively sense of satisfaction, "In truth, being a king is not all dreariness—it hath its compensations and conveniences."

The earl called a page, and sent him to the captain of the guard with the order—

"Let the mob be halted, and inquiry made concerning the occasion of its movement. By the king's command!"

A few seconds later a long rank of the royal guards, cased in flashing steel, filed out at the gates and formed across the highway in front of the multitude. A messenger returned, to report that the crowd were following a man, a woman, and a young girl to execution for crimes committed against the peace and dignity of the realm.

Death—and a violent death—for these poor unfortunates! The thought wrung Tom's heartstrings. The spirit of compassion took control of him, to the exclusion of all other considerations; he never thought of the offended laws, or of the grief or loss which these three criminals had inflicted upon their victims, he could think of nothing but the scaffold and the grisly fate hanging over the heads of the condemned. His concern made him even forget, for the moment, that he was but the false shadow of a king, not the substance; and before he knew it he had blurted out the command—

"Bring them here!"

Then he blushed scarlet, and a sort of apology sprung to his lips; but observing that his order had wrought no sort of surprise in the earl or the waiting page, he suppressed the words he was about to utter. The page, in the most matter-of-course way, made a profound obeisance and retired backward out of the room to deliver the command. Tom experienced a glow of pride and a renewed sense of the compensating advantages of the kingly office. He said to himself, "Truly it is like what I used to feel when I read the old priest's tales, and did imagine mine own self a prince, giving law and command to all, saying, 'Do this, do that,' while none durst offer let or hindrance to my will."

Now the doors swung open; one high-sounding title after another was announced, the personages owning them followed, and the place was quickly half filled with noble folk and finery. But Tom was hardly conscious of the presence of these people, so wrought up was he and so intensely absorbed in that other and more interesting matter. He seated himself, absently, in his chair of state, and turned his eyes upon the door with manifestations of impatient expectancy; seeing which, the company forbore to trouble him, and fell to chatting a mixture of public business and court gossip one with another.

In a little while the measured tread of military men was heard approaching, and the culprits entered the presence in charge of an under-sheriff and escorted by a detail of the King's Guard. The civil officer knelt before Tom, then stood aside; the three doomed persons knelt also, and remained so; the guard took position behind Tom's chair. Tom scanned the prisoners curiously. Something about the dress or appearance of the man had stirred a vague memory in him. "Methinks I have seen this man ere now . . . but the when or the where fail me"—such was Tom's thought. Just then the man glanced meekly up, and quickly dropped his face again, not being able to endure the awful port of sovereignty; but the one full glimpse of the face, which Tom got, was sufficient. He said to himself: "Now is the matter clear; this is the stranger that plucked Giles Witt out of the Thames, and saved his life that windy, bitter, first day of the New Year—a brave, good deed—pity he hath been doing baser ones and got himself in this sad case . . . I have not forgot the day, neither the hour; by reason that an hour after, upon the stroke of eleven, I did get a hiding by the hand of Gammer Canty which was of so goodly and admired severity that all that went before or followed after it were but fondlings and caresses by comparison."

Tom now ordered that the woman and the girl be removed from the presence for a little time; then addressed himself to the under-sheriff, saying—

"Good sir, what is this man's offense?"

The officer knelt, and answered—

"So please your majesty, he hath taken the life of a subject by poison."

Tom's compassion for the prisoner, and admiration of him as the daring rescuer of a drowning boy, experienced a most damaging shock.

"The thing was proven upon him?" he asked.

"Most clearly, sire."

Tom sighed, and said—

"Take him away—he hath earned his death. 'tis a pity, for he was a brave heart—na-na, I mean he hath the *look* of it!"

The prisoner clasped his hands together with sudden energy, and wrung them despairingly, at the same time appealing imploringly to the "king" in broken and terrified phrases—

"O my lord the king, an' thou canst pity the lost, have pity upon me! I am innocent—neither hath that wherewith I am charged been more than but lamely proved—yet I speak not of that; the judgment is gone forth against me and may not suffer alteration; yet in mine extremity I beg a boon, for my doom is more than I can bear. A grace, a grace, my lord the king! in thy royal compassion grant my prayer—give commandment that I be hanged!"

Tom was amazed. This was not the outcome he had looked for.

"Odds my life, a strange *boon!* Was it not the fate intended thee?"

"O good my liege, not so! It is ordered that I be *boiled alive!*"

The hideous surprise of these words almost made Tom spring from his chair. As soon as he could recover his wits he cried out—

"Have thy wish, poor soul! an' thou had poisoned a hundred men thou shouldst not suffer so miserable a death."

The prisoner bowed his face to the ground and burst into passionate expressions of gratitude—ending with—

"If ever thou shouldst know misfortune—which God forefend!—may thy goodness to me this day be remembered and requited!"

Tom turned to the Earl of Hertford, and said—

"My lord, is it believable that there was warrant for this man's ferocious doom?"

"It is the law, your grace—for poisoners. In Germany coiners be boiled to death in *oil*—not cast in of a sudden, but by a rope let down into the oil by degrees, and slowly; first the feet, then the legs, then—"

"Oh, prithee, no more, my lord, I cannot bear it!" cried Tom, covering his eyes with his hands to shut out the picture. "I beseech your good lordship that order be taken to change this law—O, let no more poor creatures be visited with its tortures."

The earl's face showed profound gratification, for he was a man of merciful and generous impulses—a thing not very common with his class in that fierce age. He said—

"These your grace's noble words have sealed its doom. History will remember it to the honor of your royal house."

The under-sheriff was about to remove his prisoner; Tom gave him a sign to wait; then he said—

"Good sir, I would look into this matter further. The man has said his deed was but lamely proved. Tell me what thou knowest."

"If the king's grace please, it did appear upon the trial, that this man entered into a house in the hamlet of Islington where one lay sick—three witnesses say it was at ten of the clock in the morning and two say it was some minutes later—the sick man being alone at the time, and sleeping—and presently the man came forth again, and went his way. The sick man died within the hour, being torn with spasm and retchings."

"Did any see the poison given? Was poison found?"

"Marry, no, my liege."

"Then how doth one know there was poison given at all?"

"Please your majesty, the doctors testified that none die with such symptoms but by poison."

Weighty evidence, this—in that simple age. Tom recognized its formidable nature, and said—

"The doctor knoweth his trade—belike they were right. The matter hath an ill look for this poor man."

"Yet was not this all, your majesty; there is more and worse. Many testified that a witch, since gone from the village, none know whither, did foretell, and speak it privately in their ears, that the sick man *would die by poison*—and more, that a stranger would give it—a stranger with brown hair and clothed in a worn and common garb; and surely this prisoner doth answer woundily to the bill. Please, your majesty, to give the circumstance that solemn weight which is its due, seeing it was *foretold*."

This was an argument of tremendous force, in that superstitious day. Tom felt that the thing was settled; if evidence was worth anything, this poor fellow's guilt was proved. Still he offered the prisoner a chance, saying—

"If thou canst say aught in thy behalf, speak."

"Naught that will avail, my king. I am innocent, yet cannot I make it appear. I have no friends, else might I show that I was not in Islington that day; so also might I show that at that hour they name I was above a league away, seeing I was at Wapping Old Stairs; yea more, my king, for I could show, that while they say I was taking life, I was *saving* it. A drowning boy"—

"Peace! Sheriff, name the day the deed was done!"

"At ten in the morning, or some minutes later, the first day of the new year, most illustrious"—

"Let the prisoner go free—it is the king's will!"

Another blush followed this unregal outburst, and he covered his indecorum as well as he could by adding—

"It enrageth me that a man should be hanged upon such idle, hare-brained evidence!"

A low buzz of admiration swept through the assemblage. It was not admiration of the decree that had been delivered by Tom, for the propriety or expediency of pardoning a convicted poisoner was a thing which few there would have felt justified in either admitting or admiring—no, the admiration was for the intelligence and spirit which Tom had displayed. Some of the low-voiced remarks were to this effect—

"This is no mad king—he hath his wits sound."

"How sanely he put his questions—how like his former natural self was this abrupt, imperious disposal of the matter!"

"God be thanked his infirmity is spent! This is no weakling, but a king. He hath borne himself like to his own father."

The air being filled with applause, Tom's ear necessarily caught a little of it. The effect which this had upon him was to put him greatly at his ease, and also to charge his system with very gratifying sensations.

However, his juvenile curiosity soon rose superior to these pleasant thoughts and feelings; he was eager to know what sort of deadly mischief the woman and the little girl could have been about; so, by his command the two terrified and sobbing creatures were brought before him.

"What is it that these have done?" he inquired of the sheriff.

"Please your majesty, a black crime is charged upon them, and clearly proven; wherefore the judges have decreed, according to the law, that they be hanged. They sold themselves to the devil—such is their crime."

Tom shuddered. He had been taught to abhor people who did this wicked thing. Still, he was not going to deny himself the pleasure of feeding his curiosity, for all that; so he asked—

"Where was this done?—and when?"

"On a midnight, in December—in a ruined church, your majesty."

Tom shuddered again.

"Who was there present?"

"Only these two, your grace—and *that other*."

"Have these confessed?"

"Nay, not so, sire—they do deny it."

"Then, prithee, how was it known?"

"Certain witnesses did see them wending thither, good your majesty; this bred the suspicion, and dire effects have since confirmed and justified it. In particular, it is in evidence that through the wicked power so obtained, they did invoke and bring about a storm that wasted all the region round about. Above forty witnesses have proved the storm; and sooth one might have had a thousand, for all had reason to remember it, sith all had suffered by it."

"Certes this is a serious matter." Tom turned this dark piece of scoundrelism over in his mind awhile, then asked—

"Suffered the woman, also, by the storm?"

Several old heads among the assemblage nodded their recognition of the wisdom of this question. The sheriff, however, saw nothing consequential in the inquiry; he answered, with simple directness.

"Indeed, did she, your majesty, and most righteously, as all aver. Her habitation was swept away, and herself and child left shelterless."

"Methinks the power to do herself so ill a turn was dearly bought. She had been cheated, had she paid but a farthing for it; that she paid her soul, and her child's, argueth that she is mad; if she is mad she knoweth not what she doth, therefore sinneth not."

The elderly heads nodded recognition of Tom's wisdom once more, and one individual murmured, "An' the king be mad himself, according to report, then it is a madness of a sort that would improve the sanity of some I wot of, if by the gentle providence of God they could but catch it."

"What age hath the child?" asked Tom.

"Nine years, please your majesty."

"By the law of England may a child enter into covenant and sell itself, my lord?" asked Tom, turning to a learned judge.

"The law doth not permit a child to make or meddle in any weighty matter, good my liege, holding that its callow wit unfitteth it to cope with the riper wit and evil schemings of them that are its elders. The devil may buy a child, if he so choose, and the child agree thereto, but not an Englishman—in this latter case the contract would be null and void."

"It seemeth a rude unchristian thing, and ill contrived, that English law denieth privileges to Englishmen, to waste them on the devil!" cried Tom, with honest heat.

This novel view of the matter excited many smiles, and was stored away in many heads to be repeated about the court as evidence of Tom's originality as well as progress toward mental health.

The elder culprit had ceased from sobbing, and was hanging upon Tom's words with an excited interest and a growing hope. Tom noticed this, and it strongly inclined his sympathies toward her in her perilous and unfriended situation. Presently he asked—

"How wrought they, to bring the storm?"

"*By pulling off their stockings*, sire."

This astonished Tom, and also fired his curiosity to fever heat. He said eagerly—

"It is wonderful! Hath it always this dread effect?"

"Always, my liege—at least if the woman desire it, and utter the needful words, either in her mind or with her tongue."

Tom turned to the woman, and said with impetuous zeal—

"Exert thy power—I would see a storm."

There was a sudden paling of cheeks in the superstitious assemblage, and a general, though unexpressed, desire to get out of the place—all of which was

Gradually realizing that he has real power, the pauper king nervously commands the accused witch to brew up a storm—but not a harmful one.

lost upon Tom, who was dead to everything but the proposed cataclysm. Seeing a puzzled and astonished look in the woman's face, he added, excitedly—

"Never fear—thou shalt be blameless. More—thou shalt go free—none shall touch thee. Exert thy power."

"O, my lord the king, I have it not—I have been falsely accused."

"Thy fears stay thee. Be of good heart, thou shalt suffer no harm. Make a storm—it mattereth not how small a one—I require naught great or harmful, but indeed prefer the opposite—do this and thy life is spared—thou shalt go out free, with thy child, bearing the king's pardon, and safe from hurt or malice from any in the realm."

The woman prostrated herself, and protested, with tears, that she had no power to do the miracle, else she would gladly win her child's life alone, and be content to lose her own, if by obedience to the king's command so precious a grace might be acquired.

Tom urged—the woman still adhered to her declarations. Finally, he said—

"I think the woman hath said true. An' *my* mother were in her place and gifted with the devil's functions, she had not stayed a moment to call her storms and lay the whole land in ruins, if the saving of my forfeit life were the price she got! It is argument that other mothers are made in like mold. Thou art free, good wife—thou and thy child—for I do think thee innocent. *Now* thou'st naught to fear, being pardoned—pull off thy stockings!—an' thou canst make me a storm, thou shalt be rich!"

The redeemed creature was loud in her gratitude, and proceeded to obey, while Tom looked on with eager expectancy, a little marred by apprehension; the courtiers at the same time manifesting decided discomfort and uneasiness. The woman stripped her own feet and her little girl's also, and plainly did her best to reward the king's generosity with an earthquake, but it was all a failure and a disappointment. Tom sighed and said—

"There, good soul, trouble thyself no further, thy power is departed out of thee. Go thy way in peace; and if it return to thee at any time, forget me not, but fetch me a storm."

—*The Prince and the Pauper* (1881), chapter 15

———————— ••• ◆ ••• ————————

Mark Twain's endnote to this tale calls attention to the fact that an English woman and her nine-year-old daughter had once been hanged for selling their souls to the devil by pulling off their stockings to raise a storm. That remark is a nice counterpoint to The Prince and the Pauper's *prelude, which states, "It may have happened, it may not have happened: but it could have happened."*

———————— ••• ◆ ••• ————————

4.

"OUT OF FOCUS IMAGINATIONS"

———————•———————

During the late 1890s, Mark Twain wrote, "You can't depend on your judgment when your imagination is out of focus." Rarely do people's imaginations get more out of focus than those of the two men in this simple tale. The narrator is a young man escorting the body of a recently deceased friend on a long train ride on a cold winter's night. The other, older, man is a railroad expressman posted to a baggage car. All they are doing is chaperoning a box on a long trip. It happens that the box they are escorting is the wrong one, but that is not what drives their imaginations out of focus.

———————•———————

I seem sixty and married, but these effects are due to my condition and sufferings, for I am a bachelor, and only forty-one. It will be hard for you to believe that I, who am now but a shadow, was a hale, hearty man two short years ago—a man of iron, a very athlete!—yet such is the simple truth. But stranger still than this fact is the way in which I lost my health. I lost it through helping to take care of a box of guns on a two-hundred-mile railway journey one winter's night. It is the actual truth, and I will tell you about it.

I belong in Cleveland, Ohio. One winter's night, two years ago, I reached home just after dark, in a driving snow-storm, and the first thing I heard when I entered the house was that my dearest boyhood friend and schoolmate, John B. Hackett, had died the day before, and that his last utterance had been a desire that I would take his remains home to his poor old father and mother in Wisconsin. I was greatly shocked and grieved, but there was no time to waste in emotions; I must start at once. I took the card, marked "Deacon Levi Hackett, Bethlehem, Wisconsin," and hurried off through the whistling storm to the railway station. Arrived there I found the long white-pine box which had been described to me; I fastened the card to it with some tacks, saw it put safely aboard the express car, and then ran into the eating-room to provide myself with a sandwich and some cigars. When I returned, presently, there was my coffin-box *back again*, apparently, and a young fellow examining around it, with a card in his hand, and some tacks and a hammer! I was astonished and puzzled. He began to nail on his card, and I rushed out to the express car, in a good deal of a state of mind, to ask for an explanation. But no—there was my box, all right, in the express car; it hadn't been disturbed. [The fact is that without my suspecting it a prodigious mistake had been made. I was carrying off a box of *guns* which that young fellow had come to the station to ship to a rifle company in Peoria, Illinois, and he had got my corpse!]

Just then the conductor sung out "All aboard," and I jumped into the express car and got a comfortable seat on a bale of buckets. The expressman was there, hard at work—a plain man of fifty, with a simple, honest, good-natured face, and a breezy, practical heartiness in his general style. As the train moved off a stranger skipped into the car and set a package of peculiarly mature and capable Limburger cheese on one end of my coffin-box—I mean my box of guns. That is to say, I know *now* that it was Limburger cheese, but at that time I never had heard of the article in my life, and of course was wholly ignorant of its character. Well, we sped through the wild night, the bitter storm raged on, a cheerless misery stole over me, my heart went down, down, down ! The old expressman made a brisk remark or two about the tempest and the arctic weather, slammed his sliding doors to, and bolted them, closed his window down tight, and then went bustling around, here and there and yonder, setting things to rights, and all the time contentedly humming "Sweet By and By," in a low tone, and flatting a good deal. Presently I began to detect a most evil and searching odor stealing about on the frozen air. This depressed my spirits still more, because of course I attributed it to my poor departed friend. There was something infinitely saddening about his calling himself to my remembrance in this dumb pathetic way, so it was hard to keep the tears back. Moreover, it distressed me on account of the old expressman, who, I was afraid, might notice it. However, he went humming tranquilly on, and gave no sign; and for this I was grateful.

Grateful, yes, but still uneasy; and soon I began to feel more and more uneasy every minute, for every minute that went by that odor thickened up the more, and got to be more and more gamey and hard to stand. Presently, having got things arranged to his satisfaction, the expressman got some wood and made up a tremendous fire in his stove. This distressed me more than I can tell, for I could not but feel that it was a mistake. I was sure that the effect would be deleterious upon my poor departed friend. Thompson—the expressman's name was Thompson, as I found out in the course of the night—now went poking around his car, stopping up whatever stray cracks he could find, remarking that it didn't make any difference what kind of a night it was outside, he calculated to make us comfortable, anyway. I said nothing, but I believed he was not choosing the right way. Meantime he was humming to himself just as before; and meantime, too, the stove was getting hotter and hotter, and the place closer and closer. I felt myself growing pale and qualmish, but grieved in silence and said nothing. Soon I noticed that the "Sweet By and By" was gradually fading out; next it ceased altogether, and there was an ominous stillness. After a few moments Thompson said—

"Pfew! I reckon it ain't no cinnamon 't I've loaded up thish-yer stove with!"

He gasped once or twice, then moved toward the cof—gun-box, stood over that Limburger cheese part of a moment, then came back and sat down near me, looking a good deal impressed. After a contemplative pause, he said, indicating the box with a gesture—

"Friend of yourn?"

"Yes," I said with a sigh.

Alarmed by the fetid stench in the train's baggage car, the two men carefully examine the crate.

"He's pretty ripe, *ain't* he!"

Nothing further was said for perhaps a couple of minutes, each being busy with his own thoughts; then Thompson said, in a low, awed voice—

"Sometimes it's uncertain whether they're really gone or not—seem gone, you know—body warm, joints limber—and so, although you *think* they're gone, you don't really know. I've had cases in my car. It's perfectly awful, becuz *you* don't know what minute they'll rise right up and look at you!" Then, after a pause, and slightly lifting his elbow toward the box—"But *he* ain't in no trance! No, sir, I go bail for *him!*"

We sat some time, in meditative silence, listening to the wind and the roar of the train; then Thompson said, with a good deal of feeling—

"Well-a-well, we've all got to go, they ain't no getting around it. Man that is born of woman is of few days and far between, as Scriptur' says. Yes, you look at it any way you want to, it's awful solemn and cur'us: they ain't *nobody* can get around it; *all's* got to go—just everybody, as you may say. One day you're hearty and strong"—here scrambled to his feet and broke a pane and stretched his nose out at it a moment or two, then sat down again while I struggled up and thrust my nose out at the same place, and this we kept on doing every now and then—"and next day he's cut down like the grass, and the places which knows him no more forever, as Scriptur' says. Yes-'ndeedy, it's awful solemn and cur'us; but we've all got to go, one time or another; they ain't no getting around it."

There was another long pause; then—

"What did he die of?"

I said I didn't know.

"How long has he ben dead?"

It seemed judicious to enlarge the facts to fit the probabilities; so I said—

"Two or three days."

But it did no good; for Thompson received it with an injured look which plainly said, "Two or three *years*, you mean." Then he went right along, placidly ignoring my statement, and gave his views at considerable length upon the unwisdom of putting off burials too long. Then he lounged off toward the box, stood a moment, then came back on a sharp trot and visited the broken pane, observing—

"'T would 'a' ben a dum sight better, all around, if they'd started him along last summer."

Thompson sat down and buried his face in his red silk handkerchief, and began to slowly sway and rock his body like one who is doing his best to endure the almost unendurable. By this time the fragrance—if you may call it fragrance—was just about suffocating, as near as you can come at it. Thompson's face was turning gray; I knew mine hadn't any color left in it. By and by Thompson rested his forehead in his left hand, with his elbow on his knee, and sort of waved his red handkerchief towards the box with his other hand, and said—

"I've carried a many a one of 'em—some of 'em considerable overdue, too—but, lordy, he just lays over 'em all!—and does it easy. Cap., they was heliotrope to *him!*"

This recognition of my poor friend gratified me, in spite of the sad circumstances, because it had so much the sound of a compliment.

Pretty soon it was plain that something had got to be done. I suggested cigars. Thompson thought it was a good idea. He said—

"Likely it'll modify him some."

We puffed gingerly along for a while, and tried hard to imagine that things were improved. But it wasn't any use. Before very long, and without any consultation, both cigars were quietly dropped from our nerveless fingers at the same moment. Thompson said, with a sigh—

"No, Cap., it don't modify him worth a cent. Fact is, it makes him worse, becuz it appears to stir up his ambition. What do you reckon we better do, now?"

I was not able to suggest anything; indeed, I had to be swallowing and swallowing, all the time, and did not like to trust myself to speak. Thompson fell to maundering, in a desultory and low-spirited way, about the miserable experiences of this night; and he got to referring to my poor friend by various titles—sometimes military ones, sometimes civil ones; and I noticed that as fast as my poor friend's effectiveness grew, Thompson promoted him accordingly—gave him a bigger title. Finally he said—

"I've got an idea. Suppos'n' we buckle down to it and give the Colonel a bit of a shove towards t' other end of the car?—about ten foot, say. He wouldn't have so much influence, then, don't you reckon?"

I said it was a good scheme. So we took in a good fresh breath at the broken pane, calculating to hold it till we got through; then we went there and bent down over that deadly cheese and took a grip on the box. Thompson nodded "All ready," and then we threw ourselves forward with all our might; but Thompson slipped, and slumped down with his nose on the cheese, and his breath got loose. He gagged and gasped, and floundered up and made a break for the door, pawing the air and saying, hoarsely, "Don't header me!—gimme the road! I'm a-dying; gimme the road!" Out on the cold platform I sat down and held his head a while, and he revived. Presently he said—

"Do you reckon we startled the Gen'rul any?"

I said no; we hadn't budged him.

"Well, then, *that* idea's up the flume. We got to think up something else. He's suited wher' he is, I reckon; and if that's the way he feels about it, and has made up his mind that he don't wish to be disturbed, you bet you he's a-going to have his own way in the business. Yes, better leave him right wher' he is, long as he wants it so; becuz he holds all the trumps, don't you know, and so it stands to reason that the man that lays out to alter his plans for him is going to get left."

But we couldn't stay out there in that mad storm; we should have frozen to death. So we went in again and shut the door, and began to suffer once more and take turns at the break in the window. By and by, as we were starting away from a station where we had stopped a moment Thompson pranced in cheerily, and exclaimed—

"We're all right, now! I reckon we've got the Commodore this time. I judge I've got the stuff here that'll take the tuck out of him."

It was carbolic acid. He had a carboy of it. He sprinkled it all around everywhere; in fact he drenched everything with it, rifle-box, cheese, and all. Then we sat down, feeling pretty hopeful. But it wasn't for long. You see the two perfumes began to mix, and then—well, pretty soon we made a break for the door; and out there Thompson swabbed his face with his bandanna and said in a kind of disheartened way—

"It ain't no use. We can't buck agin *him*. He just utilizes everything we put up to modify him with, and gives it his own flavor and plays it back on us. Why, Cap., don't you know, it's as much as a hundred times worse in there now than it was when he first got a-going. I never *did* see one of 'em warm up to his work so, and take such a dumnation interest in it. No, sir, I never did, as long as I've ben on the road; and I've carried a many a one of 'em, as I was telling you."

We went in again, after we were frozen pretty stiff; but my, we couldn't *stay* in, now. So we just waltzed back and forth, freezing, and thawing, and stifling, by turns. In about an hour we stopped at another station; and as we left it Thompson came in with a bag, and said—

"Cap., I'm a-going to chance him once more—just this once; and if we don't fetch him this time, the thing for us to do, is to just throw up the sponge and withdraw from the canvass. That's the way *I* put it up."

He had brought a lot of chicken feathers, and dried apples, and leaf tobacco, and rags, and old shoes, and sulphur, and assafoetida, and one thing or another; and he piled them on a breadth of sheet iron in the middle of the floor, and set fire to them. When they got well started, I couldn't see, myself, how even the corpse could stand it. All that went before was just simply poetry to that smell—but mind you, the original smell stood up out of it just as sublime as ever—fact is, these other smells just seemed to give it a better hold; and my, how rich it was! I didn't make these reflections there—there wasn't time—made them on the platform. And breaking for the platform, Thompson got suffocated and fell; and before I got him dragged out, which I did by the collar, I was mighty near gone myself. When we revived, Thompson said dejectedly—

"We got to stay out here, Cap. We got to do it. They ain't no other way. The Governor wants to travel alone, and he's fixed so he can outvote us."

And presently he added—

"And don't you know, we're *pisoned*. It's *our* last trip, you can make up your mind to it. Typhoid fever is what's going to come of this. I feel it a-coming right now. Yes, sir, we're elected, just as sure as you're born."

We were taken from the platform an hour later, frozen and insensible, at the next station, and I went straight off into a virulent fever, and never knew anything again for three weeks. I found out, then, that I had spent that awful night with a harmless box of rifles and a lot of innocent cheese; but the news was too late to save *me*; imagination had done its work, and my health was permanently shattered; neither Bermuda nor any other land can ever bring it back to me. This is my last trip; I am on my way home to die.

—"The Invalid's Story" (1882)

***

Limburger cheese is notorious for smelling like unpleasant human body odor as it ferments, but the increasingly horrible stench the men in this tale sense exists more in their out-of-focus imaginations than in their noses because of what they think they are smelling.

***

5.

"THE DEAD-HOUSE"

This tale concerns the long-forgotten Arkansas hamlet of Napoleon, a once flourishing little Mississippi River town nestled beside that great river's confluence with the Arkansas River. Mark Twain often visited the town when he piloted steamboats on the river during the 1850s. Life on the Mississippi *describes his return there in 1882, when he traveled down the river with two companions. He looked forward to performing an important errand there, but before describing what he found in Napoleon he related the macabre tale that follows.*

We were approaching Napoleon, Arkansas. So I began to think about my errand there. . . .

I got my friends into my stateroom, and said I was sorry to create annoyance and disappointment, but that upon reflection it really seemed best that we put our luggage ashore and stop over at Napoleon. Their disapproval was prompt and loud; their language mutinous. Their main argument was one which has always been the first to come to the surface, in such cases, since the beginning of time: "But you decided and *agreed* to stick to this boat, etc.;" as if, having determined to do an unwise thing, one is thereby bound to go ahead and make *two* unwise things of it, by carrying out that determination.

I tried various mollifying tactics upon them, with reasonably good success: under which encouragement, I increased my efforts; and, to show them that *I* had not created this annoying errand, and was in no way to blame for it, I presently drifted into its history—substantially as follows:

Toward the end of last year, I spent a few months in Munich, Bavaria. In November I was living in Fräulein Dahlweiner's *pension 1a* Karlstrasse; but my working quarters were a mile from there, in the house of a widow who supported herself by taking lodgers. She and her two young children used to drop in every morning and talk German to me—by request. One day, during a ramble about the city, I visited one of the two establishments where the Government keeps and watches corpses until the doctors decide that they are permanently dead, and not in a trance state. It was a grisly place, that spacious room. There were thirty-six corpses of adults in sight, stretched on their backs on slightly slanted boards, in three long rows—all of them with wax-white, rigid faces, and all of them wrapped in white shrouds. Along the sides of the room were deep alcoves, like bay windows; and in each of these lay several marble-visaged babes, utterly hidden and buried under banks of fresh flowers, all but their faces and crossed hands.

Around a finger of each of these fifty still forms, both great and small, was a ring; and from the ring a wire led to the ceiling, and thence to a bell in a watch-room yonder, where, day and night, a watchman sits always alert and ready to spring to the aid of any of that pallid company who, waking out of death, shall

Night watchman looking after corpses in a Munich "dead-house."

make a movement—for any even the slightest movement will twitch the wire and ring that fearful bell. I imagined myself a death-sentinel drowsing there alone, far in the dragging watches of some wailing, gusty night, and having in a twinkling all my body stricken to quivering jelly by the sudden clamor of that awful summons! So I inquired about this thing; asked what resulted usually? if the watchman died, and the restored corpse came and did what it could to make his last moments easy? But I was rebuked for trying to feed an idle and frivolous curiosity in so solemn and so mournful a place; and went my way with a humbled crest.

Next morning I was telling the widow my adventure, when she exclaimed—

"Come with me! I have a lodger who shall tell you all you want to know. He has been a night watchman there."

He was a living man, but he did not look it. He was abed, and had his head propped high on pillows; his face was wasted and colorless, his deep-sunken eyes were shut; his hand, lying on his breast, was talon-like, it was so bony and long-fingered. The widow began her introduction of me. The man's eyes opened slowly, and glittered wickedly out from the twilight of their caverns; he frowned a black frown; he lifted his lean hand and waved us peremptorily away. But the widow kept straight on, till she had got out the fact that I was a stranger and an American. The man's face changed at once; brightened, became even eager—and the next moment he and I were alone together.

I opened up in cast-iron German; he responded in quite flexible English; thereafter we gave the German language a permanent rest.

This consumptive and I became good friends. I visited him every day, and we talked about everything. At least, about everything but wives and children. Let anybody's wife or anybody's child be mentioned, and three things always followed: the most gracious and loving and tender light glimmered in the man's eyes for a moment; faded out the next, and in its place came that deadly look which had flamed there the first time I ever saw his lids unclose; thirdly, he ceased from speech, there and then for that day; lay silent, abstracted, and absorbed; apparently heard nothing that I said; took no notice of my good-byes, and plainly did not know, by either sight or hearing, when I left the room.

When I had been this Karl Ritter's daily and sole intimate during two months, he one day said, abruptly—

"I will tell you my story."

A DYING MAN'S CONFESSION

Then he went on as follows:—

I have never given up, until now. But now I have given up. I am going to die. I made up my mind last night that it must be, and very soon, too. You say you are going to revisit your river, by and by, when you find opportunity. Very well;

that, together with a certain strange experience which fell to my lot last night, determines me to tell you my history—for you will see Napoleon, Arkansas; and for my sake you will stop there, and do a certain thing for me—a thing which you will willingly undertake after you shall have heard my narrative.

Let us shorten the story wherever we can, for it will need it, being long. You already know how I came to go to America, and how I came to settle in that lonely region in the South. But you do not know that I had a wife. My wife was young, beautiful, loving, and oh, so divinely good and blameless and gentle! And our little girl was her mother in miniature. It was the happiest of happy households.

One night—it was toward the close of the [Civil] war—I woke up out of a sodden lethargy, and found myself bound and gagged, and the air tainted with chloroform! I saw two men in the room, and one was saying to the other, in a hoarse whisper, "I *told* her I would, if she made a noise, and as for the child—"

The other man interrupted in a low, half-crying voice—

"You said we'd only gag them and rob them, not hurt them; or I wouldn't have come."

"Shut up your whining; *had* to change the plan when they waked up; you done all *you* could to protect them, now let that satisfy you; come, help rummage."

Both men were masked, and wore coarse, ragged . . . clothes; they had a bull's-eye lantern, and by its light I noticed that the gentler robber had no thumb on his right hand. They rummaged around my poor cabin for a moment; the head bandit then said, in his stage whisper—

"It's a waste of time—*he* shall tell where it's hid. Undo his gag, and revive him up."

The other said—

"All right—provided no clubbing."

"No clubbing it is, then—provided he keeps still."

They approached me; just then there was a sound outside; a sound of voices and trampling hoofs; the robbers held their breath and listened; the sounds came slowly nearer and nearer; then came a shout—

"*Hello*, the house! Show a light, we want water."

"The captain's voice, by G—!" said the stage-whispering ruffian, and both robbers fled by the way of the back door, shutting off their bull's-eye as they ran.

The strangers shouted several times more, then rode by—there seemed to be a dozen of the horses—and I heard nothing more.

I struggled, but could not free myself from my bonds. I tried to speak, but the gag was effective; I could not make a sound. I listened for my wife's voice and my child's—listened long and intently, but no sound came from the other end of the room where their bed was. This silence became more and more awful, more and more ominous, every moment. Could you have endured an hour of it, do you think? Pity me, then, who had to endure three. Three hours?—it was three ages! Whenever the clock struck, it seemed as if years had gone by since I had heard it last. All this time I was struggling in my bonds; and at last, about dawn, I got myself free, and rose up and stretched my stiff limbs. I was able to distinguish details pretty well. The floor was littered with things thrown there by the robbers during their search for my savings. The first object that caught my particular attention was a document of mine which I had seen the rougher of the two ruffians glance at and then cast away. It had blood on it! I staggered to the other end of the room. Oh, poor unoffending, helpless ones, there they lay, their troubles ended, mine begun!

Did I appeal to the law—I? Does it quench the pauper's thirst if the King drink for him? Oh, no, no, no—I wanted no impertinent interference of the law. Laws and the gallows could not pay the debt that was owing to me! Let the laws leave the matter in my hands, and have no fears: I would find the debtor and collect the debt. How accomplish this, do you say? How accomplish it, and feel so sure about it, when I had neither seen the robbers' faces, nor heard their natural voices, nor had any idea who they might be? Nevertheless, I *was* sure—quite sure, quite confident. I had a clue—a clue which you would not have valued—a clue which would not have greatly helped even a detective, since he would lack the secret of how to apply it. I shall come to that, presently—you shall see. Let us go on, now, taking things in their due order. There was one circumstance which gave me a slant in a definite direction to begin with: Those two robbers were manifestly soldiers in tramp disguise; and not new to military service, but old in it—regulars, perhaps; they did not acquire their soldierly attitude, gestures, carriage, in a day, nor a month, nor yet in a year. So I thought, but said nothing. And one of them had said, "the captain's voice, by G—!"—the one whose life I would have. Two miles away, several regiments were in camp, and two companies of U.S. cavalry. When I learned that Captain Blakely, of Company C had passed our way, that night, with an escort, I said nothing, but in that company I resolved to seek my man. In conversation I studiously and persistently described the robbers as tramps, camp followers; and among this class the people made useless search, none suspecting the soldiers but me.

Working patiently, by night, in my desolated home, I made a disguise for myself out of various odds and ends of clothing; in the nearest village I bought a pair of blue goggles. By and by, when the military camp broke up, and Company C was ordered a hundred miles north, to Napoleon, I secreted my small hoard of money in my belt, and took my departure in the night. When Company C arrived in Napoleon, I was already there. Yes, I was there, with a new trade—fortune-teller. Not to seem partial, I made friends and told fortunes among all the companies garrisoned there; but I gave Company C the great bulk of my attentions. I made

Wearing a shabby overcoat, slouch hat, and dark-blue goggles, Karl Ritter visited Union Army camps to ingratiate himself with soldiers by telling fortunes.

myself limitlessly obliging to these particular men; they could ask me no favor, put upon me no risk, which I would decline. I became the willing butt of their jokes; this perfected my popularity; I became a favorite.

I early found a private who lacked a thumb—what joy it was to me! And when I found that he alone, of all the company, had lost a thumb, my last misgiving vanished; I was *sure* I was on the right track. This man's name was Kruger, a German. There were nine Germans in the company. I watched, to see who might be his intimates; but he seemed to have no especial intimates. But *I* was his intimate; and I took care to make the intimacy grow. Sometimes I so hungered for my revenge that I could hardly restrain myself from going on my knees and begging him to point out the man who had murdered my wife and child; but I managed to bridle my tongue. I bided my time, and went on telling fortunes, as opportunity offered.

My apparatus was simple: a little red paint and a bit of white paper. I painted the ball of the client's thumb, took a print of it on the paper, studied it that night, and revealed his fortune to him next day. What was my idea in this nonsense? It was this: When I was a youth, I knew an old Frenchman who had been a prison-keeper for thirty years, and he told me that there was one thing about a person which never changed, from the cradle to the grave—the lines in the ball of the thumb; and he said that these lines were never exactly alike in the thumbs of any two human beings. In these days, we photograph the new criminal, and hang his picture in the Rogues' Gallery for future reference; but that Frenchman, in his day, used to take a print of the ball of a new prisoner's thumb and put that away for future reference. He always said that pictures were no good—future disguises could make them useless; "The thumb 's the only sure thing," said he; "you can't disguise that." And he used to prove his theory, too, on my friends and acquaintances; it always succeeded.

I went on telling fortunes. Every night I shut myself in, all alone, and studied the day's thumb-prints with a magnifying-glass. Imagine the devouring eagerness with which I pored over those mazy red spirals, with that document by my side which bore the right-hand thumb-and-finger-marks of that unknown murderer, printed with the dearest blood—to me—that was ever shed on this earth! And many and many a time I had to repeat the same old disappointed remark, "will they *never* correspond!"

But my reward came at last. It was the print of the thumb of the forty-third man of Company C whom I had experimented on—private Franz Adler. An hour before, I did not know the murderer's name, or voice, or figure, or face, or nationality; but now I knew all these things! I believed I might feel sure; the Frenchman's repeated demonstrations being so good a warranty. Still, there was a way to *make* sure. I had an impression of Kruger's left thumb. In the morning I took him aside when he was off duty; and when we were out of sight and hearing of witnesses, I said, impressively:—

"A part of your fortune is so grave, that I thought it would be better for you if I did not tell it in public. You and another man, whose fortune I was studying last night—private Adler—have been murdering a woman and a child! You are being dogged: within five days both of you will be assassinated."

He dropped on his knees, frightened out of his wits; and for five minutes he kept pouring out the same set of words, like a demented person, and in the same half-crying way which was one of my memories of that murderous night in my cabin:—

"I didn't do it; upon my soul I didn't do it; and I tried to keep *him* from doing it; I did, as God is my witness. He did it alone."

This was all I wanted. And I tried to get rid of the fool; but no, he clung to me, imploring me to save him from the assassin. He said—

"I have money—ten thousand dollars—hid away, the fruit of loot and thievery; save me—tell me what to do, and you shall have it, every penny. Two thirds of it is my cousin Adler's; but you can take it all. We hid it when we first came here. But I hid it in a new place yesterday, and have not told him—shall not tell him. I was going to desert, and get away with it all. It is gold, and too heavy to carry when one is running and dodging; but a woman who has been gone over the river two days to prepare my way for me is going to follow me with it; and if I got no chance to describe the hiding-place to her I was going to slip my silver watch into her hand, or send it to her, and she would understand. There's a piece of paper in the back of the case, which tells it all. Here, take the watch—tell me what to do!"

He was trying to press his watch upon me, and was exposing the paper and explaining it to me, when Adler appeared on the scene, about a dozen yards away. I said to poor Kruger:—

"Put up your watch, I don't want it. You shan't come to any harm. Go, now; I must tell Adler his fortune. Presently I will tell you how to escape the assassin; meantime shall have to examine your thumb-mark again. Say nothing to Adler about this thing—say nothing to anybody."

He went away filled with fright and gratitude, poor devil. I told Adler a long fortune—purposely so long that I could not finish it; promised to come to him on guard, that night, and tell him the really important part of it—the tragical part of it, I said—so must be out of reach of eavesdroppers. They always kept a picket-watch outside the town—mere discipline and ceremony—no occasion for it, no enemy around.

Toward midnight I set out, equipped with the countersign, and picked my way toward the lonely region where Adler was to keep his watch. It was so dark that I stumbled right on a dim figure almost before I could get out a protecting word. The sentinel hailed and I answered, both at the same moment. I added, "It's only me—the fortune-teller." Then I slipped to the poor devil's side, and without a word I drove my dirk into his heart! *Ja wohl*, laughed I, it *was* the tragedy part of his fortune, indeed! As he fell from his horse, he clutched at me, and my blue goggles remained in his hand; and away plunged the beast dragging him, with his foot in the stirrup.

I fled through the woods, and made good my escape, leaving the accusing goggles behind me in that dead man's hand.

This was fifteen or sixteen years ago. Since then I have wandered aimlessly about the earth, sometimes at work, sometimes idle; sometimes with money, sometimes with none; but always tired of life, and wishing it was done, for my mission here was finished, with the act of that night; and the only pleasure, solace, satisfaction I had, in all those tedious years, was in the daily reflection, "I have killed him!"

Four years ago, my health began to fail. I had wandered into Munich, in my purposeless way. Being out of money, I sought work, and got it; did my duty faithfully about a year, and was then given the berth of night watchman yonder in that house which you visited lately. The place suited my mood. I liked it. I liked being with the dead—liked being alone with them. I used to wander among those rigid corpses, and peer into their austere faces, by the hour. The later the time, the more impressive it was; I preferred the late time. Sometimes I turned the lights low: this gave perspective, you see; and the imagination could play; always, the dim receding ranks of the dead inspired one with weird and fascinating fancies. Two years ago—I had been there a year then—I was sitting all alone in the watch-room, one gusty winter's night, chilled, numb, comfortless; drowsing gradually into unconsciousness; the sobbing of the wind and the slamming of distant shutters falling fainter and fainter upon my dulling ear each moment, when sharp and suddenly that dead-bell rang out a blood-curdling alarum over my head! The shock of it nearly paralyzed me; for it was the first time I had ever heard it.

I gathered myself together and flew to the corpse-room. About midway down the outside rank, a shrouded figure was sitting upright, wagging its head slowly from one side to the other—a grisly spectacle! Its side was toward me. I hurried to it and peered into its face. Heavens, it was Adler!

Can you divine what my first thought was? Put into words, it was this: "It seems, then, you escaped me once: there will be a different result this time!"

Evidently this creature was suffering unimaginable terrors. Think what it must have been to wake up in the midst of that voiceless hush, and look out over that grim congregation of the dead! What gratitude shone in his skinny white face when he saw a living form before him! And how the fervency of this mute gratitude was augmented when his eyes fell upon the life-giving cordials which I carried in my hands! Then imagine the horror which came into this pinched face when I put the cordials behind me, and said mockingly—

"Speak up, Franz Adler—call upon these dead. Doubtless they will listen and have pity; but here there is none else that will."

He tried to speak, but that part of the shroud which bound his jaws, held firm and would not let him. He tried to lift imploring hands, but they were crossed upon his breast and tied. I said—

"Shout, Franz Adler; make the sleepers in the distant streets hear you and bring help. Shout—and lose no time, for there is little to lose. What, you cannot? That is a pity; but it is no matter—it does not always bring help. When you and your cousin murdered a helpless woman and child in a cabin in Arkansas—my wife, it was, and my child!—they shrieked for help, you remember; but it did no good; you remember that it did no good, is it not so? Your teeth chatter—then why cannot you shout? Loosen the bandages with your hands—then you can. Ah, I see—your hands are tied, they cannot aid you. How strangely things repeat themselves, after long years; for *my* hands were tied, that night, you remember? Yes, tied much as yours are now—how odd that is. I could not pull free. It did not occur to you to untie me; it does not occur to me to untie you. Sh ——! there's a late footstep. It is coming this way. Hark, how near it is! One can count the foot-falls—one—two—three. There—it is just outside. Now is the time! Shout, man, shout!—it is the one sole chance between you and eternity! Ah, you see you have delayed too long—it is gone by. There—it is dying out. It is gone! Think of it—reflect upon it—you have heard a human footstep for the last time. How curious it must be, to listen to so common a sound as that, and know that one will never hear the fellow to it again."

Oh, my friend, the agony in that shrouded face was ecstasy to see! I thought of a new torture, and applied it—assisting myself with a trifle of lying invention:—

"That poor Kruger tried to save my wife and child, and I did him a grateful good turn for it when the time came. I persuaded him to rob you; and I and a woman helped him to desert, and got him away in safety."

A look as of surprise and triumph shone out dimly through the anguish in my victim's face. I was disturbed, disquieted. I said—

"What, then—didn't he escape?"

A negative shake of the head.

"No? What happened, then?"

The satisfaction in the shrouded face was still plainer. The man tried to mumble out some words—could not succeed; tried to express something with his obstructed hands—failed; paused a moment, then feebly tilted his head, in a meaning way, toward the corpse that lay nearest him.

"Dead?" I asked. "Failed to escape?—caught in the act and shot?"

Negative shake of the head.

"How, then?"

Again the man tried to do something with his hands. I watched closely, but could not guess the intent. I bent over and watched still more intently. He had twisted a thumb around and was weakly punching at his breast with it.

"Ah—stabbed, do you mean?"

Affirmative nod, accompanied by a spectral smile of such peculiar devilishness, that it struck an awakening light through my dull brain, and I cried—

"Did *I* stab him, mistaking him for you?—for that stroke was meant for none but you."

The affirmative nod of the re-dying rascal was as joyous as his failing strength was able to put into its expression.

"O, miserable, miserable me, to slaughter the pitying soul that stood a friend to my darlings when they were helpless, and would have saved them if he could! miserable, oh, miserable, miserable me!"

I fancied I heard the muffled gurgle of a mocking laugh. I took my face out of my hands, and saw my enemy sinking back upon his inclined board.

He was a satisfactory long time dying. He had a wonderful vitality, an astonishing constitution. Yes, he was a pleasant long time at it. I got a chair and a newspaper, and sat down by him and read. Occasionally I took a sip of brandy. This was necessary, on account of the cold. But I did it partly because I saw, that along at first, whenever I reached for the bottle, he thought I was going to give him some. I read aloud: mainly imaginary accounts of people snatched from the grave's threshold and restored to life and vigor by a few spoonsful of liquor and a warm bath. Yes, he had a long, hard death of it—three hours and six minutes, from the time he rang his bell.

It is believed that in all these eighteen years that have elapsed since the institution of the corpse-watch, no shrouded occupant of the Bavarian dead-houses has ever rung its bell. Well, it is a harmless belief. Let it stand at that.

The chill of that death-room had penetrated my bones. It revived and fastened upon me the disease which had been afflicting me, but which, up to that night, had been steadily disappearing. That man murdered my wife and my child; and in three days hence he will have added me to his list. No matter—God! how delicious the memory of it!—I caught him escaping from his grave, and thrust him back into it!

After that night, I was confined to my bed for a week; but as soon as I could get about, I went to the dead-house books and got the number of the house which Adler had died in. A wretched lodging-house, it was. It was my idea that he would naturally have gotten hold of Kruger's effects, being his cousin; and I wanted to get Kruger's watch, if I could. But while I was sick, Adler's things had been sold and scattered, all except a few old letters, and some odds and ends of no value. However, through those letters, I traced out a son of Kruger's, the only relative he left. He is a man of thirty, now, a shoemaker by trade, and living at No. 14 Königstrasse, Mannheim—widower, with several small children. Without explaining to him why, I have furnished two thirds of his support, ever since.

Now, as to that watch—see how strangely things happen! I traced it around and about Germany for more than a year, at considerable cost in money and vexation; and at last I got it. Got it, and was unspeakably glad; opened it, and found nothing in it! Why, I might have known that that bit of paper was not going to stay there all this time. Of course I gave up that ten thousand dollars then; gave it up, and dropped it out of my mind: and most sorrowfully, for I had wanted it for Kruger's son.

Last night, when I consented at last that I must die, I began to make ready. I proceeded to burn all useless papers; and sure enough, from a batch of Adler's, not previously examined with thoroughness, out dropped that long-desired scrap! I recognized it in a moment. Here it is—I will translate it:

"Brick livery stable, stone foundation, middle of town, corner of Orleans and Market. Corner toward Court-house. Third stone, fourth row. Stick notice there, saying how many are to come."

There—take it, and preserve it. Kruger explained that that stone was removable; and that it was in the north wall of the foundation, fourth row from the top, and third stone from the west. The money is secreted behind it. He said the closing sentence was a blind, to mislead in case the paper should fall into wrong hands. It probably performed that office for Adler.

Now I want to beg that when you make your intended journey down the river, you will hunt out that hidden money, and send it to Adam Kruger, care of the Mannheim address which I have mentioned. It will make a rich man of him, and I shall sleep the sounder in my grave for knowing that I have done what I could for the son of the man who tried to save my wife and child—albeit my hand ignorantly struck him down, whereas the impulse of my heart would have been to shield and serve him.

—*Life on the Mississippi* (1883), chapter 31

Mark Twain claims he intended to retrieve the ten thousand dollars and send it to Kruger's son, but as the steamboat approached Napoleon, his greedy companions persuaded him that so much money would only harm the German shoemaker. They then talked him into instead splitting the fortune among themselves, but when they finally reached Napoleon, they learned the town was entirely gone! Since Mark Twain's last visit there, the Arkansas River had "burst through it, tore it all to rags, and emptied it into the Mississippi!" It seems like there must be some kind of moral lesson in this tale . . . somewhere. (This story, incidentally, contains one of the earliest examples in literature of using fingerprints for identification.)

The Arkansas River washing away Napoleon.

6.

"THE CROSS OF THE MYSTERIOUS AVENGER"

———————————

On his return voyage up the Mississippi River in 1882, Mark Twain revisited his beloved hometown, Hannibal, Missouri, for the first time in many years. Like anyone else returning to scenes of his youth, he was naturally overwhelmed by nostalgia. However, not all the memories his visit evoked were those of an idyllic childhood.

———————————

During my three days' stay in the town, I woke up every morning with the impression that I was a boy—for in my dreams the faces were all young again, and looked as they had looked in the old times—but I went to bed a hundred years old, every night—for meantime I had been seeing those faces as they are now.

Of course I suffered some surprises, along at first, before I had become adjusted to the changed state of things. I met young ladies who did not seem to have changed at all; but they turned out to be the daughters of the young ladies I had in mind—sometimes their grand-daughters. When you are told that a stranger of fifty is a grandmother, there is nothing surprising about it; but if, on the contrary, she is a person whom you knew as a little girl, it seems impossible. You say to yourself, "How can a little girl be a grandmother?" It takes some little time to accept and realize the fact that while you have been growing old, your friends have not been standing still, in that matter.

I noticed that the greatest changes observable were with the women, not the men. I saw men whom thirty years had changed but slightly; but their wives had grown old. These were good women; it is very wearing to be good.

There was a saddler whom I wished to see; but he was gone. Dead, these many years, they said. Once or twice a day, the saddler used to go tearing down the street, putting on his coat as he went; and then everybody knew a steamboat was coming. Everybody knew, also, that John Stavely was not expecting anybody by the boat—or any freight, either; and Stavely must have known that everybody knew this, still it made no difference to him; he liked to seem to himself to be expecting a hundred thousand tons of saddles by this boat, and so he went on all his life, enjoying being faithfully on hand to receive and receipt for those saddles, in case by any miracle they should come. A malicious Quincy paper used always to refer to this town, in derision as "Stavely's Landing." Stavely was one of my earliest admirations; I envied him his rush of imaginary business, and the display he was able to make of it, before strangers, as he went flying down the street struggling with his fluttering coat.

But there was a carpenter who was my chiefest hero. He was a mighty liar, but I did not know that; I believed everything he said. He was a romantic, sentimental, melodramatic fraud, and his bearing impressed me with awe. I vividly remember the first time he took me into his confidence. He was planing a board, and every now and then he would pause and heave a deep sigh; and occasionally mutter broken sentences—confused and not intelligible—but out of their midst an ejaculation sometimes escaped which made me shiver and did me good: one was, "O God, it is his blood!" I sat on the tool-chest and humbly and shudderingly admired him; for I judged he was full of crime. At last he said in a low voice:—

"My little friend, can you keep a secret?"

I eagerly said I could.

"A dark and dreadful one?"

I satisfied him on that point.

"Then I will tell you some passages in my history; for oh, I *must* relieve my burdened soul, or I shall die!"

He cautioned me once more to be "as silent as the grave;" then he told me he was a "red-handed murderer." He put down his plane, held his hands out before him, contemplated them sadly, and said:—

"Look—with these hands I have taken the lives of thirty human beings!"

The effect which this had upon me was an inspiration to him, and he turned himself loose upon his subject with interest and energy. He left generalizing, and went into details—began with his first murder; described it, told what measures he had taken to avert suspicion; then passed to his second homicide, his third, his fourth, and so on. He had always done his murders with a bowie-knife, and he made all my hairs rise by suddenly snatching it out and showing it to me.

At the end of this first *séance* I went home with six of his fearful secrets among my freightage, and found them a great help to my dreams, which had been sluggish for a while back. I sought him again and again, on my Saturday holidays; in fact I spent the summer with him—all of it which was valuable to me. His fascinations never diminished, for he threw something fresh and stirring, in the way of horror, into each successive murder. He always gave names, dates, places— everything. This by and by enabled me to note two things: that he had killed his victims in every quarter of the globe, and that these victims were always named Lynch. The destruction of the Lynches went serenely on, Saturday after Saturday, until the original thirty had multiplied to sixty—and more to be heard from yet; then my curiosity got the better of my timidity, and I asked how it happened that these justly punished persons all bore the same name.

My hero said he had never divulged that dark secret to any living being; but felt that he could trust me, and therefore he would lay bare before me the story of his sad and blighted life. He had loved one "too fair for earth," and she had reciprocated "with all the sweet affection of her pure and noble nature." But he had a rival, a "base hireling" named Archibald Lynch, who said the girl should be his, or he would "dye his hands in her heart's best blood." The carpenter, "inno- cent and happy in love's young dream," gave no weight to the threat, but led his "golden-haired darling to the altar," and there, the two were made one; there also, just as the minister's hands were stretched in blessing over their heads, the fell deed was done—with a knife—and the bride fell a corpse at her husband's feet. And what did the husband do? He plucked forth that knife, and kneeling by the body of his lost one, swore to "consecrate his life to the extermination of all the human scum that bear the hated name of Lynch."

That was it. He had been hunting down the Lynches and slaughtering them, from that day to this—twenty years. He had always used that same consecrated knife; with it he had murdered his long array of Lynches, and with it he had left upon the forehead of each victim a peculiar mark—a cross, deeply incised. Said he:—-

"The cross of the Mysterious Avenger is known in Europe, in America, in China, in Siam, in the Tropics, in the Polar Seas, in the deserts of Asia, in all the earth. Wherever in the uttermost parts of the globe, a Lynch has penetrated, there has the Mysterious Cross been seen, and those who have seen it have shud- dered and said, 'it is his mark, he has been here.' You have heard of the Mysterious Avenger—look upon him, for before you stands no less a person! But beware— breathe not a word to any soul. Be silent, and wait. Some morning this town will flock aghast to view a gory corpse; on its brow will be seen the awful sign, and men will tremble and whisper, 'he has been here—it is the Mysterious Avenger's mark!' You will come here, but I shall have vanished; you will see me no more."

This ass has been reading the "Jibbenainosay," no doubt, and had had his poor romantic head turned by it; but as I had not yet seen the book then, I took his inventions for truth, and did not suspect that he was a plagiarist.

Down on his knees before Mr. Lynch, the humiliated "avenger" begs for mercy.

However, we had a Lynch living in the town; and the more I reflected upon his impending doom, the more I could not sleep. It seemed my plain duty to save him, and a still plainer and more important duty to get some sleep for myself, so at last I ventured to go to Mr. Lynch and tell him what was about to happen to him—under strict secrecy. I advised him to "fly," and certainly expected him to do it. But he laughed at me; and he did not stop there; he led me down to the carpenter's shop, gave the carpenter a jeering and scornful lecture upon his silly pretensions, slapped his face, made him get down on his knees and beg—then went off and left me to contemplate the cheap and pitiful ruin of what, in my eyes, had so lately been a majestic and incomparable hero. The carpenter blustered, flourished his knife, and doomed this Lynch in his usual volcanic style, the size of his fateful words undiminished; but it was all wasted upon me; he was a hero to me no longer but only a poor, foolish, exposed humbug. I was ashamed of him, and ashamed of myself; I took no further interest in him, and never went to his shop any more. He was a heavy loss to me, for he was the greatest hero I had ever known. The fellow must have had some talent; for some of his imaginary murders were so vividly and dramatically described that I remember all their details yet.

—*Life on the Mississippi* (1883), chapter 55

———————

Mark Twain evidently really believed the carpenter's story when he was a boy. The "Jibbenainosay" to which his tale alludes is a ruthless creature in the forests of Kentucky who savagely kills Native Americans. The creature appears in Nick of the Woods; Or, the Jibbenainosay, *a novel published by Robert Montgomery Bird in 1837—two years after Mark Twain was born. In 1839, Louisa H. Medina adapted Bird's story to a popular stage melodrama that helped to make "Jibbenainosay" a symbol for an avenging devil.*

———————

PART II.

———◆———

Unpleasant Places

Mark Twain was one of the most-well traveled Americans of his time. He journeyed across much of the present United States, lived for at least several months in most of its regions—including the Hawaiian Islands—and also crossed the Atlantic Ocean twenty-five times and spent about twelve years of his life living abroad—mainly in western Europe. It should thus not be surprising that during all his diverse residences and peregrinations he experienced more than his share of unpleasant experiences. The selection of tales in this section includes reminiscences from real places he visited and resided in in Europe and America, as well as wholly fictional stories from his rich imagination. Some of the places in these stories are decidedly spooky, others are merely uncomfortably grim. "Neglected Graveyards," for example, depicts a not terribly frightening but decidedly spooky cemetery that Mark Twain imagined while he was living in Buffalo, New York. "Repulsive Memories" and "A Grotesque & Ghastly Performance," on the other hand, are actual reminiscences—doubtless enhanced—from his first of several visits to Italy. The latter story, incidentally, also includes a spooky reminiscence from his Hannibal, Missouri, boyhood. In contrast, "Politically Correct Cannibals" is another work of pure—and gory!—imagination about passengers on a stalled train, though it was doubtless influenced by Mark Twain's having recently observed parliamentary procedure in action in Washington, D.C. There's actually nothing overtly gory in the story, unless, that is, readers pause to think about what is really happening on that train! The last two pieces, "A Hotel Unfit for Perdition" and "Forty-seven Miles in the Dark," are also based on Mark Twain's actual travel experiences—in both the United States and Europe.

7.

"NEGLECTED GRAVEYARDS"

———————————

Everyone has curious dreams, but whether the dream Mark Twain describes in this story he wrote for a newspaper actually happened is an open question. In any case, it is one of his earliest dream stories and one of the first to feature communication with the dead. It's not very scary, but it is deliciously creepy.

———————————

Night before last I had a singular dream. I seemed to be sitting on a door-step (in no particular city perhaps), ruminating, and the time of night appeared to be about twelve or one o'clock. The weather was balmy and delicious. There was no human sound in the air, not even a footstep. There was no sound of any kind to emphasize the dead stillness, except the occasional hollow barking of a dog in the distance and the fainter answer of a further dog. Presently up the street I heard a bony clack-clacking, and guessed it was the castanets of a serenading party. In a minute more a tall skeleton, hooded, and half-clad in a tattered and mouldy shroud, whose shreds were flapping about the ribby lattice-work of its person swung by me with a stately stride, and disappeared in the grey gloom of the starlight. It had a broken and worm-eaten coffin on its shoulder and a bundle of something in its hand. I knew what the clack-clacking was then; it was this party's joints working together, and his elbows knocking against his sides as he walked. I may say I was surprised. Before I could collect my thoughts and enter upon any speculations as to what this apparition might portend, I heard another one coming—for I recognized his clack-clack. He had two-thirds of a coffin on his shoulder, and some foot- and headboards under his arm. I mightily wanted to peer under his hood and speak to him, but when he turned and smiled upon me with his cavernous sockets and his projecting grin as he went by, I thought I would not detain him. He was hardly gone when I heard

In a strange dream, Mark Twain helps a skeleton in a tattered shroud carry a gravestone as more shabby specters come up the street before his home.

the clacking again, and another one issued from the shadowy half-light. This one was bending under a heavy gravestone, and dragging a shabby coffin after him by a string. When he got to me he gave me a steady look for a moment or two, and then rounded to and backed up to me, saying:

"Ease this down for a fellow, will you?"

I eased the grave-stone down till it rested on the ground, and in doing so noticed that it bore the name of "John Baxter Copmanhurst," with "May, 1839," as the date of his death. Deceased sat wearily down by me, and wiped his os frontis with his major maxillary—chiefly from former habit I judged, for I could not see that he brought away any perspiration.

"It is too bad, too bad," said he, drawing the remnant of the shroud about him and leaning his jaw pensively on his hand. Then he put his left foot up on his knee and fell to scratching his ankle bone absently with a rusty nail which he got out of his coffin.

"What is too bad, friend?"

"Oh, everything, everything. I almost wish I never had died."

"You surprise me. Why do you say this? Has anything gone wrong? What is the matter?"

"Matter! Look at this shroud—rags. Look at this gravestone, all battered up. Look at that disgraceful old coffin. All a man's property going to ruin and destruction before his eyes, and ask him if anything is wrong? Fire and brimstone!"

"Calm yourself, calm yourself," I said. "It is too bad—it is certainly too bad, but then I had not supposed that you would much mind such matters, situated as you are."

"Well, my dear sir, I do mind them. My pride is hurt, and my comfort is impaired—destroyed, I might say. I will state my case—I will put it to you in such a way that you can comprehend it, if you will let me," said the poor skeleton, tilting the hood of his shroud back, as if he were clearing for action, and thus unconsciously giving himself a jaunty and festive air very much at variance with the grave character of his position in life—so to speak—and in prominent contrast with his distressful mood.

"Proceed," said I.

"I reside in the shameful old graveyard a block or two above you here, in this street—there, now, I just expected that cartilage would let go!—third rib from the bottom, friend, hitch the end of it to my spine with a string, if you have got such a thing about you, though a bit of silver wire is a deal pleasanter, and more durable and becoming, if one keeps it polished—to think of shredding out and going to pieces in this way, just on account of the indifference and neglect of one's posterity!"—and the poor ghost grated his teeth in a way that gave me a wrench and a shiver—for the effect is mightily increased by the absence of muffling flesh and cuticle. "I reside in that old graveyard, and have for these thirty years; and I tell you things have changed since I first laid this old tired frame there, and turned over, and stretched out for a long sleep, with a delicious sense upon me of being done with bother, and grief, and anxiety, and doubt, and fear, for ever and ever, and listening with comfortable and increasing satisfaction to the sexton's work, from the startling clatter of his first spadeful on my coffin till it dulled away to the faint patting that shaped the roof of my new home—delicious! My! I wish you could try it to-night!" and out of my reverie deceased fetched me with a rattling slap with a bony hand.

"Yes, sir, thirty years ago I laid me down there, and was happy. For it was out in the country; then—out in the breezy, flowery, grand old woods, and the lazy winds gossiped with the leaves, and the squirrels capered over us and around us, and the creeping things visited us, and the birds filled the tranquil solitude with music. Ah, it was worth ten years of a man's life to be dead then! Everything was pleasant. I was in a good neighborhood, for all the dead people that lived near me belonged to the best families in the city. Our posterity appeared to think the world of us. They kept our graves in the very best condition; the fences were always in faultless repair, head-boards were kept painted or white-washed, and were replaced with new ones as soon as they began to look rusty or decayed; monuments were kept upright, railings intact and bright, the rosebushes and shrubbery trimmed, trained, and free from blemish, the walks clean and smooth and gravelled. But that day is gone by. Our descendants have forgotten us. My grandson lives in a stately house built with money made by these old hands of mine, and I sleep in a neglected grave with invading vermin that gnaw my shroud to build them nests withal! I and friends that lie with me founded and secured the prosperity of this fine city, and the stately bantling of our loves leaves us to rot in a dilapidated cemetery which neighbors curse and strangers scoff at. See the difference between the old time and this—for instance: Our graves are all caved in, now; our head-boards have rotted away and tumbled down; our railings reel this way and that, with one foot in the air, after a fashion of unseemly levity; our monuments lean wearily, and our gravestones bow their heads discouraged; there be no adornments any more—no roses, nor shrubs, nor gravelled walks, nor anything that is a comfort to the eye; and even the paintless old board fence that did make a show of holding us sacred from companionship with beasts and the defilement of heedless feet, has tottered till it overhangs the street, and only advertises the presence of our dismal resting-place and invites yet more derision to it. And now we cannot hide our poverty and tatters in the friendly woods, for the city has stretched its withering arms abroad and taken us in, and all that remains of the cheer of our old home is the cluster of lugubrious forest trees that stand, bored and weary of a city life, with their feet in our coffins, looking into the hazy distance and wishing they were there. I tell you it is disgraceful!

"You begin to comprehend—you begin to see how it is. While our descendants are living sumptuously on our money, right around us in the city, we have to fight hard to keep skull and bones together. Bless you, there isn't a grave in our cemetery that doesn't leak—not one. Every time it rains in the night we have to climb out and roost in the trees—and sometimes we are wakened suddenly by the chilly water trickling down the back of our necks. Then I tell you there is a general heaving up of old graves and kicking over of old monuments, and scampering of old skeletons for the trees! Bless me, if you had gone along there some such nights after twelve you might have seen as many as fifteen of us roosting on one limb, with our joints rattling drearily and the wind wheezing through our ribs! Many a time we have perched there for three or four dreary hours, and then come down, stiff and chilled through and drowsy, and borrowed each other's skulls to bale out our graves with—if you will glance up in my mouth, now as I tilt my head back, you can see that my head-piece is half full of old dry sediment—how top-heavy and stupid it makes me sometimes! Yes, sir, many a time if you had happened to come along just before the dawn you'd have caught us baling out the graves and hanging our shrouds on the fence to dry. Why, I had an elegant shroud stolen from there one morning—think a party by the name of Smith took it, that resides in a plebeian graveyard over yonder—I think so because the first time I ever saw him he hadn't anything on but a check-shirt, and the last time I saw him, which was at a social gathering in the new cemetery, he was the best dressed corpse in the company—and it is a significant fact that he left when he saw me; and presently an old woman from here missed her coffin—she generally took it with her when she went anywhere, because she was liable to take cold and bring on the spasmodic rheumatism that originally killed her if she exposed herself to the night air much. She was named Hotchkiss—Anna Matilda Hotchkiss—you might know her? She has two upper front teeth, is tall, but a good deal inclined to stoop, one rib on the left side gone, has one shred of rusty hair hanging from the left side of her head, and one little tuft just above and a little forward of her right ear, has her under jaw wired on one side where it had worked loose, small bone of

Mark Twain converses with one of the skeletons in the decaying graveyard.

left forearm gone—lost in a fight—has a kind of swagger in her gait and a 'gallus' way of going with her arms akimbo and her nostrils in the air—has been pretty free and easy, and is all damaged and battered up till she looks like a queen's-ware crate in ruins—maybe you have met her?"

"God forbid!" I involuntarily ejaculated, for somehow I was not looking for that form of question, and it caught me a little off my guard. But I hastened to make amends for my rudeness, and say, "I simply meant I had not had the honor—for I would not deliberately speak discourteously of a friend of yours. You were saying that you were robbed—and it was a shame, too—but it appears by what is left of the shroud you have on that it was a costly one in its day. How did—"

A most ghastly expression began to develop among the decayed features and shriveled integuments of my guest's face, and I was beginning to grow uneasy and distressed, when he told me he was only working up a deep, sly smile, with a wink in it, to suggest that about the time he acquired his present garment a ghost in a neighboring cemetery missed one. This reassured me, but I begged him to confine himself to speech thenceforth because his facial expression was uncertain. Even with the most elaborate care it was liable to miss fire. Smiling should especially be avoided. What he might honestly consider a shining success was likely to strike me in a very different light. I said I liked to see a skeleton cheerful, even decorously playful, but I did not think smiling was a skeleton's best hold.

"Yes, friend," said the poor skeleton, "the facts are just as I have given them to you. Two of these old graveyards—the one that I resided in and one further along—have been deliberately neglected by our descendants of to-day until there is no occupying them any longer. Aside from the osteological discomfort of it—and that is no light matter this rainy weather—the present state of things is ruinous to property. We have got to move or be content to see our effects wasted away and utterly destroyed. Now, you will hardly believe it, but it is true, nevertheless, that there isn't a single coffin in good repair among all my acquaintance—now that is an absolute fact. I do not refer to low people who come in a pine box mounted on an express wagon, but I am talking about your high-toned, silver mounted burial-case, your monumental sort, that travel under black plumes at the head of a procession and have choice of cemetery lots—I mean folks like the Jarvises, and the Bledsoes and Burlings, and such. They are all about ruined. The most substantial people in our set, they were. And now look at them—utterly used up and poverty-stricken. One of the Bledsoes actually traded his monument to a late bar-keeper for some fresh shavings to put under his head. I tell you it speaks volumes, for there is nothing a corpse takes so much pride in as his monument. He loves to read the inscription. He comes after a while to believe what it says himself, and then you may see him sitting on the fence night after night enjoying it. Epitaphs are cheap, and they do a poor chap a world of good after he is dead, especially if he had hard luck while he was alive. I wish they were used more. Now, I don't complain, but confidentially I do think it was a little shabby in my descendants to give me nothing but this old slab of a gravestone—and all the more that there isn't a compliment on it. It used to have

'GONE TO HIS JUST REWARD'

on it, and I was proud when I first saw it, but by-and-by I noticed that whenever an old friend of mine came along he would hook his chin on the railing and pull a long face and read along down till he came to that and then he would chuckle to himself and walk off, looking satisfied and comfortable. So I scratched it off to get rid of those fools. But a dead man always takes a deal of pride in his monument. Yonder goes half-a-dozen of the Jarvises, now, with the family monument along. And Smithers and some hired spectres went by with him a while ago. Hello, Higgins, good-bye, old friend! That's Meredith Higgins—died in '44—belongs to our set in the cemetery—fine old family—great-grandmother was an Injun—I am on the most familiar terms with him—he didn't hear me was the reason he didn't answer me. And I am sorry, too, because I would have liked to introduce you. You would admire him. He is the most disjointed, sway-backed, and generally distorted old skeleton you ever saw, but he is full of fun. When he laughs it sounds like rasping two stones together, and he always starts it off with a cheery screech like raking a nail across a window-pane. Hey, Jones! That is old Columbus Jones—shroud cost four hundred dollars—entire trousseau, including monument, twenty-seven hundred. This was in the Spring of '26. It was enormous style for those days. Dead people came all the way from the Alleghenies to see his things—the party that occupied the grave next to mine remembers it well. Now do you see that individual going along with a piece of a head-board under his arm, one leg-bone below his knee gone, and not a thing in the world one? That is Barstow Dalhousie, and next to Columbus Jones he was the most sumptuously outfitted person that ever entered our cemetery. We are all leaving. We cannot tolerate the treatment we are receiving at the hands of our descendants. They open new cemeteries, but they leave us to our ignominy. They mend the streets, but they never mend anything that is about us or belongs to us. Look at that coffin of mine—yet I tell you in its day it was a piece of furniture that would have attracted attention in any drawing-room in this city. You may have it if you want it—I can't afford to repair it. Put a new bottom in her, and art of a new top, and a bit of fresh lining along the left side, and you'll find her about as comfortable as any receptacle of her species you ever tried. No thanks—no, don't mention it—you have been civil to me, and I would give you all the property I have got before I would seem ungrateful. Now this winding-sheet is a kind of a sweet thing in its way, if you would like to—. No? Well, just as you say, but I wished to be fair and liberal—there's nothing mean about me. Good-by, friend, I must be going. I may have a good way to go to-night—don't know. I only know one thing for certain, and that is, that I am on the emigrant trail, now, and I'll never sleep in that crazy old cemetery again. I will travel till I find respectable quarters if I have to hoof it to New Jersey. All the boys are going. It was decided in public conclave, last night, to emigrate, and by the time the sun rises there won't be a bone left in our old habitations. Such cemeteries may suit my surviving friends, but they do not suit the remains that have the honor to make these remarks. My opinion is the general opinion. If you doubt it, go and see how the departing ghosts upset things before they started. They were almost riotous in their demonstrations of distaste. Hello, here are some of the Bledsoes, and if you will give me a lift with this tombstone I guess I will join company and jog along with them—mighty respectable old family, the Bledsoes, and used to always come out in six-horse hearses, and all that sort of thing fifty years ago when I walked these streets in daylight. Good-by, friend."

And with his gravestone on his shoulder he joined the grisly procession, dragging his damaged coffin after him, for notwithstanding he pressed it upon me so earnestly, I utterly refused his hospitality. I suppose that for as much as two hours these sad outcasts went clacking by, laden with their dismal effects, and all that time I sat pitying them. One or two of the youngest and least dilapidated among them inquired about midnight trains on the railways, but the rest seemed unacquainted with that mode of travel, and merely asked about common public roads to various towns and cities, some of which are not on the map now, and vanished from it and from the earth as much as thirty years ago, and some few of them never had existed anywhere but on maps, and private ones in real estate agencies at that. And they asked about the condition of the cemeteries in these towns and cities, and about the reputation the citizens bore as to reverence for the dead.

This whole matter interested me deeply, and likewise compelled my sympathy for these homeless ones. And it all seeming real, and I not knowing it was a dream, I mentioned to one shrouded wanderer an idea that had entered my head to publish an account of this curious and very sorrowful exodus, but said also that I could not describe it truthfully, and just as it occurred, without seeming to trifle with a grave subject and exhibit an irreverence for the dead that would shock and distress their surviving friends. But this bland and stately remnant of a former citizen leaned him far over my gate and whispered in my ear, and said: -

Do not let that disturb you. The community that can stand such graveyards as those we are emigrating from can stand anything a body can say about the neglected and forsaken dead that lie in them.

At that very moment a cock crowed, and the weird procession vanished and left not a shred or a bone behind. I awoke, and found myself lying with my head out of the bed and "sagging" downwards considerably—a position favorable to dreaming dreams with morals in them, maybe, but not poetry.

Note:—The reader is assured that if the cemeteries in his town are kept in good order, this Dream is not leveled at his town at all, but is leveled particularly and venomously at the next town.

—"A Curious Dream" (1870 & 1875)

———— •••◆◆◆••• ————

Mark Twain wrote this sketch while he was living in Buffalo, New York, and editing the town's Express newspaper. Although the piece specifies that it is set in "no particular city," he actually wrote it to call attention to a badly neglected cemetery in Buffalo. According to his biographer, Albert Bigelow Paine, the story's publication, twice, in the Express helped to launch a cemetery reform movement. The sketch was later reprinted several times and was adapted to a now-lost silent film in 1907.

———— •••◆◆◆••• ————

8.

"REPULSIVE MEMORIES"

———————•———————

During Mark Twain's famous Quaker City *cruise to Europe and the Holy Land in 1867, he and several companions left the ship long enough to make an overland journey through Italy. A highlight of that interlude was their visit to the famous Milan Cathedral, where Mark Twain saw something he wished he could forget, and in describing that unpleasant memory he recalled another one from his youth.*

———————•———————

Toward dusk we drew near Milan, and caught glimpses of the city and the blue mountain peaks beyond. But we were not caring for these things—they did not interest us in the least. We were in a fever of impatience; we were dying to see the renowned Cathedral! We watched—in this direction and that—all around—every where. We needed no one to point it out—we did not wish any one to point it out—we would recognize it, even in the desert of the great Sahara.

At last, a forest of graceful needles, shimmering in the amber sunlight, rose slowly above the pigmy house-tops, as one sometimes sees, in the far horizon, a gilded and pinnacled mass of cloud lift itself above the waste of waves, at sea—the Cathedral! We knew it in a moment. . . .

At nine o'clock in the morning we went and stood before this marble colossus. The central one of its five great doors is bordered with a bas-relief of birds and fruits and beasts and insects, which have been so ingeniously carved out of the marble that they seem like living creatures—and the figures are so numerous and the design so complex, that one might study it a week without exhausting its interest. On the great steeple—surmounting the myriad of spires—inside of the spires—over the doors, the windows—in nooks and corners—every where that a niche or a perch can be found about the enormous building, from summit to base, there is a marble statue, and every statue is a study in itself! . . .

Taking notes on the statuary in the Milan Cathedral.

———————•——————

After climbing to the roof of the cathedral, the travelers descended into its cavernous nave, where they were shown the cathedral's most famous statue—Marco d'Agrate's sixteenth-century sculpture of the martyred Saint Bartholomew.

———————•——————

The guide showed us a coffee-colored piece of sculpture which he said was considered to have come from the hand of Phidias, since it was not possible that any other artist, of any epoch, could have copied nature with such faultless accuracy. The figure was that of a man without a skin; with every vein, artery, muscle, every fibre and tendon and tissue of the human frame, represented in minute detail. It looked natural, because somehow it looked as if it were in pain. A skinned man would be likely to look that way, unless his attention were occupied with some other matter. It was a hideous thing, and yet there was a fascination about it some where. I am very sorry I saw it, because I shall always see it, now. I shall dream of it, sometimes. I shall dream that it is resting its corded arms on the bed's head and looking down on me with its dead eyes; I shall dream that it is stretched between the sheets with me and touching me with its exposed muscles and its stringy cold legs.

It is hard to forget repulsive things. I remember yet how I ran off from school once, when I was a boy, and then, pretty late at night, concluded to climb into the window of my father's office and sleep on a lounge, because I had a delicacy about going home and getting thrashed. As I lay on the lounge and my eyes grew accustomed to the darkness, I fancied I could see a long, dusky, shapeless thing stretched upon the floor. A cold shiver went through me. I turned my face to the wall. That did not answer. I was afraid that that thing would creep over and seize me in the dark. I turned back and stared at it for minutes and minutes—they seemed hours. It appeared to me that the lagging moonlight never, never would get to it. I turned to the wall and counted twenty, to pass the feverish time away. I looked—the pale square was nearer. I turned again and counted fifty—it was almost touching it. With desperate will I turned again and counted one hundred, and faced about, all in a tremble. A white human hand lay in the moonlight! Such an awful sinking at the heart—such a sudden gasp for breath! I felt—I can not tell what I felt. When I recovered strength enough, I faced the wall again. But no boy could have remained so, with that mysterious hand behind him. I counted again, and looked—the most of a naked arm was exposed. I put my hands over my eyes and counted till I could stand it no longer, and then—the pallid face of a man was there, with the corners of the mouth drawn down, and the eyes fixed and glassy in death! I raised to a sitting posture and glowered on that corpse till the light crept down the bare breast—line by line—inch by inch—past the nipple—and then it disclosed a ghastly stab!

I went away from there. I do not say that I went away in any sort of a hurry, but I simply went—that is sufficient. I went out at the window, and I carried the sash along with me. I did not need the sash, but it was handier to take it than it was to leave it, and so I took it.—I was not scared, but I was considerably agitated.

When I reached home, they whipped me, but I enjoyed it. It seemed perfectly delightful. That man had been stabbed near the office that afternoon, and they carried him in there to doctor him, but he only lived an hour. I have slept in the same room with him often, since then—in my dreams.

Now we will descend into the crypt, under the grand altar of Milan Cathedral, and receive an impressive sermon from lips that have been silent and hands that have been gestureless for three hundred years.

Not exactly scared, but considerably agitated, the young boy leaves his father's office by the most convenient route.

The priest stopped in a small dungeon and held up his candle. This was the last resting-place of a good man, a warm-hearted, unselfish man; a man whose whole life was given to succoring the poor, encouraging the faint-hearted, visiting the sick; in relieving distress, whenever and wherever he found it. His heart, his hand and his purse were always open. With his story in one's mind he can almost see his benignant countenance moving calmly among the haggard faces of Milan in the days when the plague swept the city, brave where all others were cowards, full of compassion where pity had been crushed out of all other breasts by the instinct of self-preservation gone mad with terror, cheering all, praying with all, helping all, with hand and brain and purse, at a time when parents forsook their children, the friend deserted the friend, and the brother turned away from the sister while her pleadings were still wailing in his ears.

This was good St. Charles Borroméo, Bishop of Milan. The people idolized him; princes lavished uncounted treasures upon him. We stood in his tomb. Near by was the sarcophagus, lighted by the dripping candles. The walls were faced with bas-reliefs representing scenes in his life done in massive silver. The priest put on a short white lace garment over his black robe, crossed himself, bowed reverently, and began to turn a windlass slowly. The sarcophagus separated in two parts, lengthwise, and the lower part sank down and disclosed a coffin of rock crystal as clear as the atmosphere. Within lay the body, robed in costly habiliments covered with gold embroidery and starred with scintillating gems. The decaying head was black with age, the dry skin was drawn tight to the bones, the eyes were gone, there was a hole in the temple and another in the cheek, and the skinny lips were parted as in a ghastly smile! Over this dreadful face, its dust and decay, and its mocking grin, hung a crown sown thick with flashing brilliants; and upon the breast lay crosses and croziers of solid gold that were splendid with emeralds and diamonds.

How poor, and cheap, and trivial these gew-gaws seemed in presence of the solemnity, the grandeur, the awful majesty of Death! Think of Milton, Shakspeare, Washington, standing before a reverent world tricked out in the glass beads, the brass ear-rings and tin trumpery of the [Indians] of the plains!

Dead Bartoloméo preached his pregnant sermon, and its burden was: You that worship the vanities of earth—you that long for worldly honor, worldly wealth, worldly fame—behold their worth!

To us it seemed that so good a man, so kind a heart, so simple a nature, deserved rest and peace in a grave sacred from the intrusion of prying eyes, and believed that he himself would have preferred to have it so, but peradventure our wisdom was at fault in this regard.

As we came out upon the floor of the church again, another priest volunteered to show us the treasures of the church. What, more? The furniture of the narrow chamber of death we had just visited, weighed six millions of francs in ounces and carats alone, without a penny thrown into the account for the costly workmanship bestowed upon them! But we followed into a large room filled with tall wooden presses like wardrobes. He threw them open, and behold, the cargoes of "crude bullion" of the assay offices of Nevada faded out of my memory. There were Virgins and bishops there, above their natural size, made of solid silver, each worth, by weight, from eight hundred thousand to two millions of francs, and bearing gemmed books in their hands worth eighty thousand; there were bas-reliefs that weighed six hundred pounds, carved in solid silver; croziers and crosses, and candlesticks six and eight feet high, all of virgin gold, and brilliant with precious stones; and beside these were all manner of cups and vases, and such things, rich in proportion. It was an Aladdin's palace. The treasures here, by simple weight, without counting workmanship, were valued at fifty millions of francs! If I could get the custody of them for a while, I fear me the market price of silver bishops would advance shortly, on account of their exceeding scarcity in the Cathedral of Milan.

The priests showed us two of St. Paul's fingers, and one of St. Peter's; a bone of Judas Iscariot, (it was black,) and also bones of all the other disciples; a hand- kerchief in which the Saviour had left the impression of his face. Among the most precious of the relics were a stone from the Holy Sepulchre, part of the crown of thorns, (they have a whole one at Notre Dame,) a fragment of the purple robe worn by the Saviour, a nail from the Cross, and a picture of the Virgin and Child painted by the veritable hand of St. Luke. This is the second of St. Luke's Virgins we have seen. Once a year all these holy relics are carried in procession through the streets of Milan.

—*The Innocents Abroad*, chapter 18

Mark Twain was not the only visitor to Milan's cathedral to be repulsed by the graphic realism of the statue of Saint Bartholomew. His description doesn't even mention one of the statue's most disturbing features: What appears to be a long stole wrapped around Bartholomew's flayed body is actually Bartholomew's own skin!

9.

"A GROTESQUE & GHASTLY PERFORMANCE"

———•———

After touring northern Italian towns, Mark Twain and his companions went to Rome, where their explorations of the famous catacombs included a visit to the strange and spooky crypt of monks below the church of Santa Maria della Concezione dei Cappuccini.

———•———

From the sanguinary sports of the Holy Inquisition; the slaughter of the Coliseum; and the dismal tombs of the Catacombs, I naturally pass to the picturesque horrors of the Capuchin Convent. We stopped a moment in a small chapel in the church to admire a picture of St. Michael vanquishing Satan—a picture which is so beautiful that I can not but think it belongs to the reviled *"Renaissance,"* notwithstanding I believe they told us one of the ancient old masters painted it—and then we descended into the vast vault underneath.

Here was a spectacle for sensitive nerves! Evidently the old masters had been at work in this place. There were six divisions in the apartment, and each division was ornamented with a style of decoration peculiar to itself—and these decorations were in every instance formed of human bones! There were shapely arches, built wholly of thigh bones; there were startling pyramids, built wholly of grinning skulls; there were quaint architectural structures of various kinds, built of shin bones and the bones of the arm; on the wall were elaborate frescoes, whose curving vines were made of knotted human vertebrae; whose delicate tendrils were made of sinews and tendons; whose flowers were formed of knee-caps and toe-nails. Every lasting portion of the human frame was represented in these intricate designs . . . and there was a careful finish about the work, and an attention to details that betrayed the artist's love of his labors as well as his schooled ability. I asked the good-natured monk who accompanied us, who did this? And he said,

"We did it"—meaning himself and his brethren up stairs. I could see that the old friar took a high pride in his curious show. We made him talkative by exhibiting an interest we never betrayed to guides.

"Who were these people?"

"We—up stairs—Monks of the Capuchin order—my brethren."

"How many departed monks were required to upholster these six parlors?"

"These are the bones of four thousand."

"It took a long time to get enough?"

"Many, many centuries."

"Their different parts are well separated—skulls in one room, legs in another, ribs in another—there would be stirring times here for a while if the last trump should blow. Some of the brethren might get hold of the wrong leg, in the confusion, and the wrong skull, and find themselves limping, and looking through eyes that were wider apart or closer together than they were used to. You can not tell any of these parties apart, I suppose?"

"Oh, yes, I know many of them."

He put his finger on a skull. "This was Brother Anselmo—dead three hundred years—a good man."

He touched another. "This was Brother Alexander—dead two hundred and eighty years. This was Brother Carlo—dead about as long."

Then he took a skull and held it in his hand, and looked reflectively upon it, after the manner of the grave-digger when he discourses of Yorick.

"This," he said, "was Brother Thomas. He was a young prince, the scion of a proud house that traced its lineage back to the grand old days of Rome well nigh two thousand years ago. He loved beneath his estate. His family persecuted him; persecuted the girl, as well. They drove her from Rome; he followed; he sought her far and wide; he found no trace of her. He came back and offered his broken heart at our altar and his weary life to the service of God. But look you. Shortly his father died, and likewise his mother. The girl returned, rejoicing. She sought every where for him whose eyes had used to look tenderly into hers out of this poor skull, but she could not find him. At last, in this coarse garb we wear, she recognized him in the street. He knew her. It was too late. He fell where he stood. They took him up and brought him here. He never spoke afterward. Within the week he died. You can see the color of his hair—faded, somewhat—by this thin shred that clings still to the temple. This," [taking up a thigh bone,] "was his. The veins of this leaf in the decorations over your head, were his finger-joints, a hundred and fifty years ago."

This business-like way of illustrating a touching story of the heart by laying the several fragments of the lover before us and naming them, was as grotesque a performance, and as ghastly, as any I ever witnessed. I hardly knew whether to

During the monk's grotesque performance, Mark Twain hardly knows whether to smile or shudder.

smile or shudder. There are nerves and muscles in our frames whose functions and whose methods of working it seems a sort of sacrilege to describe by cold physiological names and surgical technicalities, and the monk's talk suggested to me something of this kind. Fancy a surgeon, with his nippers lifting tendons, muscles and such things into view, out of the complex machinery of a corpse, and observing, "Now this little nerve quivers—the vibration is imparted to this muscle—from here it is passed to this fibrous substance; here its ingredients are separated by the chemical action of the blood—one part goes to the heart and thrills it with what is popularly termed emotion, another part follows this nerve to the brain and communicates intelligence of a startling character—the third part glides along this passage and touches the spring connected with the fluid receptacles that lie in the rear of the eye. Thus, by this simple and beautiful process, the party is informed that his mother is dead, and he weeps." Horrible!

I asked the monk if all the brethren up stairs expected to be put in this place when they died. He answered quietly:

"We must all lie here at last."

See what one can accustom himself to.—The reflection that he must some day be taken apart like an engine or a clock, or like a house whose owner is gone, and worked up into arches and pyramids and hideous frescoes, did not distress this monk in the least. I thought he even looked as if he were thinking, with complacent vanity, that his own skull would look well on top of the heap and his own ribs add a charm to the frescoes which possibly they lacked at present.

Here and there, in ornamental alcoves, stretched upon beds of bones, lay dead and dried-up monks, with lank frames dressed in the black robes one sees ordinarily upon priests. We examined one closely. The skinny hands were clasped upon the breast; two lustreless tufts of hair stuck to the skull; the skin was brown and sunken; it stretched tightly over the cheek bones and made them stand out sharply; the crisp dead eyes were deep in the sockets; the nostrils were painfully prominent, the end of the nose being gone; the lips had shriveled away from the yellow teeth: and brought down to us through the circling years, and petrified there, was a weird laugh a full century old!

It was the jolliest laugh, but yet the most dreadful, that one can imagine. Surely, I thought, it must have been a most extraordinary joke this veteran produced with his latest breath, that he has not got done laughing at it yet. At this moment I saw that the old instinct was strong upon the boys, and I said we had better hurry to St. Peter's. . . .

—*The Innocents Abroad* (1869), chapter 28

In his description of the grisly statue of Saint Bartholomew in Milan, Mark Twain remarks on the difficult of forgetting repulsive things. The bones and desiccated body parts of the Capuchin monks of Rome are difficult to forget, even if one is merely reading about them.

10.

"POLITICALLY CORRECT CANNIBALS"

The year is 1853—more than two decades before publication of Robert's Rules of Order, *the manual governing parliamentary procedure in legislative bodies. The author of that famous manual would probably recoil from the subject of the deliberations described in the tale that follows, but he doubtless would approve their punctiliously correct form. The auditor's informant in this tale is clearly conversant with the procedures of legislative bodies, but we have to wonder what other kinds of bodies he was familiar with.*

I visited St. Louis lately, and on my way west, after changing cars at Terre Haute, Indiana, a mild, benevolent-looking gentleman of about forty-five, or may be fifty, came in at one of the way-stations and sat down beside me. We talked together pleasantly on various subjects for an hour, perhaps, and I found him exceedingly intelligent and entertaining. When he learned that I was from Washington, he immediately began to ask questions about various public men, and about Congressional affairs; and I saw very shortly that I was conversing with a man who was perfectly familiar with the ins and outs of political life at the Capital, even to the ways and manners, and customs of procedure of Senators and Representatives in the Chambers of the National Legislature. Presently two men halted near us for a single moment, and one said to the other:

"Harris, if you'll do that for me, I'll never forget you, my boy."

My new comrade's eyes lighted pleasantly. The words had touched upon a happy memory, I thought. Then his face settled into thoughtfulness—almost into gloom. He turned to me and said, "Let me tell you a story; let me give you a secret chapter of my life—a chapter that has never been referred to by me since its events transpired. Listen patiently, and promise that you will not interrupt me."

I said I would not, and he related the following strange adventure, speaking sometimes with animation, sometimes with melancholy, but always with feeling and earnestness.

THE STRANGER'S NARRATIVE

"On the 19th of December, 1853, I started from St. Louis on the evening train bound for Chicago. There were only twenty-four passengers, all told. There were no ladies and no children. We were in excellent spirits, and pleasant acquaintanceships were formed. The journey bade fair to be a happy one; and no individual in the party, I think, had even the vaguest presentment of the horrors we were soon to undergo.

"At 11 P.M. it began to snow hard. Shortly after leaving the small village of Welden, we entered upon that tremendous prairie solitude that stretches its leagues on leagues of houseless dreariness far away towards the Jubilee Settlements. The winds, unobstructed by trees or hills, or even vagrant rocks, whistled fiercely across the level desert, driving the falling snow before it like spray from the crested waves of a stormy sea. The snow was deepening fast; and we knew, by the diminished speed of the train, that the engine was ploughing through it with steadily increasing difficulty. Indeed, it almost came to a dead halt sometimes, in the midst of great drifts that piled themselves like colossal graves across the track. Conversation began to flag. Cheerfulness gave place to grave concern. The possibility of being imprisoned in the snow, on the bleak prairie, fifty miles from any house, presented itself to every mind, and extended its depressing influence over every spirit.

"At two o'clock in the morning I was aroused out of an uneasy slumber by the ceasing of all motion about me. The appalling truth flashed upon me instantly— we were captives in a snow-drift! 'All hands to the rescue!' Every man sprang to obey. Out into the wild night, the pitchy darkness, the billowy snow, the driving storm, every soul leaped, with the consciousness that a moment lost now might bring destruction to us all. Shovels, hands, boards—anything, everything that could displace snow, was brought into instant requisition. It was a weird picture, that small company of frantic men fighting the banking snows, half in the blackest shadow and half in the angry light of the locomotive's reflector.

"One short hour sufficed to prove the utter uselessness of our efforts. The storm barricaded the track with a dozen drifts while we dug one away. And worse than this, it was discovered that the last grand charge the engine had made upon the enemy had broken the fore-and-aft shaft of the driving-wheel! With a free track before us we should still have been helpless. We entered the car wearied with labor, and very sorrowful. We gathered about the stoves, and gravely canvassed our situation. We had no provisions whatever—in this lay our chief distress. We could not freeze, for there was a good supply of wood in the tender. This was our only comfort. The discussion ended at last in accepting the

The severe blizzard brings the St. Louis-to-Chicago passenger train to a dead stop in the middle of a vast prairie.

disheartening decision of the conductor, viz., that it would be death for any man to attempt to travel fifty miles on foot through snow like that. We could not send for help; and even if we could, it could not come. We must submit, and await, as patiently as we might, succor or starvation! I think the stoutest heart there felt a momentary chill when those words were uttered.

"Within the hour conversation subsided to a low murmur here and there about the car, caught fitfully between the rising and falling of the blast; the lamps grew dim; and the majority of the castaways settled themselves among the flickering shadows to think—to forget the present, if they could—to sleep, if they might.

"The eternal night—it surely seemed eternal to us—wore its lagging hours away at last, and the cold grey dawn broke in the east. As the light grew stronger the passengers began to stir and give signs of life, one after another, and each in turn pushed his slouched hat up from his forehead, stretched his stiffened limbs, and glanced out at the windows upon the cheerless prospect. It was cheerless indeed!—not a living thing visible anywhere, not a human habitation; nothing but a vast white desert; uplifted sheets of snow drifting hither and thither before the wind—a world of eddying flakes shutting out the firmament above.

"All day we moped about the cars, saying little, thinking much. Another lingering dreary night—and hunger.

"Another dawning—another day of silence, sadness, wasting hunger, hopeless watching for succor that could not come. A night of restless slumber, filled with dreams of feasting—wakings distressed with the gnawings of hunger.

"The fourth day came and went—and the fifth! Five days of dreadful imprisonment! A savage hunger looked out at every eye. There was in it a sign of awful import—the foreshadowing of a something that was vaguely shaping itself in every heart—a something which no tongue dared yet to frame into words.

"The sixth day passed—the seventh dawned upon as gaunt and haggard and hopeless a company of men as ever stood in the shadow of death. It must out now! That thing which had been growing up in every heart was ready to leap from every lip at last! Nature had been taxed to the utmost—she must yield. RICHARD H. GASTON, of Minnesota, tall, cadaverous, and pale, rose up. All knew what was coming. All prepared—every emotion, every semblance of excitement was smothered—only a calm, thoughtful seriousness appeared in the eyes that were lately so wild.

"'Gentlemen—It cannot be delayed longer! The time is at hand! We must determine which of us shall die to furnish food for the rest!'

"Mr. JOHN J. WILLIAMS, of Illinois, rose and said: Gentlemen—I nominate the Rev. James Sawyer, of Tennessee.'

"Mr. WM. R. ADAMS, of Indiana, said: I nominate Mr. Daniel Slote, of New York.'

"Mr. CHARLES J. LANGDON: I nominate Mr. Samuel A. Bowen, of St. Louis.'

"Mr. SLOTE: Gentlemen—I desire to decline in favor of Mr. John A. Van Nostrand, Jun., of New Jersey.'

"Mr. GASTON: If there be no objection, the gentleman's desire will be acceded to.'

"Mr. VAN NOSTRAND objecting, the resignation of Mr. Slote was rejected. The resignations of Messrs. Sawyer and Bowen were also offered, and refused upon the same grounds.

"Mr. A. L. BASCOM, of Ohio: I move that the nominations now close, and that the House proceed to an election by ballot.'

"Mr. SAWYER: Gentlemen—I protest earnestly against these proceedings. They are, in every way, irregular and unbecoming. I must beg to move that they be dropped at once, and that we elect a chairman of the meeting and proper officers to assist him, and then we can go on with the business before us understandingly.'

"Mr. BELL, of Iowa: Gentlemen—I object. This is no time to stand upon forms and ceremonious observances. For more than seven days we have been without food. Every moment we lose in idle discussion increases our distress. I am satisfied with the nominations that have been made—every gentleman present is, I believe—and I, for one, do not see why we should not proceed at once to elect one or more of them. I wish to offer a resolution—'

"Mr. GASTON: It would be objected to, and have to lie over one day under the rules, thus bringing about the very delay you wish to avoid. The gentleman from New Jersey—'

After a fiery debate, the well-chilled passengers begin voting.

"Mr. VAN NOSTRAND: Gentlemen—I am a stranger among you; I have not sought the distinction that has been conferred upon me, and I feel a delicacy—'

"Mr. MORGAN, of Alabama (interrupting): I move the previous question.'

"The motion was carried, and further debate shut off, of course. The motion to elect officers was passed, and under it Mr. Gaston was chosen chairman, Mr. Blake secretary, Messrs. Holcomb, Dyer, and Baldwin, a committee on nominations, and Mr. R. M. Howland, purveyor, to assist the committee in making selections.

"A recess of half an hour was then taken, and some little caucusing followed. At the sound of the gavel the meeting reassembled, and the committee reported in favor of Messrs. George Ferguson, of Kentucky, Lucien Herrman, of Louisiana, and W. Messick, of Colorado, as candidates. The report was accepted.

"Mr. ROGERS, of Missouri: Mr. President—The report being properly before the House now, I move to amend it by substituting for the name of Mr. Herrman that of Mr. Lucius Harris, of St. Louis, who is well and honorably known to us all. I do not wish to be understood as casting the least reflection upon the high character and standing of the gentleman from Louisiana—far from it. I respect and esteem him as much as any gentleman here present possibly can; but none of us can be blind to the fact that he has lost more flesh during the week that we have lain here than any among us—none of us can be blind to the fact that the committee has been derelict to its duty, either through negligence or a graver fault, in thus offering for our suffrages a gentleman who, however pure his own—motives may be, has really less nutriment in him—'

"The Chair: The gentleman from Missouri will take his seat. The Chair cannot allow the integrity of the Committee to be questioned save by the regular course, under the rules. What action will the House take upon the gentleman's motion?'

"Mr. Halliday, of Virginia: I move to further amend the report by substituting Mr. Harvey Davis, of Oregon, for Mr. Messick. It may be urged by gentlemen that the hardships and privations of a frontier life have rendered Mr. Davis tough; but, gentlemen, is this a time to cavil at toughness? is this a time to be fastidious concerning trifles? is this a time to dispute about matters of paltry significance? No, gentlemen, bulk is what we desire—substance, weight, bulk—these are the supreme requisites now—not talent, not genius, not education. I insist upon my motion.'

"Mr. Morgan (excitedly): Mr. Chairman—I do most strenuously object to this amendment. The gentleman from Oregon is old, and furthermore is bulky only in bone—not in flesh. I ask the gentleman from Virginia if it is soup we want instead of solid sustenance? if he would delude us with shadows? if he would mock our suffering with an Oregonial spectre? I ask him if he can look upon the anxious faces around him, if he can gaze into our sad eyes, if he can listen to the beating of our expectant hearts, and still thrust this famine-stricken fraud upon us! I ask him if he can think of our desolate state, of our past sorrows, of our dark future, and still unpityingly foist upon us this wreck, this ruin, this tottering swindle, this gnarled and blighted and sapless vagabond from Oregon's inhospitable shores? Never!' (Applause.)

"The amendment was put to vote, after a fiery debate, and lost. Mr. Harris was substituted on the first amendment. The balloting then began. Five ballots were held without a choice. On the sixth, Mr. Harris was elected, all voting for him but himself. It was then moved that his election should be ratified by acclamation, which was lost, in consequence of his again voting against himself.

"Mr. Radway moved that the House now take up the remaining candidates, and go into an election for breakfast. This was carried.

"On the first ballot there was a tie, half the members favoring one candidate on account of his youth, and half favoring the other on account of his superior size. The President gave the casting vote for the latter, Mr. Messick. This decision created considerable dissatisfaction among the friends of Mr. Ferguson, the defeated candidate, and there was some talk of demanding a new ballot; but in the midst of it, a motion to adjourn was carried, and the meeting broke up at once.

More chilled than ever, the hungry passengers demonstrate their appreciation of the late winners of their first election.

"The preparations for supper diverted the attention of the Ferguson faction from the discussion of their grievance for a long time, and then, when they would have taken it up again, the happy announcement that Mr. Harris was ready, drove all thought of it to the winds.

"We improvised tables by propping up the backs of car-seats, and sat down with hearts full of gratitude to the finest supper that had blessed our vision for seven torturing days. How changed we were from what we had been a few short hours before! Hopeless, sad-eyed misery, hunger, feverish anxiety, desperation, then—thankfulness, serenity, joy too deep for utterance now. That I know was the cheeriest hour of my eventful life. The wind howled, and blew the snow wildly about our prison-house, but they were powerless to distress us any more. I liked Harris. He might have been better done, perhaps, but I am free to say that no man ever agreed with me better than Harris, or afforded me so large a degree of satisfaction. Messick was very well, though rather high-flavored, but for genuine nutritiousness and delicacy of fibre, give me Harris. Messick had his good points—I will not attempt to deny it, nor do I wish to do it—but he was no more fitted for breakfast than a mummy would be, sir—not a bit. Lean?—why, bless me!—and tough? Ah, he was very tough! You could not imagine it—you could never imagine anything like it."

"Do you mean to tell me that—"

"Do not interrupt me, please. After breakfast we elected a man by the name of Walker, from Detroit, for supper. He was very good. I wrote his wife so afterwards. He was worthy of all praise. I shall always remember Walker. He was a little rare, but very good. And then the next morning we had Morgan, of Alabama, for breakfast. He was one of the finest men I ever sat down to—handsome, educated, refined, spoke several languages fluently—a perfect gentleman—he was a perfect gentleman, and singularly juicy. For supper we had that Oregon patriarch, and he *was* a fraud, there is no question about it—old, scraggy, tough, nobody can picture the reality. I finally said, gentlemen, you can do as you like, but I will wait for another election. And Grimes, of Illinois, said, Gentlemen, *I* will wait also. When you elect a man that has *something* to recommend him, I shall be glad to join you again.' It soon became evident that there was general dissatisfaction with Davis, of Oregon, and so, to preserve the good-will that had prevailed so pleasantly since we had had Harris, an election was called, and the result of it was that Baker, of Georgia, was chosen. He was splendid! Well, well—after that we had Doolittle and Hawkins, and McElroy (there was some complaint about McElroy, because he was uncommonly short and thin), and Penrod, and two Smiths, and Bailey (Bailey had a wooden leg, which was clear loss, but he was otherwise good), and an Indian boy, and an organ grinder, and a gentleman by the name of Buckminster—a poor stick of a vagabond that wasn't any good for company and no account for breakfast. We were glad we got him elected before relief came."

"And so the blessed relief *did* come at last?"

"Yes, it came one bright, sunny morning, just after election. John Murphy was the choice, and there never was a better, I am willing to testify; but John Murphy came home with us, in the train that came to succor us, and lived to marry the widow Harris—"

"Relict o—"

"Relict of our first choice. He married her, and is happy and respected and prosperous yet. Ah, it was like a novel, sir—it was like a romance. This is my stopping-place, sir; I must bid you good-by. Any time that you can make it convenient to tarry a day or two with me, I shall be glad to have you. I like you, sir; I have conceived an affection for you. I could like you as well as I liked Harris himself, sir. Good day, sir, and a pleasant journey."

He was gone. I never felt so stunned, so distressed, so bewildered in my life. But in my soul I was glad he was gone. With all his gentleness of manner and his soft voice, I shuddered whenever he turned his hungry eye upon me; and when I heard that I had achieved his perilous affection, and that I stood almost with the late Harris in his esteem, my heart fairly stood still!

I was bewildered beyond description. I did not doubt his word; I could not question a single item in a statement so stamped with the earnestness of truth as his; but its dreadful details overpowered me, and threw my thoughts into hopeless confusion. I saw the conductor looking at me. I said, "Who is that man?"

"He was a member of Congress once, and a good one. But he got caught in a snowdrift in the cars, and like to been starved to death. He got so frostbitten and frozen up generally, and used up for want of something to eat, that he was sick and out of his head two or three months afterwards. He is all right now, only he is a monomania, and when he gets on that old subject he never stops till he has eat up that whole car-load of people he talks about. He would have finished the crowd by this time, only he had to get out here. He has got their names as pat as A, B, C. When he gets them all eat up but himself, he always says:—Then the hour for the usual election for breakfast having arrived, and there being no opposition, I was duly elected, after which, there being no objections offered, I resigned. Thus I am here.'"

I felt inexpressively relieved to know that I had only been listening to the harmless vagaries of a madman instead of the genuine experiences of a bloodthirsty cannibal.

—"Cannibalism in the Cars" (1868)

Like the unnamed auditor in this tale, we are relieved to know that we have only been listening to the harmless prattling of a madman, not the genuine experiences of a bloodthirsty cannibal. However, given Mark Twain's propensity for mixing truth and fiction, how sure can we be that this story didn't really happen? After all, many of the names in it—such as Daniel Slote, John van Nostrand, and Charles Langdon—belonged to men whom Mark Twain knew personally. The story may actually have been inspired by an article published in Mark Twain's brother's Muscatine, Ohio, newspaper in 1855 about government legislators whose train got stuck in snow for several days, forcing them to eat their dogs to stay alive. This story's careful use of correct parliamentary procedures doubtless also owed much to Mark Twain's experience reporting on legislative bodies in Washington, D.C., and Carson City.

11.

"A HOTEL UNFIT FOR PERDITION"

One of Mark Twain's most characteristic traits as a writer was his tendency to change subjects suddenly and even wildly. This digression about a dismal hotel in the American Midwest appears within his account of his visit to Egypt in his first travel book, The Innocents Abroad *(1869). By the time he traveled in the Holy Land and North Africa in 1867, he had already spent enough nights in bad hotels in the United States and other parts of the world so that staying in a really terrible one in Egypt was nothing new to him. Perhaps calling that Egyptian hotel "the worst on earth" was what made him recall one in the United States that was even worse.*

Alexandria was too much like a European city to be novel, and we soon tired of it. We took the cars and came up here to ancient Cairo, which is an Oriental city and of the completest pattern. There is little about it to disabuse one's mind of the error if he should take it into his head that he was in the heart of Arabia. Stately camels and dromedaries, swarthy Egyptians, and likewise Turks and black Ethiopians, turbaned, sashed, and blazing in a rich variety of Oriental costumes of all shades of flashy colors, are what one sees on every hand crowding the narrow streets and the honeycombed bazaars. We are stopping at Shepherd's Hotel, which is the worst on earth except the one I stopped at once in a small town in the United States. It is pleasant to read this sketch in my note-book, now, and know that I can stand Shepherd's Hotel, sure, because I have been in one just like it in America and survived:

> I stopped at the Benton House. It used to be a good hotel, but that proves nothing—I used to be a good boy, for that matter. Both of us have lost character of late

years. The Benton is not a good hotel. The Benton lacks a very great deal of being a good hotel. Perdition is full of better hotels than the Benton.

It was late at night when I got there, and I told the clerk I would like plenty of lights, because I wanted to read an hour or two. When I reached No. 15 with the porter (we came along a dim hall that was clad in ancient carpeting, faded, worn out in many places, and patched with old scraps of oil cloth—a hall that sank under one's feet, and creaked dismally to every footstep,) he struck a light—two inches of sallow, sorrowful, consumptive tallow candle, that burned blue, and sputtered, and got discouraged and went out. The porter lit it again, and I asked if that was all the light the clerk sent. He said, "Oh no, I've got another one here," and he produced another couple of inches of tallow candle. I said, "Light them both—I'll have to have one to see the other by." He did it, but the result was drearier than darkness itself. He was a cheery, accommodating rascal. He said he would go " somewheres" and steal a lamp. I abetted and encouraged him in his criminal design. I heard the landlord get after him in the hall ten minutes afterward.

"Where are you going with that lamp?"

"Fifteen wants it, sir."

"Fifteen! why he's got a double lot of candles—does the man want to illuminate the house?—does he want to get up a torch-light procession?—what is he up to, any how?"

"He don't like them candles—says he wants a lamp."

"Why what in the nation does—why I never heard of such a thing? What on earth can he want with that lamp?"

"Well, he only wants to read—that's what he says."

"Wants to read, does he?—ain't satisfied with a thousand candles, but has to have a lamp!—I do wonder what the devil that fellow wants that lamp for? Take him another candle, and then if—"

"But he wants the lamp—says he'll burn the d—d old house down if he don't get a lamp!" (a remark which I never made.)

"I'd like to see him at it once. Well, you take it along—but I swear it beats my time, though—and see if you can't find out what in the very nation he wants with that lamp."

And he went off growling to himself and still wondering and wondering over the unaccountable conduct of No. 15. The lamp was a good one, but it revealed some disagreeable things—a bed in the suburbs of a desert of room—a bed that had hills and valleys in it, and you'd have to accommodate your body to the impression left in it by the man that slept there last, before you could lie comfortably; a carpet that had seen better days; a melancholy washstand in a remote corner, and a dejected pitcher on it sorrowing over a broken nose; a looking-glass split across the centre, which chopped your head off at the chin, and made you look like some dreadful unfinished monster or other; the paper peeling in shreds from the walls.

I sighed and said: "This is charming; and now don't you think you could get me something to read?"

The porter said, "Oh, certainly; the old man's got dead loads of books;" and he was gone before I could tell him what sort of literature I would rather have. And yet his countenance expressed the utmost confidence in his ability to execute the commission with credit to himself. The old man made a descent on him.

"What are you going to do with that pile of books?"

"Fifteen wants 'em, sir."

"Fifteen, is it? He'll want a warming-pan, next—he'll want a nurse! Take him every thing there is in the house—take him the bar-keeper—take him the bag-gage-wagon—take him a chamber-maid! Confound me, I never saw any thing like it. What did he say he wants with those books?"

"Wants to read 'em, like enough; it ain't likely he wants to eat 'em, I don't reckon."

"Wants to read 'em—wants to read 'em this time of night, the infernal lunatic! Well, he can't have them."

"But he says he's mor'ly bound to have 'em; he says he'll just go a-rairin' and a-chargin' through this house and raise more—well, there's no tellin' what he won't do if he don't get 'em; because he's drunk and crazy and desperate, and nothing'll soothe him down but them cussed books." [I had not made any threats, and was not in the condition ascribed to me by the porter.]

Mark Twain settles into bed with just enough light to read in the dismal hotel room.

"Well, go on; but I will be around when he goes to raiding and charging, and the first air he makes I'll make him air out of the window." And then the old gentleman went off, growling as before.

The genius of that porter was something wonderful. He put an armful of books on the bed and said "Good night" as confidently as if he knew perfectly well that those books were exactly my style of reading matter. And well he might. His selection covered the whole range of legitimate literature. It comprised "The Great Consummation," by Rev. Dr. Cummings—theology; "Revised Statutes of the State of Missouri"—law; "The Complete Horse-Doctor"—medicine; "The Toilers of the Sea," by Victor Hugo—romance; "The works of William Shakspeare"—poetry. I shall never cease to admire the tact and the intelligence of that gifted porter.

—*Innocents Abroad* (1869), chapter 57

The Innocents Abroad *took this account from a travel letter Mark Twain had published in San Francisco's* Alta California *newspaper shortly before he left for Europe and the Holy Land in June 1867. That letter calls the hotel the "Heming House," but the establishment's actual name was the "Deming House." It was one of Keokuk, Iowa's, two hotels—both owned by J. R. Tepfer. Mark Twain may have happened to stay in the hotel on a bad night, as the following year an editorial in Keokuk's* Gate City *newspaper said the Deming had "the well-established reputation . . . as one of the best hotels in the West." Whatever the truth about the hotel, Mark Twain would visit even more unpleasant places in the future.*

12.

"FORTY-SEVEN MILES IN THE DARK"

———————

After Mark Twain published A Tramp Abroad *in 1880, he got a letter from a perplexed reader of the book asking him "by what rule a fellow can infallibly judge when you are lying and when you are telling the truth?" The reader added the suggestion that in the next volume Mark Twain published he had "the truth printed in italics." The reader who made that suggestion may have had in mind the following passage about Mark Twain's spooky experience in a German hotel. Did the incident actually happen? Inquiring typesetters need to know!*

———————

When we got back to the hotel I wound and set the pedometer and put it in my pocket, for I was to carry it next day and keep record of the miles we made. The work which we had given the instrument to do during the day which had just closed had not fatigued it perceptibly.

We were in bed by ten, for we wanted to be up and away on our tramp homeward with the dawn. I hung fire, but Harris went to sleep at once. I hate a man who goes to sleep at once; there is a sort of indefinable something about it which is not exactly an insult, and yet is an insolence; and one which is hard to bear, too. I lay there fretting over this injury, and trying to go to sleep; but the harder I tried, the wider awake I grew. I got to feeling very lonely in the dark, with no company but an undigested dinner. My mind got a start by and by, and began to consider the beginning of every subject which has ever been thought of; but it never went further than the beginning; it was touch and go; it fled from topic to topic with a frantic speed. At the end of an hour my head was in a perfect whirl and I was dead tired, fagged out.

The fatigue was so great that it presently began to make some head against the nervous excitement; while imagining myself wide awake, I would really doze into momentary unconsciousness, and come suddenly out of them with a physical jerk which nearly wrenched my joints apart—the delusion of the instant being that I was tumbling backwards over a precipice. After I had fallen over eight or nine precipices and thus found out that one-half of my brain had been asleep eight or nine times without the wide-awake, hard-working other half suspecting it, the periodical unconsciousness began to extend their spell gradually over more of my brain-territory, and at last I sank into a drowse which grew deeper and deeper and was doubtless just on the very point of becoming a solid, blessed, dreamless stupor, when—what was that?

My dulled faculties dragged themselves partly back to life and took a receptive attitude. Now out of an immense, a limitless distance, came a something which grew and grew, and approached, and presently was recognizable as a sound—it had rather seemed to be a feeling, before. This sound was a mile away, now—perhaps it was the murmur of a storm; and now it was nearer—not a quarter of a mile away; was it the muffled rasping and grinding of distant machinery? No, it came still nearer; was it the measured tramp of a marching troop? But it came nearer still, and still nearer—and at last it was right in the room: it was merely a mouse gnawing the woodwork. So I had held my breath all that time for such a trifle.

Well, what was done could not be helped: I would go to sleep at once and make up the lost time. That was a thoughtless thought. Without intending it—hardly knowing it—I fell to listening intently to that sound, and even unconsciously counting the strokes of the mouse's nutmeg-grater. Presently I was deriving exquisite suffering from this employment, yet maybe I could have endured it if the mouse had attended steadily to his work; but he did not do that; he stopped every now and then, and I suffered more while waiting and listening for him to begin again than I did while he was gnawing. Along at first I was mentally offering a reward of five—six—seven—ten—dollars for that mouse; but toward the last I was offering rewards which were entirely beyond my means. I close-reefed my ears—that is to say, I bent the flaps of them down and furled them into five or six folds, and pressed them against the hearing-orifice—but it did no good: the faculty was so sharpened by nervous excitement that it was become a microphone and could hear through the overlays without trouble.

My anger grew to a frenzy. I finally did what all persons before me have done, clear back to Adam—resolved to throw something. I reached down and got my walking-shoes, then sat up in bed and listened, in order to exactly locate the noise. But I couldn't do it; it was as unlocatable as a cricket's noise; and where one thinks that that is, is always the very place where it isn't. So I presently hurled a shoe at random, and with a vicious vigor. It struck the wall over Harris's head and fell down on him; I had not imagined I could throw so far. It woke Harris, and I was glad of it until I found he was not angry; then I was sorry. He soon went to sleep again, which pleased me; but straightway the mouse began again, which roused my temper once more. I did not want to wake Harris a second time, but the gnawing continued until I was compelled to throw the other shoe. This time I broke a mirror—there were two in the room—I got the largest one, of course. Harris woke again, but did not complain, and I was sorrier than ever. I resolved that I would suffer all possible torture before I would disturb him a third time.

The mouse eventually retired, and by and by I was sinking to sleep, when a clock began to strike; I counted till it was done, and was about to drowse again when another clock began; I counted; then the two great Rathhaus clock angels began to send forth soft, rich, melodious blasts from their long trumpets. I had never heard anything that was so lovely, or weird, or mysterious—but when they got to blowing the quarter-hours, they seemed to me to be overdoing the thing. Every time I dropped off for a moment, a new noise woke me. Each time I woke I missed my coverlet, and had to reach down to the floor and get it again.

At last all sleepiness forsook me. I recognized the fact that I was hopelessly and permanently wide-awake. Wide-awake, and feverish and thirsty. When I had lain tossing there as long as I could endure it, it occurred to me that it would be a good idea to dress and go out in the great square and take a refreshing wash in the fountain, and smoke and reflect there until the remnant of the night was gone.

I believed I could dress in the dark without waking Harris. I had banished my shoes after the mouse, but my slippers would do for a summer night. So I rose softly, and gradually got on everything—down to one sock. I couldn't seem to get on the track of that sock, any way I could fix it. But I had to have it; so I went down on my hands and knees, with one slipper on and the other in my hand, and began to paw gently around and rake the floor, but with no success. I enlarged my circle, and went on pawing and raking. With every pressure of my knee, how the floor creaked! and every time I chanced to rake against any article, it seemed to give out thirty-five or thirty-six times more noise than it would have done in the daytime. In those cases I always stopped and held my breath till I was sure Harris had not awakened—then I crept along again. I moved on and on, but I could not find the sock; I could not seem to find anything but furniture. I could not remember that there was much furniture in the room when I went to bed, but the place was alive with it now—especially chairs—chairs everywhere—had a couple of families moved in, in the meantime? And I never could seem to glance on one of those chairs, but always struck it full and square with my head. My temper rose, by steady and sure degrees, and as I pawed on and on, I fell to making vicious comments under my breath.

Groping in the dark for the missing sock in the cavernous German hotel room.

Finally, with a venomous access of irritation, I said I would leave without the sock; so I rose up and made straight for the door—as I supposed—and suddenly confronted my dim spectral image in the unbroken mirror. It startled the breath out of me, for an instant; it also showed me that I was lost, and had no sort of idea where I was. When I realized this, I was so angry that I had to sit down on the floor and take hold of something to keep from lifting the roof off with an explosion of opinion. If there had been only one mirror, it might possibly have helped to locate me; but there were two, and two were as bad as a thousand; besides, these were on opposite sides of the room. I could see the dim blur of the windows, but in my turned-around condition they were exactly where they ought not to be, and so they only confused me instead of helping me.

I started to get up, and knocked down an umbrella; it made a noise like a pistol-shot when it struck that hard, slick, carpetless floor; I grated my teeth and held my breath—Harris did not stir. I set the umbrella slowly and carefully on end against the wall, but as soon as I took my hand away, its heel slipped from under it, and down it came again with another bang. I shrunk together and listened a moment in silent fury—no harm done, everything quiet. With the most painstaking care and nicety I stood the umbrella up once more, took my hand away, and down it came again.

I have been strictly reared, but if it had not been so dark and solemn and awful there in that lonely, vast room, I do believe I should have said something then which could not be put into a Sunday-school book without injuring the sale of it. If my reasoning powers had not been already sapped dry by my harassments, I would have known better than to try to set an umbrella on end on one of those glassy German floors in the dark; it can't be done in the daytime without four failures to one success. I had one comfort, though—Harris was yet still and silent—he had not stirred.

The umbrella could not locate me—there were four standing around the room, and all alike. I thought I would feel along the wall and find the door in that way. I rose up and began this operation, but raked down a picture. It was not a large one, but it made noise enough for a panorama. Harris gave out no sound, but I felt that if I experimented any further with the pictures I should be sure to wake him. Better give up trying to get out. Yes, I would find King Arthur's Round Table once more—I had already found it several times—and use it for a base of departure on an exploring tour for my bed; if I could find my bed I could then find my water-pitcher; I would quench my raging thirst and turn in. So I started on my hands and knees, because I could go faster that way, and with more confidence, too, and not knock down things. By and by I found the table—with my head—rubbed the bruise a little, then rose up and started, with hands abroad and fingers spread, to balance myself. I found a chair; then the wall; then another chair; then a sofa; then an alpenstock, then another sofa; this confounded me, for I had thought there was only one sofa. I hunted up the table again and took a fresh start; found some more chairs.

It occurred to me, now, as it ought to have done before, that as the table was round, it was therefore of no value as a base to aim from; so I moved off once more, and at random among the wilderness of chairs and sofas—wandered off into unfamiliar regions, and presently knocked a candlestick off a mantelpiece; grabbed at the candlestick and knocked off a lamp, grabbed at the lamp and knocked off a water-pitcher with a rattling crash, and thought to myself, "I've found you at last—I judged I was close upon you." Harris shouted "murder," and "thieves," and finished with "I'm absolutely drowned."

The crash had roused the house. Mr. X. pranced in, in his long night-garment, with a candle, young Z. after him with another candle; a procession swept in at another door, with candles and lanterns—landlord and two German guests in their nightgowns, and a chambermaid in hers.

I looked around; I was at Harris's bed, a Sabbath day's journey from my own. There was only one sofa; it was against the wall; there was only one chair where a body could get at it—I had been revolving around it like a planet, and colliding with it like a comet half the night.

I explained how I had been employing myself, and why. Then the landlord's party left, and the rest of us set about our preparations for breakfast, for the dawn was ready to break. I glanced furtively at my pedometer, and found I had made 47 miles. But I did not care, for I had come out for a pedestrian tour anyway.

—*A Tramp Abroad* (1880), chapter 13

———————•———————

This incident—or something like it—actually happened. However, the traveling companion "Harris" whom it describes was a pure fiction. Mark Twain actually shared the hotel room with his wife, Livy. When he accidentally woke her up and explained he was hunting for his sock, she replied, "Are you hunting for it with a club?" Incidentally, if Mark Twain actually made forty-seven miles during his nocturnal travels in the hotel room, that would be ironic. The story appears in A Tramp Abroad, which describes itself as an account of "a man adventurous enough to undertake a journey through Europe on foot." That claim is a joke, however, as the book's narrator journeys through Europe by almost every possible means of conveyance except on foot. If the narrator actually walked forty-seven miles in his hotel room, that may have been farther than he walked anywhere else in Europe.

———————•———————

PART III.

Remarkable Characters

Given the great amount of fiction and wildly divergent genres in which Mark Twain wrote, it should not be surprising that he created many remarkable and strange characters. Some of the most unusual characters in his best-known works, *Tom Sawyer* and *Huckleberry Finn*, include the despicable Injun Joe and Pap Finn and those devious scalawags who called themselves the "King of France" and the "Duke of Bridgewater." However, even they seem almost commonplace compared to some of those whom he created for other works. "The Mysterious New Boy," for example, introduces a boy with both the unlikely name "Forty-four" and incredible supernatural powers. Perhaps the most extraordinary character Mark Twain ever created, he is, unfortunately, little known because he appears only in an unfinished story excerpted here—"Schoolhouse Hill"—which wasn't published until nearly sixty years after Mark Twain died. "Scaring Nicodemus to Death" presents the opposite of Forty-four—an apparent simpleton, modeled on a person Mark Twain knew as a youth. However, people who attempt to play cruel tricks on this country bumpkin are in for big surprises! "Murder Will Out!" is based on another of Mark Twain's boyhood reminiscences—this one about his own guilt in the flaming death of the town drunk. "The Incredible Shrinking Young Man" is a return to Mark Twain's earliest works of pure imagination. Originally titled "Aurelia's Unfortunate Young Man," it contains an unstated mystery, namely: Which character is the *more* remarkable—the steadily disintegrating young man? Or his inexplicably devoted lover, Aurelia? Finally, the last piece, "The War Prayer," is another work of pure imagination that goes in a startling different direction. Written late in Mark Twain's life and not published until after he died, it is a powerful sketch that presents a man claiming to be a messenger sent directly from God to make a powerful argument against war that will ever remain timeless.

13.

"THE MYSTERIOUS NEW BOY"

---•◆•---

In Tom Sawyer and Huck Finn's sleepy little rustic hometown, the arrival of a new boy is a rarer sight than a new comet. When the handsome new boy in this tale appears at the village school, all attention is naturally focused on him. This boy, however, is something much more than a mere stranger. He is, in fact, the most marvelous and most awe-inspiring person anyone in the village—or anywhere else on earth—has ever seen. Even Tom Sawyer is impressed! But, who is he? And where does he come from?

---•◆•---

It was not much short of fifty years ago—and a frosty morning. Up the naked long slant of Schoolhouse Hill the boys and girls of Petersburg village were struggling from various directions against the fierce wind, and making slow and difficult progress. The wind was not the only hindrance, nor the worst; the slope was steel-clad in frozen snow, and the foothold offered was far from trustworthy. Every now and then a boy who had almost gained the schoolhouse stepped out with too much confidence, thinking himself safe, lost his footing, struck upon his back and went skimming down the hill behind his freed sled, the straggling schoolmates scrambling out of his way and applauding as he sailed by; and in a few seconds he was at the bottom with all his work to do over again. But this was fun; fun for the boy, fun for the witnesses, fun all around; for boys and girls are ignorant and do not know trouble when they see it.

Sid Sawyer, the good boy, the model boy, the cautious boy, did not lose his footing. He brought no sled, he chose his steps with care, and he arrived in safety. Tom Sawyer brought his sled and he, also, arrived without adventure, for Huck Finn was along to help, although he was not a member of the school in these days; he merely came in order to be with Tom until school "took in." Henry Bascom arrived safely, too—Henry Bascom the new boy of last year, whose papa was a

Children arriving at the village schoolhouse are greeted by the master outside the building.

[slave] trader and rich; a mean boy, he was, and proud of his clothes, and he had a play-slaughterhouse at home, with all the equipment, in little of a regular slaughterhouse, and in it he slaughtered puppies and kittens exactly as beeves were done to death down at the "point"; and he was this year's school-bully, and was dreaded and flattered by the timid and the weak and disliked by everybody. He arrived safely because his [servant] Jake helped him up the hill and drew his sled for him; and it wasn't a home-made sled but a "store" sled, and was painted, and had iron-tyred runners, and came from St. Louis, and was the only store-sled in the village.

All the twenty-five or thirty boys and girls arrived at last, red and panting, and still cold, notwithstanding their yarn comforters and mufflers and mittens; and the girls flocked into the little schoolhouse and the boys packed themselves together in the shelter of its lee.

It was noticed now that a new boy was present, and this was a matter of extraordinary interest, for a new boy in the village was a rarer sight than a new comet in the sky. He was apparently about fifteen; his clothes were neat and tasty above the common, he had a good and winning face, and he was surprisingly hand-some—handsome beyond imagination! His eyes were deep and rich and beautiful, and there was a modesty and dignity and grace and graciousness and charm about him which some of the boys, with a pleased surprise, recognized at once as famil-iar—they had encountered it in books about fairy-tale princes and that sort. They stared at him with a trying backwoods frankness, but he was tranquil and did not seem troubled by it. After looking him over, Henry Bascom pushed forward in front of the others and began in an insolent tone to question him:

"Who are you? What's your name?"

The boy slowly shook his head, as if meaning by that that he did not understand.

"Do you hear? Answer up!"

Another slow shake.

"Answer up, I tell you, or I'll make you!"

Tom Sawyer said—

"That's no way, Henry Bascom—it's against the rules. If you want your fuss, and can't wait till recess, which is regular, go at it right and fair; put a chip on your shoulder and dare him to knock it off."

"All right; he's got to fight, and fight now, whether he answers or not; and I'm not particular about how it's got at." He put a flake of ice on his shoulder and said, "There—knock it off if you dare!"

The boy looked inquiringly from face to face, and Tom stepped up and answered by signs. He touched the boy's right hand, then flipped off the ice with his own, put it back in its place, and indicated that that was what the boy must do. The lad smiled, put out his hand, and touched the ice with his finger. Bascom launched a blow at his face which seemed to miss; the energy of it made Bascom slip on the ice, and he departed on his back to the bottom of the hill, with cordial laughter and mock applause from the boys to cheer his way.

The bell began to ring, and the little crowd swarmed into the schoolhouse and hurried to their places. The stranger found a seat apart, and was at once a target for the wondering eyes and eager whisperings of the girls. School now "began." Archibald Ferguson, the old Scotch schoolmaster, rapped upon his desk with his ruler, rose upon his dais and stood, with his hands together, and said, "Let us pray." After the prayer there was a hymn, then the buzz of study began, and the multiplication class was called up. It recited, up to "twelve times twelve;" then the arithmetic class followed and exposed its slates to much censure and little commendation; next came the grammar class of parsing parrots, who knew everything about grammar except how to utilize its rules in common speech.

"Spelling class!" The schoolmaster's wandering eye now fell upon the new boy, and he countermanded that order. "Hm—a stranger? Who is it? What is your name, my boy?"

The lad rose and bowed, and said—

"Pardon, monsieur—je ne comprehends pas."

Ferguson looked astonished and pleased, and said in French—

"Ah, French—how pleasant! It is the first time I have heard that tongue in many years. I am the only person in this village who speaks it. You are very welcome; I shall be glad to renew my practice. You speak no English?"

"Not a word, sir."

"You must try to learn it."

"Gladly, sir."

"It is your purpose to attend my school regularly?"

"If I may have the privilege, sir."

"That is well. Take English only, for the present. The grammar has about thirty rules. It will be necessary to learn them by heart."

"I already know them, sir, but I do not know what the words mean."

"What is it you say? You know the rules of the grammar, and yet don't know English? How can that be? When did you learn them?"

"I heard your grammar class recite the rules before entering upon the rest of their lesson."

The teacher looked over his glasses at the boy a while, in a puzzled way, then said—

"If you know no English words, how did you know it was a grammar lesson?"

"From similarities to the French—like the word grammar itself."

"True! You have a headpiece! You will soon get the rules by heart."

"I know them by heart, sir."

"Impossible! You are speaking extravagantly; you do not know what you are saying."

The boy bowed respectfully, resumed his upright position, and said nothing. The teacher felt rebuked, and said gently—

"I should not have spoke so, and am sorry. Overlook it, my boy; recite me a rule of grammar—as well as you can—never mind the mistakes."

The boy began with the first rule and went along with his task quite simply and comfortably, dropping rule after rule unmutilated from his lips, while the teacher and the school sat with parted lips and suspended breath, listening in mute wonder. At the finish the boy bowed again, and stood, waiting. Ferguson sat silent a moment or two in his great chair, then said—

"On your honor—those rules were wholly unknown to you when you came into this house?"

Tom Sawyer's classmates stare in bewilderment at the handsome new boy after he dazzles the master with his let-ter-perfect recitation of English grammar rules.

"Yes, sir."

"Upon my word I believe you, on the veracity that is written in your face. No—I don't—I can't. It is beyond the reach of belief. A memory like that—an ear for pronunciation like that, is of course im—why, *no* one in the earth has such a memory as that!"

The boy bowed, and said nothing. Again the old Scot felt rebuked, and said—

"Of course I don't mean—I don't really mean—er—tell me: if you could *prove* in some way that you have never until now—for instance, if you could repeat other things which you have heard here. Will you try?"

With engaging simplicity and serenity, and with apparently no intention of being funny, the boy began on the arithmetic lesson, and faithfully put into his report everything the teacher had said and everything the pupils had said, and imitated the voice and style of all concerned—as follows:

"Well, I give you my word it's enough to drive a man back to the land of his fathers, and make him hide his head in the charitable heather and never more give out that *he* can teach the race! Five slates—five of the chiefest intelligences in the school—and look at them! Scots wha hae wi' Wallace bled—Harry Slater! *Yes, sir.* Since when, is it, that 17, and 45, and 68 and 21 make 155, ye unspeakable creature? *I—I—if you please, sir, Sally Fitch hunched me and I reckon it made me make a figure 9 when I was intending to make a—* There's not a 9 in the sum, you blockhead!—and ye'll get a black mark for the lie you've told; a foolish lie, ill wrought and clumsy in the invention; you have no talent—stock to the truth. Becky Thatcher! *Yes, sir, please.* Make the curtsy over again, and do it better. *Yes, sir.* Lower, still! *Yes, sir.* Very good. Now I'll just ask you how you make that 58 from 156 leaves 43? *If you please, sir, I subtracted the 8 from the 6, which leaves—which leaves—I* THINK *it leaves 3—and then—* Peace! ye banks and braes o' bonny Doon but it's a rare answer and a credit to my patient teaching! Jack Stillson! *Yes, sir.* Straighten up, and don't d-r-a-w-l like that—it's a fatigue to hear ye! And what *have* you been setting down here: If a horse travels 96 feet in 4 seconds and two-tenths of a second, how much will a barrel of mackerel cost when potatoes are 22 cents a bushel? Answer—eleven dollars and forty-six cents. You incurable ass, don't you see that ye've mixed three questions into one? The gauds and vanities o'learning! Oh, here's a hand, my trusty fere, and gie's a hand o'thing, and we'll—out of my sight, yet maundering idiot!—"

The show was become unendurable. the boy had forgotten not a word, not a tone, nor a look, nor a gesture, nor any shade or trifle of detail—he was letter-perfect, and the house could shut its eyes anywhere in the performance and know which individual was being imitated. The boy's deep gravity and sincerity made the exhibition more and more trying the longer he went on. For a time, in decorous, disciplined and heroic silence, house and teacher sat bursting to laugh, with the tears running down, the regulations requiring noiseless propriety and solemnity; but when the stranger recited the answer to the triple sum and then put his hands together and raised his despairing eyes toward heaven in exact imitation of Mr. Ferguson's manner, the teacher's face broke up; and with that concession the house let go with a crash and laughed its fill thenceforth. But the boy went tranquilly on and on, unheeding the screams and throes and explosions, clear to the finish; then made his bow and straightened up and stood, bland and waiting.

It took some time to quiet the school; then Mr. Ferguson said—

"It is the most extraordinary thing I have seen in my life. In this world there is not another talent like yours, lad; be grateful for it, and for the noble modesty with which you bear about such a treasure. How long would you be able to keep in your memory the things which you have been uttering?"

"I cannot forget anything that I see or hear, sir."

"At all?"

"No, sir."

"It seems incredible—just impossible. Let me experiment a little—for the pure joy of it. Take my English-French dictionary and sit down and study it while I go with the school's exercises. Shall you be disturbed by us?"

"No, sir."

He took the dictionary and began to skim the pages swiftly, one after another. Evidently he dwelt upon no page, but merely gave it a lick from top to bottom with his eye and turned it over. The school-work rambled on after a fashion, but it consisted of blunders, mainly, for the fascinated eyes and minds of school and teacher were oftener on the young stranger than elsewhere. At the end of twenty minutes the boy laid the book down. Mr. Ferguson noticed this, and said, with a touch of disappointment in his tone—

"I am sorry. I saw that it did not interest you."

The boy rose and said—

"Oh, sir, on the contrary!" This in French; then in English, "I have now the words of your language, but the forms not—perhaps, how you call?—the pronunciation also."

"You have the words? How many of the words do you know?"

"All, sir."

"No—no—there are 645 octavo pages—you couldn't have examined a tenth of them in this short time. A page in two seconds?—it is impossible."

The boy bowed respectfully, and said nothing.

"There—I am in fault again. I shall learn of you—courtesy. Give me the book. Begin. Recite—recite!"

It was another miracle. The boy poured out, in a rushing stream, the words, the definitions, the accompanying illustrative phrases and sentences, the signs indicating the parts of speech—everything; he skipped nothing, he put in all the details, and he even got the pronunciations substantially right, since it was a pronouncing-dictionary. Teacher and school sat in a soundless and motionless spell of awe and admiration, unconscious of the flight of time, unconscious of everything but the beautiful stranger and his stupendous performance. After a long while the juggler interrupted his recitation to say—in rather cumbrous and booky English—

"It is of necessity—what you call 'of course,' n'est-ce pas?—that I now am enabled to apply the machinery of the rules of the grammar, since the meanings of the words which constitute them were become my possession—" Here he stopped, quoted the violated rule, corrected his sentence, then went on: "And it is of course that I now understand the languages—language—appropriated to the lesson of arithmetic—yet not all, the dictionary being in the offensive. As for example, to-wit, 'Scots wha he wi' Wallace bled, Sally Fitch *hunched* me, ye banks and braes o' bonny Doon, oh here's a hand my trusty fere and gie's a hand o' thine.' Some of these words are by mischance omitted from the dictionary, and thereby results confusion. Without knowledge of the signification of *hunched* one is ignorant of the nature of the explanation preferred by the mademoiselle Thatcher; and if one shall not know what a Doon is, and whether it is a financial bank or other that is involved, one is still yet again at a loss."

Silence. The master roused himself as if from a dream, and lifted his hands and said—

"It is not a parrot—it *thinks!* Boy, ye are a marvel! With listening an hour and studying half as long, you have learned the English language. You are the only person in America who knows all its words. Let it rest, where it is—the construction will come of itself. Take up the Latin, now, and the Greek, and short-hand writing, and the mathematics. Here are the books. You shall have thirty minutes to each. Then your education will be complete. But tell me! How do you manage these things? What is your method? You do not read the page, you only skim it down with your eye, as one wipes a column of sums from a slate. You understand my English?"

"Yes, master—perfectly. I have no method—meaning I have no mystery. I only see what is on the page—that is all."

"But you see it at a glance."

"But is not the particulars of the page—" He stopped to apply the rule and correct the sentence: "are not the particulars of the page the same as the particulars of the school? I see all the pupils at once; do I not know, then, how each is dressed, and his attitude and expression, and the color of his eyes and hair, and the length of his nose, and if his shoes are tied or not? Why shall I glance twice?"

Margaret Stover, over in the corner, drew her untied shoe back out of sight.

"Ah, well, I have seen no one else who could individualize a thousand details with one sweep of the two eyes. Maybe the eyes of the admirable creature the dragon-fly can do it, but that is another matter—he has twelve thousand, and so the haul he makes with his multitudinous glance is a thing within reason and comprehension. Get at your Latin, lad." Then with a sigh, "We will proceed with our poor dull ploddings."

The boy took up the book and began to turn the pages, much as if he were carefully counting them. The school glanced with an evil joy at Henry Bascom, and was pleased to note that he was not happy. He was the only Latin pupil in the school, and his pride in this distinction was a thing through which his mates were made to endure much suffering.

The school droned and buzzed along, with the bulk of its mind and its interest not on its work but fixed in envy and discouragement upon the new scholar. At the end of half an hour it saw him lay down his Latin book and take up the Greek; it glanced contentedly at Henry Bascom, and a satisfied murmur dribbled down the benches. In turn the Greek and the mathematics were mastered, then "The New Short-Hand Method, called Phonography" was taken up. But the phonographic study was short-lived—it lasted but a minute and twenty seconds; then the boy played with several other books. The master noticed this, and by and by said—

"So soon done with the Phonography?"

"It is only a set of compact and simple *principles,* sir. They are applicable with ease and certainty—like the principles of the mathematics. Also, the examples assist; innumerable combinations of English words are given, and the vowels eliminated. It is admirable, this system, for precision and clarity; one could write Greek and Latin with it, making word-combinations with the vowels excised, and still be understood."

"Your English is improving by leaps and bounds, my boy."

"Yes, sir. I have been reading these English books. They have furnished me the forms of the language—the moulds in which it is cast—the idioms."

"I am past wondering! I think there is no miracle that a mind like this cannot do. Pray go to the blackboard and let me see what Greek may look like in phonographic word-combinations with the vowel-signs left out. I will read some passages."

The boy took the chalk, and the trial began. The master read very slowly; then a little faster; then faster still; then as fast as he could. The boy kept up, without apparent difficulty. Then the master threw in Latin sentences, English sentences, French ones, and now and then a hardy problem from Euclid to be ciphered out. The boy was competent, all the while.

"It is amazing, my child, amazing—stupefying! Do me one more miracle, and I strike my flag. Here is a page of columns of figures. Add them up. I have seen the famous lightning-calculator do it in three minutes and a quarter, and I know the answer. I will hold the watch. Beat him!"

The boy glanced at the page, made his bow and said—

"The total is 4,865,493 if the blurred twenty-third figure in the column is a 9; if it is a 7, the total is less by 2."

"Right, and he is beaten by incredible odds; but you hadn't time to even see the blurred figure, let alone note its place. Wait till I find it—the twenty-third, did you say? Here it is, but I can't tell which it is—it may be a 9, it may be a 7. But no matter, one of your answers is right, according to which name we give the figure. Dear me, can my watch be right? It is long past the noon recess, and everybody has forgotten his dinner. In my thirty years of schoolteaching experience this has not happened before. Truly it is a day of miracles. Children, we dull moles are in no condition to further plod and grub after the excitements and bewilderments of this intellectual conflagration—school is dismissed. My wonderful scholar, tell me your name."

The school crowded forward in a body to devour the stranger at close quarters with their envying eyes; all except Bascom, who remained apart and sulked.

"Quarante-quatre, sir. Forty-four."

"Why—why—that is only a number, you know, not a name."

The boy bowed. The master dropped the subject.

"When did you arrive in our town?"

"Last night, sir."

"Have you friends or relatives among us?"

"No, sir—none. Mr. Hotchkiss allows me to lodge in his house."

"You will find the Hotchkisses good people, excellent people. Had you introductions to them?"

"No, sir."

"You see I am curious; but we are all that, in this monotonous little place, and we mean no harm. How did you make them understand what you wanted?"

"Through my signs and their compassion. It was cold, and I was a stranger."

"Good—good—and well stated, without waste of words. It describes the Hotchkisses; it's a whole biography. Whence did you come—and how?"

Forty-four bowed. The master said, affably—

"It was another indiscretion—you will not remember it against—no, I mean you will forget it, in consid—what I am trying to say is, that you will overlook it—that is it, overlook it. I am glad you are come, grateful that you are come."

"I thank you—thank you deeply, sir."

"My official character requires that I precede you in leaving this house, therefore I do it. This is an apology. Adieu."

"Adieu, my master."

The school made way, and the old gentleman marched out between the ranks with a grave dignity proper to his official state.

—"Schoolhouse Hill" (1898), chapter 1

———•———

"Forty-four" is a suitably unusual name for an extraordinarily unusual boy. What makes him so unusual? Is he a magician, a warlock, or perhaps even some kind of god? Whatever he is, we can be certain that Tom Sawyer will want to know more about him. Unfortunately, Mark Twain never finished this story.

———•———

14.

"SCARING NICODEMUS TO DEATH"

---·••·---

Mark Twain regarded practical jokes as "witless inventions." Late in life, he wrote that "grown-up persons indulge in practical jokes, the fact gauges them. They have lived narrow, obscure, and ignorant lives, and at full manhood they still retain and cherish a job lot of left-over standards and ideals that would have been discarded with their boyhood if they had then moved out into the world and a broader life." Hold that thought as you read this anecdote from A Tramp Abroad, *his 1880 account of his recent tour of Europe. Here his narrator describes an argument he had with his imaginary travel companion Harris about how melodramatically grown men react to the pain they experience when they have teeth extracted. Note how the subject of their conversation gradually transitions to human skeletons!*

---·••·---

That changed the subject to dentistry. I said I believed the average man dreaded tooth-pulling more than amputation, and that he would yell quicker under the former operation than he would under the latter. The philosopher Harris said that the average man would not yell in either case if he had an audience. Then he continued:

"When our [Civil War] brigade first went into camp on the Potomac, we used to be brought up standing, occasionally, by an ear-splitting howl of anguish. That meant that a soldier was getting a tooth pulled in a tent. But the surgeons soon changed that; they instituted open-air dentistry. There never was a howl afterward—that is, from the man who was having the tooth pulled. At the daily dental hour there would always be about five hundred soldiers gathered together in the neighborhood of that dental chair waiting to see the performance—and help; and the moment the surgeon took a grip on the candidate's tooth and began to lift, every one of those five hundred rascals would clap his hand to his jaw and begin

Civil War dental surgery always produced an enormous caterwaul.

to hop around on one leg and howl with all the lungs he had! It was enough to raise your hair to hear that variegated and enormous unanimous caterwaul burst out! With so big and so derisive an audience as that, a sufferer wouldn't emit a sound though you pulled his head off. The surgeons said that pretty often a patient was compelled to laugh, in the midst of his pangs, but that they had never caught one crying out, after the open-air exhibition was instituted."

Dental surgeons suggested doctors, doctors suggested death, death suggested skeletons—and so, by a logical process the conversation melted out of one of these subjects and into the next, until the topic of skeletons raised up Nicodemus Dodge out of the deep grave in my memory where he had lain buried and forgotten for twenty-five years. When I was a boy in a printing-office in Missouri, a loose-jointed, long-legged, tow-headed, jeans-clad, countrified cub of about sixteen lounged in one day, and without removing his hands from the depths of his trousers pockets or taking off his faded ruin of a slouch hat, whose broken rim hung limp and ragged about his eyes and ears like a bug-eaten cabbage-leaf, stared indifferently around, then leaned his hip against the editor's table, crossed his mighty brogans, aimed at a distant fly from a crevice in his upper teeth, laid him low, and said with composure:

"Whar's the boss?"

"I am the boss," said the editor, following this curious bit of architecture wonderingly along up to its clock-face with his eye.

"Don't want anybody fur to learn the business 't ain't likely?"

"Well, I don't know. Would you like to learn it?"

"Pap's so po' he cain't run me no mo', so I want to git a show somers if I kin, 'tain't no diffunce what—I'm strong and hearty, and I don't turn my back on no kind of work, hard nur soft."

"Do you think you would like to learn the printing business?"

"Well, I don't re'ly k'yer a durn what I *do* learn, so's I git a chance fur to make my way. I'd jist as soon learn print'n 's anything."

"Can you read?"

"Yes—middlin'."

"Write?"

"Well, I've seed people could lay over me thar."

"Cipher?"

"Not good enough to keep store, I don't reckon, but up as fur as twelve-times-twelve I ain't no slouch. 'Tother side of that is what gits me."

"Where is your home?"

"I'm f'm old Shelby."

"What's your father's religious denomination?"

"Him? Oh, he's a blacksmith."

"No, no—I don't mean his trade. What's his *religious* denomination?"

"O—I didn't understand you befo'. He's a Freemason."

"No-no, you don't get my meaning yet. What I mean is, does he belong to any *church*?"

"*Now* you're talkin'! Couldn't make out what you was a tryin' to git through yo' head no way. B'long to a *church*! Why, boss, he's ben the pizenest kind of a Free-will Babtis' for forty year. They ain't no pizener ones 'n' what *he* is. Mighty good man, pap is. Everybody says that. If they said any diffrunt they wouldn't say it whar *I* wuz—not much they wouldn't."

"What is your own religion?"

"Well, boss, you've kind o' got me, thar—and yit you hain't got me so mighty much, nuther. I think 't if a feller he'ps another feller when he's in trouble, and don't cuss, and don't do no mean things, nur noth'n' he ain' no business to do, and don't spell the Saviour's name with a little *g*, he ain't runnin' no resks—he's about as saift as if he b'longed to a church."

"But suppose he did spell it with a little *g*—what then?"

"Well, if he done it a-purpose, I reckon he wouldn't stand no chance—he *oughtn't* to have no chance, anyway, I'm most rotten certain 'bout that."

"What is your name?"

"Nicodemus Dodge."

"I think maybe you'll do, Nicodemus. We'll give you a trial, anyway."

"All right."

"When would you like to begin?"

"Now."

So, within ten minutes after we had first glimpsed this nondescript he was one of us, and with his coat off and hard at it.

Beyond that end of our establishment which was furthest from the street, was a deserted garden, pathless, and thickly grown with the bloomy and villainous "jimpson" weed and its common friend the stately sunflower. In the midst of this mournful spot was a decayed and aged little "frame" house with but one room, one window, and no ceiling—it had been a smoke-house a generation before. Nicodemus was given this lonely and ghostly den as a bedchamber.

The village smarties recognized a treasure in Nicodemus, right away—a butt to play jokes on. It was easy to see that he was inconceivably green and confiding. George Jones had the glory of perpetrating the first joke on him; he gave him a cigar with a fire-cracker in it and winked to the crowd to come; the thing exploded presently and swept away the bulk of Nicodemus's eyebrows and eyelashes. He simply said—

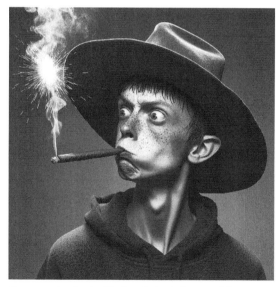

First tremors signaling that Nicodemus's cigar is about to explode.

"I consider them kind of seeg'yars dangersome,"—and seemed to suspect nothing. The next evening Nicodemus waylaid George and poured a bucket of ice-water over him.

One day, while Nicodemus was in swimming, Tom McElroy "tied" his clothes. Nicodemus made a bonfire of Tom's by way of retaliation.

A third joke was played upon Nicodemus a day or two later—he walked up the middle aisle of the village church, Sunday night, with a staring handbill pinned between his shoulders. The joker spent the remainder of the night, after church, in the cellar of a deserted house, and Nicodemus sat on the cellar door till toward breakfast-time to make sure that the prisoner remembered that if any noise was made, some rough treatment would be the consequence. The cellar had two feet of stagnant water in it, and was bottomed with six inches of soft mud.

But I wander from the point. It was the subject of skeletons that brought this boy back to my recollection. Before a very long time had elapsed, the village smarties began to feel an uncomfortable consciousness of not having made a very shining success out of their attempts on the simpleton from "old Shelby." Experimenters grew scarce and chary. Now the young doctor came to the rescue. There was delight and applause when he proposed to scare Nicodemus to death, and explained how he was going to do it. He had a noble new skeleton—the skeleton of the late and only local celebrity, Jimmy Finn, the village drunkard—a grisly piece of property which he had bought of Jimmy Finn himself, at auction, for fifty dollars, under great competition, when Jimmy lay very sick in the tan-yard a fortnight before his death. The fifty dollars had gone promptly for whisky and had considerably hurried up the change of ownership in the skeleton. The doctor would put Jimmy Finn's skeleton in Nicodemus's bed!

This was done—about half-past ten in the evening. About Nicodemus's usual bedtime—midnight—the village jokers came creeping stealthily through the jimpson weeds and sunflowers toward the lonely frame den. They reached the window and peeped in. There sat the long-legged pauper, on his bed, in a very short shirt, and nothing more; he was dangling his legs contentedly back and forth, and wheezing the music of "Camptown Races" out of a paper-overlaid comb which he was pressing against his mouth; by him lay a new jewsharp, a new top, a solid india-rubber ball, a handful of painted marbles, five pounds of "store" candy, and a well-gnawed slab of gingerbread as big and as thick as a volume of sheet music. He had sold the skeleton to a traveling quack for three dollars and was enjoying the result!

—*A Tramp Abroad* (1880), chapter 23

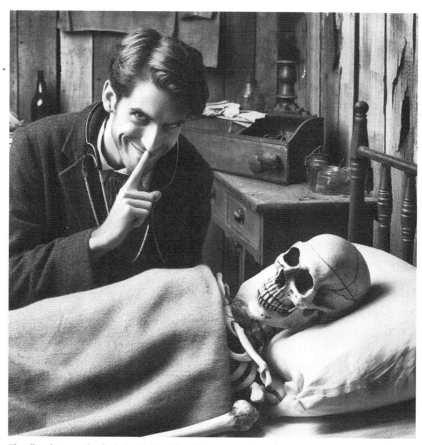

The village doctor smirks after laying his fifty-dollar skeleton on Nicodemus's bed.

There may be some truth in this anecdote. Mark Twain invented his traveling companion Harris, but he modeled "Nicodemus Dodge" on a real person named Jim Wolf with whom he had worked as a print shop apprentice when he was a boy. Ten years after writing this anecdote for his travel book, he told a different version of this story in a speech he delivered to a professional druggists convention in Washington, D.C. The preface to this tale above asked you to keep in mind Mark Twain's harsh opinion of practical jokesters. Note that A Tramp Abroad credits the village doctor with the idea of scaring Nicodemus with the skeleton he had purchased. In contrast, Mark Twain's 1890 speech admits that scaring "Nicodemus Dodge" with the skeleton was his idea and that of his fellow apprentices. "We took him for a fool," he said. He then added:

. . . and thought we would try to scare him to death. We went to the village druggist and borrowed a skeleton. The skeleton didn't belong to the druggist, but he had imported it for the village doctor because the doctor thought he would send away for it, having some delicacy about using—the price of a skeleton at that time was fifty dollars. I don't know how high they go now but probably higher on account of the tariff.

We borrowed the skeleton about nine o'clock at night and we got this man—Nicodemus Dodge was his name—we got him downtown, out of the way, and then we put the skeleton in his bed. He lived in a little one-storied log cabin in the middle of a vacant lot. We left him to get home by himself. We enjoyed the result in the light of anticipation. But by and by we began to drop into silence. The possible consequences were preying upon us. Suppose that it frightens him into madness, overturns his reason and send him screeching through the streets! We shall spend sleepless nights the rest of our days. Everybody was afraid.

By and by it was forced to the lips of one of us that we had better go at once and see what had happened. Loaded down with crime, we approached that hut and peeped through the windows. That long-legged critter was sitting on his bed with a hunk of gingerbread in his hand, and between the bites he played a tune on a jew's harp. There he sat perfectly happy, and all around him on the bed were toys and gimcracks and striped candy. The darned cuss, he had gone and sold that skeleton for five dollars.

The druggist's fifty-dollar skeleton was gone. We went in tears to the druggist and explained the matter. We couldn't have raised that fifty dollars in two hundred and fifty years. We were getting board and clothing for the first year, clothing and board for the second year, and both of them for the third year. The druggist forgave us on the spot but he said he would like us to let him have our skeletons when we were done with them. There couldn't be anything fairer than that. We spouted our skeletons and went away comfortable.

But from that time the druggist's prosperity ceased. This was one of the most unfortunate speculations he ever went into. After some years one of the boys went and got drowned. That was one skeleton gone, and I tell you the druggist felt pretty badly about it. A few years after, another of the boys went up in a balloon. He was to get five dollars an hour for it. When he gets back they will be owing him one million dollars. The druggist's property was decreasing right along.

After a few more years the third boy tried an experiment to see if a dynamite charge would go. It went all right. They found some of him, perhaps a vest pocketful. Still, it was enough to show that some more of that estate had gone.

The druggist was getting along in years and he commenced to correspond with me. I have been the best correspondent he has. He is the sweetest-natured man I ever saw—always mild and polite and never wants to hurry me at all.

I get a letter from him every now and then, and he never refers to my form as a skeleton. Says, "Well, how is it getting along. Is it in good repair?"

I got a night-rate message from him recently. Said he was getting old and the property was depreciating in value, and if I could let him have a part of it now he would give time on the balance.

Think of the graceful way in which he does everything, the generosity of it all. You cannot find a finer character than that. It is the gracious characteristic of all druggists. So, out of my heart, I wish you all prosperity and every happiness.
—Address before National Wholesale Druggists Association,
Washington, D.C., fall 1890

15.

"MURDER WILL OUT!"

———————————————

In the previous chapter, Mark Twain describes a real-life drunkard named Jimmy Finn apparently drinking himself to death when he was ill. In this chapter, he tells a different story about Finn's demise. It's not unreasonable, incidentally, to suspect that the real Jimmy Finn was one of the models for Huck's drunken father, Pap Finn, in Huckle-berry Finn, in which Pap meets yet another kind of end. What this tale says about the real Jimmy certainly fits the fictional Pap's description; however, this tale is not so much about Jimmy Finn as it is about Mark Twain himself and a particularly unpleasant memory from his boyhood. He wrote this passage shortly after revisiting his hometown of Hannibal, Missouri, for the first time in many years in 1882.

———————————————

The slaughter-house is gone from the mouth of Bear Creek and so is the small jail (or "calaboose") which once stood in its neighborhood. A citizen asked, "Do you remember when Jimmy Finn, the town drunkard, was burned to death in the calaboose?"

Observe, now, how history becomes defiled, through lapse of time and the help of the bad memories of men. Jimmy Finn was not burned in the calaboose, but died a natural death in a tan vat, of a combination of delirium tremens and spontaneous combustion. When I say natural death, I mean it was a natural death for Jimmy Finn to die. The calaboose victim was not a citizen; he was a poor stranger, a harmless whiskey-sodden tramp. I know more about his case than anybody else; I knew too much of it, in that bygone day, to relish speaking of it. That tramp was wandering about the streets one chilly evening, with a pipe in his mouth, and begging for a match; he got neither matches nor courtesy; on the contrary, a troop of bad little boys followed him around and amused themselves with nagging and annoying him. I assisted; but at last, some appeal which the

Ashamed of having helped pester the drunken Jimmy Finn, young Sammy Clemens sneaks matches to him.

wayfarer made for forbearance, accompanying it with a pathetic reference to his forlorn and friendless condition, touched such sense of shame and remnant of right feeling as were left in me, and I went away and got him some matches, and then hied me home and to bed, heavily weighted as to conscience, and unbuoyant in spirit. An hour or two afterward, the man was arrested and locked up in the calaboose by the marshal—large name for a constable, but that was his title. At two in the morning, the church bells rang for fire, and everybody turned out, of course—I with the rest. The tramp had used his matches disastrously: he had set his straw bed on fire, and the oaken sheathing of the room had caught. When I reached the ground, two hundred men, women, and children stood massed together, transfixed with horror, and staring at the grated windows of the jail. Behind the iron bars, and tugging frantically at them, and screaming for help, stood the tramp; he seemed like a black object set against a sun, so white and intense was the light at his back. That marshal could not be found, and he had the only key. A battering-ram was quickly improvised, and the thunder of its blows upon the door had so encouraging a sound that the spectators broke into wild cheering, and believed the merciful battle won. But it was not so. The timbers were too strong; they did not yield. It was said that the man's death-grip still held fast to the bars after he was dead; and that in this position the fires wrapped him about and consumed him. As to this, I do not know. What was seen after I recognized the face that was pleading through the bars was seen by others, not by me.

I saw that face, so situated, every night for a long time afterward; and I believed myself as guilty of the man's death as if I had given him the matches purposely that he might burn himself up with them. I had not a doubt that I should be hanged if my connection with this tragedy were found out. The happenings and the impressions of that time are burnt into my memory, and the study of them entertains me as much now as they themselves distressed me then. If anybody spoke of that grisly matter, I was all ears in a moment, and alert to hear what might be said, for I was always dreading and expecting to find out that I was suspected; and so fine and so delicate was the perception of my guilty conscience, that it often detected suspicion in the most purposeless remarks, and in looks, gestures, glances of the eye which had no significance, but which sent me shivering away in a panic of fright, just the same. And how sick it made me when somebody dropped, howsoever carelessly and barren of intent, the remark that "murder will out!" For a boy of ten years, I was carrying a pretty weighty cargo.

All this time I was blessedly forgetting one thing—the fact that I was an inveterate talker in my sleep. But one night I awoke and found my bed-mate—my younger brother—sitting up in bed and contemplating me by the light of the moon. I said:—

"What is the matter?"

"You talk so much I can't sleep."

I came to a sitting posture in an instant, with my kidneys in my throat and my hair on end.

"What did I say? Quick—out with it—what did I say?"

"Nothing much."

"It's a lie—you know everything."

"Everything about what?"

"You know well enough. About *that*."

"About *what*?—I don't know what you are talking about. I think you are sick or crazy or something. But anyway, you're awake, and I'll get to sleep while I've got a chance."

He fell asleep and I lay there in a cold sweat, turning this new terror over in the whirling chaos which did duty as my mind. The burden of my thought was,

Feeling even more guilty than before after Finn burns himself alive in his jail cell, Sammy is plagued by nightmares of Finn's terrible death.

How much did I divulge? How much does he know?—what a distress is this uncertainty! But by and by I evolved an idea—I would wake my brother and probe him with a supposititious case. I shook him up, and said—

"Suppose a man should come to you drunk—"

"This is foolish—I never get drunk."

"I don't mean you, idiot—I mean the man. Suppose a *man* should come to you drunk, and borrow a knife, or a tomahawk, or a pistol, and you forgot to tell him it was loaded, and—"

"How could you load a tomahawk?"

"I don't mean the tomahawk, and I didn't *say* the tomahawk; I said the pistol. Now don't you keep breaking in that way, because this is serious. There's been a man killed."

"What! In this town?"

"Yes, in this town."

"Well, go on—I won't say a single word."

"Well, then, suppose you forgot to tell him to be careful with it, because it was loaded, and he went off and shot himself with that pistol—fooling with it, you know, and probably doing it by accident, being drunk. Well, would it be murder?"

"No—suicide."

"No, no. I don't mean *his* act, I mean yours: would you be a murderer for letting him have that pistol?"

After deep thought came this answer—

"Well, I should think I was guilty of something—maybe murder—yes, probably murder, but I don't quite know."

This made me very uncomfortable. However, it was not a decisive verdict. I should have to set out the real case—there seemed to be no other way. But I would do it cautiously, and keep a watch out for suspicious effects. I said:—

"I was supposing a case, but I am coming to the real one now. Do you know how the man came to be burned up in the calaboose?"

"No."

"Haven't you the least idea?"

"Not the least."

"Wish you may die in your tracks if you have?"

"Yes, wish I may die in my tracks."

"Well, the way of it was this. The man wanted some matches to light his pipe. A boy got him some. The man set fire to the calaboose with those very matches, and burnt himself up."

"Is that so?"

"Yes, it is. Now, is that boy a murderer, do you think?"

"Let me see. The man was drunk?"

"Yes, he was drunk."

"Very drunk?"

"Yes."

"And the boy knew it?"

"Yes, he knew it."

There was a long pause. Then came this heavy verdict:—

"If the man was drunk, and the boy knew it, the boy murdered that man. This is certain."

Faint, sickening sensations crept along all the fibres of my body, and I seemed to know how a person feels who hears his death sentence pronounced from the bench. I waited to hear what my brother would say next. I believed I knew what it would be, and I was right. He said—-

"I know the boy."

I had nothing to say; so I said nothing. I simply shuddered. Then he added—

"Yes, before you got half through telling about the thing, I knew perfectly well who the boy was; it was Ben Coontz!"

I came out of my collapse as one who rises from the dead. I said, with admiration:—

"Why, how in the world did you ever guess it?"

"You told it in your sleep."

I said to myself, "How splendid that is! This is a habit which must be cultivated."

My brother rattled innocently on:—

"When you were talking in your sleep, you kept mumbling something about 'matches,' which I couldn't make anything out of; but just now, when you began to tell me about the man and the calaboose and the matches, I remembered that in your sleep you mentioned Ben Coontz two or three times; so I put this and that together, you see, and right away I knew it was Ben that burnt that man up."

I praised his sagacity effusively. Presently he asked—

"Are you going to give him up to the law?"

"No," I said; "I believe that this will be a lesson to him. I shall keep an eye on him, of course, for that is but right; but if he stops where he is and reforms, it shall never be said that I betrayed him."

"How good you are!"

"Well, I try to be. It is all a person can do in a world like this."

And now, my burden being shifted to other shoulders, my terrors soon faded away.

—*Life on the Mississippi* (1883), chapter 56

———••◆•——

The obvious question this tale raises is whether any of it is true. Did a vagrant tramp really burn himself to death in a Hannibal jail with matches given to him by the young Sam Clemens? The answer is apparently yes. Mark Twain retold the story in his autobiographical dictations, which he published in a national magazine in 1907. Readers can't always be sure that stories he tells about himself in his travel books are true, but would he tell an untrue story that reflects negatively on him in a published autobiography? Tales such as this are important as expressions of the dark side of his boyhood. "A boy's life is not all comedy," he wrote in his autobiography, "much of the tragic enters into it. The drunken tramp . . . who was burned up in the village jail, lay upon my conscience a hundred nights afterward and filled them with hideous dreams—dreams in which I saw his appealing face as I had seen it in the pathetic reality, pressed against the window-bars, with the red hell glowing behind him—a face which seemed to say to me, 'If you had not given me the matches, this would not have happened; you are responsible for my death.' . . . The tramp—who was to blame—suffered ten minutes; I, who was not to blame, suffered three months."

Mark Twain used the incident in Tom Sawyer, in which Muff Potter is falsely arrested for murder and sent to languish, friendless, in the town jail. Feeling guilty for knowing that Muff is innocent and doing nothing in his defense, Tom and his pal Huck pass tobacco and matches to him through his cell window. Happily, Muff does not suffer the same fate as that real-life tramp. Ben Coontz, incidentally, was a real-life boyhood friend of Mark Twain. The latter must have kept a close eye on him, as he turned out to be one of Hannibal's leading citizens, and his son, Robert E. Coontz, rose to the highest ranks in the U.S. Navy.

16.

"THE INCREDIBLE
SHRINKING YOUNG MAN"

———————•━—•━—•———————

The chief mystery in this somewhat grisly tale is why young Aurelia persists in remaining engaged to Williamson Breckinridge Caruthers, despite the fact he is literally falling apart before her eyes. Mark Twain enjoyed inflicting strange mishaps on characters occasionally, but Caruthers's collective calamities really are off the charts! Just about every nasty thing imaginable happens to him, including falling down a well—a fate Mark Twain would later, and more famously, inflict on Stephen Dowling Bots in Huckleberry Finn.

———————•━—•━—•———————

The facts in the following case came to me by letter from a young lady who lives in the beautiful city of San José; she is perfectly unknown to me, and simply signs herself "Aurelia Maria," which may possibly be a fictitious name. But no matter, the poor girl is almost heart-broken by the misfortunes she has undergone, and so confused by the conflicting counsels of misguided friends and insidious enemies, that she does not know what course to pursue in order to extricate herself from the web of difficulties in which she seems almost hopelessly involved. In this dilemma she turns to me for help, and supplicates for my guidance and instruction with a moving eloquence that would touch the heart of a statue. Hear her sad story:

She says that when she was sixteen years old she met and loved, with all the devotion of a passionate nature, a young man from New Jersey, named Williamson Breckinridge Caruthers, who was some six years her senior. They were engaged, with the free consent of their friends and relatives, and for a time it seemed as if their career was destined to be characterized by an immunity from sorrow beyond the usual lot of humanity. But at last the tide of fortune turned; young Caruthers became infected with smallpox of the most virulent type, and when he recovered from his illness his face was pitted like a waffle-mould, and his comeliness gone for ever. Aurelia thought to break off the engagement at first, but pity for her unfortunate lover caused her to postpone the marriage-day for a season, and give him another trial.

The very day before the wedding was to have taken place, Breckinridge, while absorbed in watching the flight of a balloon, walked into a well and fractured one of his legs, and it had to be taken off above the knee. Again Aurelia was moved to break the engagement, but again love triumphed, and she set the day forward and gave him another chance to reform.

And again misfortune overtook the unhappy youth. He lost one arm by the premature discharge of a Fourth-of-July cannon, and within three months he got the other pulled out by a carding-machine. Aurelia's heart was almost crushed by these latter calamities. She could not but be deeply grieved to see her lover passing from her by piecemeal, feeling, as she did, that he could not last for ever under this disastrous process of reduction, yet knowing of no way to stop its dreadful career, and in her tearful despair she almost regretted, like brokers who hold on and lose, that she had not taken him at first, before he had suffered such an alarming depreciation. Still, her brave soul bore her up, and she resolved to bear with her friend's unnatural disposition yet a little longer.

Again the wedding-day approached, and again disappointment overshadowed it: Caruthers fell ill with the erysipelas, and lost the use of one of his eyes entirely. The friends and relatives of the bride, considering that she had already put up with more than could reasonably be expected of her, now came forward and insisted that the match should be broken off, but after wavering awhile, Aurelia, with a generous spirit which did her credit, said she had reflected calmly upon the matter, and could not discover that Breckinridge was to blame.

So she extended the time once more, and he broke his other leg.

It was a sad day for the poor girl when she saw the surgeons reverently bearing away the sack whose uses she had learned by previous experience, and her heart told her the bitter truth that some more of her lover was gone. She felt that the field of her affections was growing more and more circumscribed every day, but once more she frowned down her relatives and renewed her betrothal.

Shortly before the time set for the nuptials another disaster occurred. There was but one man scalped by the Owens River Indians last year. That man was Williamson Breckinridge Caruthers, of New Jersey. He was hurrying home with happiness in his heart, when he lost his hair forever, and in that hour of bitterness he almost cursed the mistaken mercy that had spared his head.

At last Aurelia is in serious perplexity as to what she ought to do. She still loves her Breckinridge, she writes, with truly womanly feeling—she still loves what is left of him—but her parents are bitterly opposed to the match, because he has

Aurelia with her young lover before an unfortunate encounter with a carding-machine makes him shrink even more.

no property and is disabled from working, and she has not sufficient means to support both comfortably. "Now, what should she do?" she asks with painful and anxious solicitude.

It is a delicate question; it is one which involves the life-long happiness of a woman, and that of nearly two-thirds of a man, and I feel that it would be assuming too great a responsibility to do more than make a mere suggestion in the case. How would it do to build to him? If Aurelia can afford the expense, let her furnish her mutilated lover with wooden arms and wooden legs, and a glass eye and a wig, and give him another show; give him ninety days, without grace, and if he does not break his neck in the meantime, marry him and take the chances. It does not seem to me that there is much risk, any way, Aurelia, because if he sticks to his singular propensity for damaging himself every time he sees a good opportunity, his next experiment is bound to finish him, and then you are safe, married or single. If married, the wooden legs and such other valuables as he may possess revert to the widow, and you see you sustain no actual loss save the cherished fragment of a noble but most unfortunate husband, who honestly strove to do right, but whose extraordinary instincts were against him. Try it, Maria. I have thought the matter over carefully and well, and it is the only chance I see for you. It would have been a happy conceit on the part of Caruthers if he had started with his neck and broken that first; but since he has seen fit to choose a different policy and string himself out as long as possible, I do not think we ought to upbraid him for it if he has enjoyed it. We must do the best we can under the circumstances and try not to feel exasperated at him.

—"Aurelia's Unfortunate Young Man" (1864)

———————————◆———————————

In "Those Extraordinary Twins," an unfinished story that Mark Twain later wrote as a kind of warm-up for Pudd'nhead Wilson, *he said he so much liked the idea of "weeding out" unwanted characters by having them fall down a well that he got rid of five characters that way and "was going to drown some of the others, but I gave up the idea, partly because I believed that if I kept that up it would arouse attention, and perhaps sympathy with those people, and partly because it was not a large well and would not hold any more anyway." Happily, when young Caruthers fell down a well, he merely broke his leg—but perhaps that was only because Mark Twain was saving him for even nastier mishaps.*

———————————◆———————————

17.

"THE WAR PRAYER"

———————•———————

No one need be reminded that war is a terrible thing. For every victory, there is a defeat. For all the victors, there are the vanquished. What this brief tale reminds us of is that when we ask a higher power for help in achieving victory, we are also asking that abject misery and devastation engulf our foes. That is not the kind of lesson overlooked in Mark Twain's writings when he expresses his sincere beliefs.

———————•———————

It was a time of great and exalting excitement. The country was up in arms, the war was on, in every breast burned the holy fire of patriotism; the drums were beating, the bands playing, the toy pistols popping, the bunched firecrackers hissing and spluttering; on every hand and far down the receding and fading spread of roofs and balconies a fluttering wilderness of flags flashed in the sun; daily the young volunteers marched down the wide avenue gay and fine in their new uniforms, the proud fathers and mothers and sisters and sweethearts cheering them with voices choked with happy emotion as they swung by; nightly the packed mass-meetings listened, panting, to patriot oratory which stirred the deepest deeps of their hearts, and which they interrupted at briefest intervals with cyclones of applause, the tears running down their cheeks the while; in the churches the pastors preached devotion to flag and country, and invoked the God of Battles, beseeching His aid in our good cause in outpourings of fervid eloquence which moved every listener. It was indeed a glad and gracious time, and the half dozen rash spirits that ventured to disapprove of the war and cast a doubt upon its righteousness straightaway got such a stern and angry warning that for their personal safety's sake they quickly shrank out of sight and offended no more in that way.

Sunday morning came—next day the battalions would leave for the front; the church was filled; the volunteers were there, their young faces alight with martial dreams—visions of the stern advance, the gathering momentum, the rushing charge, the flashing sabres, the flight of the foe, the tumult, the enveloping smoke, the fierce pursuit, the surrender!—then home from the war, bronzed heroes,

With their country up in arms, enthusiastic crowds gather to cheer their gallant troops marching off to war!

welcomed, adored, submerged in golden seas of glory! With the volunteers sat their dear ones, proud, happy, and envied by the neighbors and friends who had no sons and brothers to send forth to the field of honor, there to win for the flag, or, failing, die the noblest of noble deaths. The service proceeded; a war-chapter from the Old Testament was read; the first prayer was said; it was followed by an organ-burst that shook the building, and with one impulse the house rose, with glowing eyes and beating hearts and poured out that tremendous invocation—

> God the all-terrible! Thou who ordainest,
> Thunder thy clarion and lightning thy sword!

Then came the "long" prayer. None could remember the like of it for passionate pleading and moving and beautiful language. The burden of its supplication was, that the ever-merciful and benignant Father of us would watch over our noble young soldiers, and aid, comfort, and encourage them in their patriotic work;

bless them, shield them in His mighty hand, make them strong and confident, invincible in the bloody onset, help them to crush the foe, grant to them and to their flag and country imperishable honor and glory—

An aged stranger entered, and moved with slow and noiseless step up the main aisle, his eyes fixed upon the minister, his long body clothed in a robe that reached to his feet, his head bare, his white hair descending in a frothy cataract to his shoulders, his seamy face unnaturally pale, pale even to ghastliness. With all eyes following him and wondering, he made his silent way; without pausing, he ascended to the preacher's side and stood there, waiting. With shut lids the preacher, unconscious of his presence, continued his moving prayer, and at last finished it with the words, uttered in fervent appeal, "Bless our arms, grant us the victory, O Lord our God, Father and Protector of our land and flag!"

The stranger touched his arm, motioned him to step aside—which the startled minister did—and took his place. During some moments he surveyed the spellbound audience with solemn eyes, in which burned an uncanny light; then in a deep voice he said—

"I come from the Throne—bearing a message from the Almighty God!" The words smote the house with a shock; if the stranger perceived it he gave it no attention. "He has heard the prayer of His servant your shepherd, and will grant it if such shall be your desire after I, His messenger, shall have explained to you its import—that is to say, its full import. For it is like unto many of the prayers of men, in that it asks for more than he who utters it is aware of—except he pause and think.

"God's servant and yours has prayed his prayer. Has he paused, and taken thought? Is it one prayer? No, it is two—one uttered, the other not. Both have reached the ear of Him who heareth all supplications, the spoken and the unspoken. Ponder this—keep it in mind. If you would beseech a blessing upon yourself, beware! lest without intent you invoke a curse upon your neighbor at the same time. If you pray for the blessing of rain upon your crop which needs it, by that act you are possibly praying for a curse upon some neighbor's crop which may not need rain and can be injured by it.

"You have heard your servant's prayer—the uttered part of it. I am commissioned of God to put into words the other part of it—that part which the pastor—and also you in your hearts—fervently prayed silently. And ignorantly and unthinkingly? God grant that it was so! You heard these words: 'Grant us the victory, O Lord our God!' That is sufficient. The *whole* of the uttered prayer is compacted into those pregnant words. Elaborations were not necessary. When you have prayed for victory you have prayed for many unmentioned results which follow victory—*must* follow it, cannot help but follow it. Upon the listening spirit of God the Father fell also the unspoken part of the prayer. He commandeth me to put it into words. Listen!

"O Lord, our Father, our young patriots, idols of our hearts, go forth to battle—be Thou near them! With them—in spirit—we also go forth from the sweet peace of our beloved firesides to smite the foe. O Lord, our God, help us to tear their soldiers to bloody shreds with our shells; help us to cover their smiling fields with the pale forms of their patriot dead; help us to drown the thunder of the guns with the shrieks of their wounded, writhing in pain; help us to lay waste their humble homes with a hurricane of fire; help us to wring the hearts of their unoffending widows with unavailing grief; help us to turn them out roofless with their little children to wander unfriended the wastes of their desolated land in rags and hunger and thirst, sport of the sun-flames of summer and the icy winds of winter, broken in spirit, worn with travail, imploring Thee for the refuge of the grave and denied it—for our sakes who adore Thee, Lord, blast their hopes, blight their lives, protract their bitter pilgrimage, make heavy their steps, water

Taking the place of the congregation's minister, the stranger raises his arms in supplication, proclaiming he bears a message from God.

their way with their tears, stain the white snow with the blood of their wounded feet! We ask it, in the spirit of love, of Him Who is the Source of Love, and Who is the ever-faithful refuge and friend of all that are sore beset and seek His aid with humble and contrite hearts. Amen."

(*After a pause.*) "Ye have prayed it; if ye still desire it, speak!—The messenger of the Most High waits."

It was believed afterwards, that the man was a lunatic, because there was no sense in what he said.

—"The War Prayer" (written ca. early 1905)

———————

The beauty of this parable is its relevance to every armed conflict in human history. A man like its stranger may be seen as a lunatic by many people in the real world, but he makes perfect sense in Mark Twain's macabre world. Mark Twain wrote this piece around 1904 but was hesitant to publish it for fear he would be the one considered a lunatic. This is the version that was first published in 1923.

———————

PART IV.

————·————

Curious Talk & Strange Obsessions

Mark Twain was a master of writing dialogue. Some of his most fascinating prose passages are conversations—especially those among characters talking at cross purposes. This section opens with "Facing One's Most Pitiless Enemy," which is mostly a long-running dialogue in which the unnamed narrator—who bears an uncanny resemblance to his creator—argues with a flesh-and-blood incarnation of his own conscience. Because no meeting of the minds is possible, verbal fireworks eventually evolve into violence. The next selection, "Nothing Exists but Mind," extracted from Mark Twain's *Christian Science* (1907), is another example of a conversation in which no agreement is possible. This time Mark Twain himself is directly involved, but we have to doubt that the painful experience he describes actually happened. "A Corpse Not Particular about Style," another of Mark Twain's early sketches, is not so much a dialogue as a report on the opinions expressed by a gratified undertaker's very congenial client, who happens to be dead. And speaking of dead people, "That Mysterious Country from Whose Bourne No Traveler Returns," extracted from *Roughing It* (1872), is another extended dialogue between very different characters who have grave difficulty understanding each other, despite their mutual good will. The "Mysterious Country" to which the title alludes is clearly the "undiscovered country" Hamlet mentions in his famous soliloquy; it is an expression for death, which is appropriate since the story's two men are discussing funeral arrangements. However, the true mystery in this sketch is how in the world they ever manage to understand each other. The last two pieces in this section move away from dialogue. "Poetry That Softens the Terror of Death" is an essay expressing Mark Twain's strong feelings about the trite language of funerary poems. "A Literary Nightmare" may be the most dangerous tale in this volume. In demonstrating how simple but devilishly arranged words can take control of one's mind, it may just take control of its readers' minds!

18.

"FACING ONE'S MOST PITILESS ENEMY"

———————

Throughout Adventures of Huckleberry Finn, the novel's young protagonist strug-gles with his conscience over the question of whether he is doing the right thing or the wrong thing in helping the fugitive Jim find freedom. Unable to make up his mind, he concludes, "It don't make no difference whether you do right or wrong, a person's conscience ain't got no sense, and just goes for him anyway." That is a sentiment with which the narrator of this grim tale would certainly agree. Like many people with uneasy consciences, he would love to be able to turn the tables on his badgering inner voice. Unlike most people, he actually gets just such a chance!

———————

I was feeling blithe, almost jocund. I put a match to my cigar, and just then the morning's mail was handed in. The first superscription I glanced at was in a handwriting that sent a thrill of pleasure through and through me. It was Aunt Mary's; and she was the person I loved and honored most in all the world, outside of my own household. She had been my boyhood's idol; maturity, which is fatal to so many enchantments, had not been able to dislodge her from her pedestal; no, it had only justified her right to be there, and placed her dethronement perma-nently among the impossibilities. To show how strong her influence over me was, I will observe that long after everybody else's *"do*-stop-smoking" had ceased to affect me in the slightest degree, Aunt Mary could still stir my torpid conscience into faint signs of life when she touched upon the matter. But all things have their limit, in this world. A happy day came at last, when even Aunt Mary's words could no longer move me. I was not merely glad to see that day arrive; I was more than glad—I was grateful; for when its sun had set, the one alloy that was able to mar my enjoyment of my aunt's society was gone. The remainder of her stay with us that winter was in every way a delight. Of course she pleaded with me just as earnestly as ever, after that blessed day, to quit my pernicious habit, but to no purpose whatever; the moment she opened the subject I at once became calmly, peacefully, contentedly indifferent—absolutely, adamantinely indifferent. Consequently the closing weeks of that memorable visit melted away as pleasantly as a dream, they were so freighted, for me, with tranquil satisfaction. I could not have enjoyed my pet vice more if my gentle tormentor had been a smoker herself, and an advocate of the practice. Well, the sight of her handwriting reminded me that I was getting very hungry to see her again. I easily guessed what I should find in her letter. I opened it. Good! just as I expected; she was coming! Coming this very day, too, and by the morning train; I might expect her any moment.

I said to myself, "I am thoroughly happy and content, now. If my most pitiless enemy could appear before me at this moment, I would freely right any wrong I may have done him."

Delighted by his aunt's letter, the narrator is so happy he feels ready to face his most pitiless enemy—who will soon appear!

Straightway the door opened, and a shrivelled, shabby dwarf entered. He was not more than two feet high. He seemed to be about forty years old. Every feature and every inch of him was a trifle out of shape; and so, while one could not put his finger upon any particular part and say, "This is a conspicuous deformity," the spectator perceived that this little person was a deformity as a whole—a vague, general, evenly blended, nicely adjusted deformity. There was a foxlike cunning in the face and the sharp little eyes, and also alertness and malice. And yet, this vile bit of human rubbish seemed to bear a sort of remote and ill-defined resemblance to me! It was dully perceptible in the mean form, the countenance, and even the clothes, gestures, manner, and attitudes of the creature. He was a far-fetched, dim suggestion of a burlesque upon me, a caricature of me in little. One thing about him struck me forcibly, and most unpleasantly: he was covered all over with a fuzzy, greenish mould, such as one sometimes sees upon mildewed bread. The sight of it was nauseating.

He stepped along with a chipper air, and flung himself into a doll's chair in a very free and easy way, without waiting to be asked. He tossed his hat into the waste basket. He picked up my old chalk pipe from the floor, gave the stem a wipe or two on his knee, filled the bowl from the tobacco-box at his side, and said to me in a tone of pert command—

"Gimme a match!"

I blushed to the roots of my hair; partly with indignation, but mainly because it somehow seemed to me that this whole performance was very like an exaggeration of conduct which I myself had sometimes been guilty of in my intercourse with familiar friends—but never, never with strangers, I observed to myself. I wanted to kick the pygmy into the fire, but some incomprehensible sense of being legally and legitimately under his authority forced me to obey his order. He applied the match to the pipe, took a contemplative whiff or two, and remarked, in an irritatingly familiar way—

"Seems to me it's devilish odd weather for this time of year."

I flushed again, and in anger and humiliation as before; for the language was hardly an exaggeration of some that I have uttered in my day, and moreover was delivered in a tone of voice and with an exasperating drawl that had the seeming of a deliberate travesty of my style. Now there is nothing I am quite so sensitive about as a mocking imitation of my drawling infirmity of speech. I spoke up sharply and said—

"Look here, you miserable ash-cat! you will have to give a little more attention to your manners, or I will throw you out of the window!"

The manikin smiled a smile of malicious content and security, puffed a whiff of smoke contemptuously toward me, and said, with a still more elaborate drawl—

"Come—go gently, now; don't put on *too* many airs with your betters."

This cool snub rasped me all over, but it seemed to subjugate me, too, for a moment. The pygmy contemplated me awhile with his weasel eyes, and then said, in a peculiarly sneering way—

"You turned a tramp away from your door this morning."

I said crustily—

"Perhaps I did, perhaps I didn't. How do you know?"

"Well, I know. It isn't any matter *how* I know."

"Very well. Suppose I *did* turn a tramp away from the door—what of it?"

"Oh, nothing; nothing in particular. Only you lied to him."

"I *didn't!* That is, I—"

"Yes, but you did; you lied to him."

I felt a guilty pang—in truth I had felt it forty times before that tramp had travelled a block from my door—but still I resolved to make a show of feeling slandered; so I said—

"This is a baseless impertinence. I said to the tramp—"

"There—wait. You were about to lie again. *I* know what you said to him. You said the cook was gone down town and there was nothing left from breakfast. Two lies. You knew the cook was behind the door, and plenty of provisions behind *her.*"

This astonishing accuracy silenced me; and it filled me with wondering speculations, too, as to how this cub could have got his information. Of course he could have culled the conversation from the tramp, but by what sort of magic had he contrived to find out about the concealed cook? Now the dwarf spoke again:—

"It was rather pitiful, rather small, in you to refuse to read that poor young woman's manuscript the other day, and give her an opinion as to its literary value; and she had come so far, too, and so hopefully. Now *wasn't* it?"

I felt like a cur! And I had felt so every time the thing had recurred to my mind, I may as well confess. I flushed hotly and said—

"Look here, have you nothing better to do than prowl around prying into other people's business? Did that girl tell you that?"

"Never mind whether she did or not. The main thing is, you did that contemptible thing. And you felt ashamed of it afterwards. Aha! you feel ashamed of it *now!*"

This with a sort of devilish glee. With fiery earnestness I responded—

"I told that girl, in the kindest, gentlest way, that I could not consent to deliver judgment upon any one's manuscript, because an individual's verdict was worthless. It might underrate a work of high merit and lose it to the world, or it might overrate a trashy production and so open the way for its infliction upon the world. I said that the great public was the only tribunal competent to sit in judgment upon a literary effort, and therefore it must be best to lay it before that tribunal in the outset, since in the end it must stand or fall by that mighty court's decision any way."

"Yes, you said all that. So you did, you juggling, small-souled shuffler! And yet when the happy hopefulness faded out of that poor girl's face, when you saw her furtively slip beneath her shawl the scroll she had so patiently and honestly scribbled at—so ashamed of her darling now, so proud of it before—when you saw the gladness go out of her eyes and the tears come there, when she crept away so humbly who had come so—"

"Oh, peace! peace! peace! Blister your merciless tongue, haven't all these thoughts tortured me enough, without *your* coming here to fetch them back again?"

Remorse! remorse! It seemed to me that it would eat the very heart out of me! And yet that small fiend only sat there leering at me with joy and contempt, and placidly chuckling. Presently he began to speak again. Every sentence was an accusation, and every accusation a truth. Every clause was freighted with sarcasm and derision, every slow-dropping word burned like vitriol. The dwarf reminded me of times when I had flown at my children in anger and punished them for faults which a little inquiry would have taught me that others, and not they, had committed. He reminded me of how I had disloyally allowed old friends to be traduced in my hearing, and been too craven to utter a word in their defence.He reminded me of many dishonest things which I had done; of many which I had procured to be done by children and other irresponsible persons; of some which I had planned, thought upon, and longed to do, and been kept from the performance by fear of consequences only. With exquisite cruelty he recalled to my mind, item by item, wrongs and unkindnesses I had inflicted and humiliations I had put upon friends since dead, "who died thinking of those injuries, maybe, and grieving over them," he added, by way of poison to the stab.

"For instance," said he, "take the case of your younger brother, when you two were boys together, many a long year ago. He always lovingly trusted in you with a fidelity that your manifold treacheries were not able to shake. He followed you about like a dog, content to suffer wrong and abuse if he might only be with you; patient under these injuries so long as it was your hand that inflicted them. The latest picture you have of him in health and strength must be such a comfort to you! You pledged your honor that if he would let you blindfold him no harm should come to him; and then, giggling and choking over the rare fun of the joke, you led him to a brook thinly glazed with ice, and pushed him in; and how you did laugh! Man, you will never forget the gentle, reproachful look he gave you as he struggled shivering out, if you live a thousand years! Oho! you see it now, you see it *now!*"

"Beast, I have seen it a million times, and shall see it a million more! and may you rot away piecemeal, and suffer till doomsday what I suffer now, for bringing it back to me again!"

The dwarf chuckled contentedly, and went on with his accusing history of my career. I dropped into a moody, vengeful state, and suffered in silence under the merciless lash. At last this remark of his gave me a sudden rouse:—

"Two months ago, on a Tuesday, you woke up, away in the night, and fell to thinking, with shame, about a peculiarly mean and pitiful act of yours toward a poor [uneducated] Indian in the wilds of the Rocky Mountains in the winter of eighteen hundred and—"

"Stop a moment, devil! Stop! Do you mean to tell me that even my very *thoughts* are not hidden from you?"

"It seems to look like that. Didn't you think the thoughts I have just mentioned?"

"If I didn't, I wish I may never breathe again! Look here, friend—look me in the eye. Who *are* you?"

"Well, who do you think?"

"I think you are Satan himself. I think you are the devil."

"No."

"No? Then who can you be?"

"Would you really like to know?"

"*Indeed* I would."

"Well, I am your *Conscience!*"

In an instant I was in a blaze of joy and exultation. I sprang at the creature, roaring—

"Curse you, I have wished a hundred million times that you were tangible, and that I could get my hands on your throat once! Oh, but I will wreak a deadly vengeance on—"

Folly! Lightning does not move more quickly than my Conscience did! He darted aloft so suddenly that in the moment my fingers clutched the empty air he was already perched on the top of the high book-case, with his thumb at his nose in token of derision. I flung the poker at him, and missed. I fired the boot-jack. In a blind rage I flew from place to place, and snatched and hurled any missile that came handy; the storm of books, inkstands, and chunks of coal gloomed the air and beat about the manikin's perch relentlessly, but all to no purpose; the nimble figure dodged every shot; and not only that, but burst into a cackle of sarcastic and triumphant laughter as I sat down exhausted. While I puffed and gasped with fatigue and excitement, my Conscience talked to this effect:—

"My good slave, you are curiously witless—no, I mean characteristically so. In truth, you are always consistent, always yourself, always an ass. Otherwise it must have occurred to you that if you attempted this murder with a sad heart and a heavy conscience, I would droop under the burdening influence instantly. Fool, I should have weighed a ton, and could not have budged from the floor; but instead, you are so cheerfully anxious to kill me that your conscience is as light as a feather; hence I am away up here out of your reach. I can almost respect a mere ordinary sort of fool; but *you*—pah!"

I would have given anything, then, to be heavy-hearted, so that I could get this person down from there and take his life, but I could no more be heavy-hearted over such a desire than I could have sorrowed over its accomplishment. So I could only look longingly up at my master, and rave at the ill-luck that denied me a heavy conscience the one only time that I had ever wanted such a thing in my life. By and by I got to musing over the hour's strange adventure, and of course my human curiosity began to work. I set myself to framing in my mind some questions for this fiend to answer. Just then one of my boys entered, leaving the door open behind him, and exclaimed—

"My! what *has* been going on, here? The book-case is all one riddle of—"

I sprang up in consternation, and shouted—

"Out of this! Hurry! Jump! Fly! Shut the door! Quick, or my Conscience will get away!"

The door slammed to, and I locked it. I glanced up and was grateful, to the bottom of my heart, to see that my owner was still my prisoner. I said—

"Hang you, I might have lost you! Children are the heedlessest creatures. But look here, friend, the boy did not seem to notice you at all; how is that?"

The dwarf does everything he can to make himself annoying.

"For a very good reason. I am invisible to all but you."

I made mental note of that piece of information with a good deal of satisfaction. I could kill this miscreant now, if I got a chance, and no one would know it. But this very reflection made me so light-hearted that my Conscience could hardly keep his seat, but was like to float aloft toward the ceiling like a toy balloon. I said, presently—

"Come, my Conscience, let us be friendly. Let us fly a flag of truce for a while. I am suffering to ask you some questions."

"Very well. Begin."

"Well, then, in the first place, why were you never visible to me before?"

"Because you never asked to see me before; that is, you never asked in the right spirit and the proper form before. You were just in the right spirit this time, and when you called for your most pitiless enemy I was that person by a very large majority, though you did not suspect it."

"Well, did that remark of mine turn you into flesh and blood?"

"No. It only made me visible to you. I am unsubstantial, just as other spirits are."

This remark prodded me with a sharp misgiving. If he was unsubstantial, how was I going to kill him? But I dissembled, and said persuasively—

"Conscience, it isn't sociable of you to keep at such a distance. Come down and take another smoke."

This was answered with a look that was full of derision, and with this observation added:—

"Come where you can get at me and kill me? The invitation is declined with thanks."

"All right," said I to myself; "so it seems a spirit can be killed, after all; there will be one spirit lacking in this world, presently, or I lose my guess." Then I said aloud—

"Friend—"

"There; wait a bit. I am not your friend, I am your enemy; I am not your equal, I am your master. Call me 'my lord,' if you please. You are too familiar."

"I don't like such titles. I am willing to call you *sir*. That is as far as—"

"We will have no argument about this. Just obey; that is all. Go on with your chatter."

"Very well, my lord—since nothing but my lord will suit you—I was going to ask you how long you will be visible to me?"

"Always!"

I broke out with strong indignation: "This is simply an outrage. That is what I think of it. You have dogged, and dogged, and *dogged* me, all the days of my life, invisible. That was misery enough; now to have such a looking thing as you tagging after me like another shadow all the rest of my days is an intolerable prospect. You have my opinion, my lord; make the most of it."

"My lad, there was never so pleased a conscience in this world as I was when you made me visible. It gives me an inconceivable advantage. *Now,* I can look you straight in the eye, and call you names, and leer at you, jeer at you, sneer at you; and *you* know what eloquence there is in visible gesture and expression, more especially when the effect is heightened by audible speech. I shall always address you henceforth in your o-w-n s-n-i-v-e-l-l-i-n-g d-r-a-w-l—baby!"

I let fly with the coal-hod. No result. My lord said—

"Come, come! Remember the flag of truce!"

"Ah, I forgot that. I will try to be civil; and you try it, too, for a novelty. The idea of a *civil* conscience! It is a good joke; an excellent joke. All the consciences *I* have ever heard of were nagging, badgering, fault-finding, execrable savages! Yes; and always in a sweat about some poor little insignificant trifle or other—destruction catch the lot of them, *I* say! I would trade mine for the small-pox and seven kinds of consumption, and be glad of the chance. Now tell me, why is it that a conscience can't haul a man over the coals once, for an offence, and then let him alone? Why *is* it that it wants to keep on pegging at him, day and night and night and day, week in and week out, forever and ever, about the same old thing? There is no sense in that, and no reason in it. I think a conscience that will act like that is meaner than the very dirt itself."

"Well, we like it; that suffices."

"Do you do it with the honest intent to improve a man?"

That question produced a sarcastic smile, and this reply:—

"No, sir. Excuse me. We do it simply because it is 'business.' It is our trade. The *purpose* of it *is* to improve the man, but *we* are merely disinterested agents. We are appointed by authority, and haven't anything to say in the matter. We obey orders and leave the consequences where they belong. But I am willing to admit this much: we *do* crowd the orders a trifle when we get a chance, which is most of the time. We enjoy it. We are instructed to remind a man a few times of an error; and I don't mind acknowledging that we try to give pretty good measure. And when we get hold of a man of a peculiarly sensitive nature, oh, but we do haze him! I have known consciences to come all the way from China and Russia to see a person of that kind put through his paces, on a special occasion. Why, I knew a man of that sort who had accidentally crippled a mulatto baby; the news went abroad, and I wish you may never commit another sin if the consciences didn't flock from all over the earth to enjoy the fun and help his master exercise him. That man walked the floor in torture for forty-eight hours, without eating or sleeping, and then blew his brains out. The child was perfectly well again in three weeks."

"Well, you are a precious crew, not to put it too strong. I think I begin to see, now, why you have always been a trifle inconsistent with me. In your anxiety to get all the juice you can out of a sin, you make a man repent of it in three or four different ways. For instance, you found fault with me for lying to that tramp, and I suffered over that. But it was only yesterday that I told a tramp the square truth, to wit, that, it being regarded as bad citizenship to encourage vagrancy, I would give him nothing. What did you do *then*? Why, you made me say to myself, 'Ah, it would have been so much kinder and more blameless to ease him off with a little white lie, and send him away feeling that if he could not have bread, the gentle treatment was at least something to be grateful for!' Well, I suffered all day about *that*. Three days before, I had fed a tramp, and fed him freely, supposing it a virtuous act. Straight off you said, 'O false citizen, to have fed a tramp!' and I suffered as usual. I gave a tramp work; you objected to it—*after* the contract was made, of course; you never speak up beforehand. Next, I *refused* a tramp work; you objected to *that*. Next, I proposed to kill a tramp; you kept me awake all night, oozing remorse at every pore. Sure I was going to be right *this* time, I sent the next tramp away with my benediction; and I wish you may live as long as I do, if you didn't make me smart all night again because I didn't kill him. Is there *any* way of satisfying that malignant invention which is called a conscience?"

"Ha, ha! this is luxury! Go on!"

"But come, now, answer me that question. *Is* there any way?"

"Well, none that I propose to tell you, my son. Ass! I don't care *what* act you may turn your hand to, I can straightway whisper a word in your ear and make you think you have committed a dreadful meanness. It is my *business*—and my joy—to make you repent of *every*thing you do. If I have fooled away any opportunities it was not intentional; I beg to assure you it was not intentional!"

"Don't worry; you haven't missed a trick that *I* know of. I never did a thing in all my life, virtuous or otherwise, that I didn't repent of within twenty-four hours. In church last Sunday I listened to a charity sermon. My first impulse was to give three hundred and fifty dollars; I repented of that and reduced it a hundred; repented of that and reduced it another hundred; repented of that and reduced it another hundred; repented of that and reduced the remaining fifty to twenty-five; repented of that and came down to fifteen; repented of that and dropped to two dollars and a half; when the plate came around at last, I repented once more and contributed ten cents. Well, when I got home, I did wish to goodness I had that ten cents back again! You never *did* let me get through a charity sermon without having something to sweat about."

"Oh, and I never shall, I never shall. You can always depend on me."

"I think so. Many and manys the restless night I've wanted to take you by the neck. If I could only get hold of you now!"

"Yes, no doubt. But I am not an ass; I am only the saddle of an ass. But go on, go on. You entertain me more than I like to confess."

"I am glad of that. (You will not mind my lying a little, to keep in practice.) Look here; not to be too personal, I think you are about the shabbiest and most contemptible little shrivelled-up reptile that can be imagined. I am grateful enough that you are invisible to other people, for I should die with shame to be seen with such a mildewed monkey of a conscience as you are. Now if you were five or six feet high, and—"

"Oh, come! who is to blame?"

"I don't know."

"Why, you are; nobody else."

"Confound you, I wasn't consulted about your personal appearance."

"I don't care, you had a good deal to do with it, nevertheless. When you were eight or nine years old, I was seven feet high, and as pretty as a picture."

"I wish you had died young! So you have grown the wrong way, have you?"

"Some of us grow one way and some the other. You had a large conscience once; if you've a small conscience now, I reckon there are reasons for it. However, both of us are to blame, you and I. You see, you used to be conscientious about a great many things; morbidly so, I may say. It was a great many years ago. You probably do not remember it, now. Well, I took a great interest in my work, and I so enjoyed the anguish which certain pet sins of yours afflicted you with, that I kept pelting at you until I rather overdid the matter. You began to rebel. Of course I began to lose ground, then, and shrivel a little—diminish in stature, get mouldy, and grow deformed. The more I weakened, the more stubbornly you fastened on to those particular sins; till at last the places on my person that represent those vices became as callous as shark skin. Take smoking, for instance. I played that card a little too long, and I lost. When people plead with you at this late day to quit that vice, that old callous place seems to enlarge and cover me all over like a shirt of mail. It exerts a mysterious, smothering effect; and presently I, your faithful hater, your devoted Conscience, go sound asleep! Sound? It is no name for it. I couldn't hear it thunder at such a time. You have some few other vices—perhaps eighty, or maybe ninety—that affect me in much the same way."

"This is flattering; you must be asleep a good part of your time."

"Yes, of late years. I should be asleep *all* the time, but for the help I get."

"Who helps you?"

"Other consciences. Whenever a person whose conscience I am acquainted with tries to plead with you about the vices you are callous to, I get my friend to give his client a pang concerning some villany of his own, and that shuts off his meddling and starts him off to hunt personal consolation. My field of usefulness is about trimmed down to tramps, budding authoresses, and that line of goods, now; but don't you worry—I'll harry you on *them* while they last! Just you put your trust in me."

"I think I can. But if you had only been good enough to mention these facts some thirty years ago, I should have turned my particular attention to sin, and I think that by this time I should not only have had you pretty permanently asleep on the entire list of human vices, but reduced to the size of a homoeopathic pill, at that. That is about the style of conscience *I* am pining for. If I only had you shrunk down to a homoeopathic pill, and could get my hands on you, would I put you in a glass case for a keepsake? No, sir. I would give you to a yellow dog! That is where *you* ought to be—you and all your tribe. You are not fit to be in society, in my opinion. Now another question. Do you know a good many consciences in this section?"

"Plenty of them."

"I would give anything to see some of them! Could you bring them here? And would they be visible to me?"

"Certainly not."

"I suppose I ought to have known that, without asking. But no matter, you can describe them. Tell me about my neighbor Thompson's conscience, please."

"Very well. I know him intimately; have known him many years. I knew him when he was eleven feet high and of a faultless figure. But he is very rusty and tough and misshapen, now, and hardly ever interests himself about anything. As to his present size—well, he sleeps in a cigar box."

"Likely enough. There are few smaller, meaner men in this region than Hugh Thompson. Do you know Robinson's conscience?"

"Yes. He is a shade under four and a half feet high; used to be a blonde; is a brunette, now, but still shapely and comely."

"Well, Robinson is a good fellow. Do you know Tom Smith's conscience?"

"I have known him from childhood. He was thirteen inches high, and rather sluggish, when he was two years old—as nearly all of us are, at that age. He is thirty-seven feet high, now, and the stateliest figure in America. His legs are still racked with growing-pains, but he has a good time, nevertheless. Never sleeps. He is the most active and energetic member of the New England Conscience Club; is president of it. Night and day you can find him pegging away at Smith, panting with his labor, sleeves rolled up, countenance all alive with enjoyment. He has got his victim splendidly dragooned, now. He can make poor Smith imagine that the most innocent little thing he does is an odious sin; and then he sets to work and almost tortures the soul out of him about it."

"Smith is the noblest man in all this section, and the purest; and yet is always breaking his heart because he cannot be good! Only a conscience *could* find pleasure in heaping agony upon a spirit like that. Do you know my aunt Mary's conscience?"

"I have seen her at a distance, but am not acquainted with her. She lives in the open air altogether, because no door is large enough to admit her."

"I can believe that. Let me see. Do you know the conscience of that publisher who once stole some sketches of mine for a 'series' of his, and then left me to pay the law expenses I had to incur in order to choke him off?"

"Yes. He has a wide fame. He was exhibited, a month ago, with some other antiquities, for the benefit of a recent Member of the Cabinet's conscience, that was starving in exile. Tickets and fares were high, but I travelled for nothing by pretending to be the conscience of an editor, and got in for half price by representing myself to be the conscience of a clergyman. However, the publisher's conscience, which was to have been the main feature of the entertainment, was a failure—as an exhibition. He was there, but what of that? The management had provided a microscope with a magnifying power of only thirty thousand diameters, and so nobody got to see him, after all. There was great and general dissatisfaction, of course, but—"

Just here there was an eager footstep on the stair; I opened the door, and my aunt Mary burst into the room. It was a joyful meeting, and a cheery bombardment of questions and answers concerning family matters ensued. By and by my aunt said—

"But I am going to abuse you a little now. You promised me, the day I saw you last, that you would look after the needs of the poor family around the corner as faithfully as I had done it myself. Well, I found out by accident that you failed of your promise. *Was* that right?"

In simple truth, I never had thought of that family a second time! And now such a splintering pang of guilt shot through me! I glanced up at my Conscience. Plainly, my heavy heart was affecting him. His body was drooping forward; he seemed about to fall from the book-case. My aunt continued:—

"And think how you have neglected my poor *protégée* at the almshouse, you dear, hard-hearted promise-breaker!" I blushed scarlet, and my tongue was tied. As the sense of my guilty negligence waxed sharper and stronger, my Conscience began to sway heavily back and forth; and when my aunt, after a little pause, said in a grieved tone, "Since you never once went to see her, maybe it will not distress you now to know that that poor child died, months ago, utterly friendless and forsaken!" my Conscience could no longer bear up under the weight of my sufferings, but tumbled headlong from his high perch and struck the floor with a dull, leaden thump. He lay there writhing with pain and quaking with apprehension, but straining every muscle in frantic efforts to get up. In a fever of expectancy I sprang to the door, locked it, placed my back against it, and bent a watchful gaze upon my struggling master. Already my fingers were itching to begin their murderous work.

"Oh, what can be the matter!" exclaimed my aunt, shrinking from me, and following with her frightened eyes the direction of mine. My breath was coming in short, quick gasps now, and my excitement was almost uncontrollable. My aunt cried out—

"Oh, do not look so! You appall me! Oh, what can the matter be? What is it you see? Why do you stare so? Why do you work your fingers like that?"

"Peace, woman!" I said, in a hoarse whisper. "Look elsewhere; pay no attention to me; it is nothing—nothing. I am often this way. It will pass in a moment. It comes from smoking too much."

My injured lord was up, wild-eyed with terror, and trying to hobble toward the door. I could hardly breathe, I was so wrought up. My aunt wrung her hands, and said—

"Oh, I knew how it would be; I knew it would come to this at last! Oh, I implore you to crush out that fatal habit while it may yet be time! You must not, you shall not be deaf to my supplications longer!" My struggling Conscience showed sudden signs of weariness! "Oh, promise me you will throw off this hateful slavery of tobacco!" My Conscience began to reel drowsily, and grope with his hands—enchanting spectacle! "I beg you, I beseech you, I implore you! Your reason is deserting you! There is madness in your eye! It flames with frenzy! Oh, hear me, hear me, and be saved! See, I plead with you on my very knees!" As she sank before me my Conscience reeled again, and then drooped languidly to the floor, blinking toward me a last supplication for mercy, with heavy eyes. "Oh, promise, or you are lost! Promise, and be redeemed! Promise! Promise and live!" With a long-drawn sigh my conquered Conscience closed his eyes and fell fast asleep!

With an exultant shout I sprang past my aunt, and in an instant I had my life-long foe by the throat. After so many years of waiting and longing, he was mine at last. I tore him to shreds and fragments. I rent the fragments to bits. I cast the bleeding rubbish into the fire, and drew into my nostrils the grateful incense of my burnt-offering. At last, and forever, my Conscience was dead!

I was a free man! I turned upon my poor aunt, who was almost petrified with terror, and shouted—

"Out of this with your paupers, your charities, your reforms, your pestilent morals! You behold before you a man whose life-conflict is done, whose soul is at peace; a man whose heart is dead to sorrow, dead to suffering, dead to remorse; a man Without a Conscience! In my joy I spare you, though I could throttle you and never feel a pang! Fly!"

She fled. Since that day my life is all bliss. Bliss, unalloyed bliss. Nothing in all the world could persuade me to have a conscience again. I settled all my old outstanding scores, and began the world anew. I killed thirty-eight persons during the first two weeks—all of them on account of ancient grudges. I burned a dwelling that interrupted my view. I swindled a widow and some orphans out of their last cow, which is a very good one, though not thoroughbred, I believe. I have also committed scores of crimes, of various kinds, and have enjoyed my work exceedingly, whereas it would formerly have broken my heart and turned my hair gray, I have no doubt.

Now completely rid of his conscience, the narrator revels in the prosperous trade in bodies his new freedom has brung.

In conclusion I wish to state, by way of advertisement, that medical colleges desiring assorted tramps for scientific purposes, either by the gross, by cord measurement, or per ton, will do well to examine the lot in my cellar before purchasing elsewhere, as these were all selected and prepared by myself, and can be had at a low rate, because I wish to clear out my stock and get ready for the spring trade.

—"The Facts Concerning the Recent Carnival of Crime in Connecticut" (1876)

Much of the greatness in Mark Twain's masterpiece Huckleberry Finn *derives from the emotional power of Huck's unresolved struggles with his conscience. That novel owes something to the present story for its careful development of ideas about the nature of the human conscience. It happens, incidentally, that Mark Twain wrote this story around the same he wrote* The Adventures of Tom Sawyer—*whose own protagonist also has epic struggles with his conscience.*

19.

"NOTHING EXISTS BUT MIND"

———••—•—••———

Imagine breaking almost every bone in your body and then being treated by a "doctor" who instead of patching you up merely tells you that you're perfectly fine, that all your nasty injuries exist only in your mind, so all you need to do is get your head straight. Well, that's exactly the situation in which Mark Twain found himself in Austria after falling off a cliff near Vienna!

———••—•—••———

Vienna, 1899

This last summer, when I was on my way back to Vienna from the Appetite-Cure in the mountains, I fell over a cliff in the twilight and broke some arms and legs and one thing or another, and by good luck was found by some peasants who had lost an ass, and they carried me to the nearest habitation, which was one of those large, low, thatch-roofed farm-houses, with apartments in the garret for the family, and a cunning little porch under the deep gable decorated with boxes of bright-colored flowers and cats; on the ground-floor a large and light sitting-room, separated from the milch-cattle apartment by a partition; and in the front yard rose stately and fine the wealth and pride of the house, the manure-pile. That sentence is Germanic, and shows that I am acquiring that sort of mastery of the art and spirit of the language which enables a man to travel all day in one sentence without changing cars.

There was a village a mile away, and a horse-doctor lived there, but there was no surgeon. It seemed a bad outlook; mine was distinctly a surgery case. Then it was remembered that a lady from Boston was summering in that village, and she was a Christian Science doctor and could cure anything. So she was sent for. It was night by this time, and she could not conveniently come, but sent word that it was no matter, there was no hurry, she would give me "absent treatment" now,

While returning from a mountain retreat near Vienna, Mark Twain falls from a cliff and breaks some arms and legs and one thing or another.

and come in the morning; meantime she begged me to make myself tranquil and comfortable and remember that there was nothing the matter with me. I thought there must be some mistake.

"Did you tell her I walked off a cliff seventy-five feet high?"

"Yes."

"And struck a bowlder at the bottom and bounced?"

"Yes."

"And struck another one and bounced again?"

"Yes."

"And struck another one and bounced yet again?"

"Yes."

"And broke the bowlders?"

"Yes."

"That accounts for it; she is thinking of the bowlders. Why didn't you tell her I got hurt, too?"

"I did. I told her what you told me to tell her: that you were now but an incoherent series of compound fractures extending from your scalp-lock to your heels, and that the comminuted projections caused you to look like a hat-rack."

"And it was after this that she wished me to remember that there was nothing the matter with me?"

"Those were her words."

"I do not understand it. I believe she has not diagnosed the case with sufficient care. Did she look like a person who was theorizing, or did she look like one who has fallen off precipices herself and brings to the aid of abstract science the confirmations of personal experience?"

"*Bitte?*"

It was too large a contract for the *Stubenmädchen's* vocabulary; she couldn't call the hand. I allowed the subject to rest there, and asked for something to eat and smoke, and something hot to drink, and a basket to pile my legs in; but I could not have any of these things.

"Why?"

"She said you would need nothing at all."

"But I am hungry and thirsty, and in desperate pain."

"She said you would have these delusions, but must pay no attention to them. She wants you to particularly remember that there are no such things as hunger and thirst and pain."

"She does, does she?"

"It is what she said."

"Does she seem to be in full and functionable possession of her intellectual plant, such as it is?"

"*Bitte?*"

"Do they let her run at large, or do they tie her up?"

"Tie her up?"

"There, good-night, run along; you are a good girl, but your mental *Geschirr* is not arranged for light and airy conversation. Leave me to my delusions."

★   ★   ★

It was a night of anguish, of course—at least, I supposed it was, for it had all the symptoms of it—but it passed at last, and the Christian Scientist came, and I was glad. She was middle-aged, and large and bony, and erect, and had an austere face and a resolute jaw and a Roman beak and was a widow in the third degree, and her name was Fuller. I was eager to get to business and find relief, but she was distressingly deliberate. She unpinned and unhooked and uncoupled her upholsteries one by one, abolished the wrinkles with a flirt of her hand, and hung the articles up; peeled off her gloves and disposed of them, got a book out of her hand-bag, then drew a chair to the bedside, descended into it without hurry, and I hung out my tongue. She said, with pity but without passion:

"Return it to its receptacle. We deal with the mind only, not with its dumb servants."

I could not offer my pulse, because the connection was broken; but she detected the apology before I could word it, and indicated by a negative tilt of her head that the pulse was another dumb servant that she had no use for. Then I thought I would tell her my symptoms and how I felt, so that she would understand the case; but that was another inconsequence, she did not need to know those things; moreover, my remark about how I felt was an abuse of language, a misapplication of terms.

"One does not *feel*," she explained; "there is no such thing as feeling: therefore, to speak of a non-existent thing as existent is a contradiction. Matter has no existence; nothing exists but mind; the mind cannot feel pain, it can only imagine it."

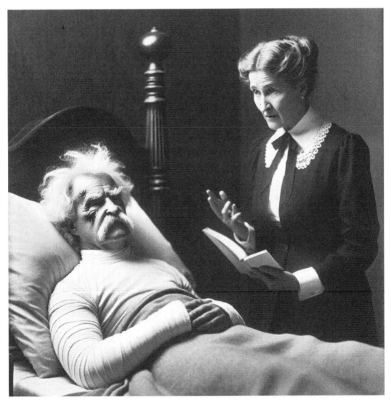

Lying in his bed of pain, Mark Twain has difficulty grasping the argument that feelings exist only in his mind.

"But if it hurts, just the same—"

"It doesn't. A thing which is unreal cannot exercise the functions of reality. Pain is unreal; hence, pain cannot hurt."

In making a sweeping gesture to indicate the act of shooing the illusion of pain out of the mind, she raked her hand on a pin in her dress, said "Ouch!" and went tranquilly on with her talk. "You should never allow yourself to speak of how you feel, nor permit others to ask you how you are feeling; you should never concede that you are ill, nor permit others to talk about disease or pain or death or similar non-existences in your presence. Such talk only encourages the mind to continue its empty imaginings." Just at that point the *Stubenmädchen* trod on the cat's tail, and the cat let fly a frenzy of cat-profanity. I asked, with caution:

"Is a cat's opinion about pain valuable?"

"A cat has no opinion; opinions proceed from mind only; the lower animals, being eternally perishable, have not been granted mind; without mind, opinion is impossible."

"She merely *imagined* she felt a pain—the cat?"

When the maid accidentally steps on its tail, the cat lets fly a frenzy of cat profanity.

"She cannot imagine a pain, for imagining is an effect of mind; without mind, there is no imagination. A cat has no imagination."

"Then she had a *real* pain?"

"I have already told you there is no such *thing* as real pain."

"It is strange and interesting. I do wonder what was the matter with the cat. Because, there being no such thing as a real pain, and she not being able to imagine an imaginary one, it would seem that God in His pity has compensated the cat with some kind of a mysterious emotion usable when her tail is trodden on which, for the moment, joins cat and Christian in one common brotherhood of—"

She broke in with an irritated—

"Peace! The cat feels nothing, the Christian feels nothing. Your empty and foolish imaginings are profanation and blasphemy, and can do you an injury. It is wiser and better and holier to recognize and confess that there is no such thing as disease or pain or death."

"I am full of imaginary tortures," I said, "but I do not think I could be any more uncomfortable if they were real ones. What must I do to get rid of them?"

"There is no occasion to get rid of them, since they do not exist. They are illusions propagated by matter, and matter has no existence; there is no such thing as matter."

"It sounds right and clear, but yet it seems in a degree elusive; it seems to slip through, just when you think you are getting a grip on it."

"Explain."

"Well, for instance: if there is no such thing as matter, how can matter propagate things?"

In her compassion she almost smiled. She would have smiled if there were any such thing as a smile.

"It is quite simple," she said; "the fundamental propositions of Christian Science explain it, and they are summarized in the four following self-evident propositions: 1. God is All in all. 2. God is good. Good is Mind. 3. God, Spirit, being all, nothing is matter. 4. Life, God, omnipotent Good, deny death, evil, sin, disease. There—now you see."

It seemed nebulous; it did not seem to say anything about the difficulty in hand—how non-existent matter can propagate illusions. I said, with some hesitancy:

"Does—does it explain?"

"*Doesn't* it? Even if read backward it will do it."

With a budding hope, I asked her to do it backward.

"Very well. Disease sin evil death deny Good omnipotent God life matter is nothing all being Spirit God Mind is Good good is God all in All is God. There—do you understand now?"

"It—it—well, it is plainer than it was before; still—"

"Well?"

"Could you try it some more ways?"

"As many as you like; it always means the same. Interchanged in any way you please it cannot be made to mean anything different from what it means when put in any other way. Because it is perfect. You can jumble it all up, and it makes no difference: it always comes out the way it was before. It was a marvellous mind that produced it. As a mental tour de force it is without a mate, it defies alike the simple, the concrete, and the occult."

"It seems to be a corker."

I blushed for the word, but it was out before I could stop it.

"A what?"

"A—wonderful structure—combination, so to speak, of profound thoughts—unthinkable ones—un—"

"It is true. Read backward, or forward, or perpendicularly, or at any given angle, these four propositions will always be found to agree in statement and proof."

"Ah—proof. Now we are coming at it. The *statements* agree; they agree with—with—anyway, they agree; I noticed that; but what is it they prove—I mean, in particular?"

"Why, nothing could be clearer. They prove: 1. GOD—Principle, Life, Truth, Love, Soul, Spirit, Mind. Do you get that?"

"I—well, I seem to. Go on, please."

"2. MAN—God's universal idea, individual, perfect, eternal. Is it clear?"

"It—I think so. Continue."

------ ••• • ••• ------

The woman goes on to amplify her principles, but mainly with the effect of adding to Mark Twain's confusion. Finally, she concludes:

------ ••• • ••• ------

"You now know the history of our dear and holy Science, sir, and that its *origin* is not of this earth, but only its *discovery*. I will leave the book with you and will go, now; but give yourself no uneasiness—I will give you absent treatment from now till I go to bed."

Under the powerful influence of the near treatment and the absent treatment together, my bones were gradually retreating inward and disappearing from view. The good work took a brisk start, now, and went on swiftly. My body was diligently straining and stretching, this way and that, to accommodate the processes of restoration, and every minute or two I heard a dull click inside and knew that the two ends of a fracture had been successfully joined. This muffled clicking and gritting and grinding and rasping continued during the next three hours, and then stopped—the connections had all been made. All except dislocations; there were only seven of these: hips, shoulders, knees, neck; so that was soon over; one after another they slipped into their sockets with a sound like pulling a distant cork, and I jumped up as good as new, as to framework, and sent for the horse-doctor.

I was obliged to do this because I had a stomach-ache and a cold in the head, and I was not willing to trust these things any longer in the hands of a woman whom I did not know, and in whose ability to successfully treat mere disease I had lost all confidence. My position was justified by the fact that the cold and the ache had been in her charge from the first, along with the fractures, but had experienced not a shade of relief; and, indeed, the ache was even growing worse and worse, and more and more bitter, now, probably on account of the protracted abstention from food and drink.

The horse-doctor came, a pleasant man and full of hope and professional interest in the case. In the matter of smell he was pretty aromatic—in fact, quite horsy—and I tried to arrange with him for absent treatment, but it was not in his line, so, out of delicacy, I did not press it. He looked at my teeth and examined my hock, and said my age and general condition were favorable to energetic measures; therefore he would give me something to turn the stomach-ache into the botts and the cold in the head into the blind staggers; then he should be on his own beat and would know what to do. He made up a bucket of bran-mash, and said a dipperful of it every two hours, alternated with a drench with turpentine and axle-grease in it, would either knock my ailments out of me in twenty-four hours, or so interest me in other ways as to make me forget they were on the premises. He administered my first dose himself, then took his leave, saying I was free to eat and drink anything I pleased and in any quantity I liked. But I was not hungry any more, and did not care for food.

I took up the Christian Science book and read half of it, then took a dipperful of drench and read the other half. The resulting experiences were full of interest and adventure. All through the rumblings and grindings and quakings and effervescings accompanying the evolution of the ache into the botts and the cold into the blind staggers I could note the generous struggle for mastery going on between the mash and the drench and the literature; and often I could tell which was ahead, and could easily distinguish the literature from the others when the others were separate, though not when they were mixed; for when a bran-mash and an eclectic drench are mixed together they look just like the Apodictical Principle out on a lark, and no one can tell it from that. The finish was reached at last, the evolutions were complete, and a fine success, but I think that this result could have been achieved with fewer materials. I believe the mash was necessary to the conversion of the stomach-ache into the botts, but I think one could develop the blind staggers out of the literature by itself; also, that blind staggers produced in this way would be of a better quality and more lasting than any produced by the artificial processes of the horse-doctor.

For of all the strange and frantic and incomprehensible and uninterpretable books which the imagination of man has created, surely this one is the prize sample. It is written with a limitless confidence and complacency, and with a dash and stir and earnestness which often compel the effects of eloquence, even when the words do not seem to have any traceable meaning. There are plenty of people who imagine they understand the book; I know this, for I have talked with them; but in all cases they were people who also imagined that there were no such things as pain, sickness, and death, and no realities in the world; nothing actually existent but Mind. It seems to me to modify the value of their testimony. . . .

—*Christian Science* (1907), book 1, chapters 1-3

We probably don't need to take seriously Mark Twain's claim to have had the painful experience he describes in this tale. We should, however, take seriously the depth of his interest in Christian Science and other forms of what might be called "mental science." He did, after all, write a 63,000-word book and a number of articles about the subject. He had strong reservations about Christian Science as a religion, but he was willing to concede that one of its central tenets—that the human mind is capable of healing the body—was at least possible.

20.

"A CORPSE NOT PARTICULAR ABOUT STYLE"

———••———

Matters of "style" always fascinated Mark Twain, and his interest in the subject even extended to funeral style. In fact, he once wrote a list of etiquette tips for funeral guests that included such suggestions as pretending not to notice when coffin handles are plated and not solid silver and ignoring the scent of oppressively odorous flowers. In view of his interest in the macabre, it should not be surprising that he even examined funeral style from the point of view of the guest of honor, that is to say, the deceased, or, more frankly, the corpse. This story, which he wrote in 1870, recalls his chat with an undertaker about a corpse indifferent to style.

———••———

"**N**ow, that corpse," said the undertaker, patting the folded hands of deceased approvingly, "was a brick—every way you took him he was a brick. He was so real accommodating, and so modest-like and simple in his last moments. Friends wanted metallic burial case—nothing else would do. *I* couldn't get it. There warn't going to be time—anybody could see that.

"Corpse said never mind, shake him up some kind of a box he could stretch out in comfortable, *he* warn't particular 'bout the general style of it. Said he went more on room than style, any way, in a last final container.

"Friends wanted a silver door-plate on the coffin, signifying who he was and wher' he was from. Now *you* know a fellow couldn't roust out such a gaily thing as that in a little country town like this. What did corpse say?

"Corpse said, whitewash his old canoe and dob his address and general destination onto it with a blacking brush and a stencil plate, 'long with a verse from some likely hymn or other, and p'int him for the tomb, and mark him C.O.D., and just let him flicker. *He* warn't distressed any more than you be—on the contrary just as

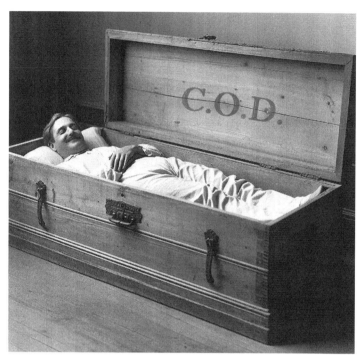

The corpse said all he wanted was a box in which he could stretch out comfortably; he wasn't particular about its style.

ca'm and collected as a hearse-horse; said he judged that wher' he was going to a body would find it considerable better to attract attention by a picturesque moral character than a natty burial case with a swell door-plate on it.

"Splendid man, he was. I'd druther do for a corpse like that 'n any I've tackled in seven year. There's some satisfaction in buryin' a man like that. You feel that what you're doing is appreciated. Lord bless you, so's he got planted before he sp'iled, he was perfectly satisfied; said his relations meant well, *perfectly* well, but all them preparations was bound to delay the thing more or less, and he didn't wish to be kept layin' around. You never see such a clear head as what he had— and so ca'm and so cool. Just a hunk of brains—that is what *he* was. Perfectly awful. It was a ripping distance from one end of that man's head to t'other. Often and over again he's had brain fever a-raging in one place, and the rest of the pile didn't know anything about it—didn't affect it any more than an Injun insurrection in Arizona affects the Atlantic States.

"Well, the relations they wanted a big funeral, but corpse said he was down on flummery—didn't want any procession—fill the hearse full of mourners, and get out a stern line and tow *him* behind. He was the most down on style of any remains I ever struck. A beautiful, simple-minded creature—it was what he was, you can depend on that. He was just set on having things the way he wanted them, and he took a solid comfort in laying his little plans. He had me measure him and take a whole raft of directions; then he had the minister stand up behind a long box with a table-cloth over it and read his funeral sermon, saying 'Angcore, angcore!' at the good places, and making him scratch out every bit of brag about him, and all the hifalutin; and then he made them trot out the choir so's he could help them pick out the tunes for the occasion, and he got them to sing 'Pop Goes the Weasel,' because he'd always liked that tune when he was down-hearted, and solemn music made him sad; and when they sung that with tears in their eyes (because they all loved him), and his relations grieving around, he just laid there as happy as a bug, and trying to beat time and showing all over how much he enjoyed it; and presently he got worked up and excited, and tried to join in, for mind you he was pretty proud of his abilities in the singing line; but the first time he opened his mouth and was just going to spread himself, his breath took a walk.

"I never see a man snuffed out so sudden. Ah, it was a great loss—it was a powerful loss to this poor little one-horse town. Well, well, well, I hain't got time to be palavering along here—got to nail on the lid and mosey along with him; and if you'll just give me a lift we'll skeet him into the hearse and meander along. Relations bound to have it so—don't pay no attention to dying injunctions, minute a corpse's gone; but if I had *my* way, if I didn't respect his last wishes and tow him behind the hearse, *I'll* be cuss'd. I consider that whatever a corpse wants done for his comfort is a little enough matter, and a man hain't got no right to deceive him or take advantage of him—and whatever a corpse trusts me to do I'm a-going to *do*, you know, even if it's to stuff him and paint him yaller and keep him for a keepsake—you hear *me!*"

He cracked his whip and went lumbering away with his ancient ruin of a hearse, and I continued my walk with a valuable lesson learned—that a healthy and wholesome cheerfulness is not necessarily impossible to any occupation. The lesson is likely to be lasting, for it will take many months to obliterate the memory of the remarks and circumstances that impressed it.

—"The Undertaker's Chat" (1875) (originally,
"A Reminiscence of the Back Settlements," 1870)

———••••—•—•••———

Not all corpses, of course, are as down on style as the one in this tale. In fact, Buck Fanshaw, the corpse in Mark Twain's next tale, may be the exact opposite. If, that is, he shares his buddy Scotty Briggs's views about how funerals should be conducted.

———••••—•—•••———

21.

"THAT MYSTERIOUS COUNTRY FROM WHOSE BOURNE NO TRAVELER RETURNS"

———————•——————

Language is an important dimension of human interaction, deserving of close attention. Or, more specifically, differences in the ways people speak are what is important. The following exchange from a mid-nineteenth-century Nevada mining town reveals the wide gulf between local slang and the refined speech of a recently arrived eastern parson. The delectable delicacies of their individual forms of expression combine to form a truly mysterious country that could exist only in Mark Twain's writings.

———————•——————

Somebody has said that in order to know a community, one must observe the style of its funerals and know what manner of men they bury with most ceremony. I cannot say which class we buried with most eclat in our "flush times," the distinguished public benefactor or the distinguished rough— possibly the two chief grades or grand divisions of society honored their illustrious dead about equally; and hence, no doubt the philosopher I have quoted from would have needed to see two representative funerals in Virginia [City] before forming his estimate of the people.

There was a grand time over Buck Fanshaw when he died. He was a representative citizen. He had "killed his man"—not in his own quarrel, it is true, but in defence of a stranger unfairly beset by numbers. He had kept a sumptuous saloon. He had been the proprietor of a dashing helpmeet whom he could have discarded without the formality of a divorce. He had held a high position in the fire department and been a very Warwick in politics. When he died there was great lamentation throughout the town, but especially in the vast bottom-stratum of society.

On the inquest it was shown that Buck Fanshaw, in the delirium of a wasting typhoid fever, had taken arsenic, shot himself through the body, cut his throat, and jumped out of a four-story window and broken his neck—and after due deliberation, the jury, sad and tearful, but with intelligence unblinded by its sorrow, brought in a verdict of death "by the visitation of God." What could the world do without juries?

Prodigious preparations were made for the funeral. All the vehicles in town were hired, all the saloons put in mourning, all the municipal and fire-company flags hung at half-mast, and all the firemen ordered to muster in uniform and bring their machines duly draped in black. Now—let us remark in parenthesis—as all the peoples of the earth had representative adventurers in the Silverland, and as each adventurer had brought the slang of his nation or his locality with him, the combination made the slang of Nevada the richest and the most infinitely varied and copious that had ever existed anywhere in the world, perhaps, except in the mines of California in the "early days." Slang was the language of Nevada. It was hard to preach a sermon without it, and be understood. Such phrases as "You bet!" "Oh, no, I reckon not!" "No Irish need apply," and a hundred others, became so common as to fall from the lips of a speaker unconsciously—and very often when they did not touch the subject under discussion and consequently failed to mean anything.

After Buck Fanshaw's inquest, a meeting of the short-haired brotherhood was held, for nothing can be done on the Pacific coast without a public meeting and an expression of sentiment. Regretful resolutions were passed and various committees appointed; among others, a committee of one was deputed to call on the minister, a fragile, gentle, spiritual new fledgling from an Eastern theological seminary, and as yet unacquainted with the ways of the mines. The committeeman, "Scotty" Briggs, made his visit; and in after days it was worth something to hear the minister tell about it. Scotty was a stalwart rough, whose customary suit, when on weighty official business, like committee work, was a fire helmet, flaming red flannel shirt, patent leather belt with spanner and revolver attached, coat hung over arm, and pants stuffed into boot tops. He formed something of a contrast to the pale theological student. It is fair to say of Scotty, however, in passing, that he had a warm heart, and a strong love for his friends, and never entered into a quarrel when he could reasonably keep out of it. Indeed, it was commonly said that whenever one of Scotty's fights was investigated, it always turned out that it had originally been no affair of his, but that out of native goodheartedness he had dropped in of his own accord to help the man who was getting the worst of it. He and Buck Fanshaw were bosom friends, for years, and had often taken adventurous "pot-luck" together. On one occasion, they had thrown off their coats and taken the weaker side in a fight among strangers, and after gaining a hard-earned victory, turned and found that the men they were helping had deserted early, and not only that, but had stolen their coats and made off with them! But to return to Scotty's visit to the minister. He was on a sorrowful mission, now, and his face was the picture of woe. Being admitted to the presence he sat down before the clergyman, placed his fire-hat on an unfinished manuscript sermon under the minister's nose, took from it a red silk handkerchief, wiped his brow and heaved a sigh of dismal impressiveness, explanatory of his business. He choked, and even shed tears; but with an effort he mastered his voice and said in lugubrious tones:

"Are you the duck that runs the gospel-mill next door?"

"Am I the—pardon me, I believe I do not understand?"

With another sigh and a half-sob, Scotty rejoined:

"Why you see we are in a bit of trouble, and the boys thought maybe you would give us a lift, if we'd tackle you—that is, if I've got the rights of it and you are the head clerk of the doxology-works next door. "

"I am the shepherd in charge of the flock whose fold is next door."

"The which?"

"The spiritual adviser of the little company of believers whose sanctuary adjoins these premises."

Scotty scratched his head, reflected a moment, and then said:

"You ruther hold over me, pard. I reckon I can't call that hand. Ante and pass the buck."

"How? I beg pardon. What did I understand you to say?"

"Well, you've ruther got the bulge on me. Or maybe we've both got the bulge, somehow. You don't smoke me and I don't smoke you. You see, one of the boys has passed in his checks and we want to give him a good send-off, and so the thing I'm on now is to roust out somebody to jerk a little chin-music for us and waltz him through handsome."

"My friend, I seem to grow more and more bewildered. Your observations are wholly incomprehensible to me. Cannot you simplify them in some way? At first I thought perhaps I understood you, but I grope now. Would it not expedite matters if you restricted yourself to categorical statements of fact unencumbered with obstructing accumulations of metaphor and allegory?"

Another pause, and more reflection. Then, said Scotty:

"I'll have to pass, I judge."

"How?"

"You've raised me out, pard."

"I still fail to catch your meaning."

"Why, that last lead of yourn is too many for me—that's the idea. I can't neither trump nor follow suit."

The clergyman sank back in his chair perplexed. Scotty leaned his head on his hand and gave himself up to thought. Presently his face came up, sorrowful but confident.

"I've got it now, so's you can savvy," he said. "What we want is a gospel-sharp. See?"

"A what?"

"Gospel-sharp. Parson."

"Oh! Why did you not say so before? I am a clergyman—a parson."

"Now you talk! You see my blind and straddle it like a man. Put it there!"—extending a brawny paw, which closed over the minister's small hand and gave it a shake indicative of fraternal sympathy and fervent gratification.

"Now we're all right, pard. Let's start fresh. Don't you mind my snuffling a little—becuz we're in a power of trouble. You see, one of the boys has gone up the flume—"

"Gone where?"

"Up the flume—throwed up the sponge, you understand."

The stalwart western ruffian Scotty Briggs shaking hands with the young gospel-sharp from the East.

"Thrown up the sponge?"

"Yes—kicked the bucket—"

"Ah—has departed to that mysterious country from whose bourne no traveler returns."

"Return! I reckon not. Why pard, he's *dead!*"

"Yes, I understand."

"Oh, you do? Well I thought maybe you might be getting tangled some more. Yes, you see he's dead again—"

"*Again?* Why, has he ever been dead before?"

"Dead before? No! Do you reckon a man has got as many lives as a cat? But you bet you he's awful dead now, poor old boy, and I wish I'd never seen this day. I don't want no better friend than Buck Fanshaw. I knowed him by the back; and when I know a man and like him, I freeze to him—you hear me. Take him all round, pard, there never was a bullier man in the mines. No man ever knowed Buck Fanshaw to go back on a friend. But it's all up, you know, it's all up. It ain't no use. They've scooped him."

"Scooped him?"

"Yes—death has. Well, well, well, we've got to give him up. Yes indeed. It's a kind of a hard world, after all, ain't it? But pard, he was a rustler! You ought to seen him get started once. He was a bully boy with a glass eye! Just spit in his face and give him room according to his strength, and it was just beautiful to see him peel and go in. He was the worst son of a thief that ever drawed breath. Pard, he was on it! He was on it bigger than an Injun!"

"On it? On what?"

"On the shoot. On the shoulder. On the fight, you understand. *He* didn't give a continental for *anybody*. *Beg* your pardon, friend, for coming so near saying a cuss-word—but you see I'm on an awful strain, in this palaver, on account of having to cramp down and draw everything so mild. But we've got to give him up. There ain't any getting around that, I don't reckon. Now if we can get you to help plant him—"

"Preach the funeral discourse? Assist at the obsequies?"

"Obs'quies is good. Yes. That's it—that's our little game. We are going to get the thing up regardless, you know. He was always nifty himself, and so you bet you his funeral ain't going to be no slouch—solid silver door-plate on his coffin, six plumes on the hearse, and a [black driver] on the box in a biled shirt and a plug hat—how's that for high? And we'll take care of *you*, pard. We'll fix you all right. There'll be a kerridge for you; and whatever you want, you just 'scape out and we'll 'tend to it. We've got a shebang fixed up for you to stand behind, in No. 1's house, and don't you be afraid. Just go in and toot your horn, if you don't sell a clam. Put Buck through as bully as you can, pard, for anybody that knowed him will tell you that he was one of the whitest men that was ever in the mines. You can't draw it too strong. He never could stand it to see things going wrong. He's done more to make this town quiet and peaceable than any man in it. I've seen him lick four Greasers in eleven minutes, myself. If a thing wanted regulating, *he* warn't a man to go browsing around after somebody to do it, but he would prance in and regulate it himself. He warn't a Catholic. Scasely. He was down on 'em. His word was, 'No Irish need apply!' But it didn't make no difference about that when it came down to what a man's rights was—and so, when some roughs jumped the Catholic bone-yard and started in to stake out town-lots in it he went for 'em! And he *cleaned* 'em, too! I was there, pard, and I seen it myself."

"That was very well indeed—at least the impulse was—whether the act was strictly defensible or not. Had deceased any religious convictions? That is to say, did he feel a dependence upon, or acknowledge allegiance to a higher power?"

More reflection.

"I reckon you've stumped me again, pard. Could you say it over once more, and say it slow?"

"Well, to simplify it somewhat, was he, or rather had he ever been connected with any organization sequestered from secular concerns and devoted to self-sacrifice in the interests of morality?"

"All down but nine—set 'em up on the other alley, pard."

"What did I understand you to say?"

"Why, you're most too many for me, you know. When you get in with your left I hunt grass every time. Every time you draw, you fill; but I don't seem to have any luck. Let's have a new deal."

"How? Begin again?"

"That's it."

"Very well. Was he a good man, and—"

"There—I see that; don't put up another chip till I look at my hand. A good man, says you? Pard, it ain't no name for it. He was the best man that ever—pard, you would have doted on that man. He could lam any galoot of his inches in America. It was him that put down the riot last election before it got a start; and everybody said he was the only man that could have done it. He waltzed in with a spanner in one hand and a trumpet in the other, and sent fourteen men home on a shutter in less than three minutes. He had that riot all broke up and prevented nice before anybody ever got a chance to strike a blow. He was always for peace, and he would have peace—he could not stand disturbances. Pard, he was a great loss to this town. It would please the boys if you could chip in something like that and do him justice. Here once when the Micks got to throwing stones through the Methodis' Sunday school windows, Buck Fanshaw, all of his own notion, shut up his saloon and took a couple of six-shooters and mounted guard over the Sunday school. Says he, 'No Irish need apply!' And they didn't. He was the bulliest man in the mountains, pard! He could run faster, jump higher, hit harder, and hold more tangle-foot whisky without spilling it than any man in seventeen counties. Put that in, pard—it'll please the boys more than anything you could say. And you can say, pard, that he never shook his mother."

"Never shook his mother?"

"That's it—any of the boys will tell you so."

"Well, but why *should* he shake her?"

"That's what *I* say—but some people does."

"Not people of any repute?"

"Well, some that averages pretty so-so."

"In my opinion the man that would offer personal violence to his own mother, ought to—"

"Cheese it, pard; you've banked your ball clean outside the string. What I was a drivin' at, was, that he never *throwed off* on his mother—don't you see? No indeedy. He give her a house to live in, and town lots, and plenty of money; and he looked after her and took care of her all the time; and when she was down with the small-pox I'm d—d if he didn't set up nights and nuss her himself! *Beg* your pardon for saying it, but it hopped out too quick for yours truly. You've treated me like a gentleman, pard, and I ain't the man to hurt your feelings intentional. I think you're white. I think you're a square man, pard. I like you, and I'll lick any man that don't. I'll lick him till he can't tell himself from a last year's corpse! Put it *there!*" [Another fraternal handshake—and exit.]

The obsequies were all that "the boys" could desire. Such a marvel of funeral pomp had never been seen in Virginia. The plumed hearse, the dirge-breathing brass bands, the closed marts of business, the flags drooping at half mast, the long, plodding procession of uniformed secret societies, military battalions and fire companies, draped engines, carriages of officials, and citizens in vehicles and on foot, attracted multitudes of spectators to the sidewalks, roofs and windows; and for years afterward, the degree of grandeur attained by any civic display in Virginia was determined by comparison with Buck Fanshaw's funeral.

Scotty Briggs, as a pall-bearer and a mourner, occupied a prominent place at the funeral, and when the sermon was finished and the last sentence of the prayer for the dead man's soul ascended, he responded, in a low voice, but with feeling:

"Amen. No Irish need apply."

As the bulk of the response was without apparent relevancy, it was probably nothing more than a humble tribute to the memory of the friend that was gone; for, as Scotty had once said, it was "his word."

In later days, Scotty Briggs achieved the distinction of becoming the only convert to religion who was ever gathered from the Virginia City roughs. The

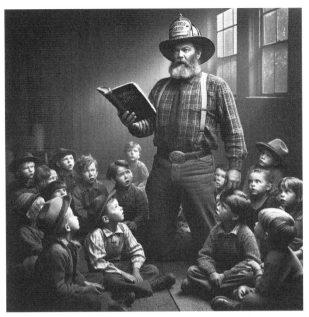

Scotty speaking to his youthful Sunday-school scholars in a language they understand.

making him one did not warp his generosity or diminish his courage; on the contrary it gave intelligent direction to the one and a broader field to the other. If his Sunday-school class progressed faster than the other classes, was it matter for wonder? I think not. He talked to his pioneer small-fry in a language they understood! It was my large privilege, a month before he died, to hear him tell the beautiful story of Joseph and his brethren to his class "without looking at the book." I leave it to the reader to fancy what it was like, as it fell, riddled with slang, from the lips of that grave, earnest teacher, and was listened to by his little learners with a consuming interest that showed that they were as unconscious as he was that any violence was being done to the sacred proprieties!

—*Roughing It* (1872), chapter 47

Scotty Briggs and the parson may as well have been speaking to each other in Choctaw and Aramaic, but they nevertheless managed to emerge from that mysterious country with a common understanding. Proof positive, if such is needed, that good hearts count for more than mere words in Mark Twain's writings.

22.

"POETRY THAT SOFTENS
THE TERROR OF DEATH"

———— ••—•—•• ————

*This essay, while not exactly spooky, is certainly creepy. It's about a very real phe-
nomenon that many people took seriously during the nineteenth century. However, as
an expression of Mark Twain's mock appreciation of poetic doggerel, the essay itself
should probably not be taken completely seriously.*

———— ••—•—•• ————

In Philadelphia they have a custom which it would be pleasant to see adopted
throughout the land. It is that of appending to published death-notices a little
verse or two of comforting poetry. Any one who is in the habit of reading the
daily Philadelphia "Ledger" must frequently be touched by these plaintive tributes
to extinguished worth. In Philadelphia, the departure of a child is a circumstance
which is not more surely followed by a burial than by the accustomed solacing
poesy in the "Public Ledger." In that city death loses half its terror because the
knowledge of its presence comes thus disguised in the sweet drapery of verse. For
instance, in a late "Ledger" I find the following (I change the surname):

Died

HAWKS. — On the 17th inst., CLARA, the daughter of Ephraim and Laura Hawks,
aged 21 months and 2 days.

> That merry shout no more I hear,
> No laughing child I see,
> No little arms are round my neck,
> No feet upon my knee;

> No kisses drop upon my cheek,
> These lips are sealed to me.
> Dear Lord, how could I give Clara up
> To any but to Thee?

A child thus mourned could not die wholly discontented. From the "Ledger" of the same date I make the following extract, merely changing the surname, as before:

BECKET. — On Sunday morning, 19th inst., JOHN P., infant son of George and Julia Becket, aged 1 year, 6 months, and 15 days.

> That merry shout no more I hear,
> No laughing child I see,
> No little arms are round my neck,
> No feet upon my knee;
> No kisses drop upon my cheek,
> These lips are sealed to me.
> Dear Lord, how could I give Johnnie up
> To any but to Thee?

The similarity of the emotions as produced in the mourners in these two instances is remarkably evidenced by the singular similarity of thought which they experienced, and the surprising coincidence of language used by them to give it expression.

In the same journal, of the same date, I find the following (surname suppressed, as before):

WAGNER. — On the 10th inst., FERGUSON G., the son of William L. and Martha Theresa Wagner, aged 4 weeks and 1 day.

> That merry shout no more I hear,
> No laughing child I see,
> No little arms are round my neck,
> No feet upon my knee;
> No kisses drop upon my cheek,
> These lips are sealed to me.
> Dear Lord, how could I give Ferguson up
> To any but to Thee?

It is strange what power the reiteration of an essentially poetical thought has upon one's feelings. When we take up the "Ledger" and read the poetry about little Clara, we feel an unaccountable depression of the spirits. When we drift further down the column and read the poetry about little Johnnie, the depression of spirits acquires an added emphasis, and we experience tangible suffering. When we saunter along down the column further still and read the poetry about little Ferguson the word torture but vaguely suggests the anguish that rends us.

In the "Ledger" (same copy referred to above) I find the following (I alter surname, as usual):

WELCH. — On the 5th inst., MARY C. WELCH, wife of William B. Welch, and daughter of Catharine and George W. Markland, in the 29th year of her age.

> A mother dear, a mother kind,
> Has gone and left us all behind.
> Cease to weep, for tears are vain,
> Mother dear is out of pain.
>
> Farewell, husband, children dear,
> Serve thy God with filial fear,
> And meet me in the land above,
> Where all is peace, and joy, and love.

What could be sweeter than that? No collection of salient facts (without reduction to tabular form) could be more succinctly stated than is done in the first stanza by the surviving relatives, and no more concise and comprehensive program of farewells, post-mortuary general orders, etc., could be framed in any form than is done in verse by deceased in the last stanza. These things insensibly make us wiser and tenderer, and better. Another extract:

BALL. — On the morning of the 15th inst., MARY E., daughter of John and Sarah F. Ball.

> 'Tis sweet to rest in lively hope
>   That when my change shall come
> Angels will hover round my bed,
>   To waft my spirit home.

The following is apparently the customary form for heads of families:

BURNS. — On the 20th inst., MICHAEL BURNS, aged 40 years.

> Dearest father, thou has left us,
>   Here thy loss we deeply feel;
> But 'tis God that has bereft us,
>   He can all our sorrows heal.
>
> Funeral at 2 o'clock sharp.

There is something very simple and pleasant about the following, which, in Philadelphia, seems to be the usual form for consumptives of long standing. (It deplores four distinct cases in the single copy of the "Ledger" which lies on the MEMORANDA editorial table):

BROMLEY. —— On the 29th inst., of consumption, PHILIP BROMLEY, in the 50th year of his age.

> Affliction sore long time he bore,
>   Physicians were in vain—
> Till God at last did hear him mourn,
>   And eased him of his pain.
>
> The friend whom death from us has torn,
>   We did not think so soon to part;
> An anxious care now sinks the thorn
>   Still deeper in our bleeding heart.

This beautiful creation loses nothing by repetition. On the contrary, the oftener one sees it in the "Ledger," the more grand and awe-inspiring it seems.

With one more extract I will close:

DOBLE. —— On the 4th inst., SAMUEL PEVERIL WORTHINGTON DOBLE, aged 4 days.

> Our little Sammy's gone,
>   His tiny spirit's fled;
> Our little boy we loved so dear
>   Lies sleeping with the dead.
>
> A tear within a father's eye,
>   A mother's aching heart,
> Can only tell the agony
>   How hard it is to part.

Could anything be more plaintive than that, without requiring further concessions of grammar? Could anything be likely to do more toward reconciling deceased to circumstances, and making him willing to go? Perhaps not. The power of song can hardly be estimated. There is an element about some poetry which is able to make even physical suffering and death cheerful things to contemplate and consummations to be desired. This element is present in the mortuary poetry of Philadelphia degree of development.

The custom I have been treating of is one that should be adopted in all the cities of the land.

—"Post-Mortem Poetry" (1870)

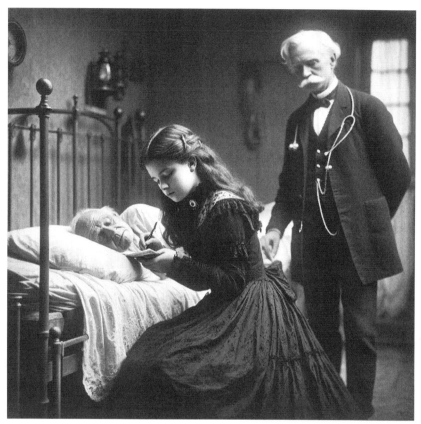

Before an elderly man's deceased body is cold, Huckleberry Finn's *Emmeline Grangerford begins composing a "tribute" to him.*

Mark Twain's fascination with funerary poetry continued in his later years and reached its highest level in his creation of the morbid teenage poetaster Emmeline Grangerford in Adventures of Huckleberry Finn *(1885). Already deceased when Huck Finn is taken into the Grangerford family, Emmeline was noted for the incredible speed with which she knocked out her funerary poems. According to Huck, whenever anyone died, "she would be on hand with her 'tribute' before he was cold. . . . it was the doctor first, then Emmeline, then the undertaker . . ." Huck so admired Emmeline's poems that he quoted one in its entirety:*

Ode to Stephen Dowling Bots, Dec'd.

And did young Stephen sicken,
    And did young Stephen die?
And did the sad hearts thicken,
    And did the mourners cry?

No; such was not the fate of
    Young Stephen Dowling Bots;
Though sad hearts round him thickened,
    'Twas not from sickness' shots.

No whooping-cough did rack his frame,
    Nor measles drear, with spots;
Not these impaired the sacred name
    Of Stephen Dowling Bots.

Despised love struck not with woe
    That head of curly knots.
Nor stomach troubles laid him low,
    Young Stephen Dowling Bots.

O No. Then list with tearful eye,
    Whilst I his fate do tell.
His soul did from this cold world fly,
    By falling down a well.

They got him out and emptied him;
    Alas it was too late;
His spirit was gone for to sport aloft
    In the realms of the good and great.

"They got him out and emptied him; alas, it was too late!"

23.

"A LITERARY NIGHTMARE"

Who among us has not had the annoying experience of hearing lines from a song or verse so catchy that they replay themselves over and over in our minds until we fear we'll go mad? No matter how hard we try, we cannot make the lines go away. Sometimes, they take such complete control of us that we are reduced to babbling jellies incapable of functioning. Such is the subject of this tale. Not surprisingly, perhaps, the lines in this tale are from a jingle deliberately, indeed, insidiously, written to be remembered.

Will the reader please to cast his eye over the following verses, and see if he can discover anything harmful in them?

> Conductor, when you receive a fare,
> Punch in the presence of the passenjare!
> A blue trip slip for an eight-cent fare,
> A buff trip slip for a six-cent fare,
> A pink trip slip for a three-cent fare,
> Punch in the presence of the passenjare!
>
> Chorus.
>
> Punch, brothers! punch with care!
> Punch in the presence of the passenjare!

I came across these jingling rhymes in a newspaper, a little while ago, and read them a couple of times. They took instant and entire possession of me. All through breakfast they went waltzing through my brain; and when, at last, I rolled up my napkin, I could not tell whether I had eaten anything or not. I had carefully laid out my day's work the day before—a thrilling tragedy in the novel which I am writing. I went to my den to begin my deed of blood. I took up my pen, but all I could get it to say was, "Punch in the presence of the passenjare." I fought hard for an hour, but it was useless. My head kept humming, "A blue trip slip for an eight-cent fare, a buff trip slip for a six-cent fare," and so on and so on, without peace or respite. The day's work was ruined—I could see that plainly enough. I gave up and drifted down town, and presently discovered that my feet were keeping time to that relentless jingle. When I could stand it no longer I altered my step. But it did no good; those rhymes accommodated themselves to the new step and went on harassing me just as before. I returned home, and suffered all the afternoon; suffered all through an unconscious and unrefreshing dinner; suffered, and cried, and jingled all through the evening; went to bed and rolled, tossed, and jingled right along, the same as ever; got up at midnight frantic, and tried to read; but there was nothing visible upon the whirling page except

Mark Twain presenting his ticket to a streetcar conductor, who prepares to punch it in his presence.

Punch, brothers! punch with care! Punch in the presence of the passenjare!

A tottering wreck, Mark Twain struggles to vanquish the catchy rhymes in his mind.

"Punch! punch in the presence of the passenjare." By sunrise I was out of my mind, and everybody marvelled and was distressed at the idiotic burden of my ravings— "Punch! oh, punch! punch in the presence of the passenjare!"

Two days later, on Saturday morning, I arose, a tottering wreck, and went forth to fulfil an engagement with a valued friend, the Rev. Mr. —— , to walk to the Talcott Tower, ten miles distant. He stared at me, but asked no questions. We started. Mr. —— talked, talked, talked—as is his wont. I said nothing; I heard nothing. At the end of a mile, Mr. —— said—

"Mark, are you sick? I never saw a man look so haggard and worn and absent-minded. Say something; do!"

Drearily, without enthusiasm, I said: "Punch, brothers, punch with care! Punch in the presence of the passenjare!"

My friend eyed me blankly, looked perplexed, then said—

"I do not think I get your drift, Mark. There does not seem to be any relevancy in what you have said, certainly nothing sad; and yet—maybe it was the way you said the words—I never heard anything that sounded so pathetic. What is—"

But I heard no more. I was already far away with my pitiless, heart-breaking "blue trip slip for an eight-cent fare, buff trip slip for a six-cent fare, pink trip slip for a three-cent fare; punch in the presence of the passenjare." I do not know what occurred during the other nine miles. However, all of a sudden Mr. —— laid his hand on my shoulder and shouted—

"Oh, wake up! wake up! wake up! Don't sleep all day! Here we are at the Tower, man! I have talked myself deaf and dumb and blind, and never got a response. Just look at this magnificent autumn landscape! look at it! Feast your eyes on it! You have travelled; you have seen boasted landscapes elsewhere. Come, now, deliver an honest opinion. What do you say to this?"

I sighed wearily, and murmured—

"A buff trip slip for a six-cent fare, a pink trip slip for a three-cent fare, punch in the presence of the passenjare."

Rev. Mr. —— stood there, very grave, full of concern, apparently, and looked long at me; then he said—

"Mark, there is something about this that I cannot understand. Those are about the same words you said before; there does not seem to be anything in them, and yet they nearly break my heart when you say them. Punch in the—how is it they go?"

I began at the beginning and repeated all the lines. My friend's face lighted with interest. He said—

"Why, what a captivating jingle it is! It is almost music. It flows along so nicely. I have nearly caught the rhymes myself. Say them over just once more, and then I'll have them, sure."

I said them over. Then Mr. —— said them. He made one little mistake, which I corrected. The next time and the next he got them right. Now a great burden seemed to tumble from my shoulders. That torturing jingle departed out of my brain, and a grateful sense of rest and peace descended upon me. I was light-hearted enough to sing; and I did sing for half an hour, straight along, as we went jogging homeward. Then my freed tongue found blessed speech again, and the pent talk of many a weary hour began to gush and flow. It flowed on and on, joyously, jubilantly, until the fountain was empty and dry. As I wrung my friend's hand at parting, I said—

"Haven't we had a royal good time! But now I remember, you haven't said a word for two hours. Come, come, out with something!"

The Rev. Mr. —— turned a lack-lustre eye upon me, drew a deep sigh, and said, without animation, without apparent consciousness—

"Punch, brothers, punch with care! Punch in the presence of the passenjare!"

A pang shot through me as I said to myself, "Poor fellow, poor fellow! *he* has got it, now."

I did not see Mr. —— for two or three days after that. Then, on Tuesday evening, he staggered into my presence and sank dejectedly into a seat. He was pale, worn; he was a wreck. He lifted his faded eyes to my face and said—

"Ah, Mark, it was a ruinous investment that I made in those heartless rhymes. They have ridden me like a nightmare, day and night, hour after hour, to this very moment. Since I saw you I have suffered the torments of the lost. Saturday evening I had a sudden call, by telegraph, and took the night train for Boston. The occasion was the death of a valued old friend who had requested that I should preach his funeral sermon. I took my seat in the cars and set myself to framing the discourse. But I never got beyond the opening paragraph; for then the train started and the car-wheels began their 'clack, clack—clack-clack-clack! clack, clack—clack-clack-clack!' and right away those odious rhymes fitted themselves to that accompaniment. For an hour I sat there and set a syllable of those rhymes to every separate and distinct clack the car-wheels made. Why, I was as fagged out, then, as if I had been chopping wood all day. My skull was splitting with headache. It seemed to me that I must go mad if I sat there any longer; so I undressed and went to bed. I stretched myself out in my berth, and—well, you know what the result was. The thing went right along, just the same. 'Clack-clack-clack, a blue trip slip, clack-clack-clack, for an eight-cent fare; clack-clack-clack, a buff trip slip, clack-clack-clack, for a six-cent fare, and so on, and so on, and so on—*punch*, in the presence of the passenjare!' Sleep? Not a single wink! I was almost a lunatic when I got to Boston. Don't ask me about the funeral. I did the best I could, but every solemn individual sentence was meshed and tangled and woven in and out with 'Punch, brothers, punch with care, punch in the presence of the passenjare.' And the most distressing thing was that my *delivery* dropped into the undulating rhythm of those pulsing rhymes, and I could actually catch absent-minded people nodding *time* to the swing of it with their stupid heads. And, Mark, you may believe it or not, but before I got through, the entire assemblage were placidly bobbing their heads in solemn unison, mourners, undertaker, and all. The moment I had finished, I fled to the anteroom in a state bordering on frenzy. Of course it would be my luck to find a sorrowing and aged maiden aunt of the deceased there, who had arrived from Springfield too late to get into the church. She began to sob, and said—

"'Oh, oh, he is gone, he is gone, and I didn't see him before he died!'

"'Yes!' I said, 'he *is* gone, he *is* gone, he *is* gone—oh, *will* this suffering never cease!'

"'*You* loved him, then! Oh, you too loved him!'

In the midst of his funeral sermon, the Reverend Mr. —— —— finds the pulsing rhymes taking control of the rhythm of his delivery.

"'Loved him! Loved *who?*'

"'Why, my poor George! my poor nephew!'

"'Oh—*him!* Yes—oh, yes, yes. Certainly—certainly. Punch—punch—oh, this misery will kill me!'

"'Bless you! bless you, sir, for these sweet words! *I*, too, suffer in this dear loss. Were you present during his last moments?'

"'Yes! I—*whose* last moments?'

"'*His.* The dear departed's.'

"'Yes! Oh, yes—yes—*yes!* I suppose so, I think so, *I* don't know! Oh, certainly— I was there—*I* was there!'

"'Oh, what a privilege! what a precious privilege! And his last words—oh, tell me, tell me his last words! What did he say?'

"'He said—he said—oh, my head, my head, my head! He said—he said—he never said anything but Punch, punch, *punch* in the presence of the passenjare! Oh, leave me, madam! In the name of all that is generous, leave me to my madness, my misery, my despair!—a buff trip slip for a six-cent fare, a pink trip slip for a three-cent fare—endurance *can* no further go!—PUNCH in the presence of the passenjare!'"

My friend's hopeless eyes rested upon mine a pregnant minute, and then he said impressively—

"Mark, you do not say anything. You do not offer me any hope. But, ah me, it is just as well—it is just as well. You could not do me any good. The time has long gone by when words could comfort me. Something tells me that my tongue is doomed to wag forever to the jigger of that remorseless jingle. There—there it is coming on me again: a blue trip slip for an eight-cent fare, a buff trip slip for a—"

Thus murmuring faint and fainter, my friend sank into a peaceful trance and forgot his sufferings in a blessed respite.

How did I finally save him from the asylum? I took him to a neighboring university and made him discharge the burden of his persecuting rhymes into the eager ears of the poor, unthinking students. How is it with *them*, now? The result is too sad to tell. Why did I write this article? It was for a worthy, even a noble, purpose. It was to warn you, reader, if you should come across those merciless rhymes, to avoid them—avoid them as you would a pestilence!

—"Punch, Brothers, Punch" (1876)

***

Modern science calls catchy ditties like "Punch, Brothers, Punch" earworms—a common form of what is known as involuntary cognition. Whatever they're called, they are certainly a fine example of the surprises awaiting readers of Mark Twain's writings.

***

PART V.

----·----

Worlds Remote in Time & Space

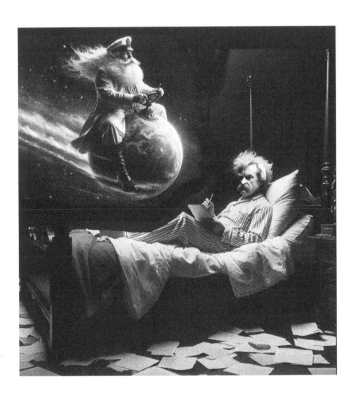

ark Twain wrote mostly about his own times and familiar American places, but there were few limits to his interests, which occasionally carried him off to other times, in the distant past and sometimes even into the future. There were also few limits to the places that interested him. He followed current developments in astronomy and occasionally wrote about other planets, such as Neptune, which was discovered during his boyhood. He was acutely aware of the fact that Halley's Comet had transited the earth when he was born in 1835 and accurately guessed that he would "go out" with that comet on its next return, which occurred in 1910. Meanwhile, during a nationwide alarm over the discovery of a new comet in 1874, he published a letter in the *New York Herald* announcing that he and showman P. T. Barnum had partnered to lease the comet, which they would outfit with a million staterooms for the purpose of providing a luxury cruise through the cosmos that would last until 1991. He then spent many years tinkering with a fictional space-travel story he published in 1909 as *Extract from Captain Stormfield's Visit to Heaven* that fleshed out his comet-tour proposal. The core of that story is excerpted here as "Heaven Is a Large Place." It is followed by several more fictional stories that reach into the remote past. "Welcome to the Sixth Century!" and "The Fragility of Fame"—both taken from *A Connecticut Yankee in King Arthur's Court* (1889)—deal with the intriguing question of what might become of an inventive and enterprising modern American mysteriously thrust back in time thirteen hundred years. The final story in this section, "The Death Disk," goes back only as far as the mid-seventeenth century. It concerns an ethical dilemma faced by England's Lord Protector Oliver Cromwell when he involves an innocent young child in the selection of a soldier to execute.

24.

"HEAVEN IS A LARGE PLACE"

———————•———————

Captain Eli Stormfield of San Francisco—a salty and sometimes profane veteran of countless sea voyages—is now nearing completion of his final voyage, one that has lasted thirty years. He is not traveling at sea, as we might expect, but through space— and at a seemingly impossible speed. Yet, despite the unimaginable distance he has navigated, this is not the strangest adventure of his life. For Captain Stormfield has been dead these past thirty years. When we meet him, he is on his way to what he expects will be Protestant heaven. What he eventually reaches, however, is not that heaven. Is it, in fact, really "heaven"?

———————•———————

W ell, when I had been dead about thirty years, I begun to get a little anxious. Mind you, I had been whizzing through space all that time, like a comet. *Like* a comet! Why, Peters, I laid over the lot of them! Of course there warn't any of them going my way, as a steady thing, you know, because they travel in a long circle like the loop of a lasso, whereas I was pointed as straight as a dart for the Hereafter; but I happened on one every now and then that was going my way for an hour or so, and then we had a bit of a brush together. But it was generally pretty one-sided, because I sailed by them the same as if they were standing still. An ordinary comet don't make more than about 200,000 miles a minute. Of course when I came across one of that sort— like Encke's and Halley's comets, for instance—it warn't anything but just a flash and a vanish, you see. You couldn't rightly call it a race. It was as if the comet was a gravel-train and I was a telegraph despatch. But after I got outside of our astronomical system, I used to flush a comet occasionally that was something *like*. *We* haven't got any such comets—ours don't begin.

One night I was swinging along at a good round gait, everything taut and trim, and the wind in my favor—I judged I was going about a million miles a minute—it might have been more, it couldn't have been less—when I flushed a most uncommonly big one about three points off my starboard bow. By his stern lights I judged he was bearing about northeast-and-by-north-half-east. Well, it was so near my course that I wouldn't throw away the chance; so I fell off a point, steadied my helm, and went for him. You should have heard me whiz, and seen the electric fur fly! In about a minute and a half I was fringed out with an electrical nimbus that flamed around for miles and miles and lit up all space like broad day. The comet was burning blue in the distance, like a sickly torch, when I first sighted him, but he begun to grow bigger and bigger as I crept up on him. I slipped up on him so fast that when I had gone about 150,000,000 miles I was close enough to be swallowed up in the phosphorescent glory of his wake, and I couldn't see anything for the glare. Thinks I, it won't do to run into him, so I shunted to one side and tore along. By and by I closed up abreast of his tail. Do you know what it was like? It was like a gnat closing up on the continent of America. I forged along. By and by I had sailed along his coast for a little upwards of a hundred and fifty million miles, and then I could see by the shape of him that I hadn't even got up to his waist-band yet. Why, Peters, *we* don't know anything about comets, down here. If you want to see comets that *are* comets, you've got to go outside of our solar system—where there's room for them, you understand. My friend, I've seen comets out there that couldn't even lay down inside the *orbits* of our noblest comets without their tails hanging over.

Well, I boomed along another hundred and fifty million miles, and got up abreast his shoulder, as you may say. I was feeling pretty fine, I tell you; but just then I noticed the officer of the deck come to the side and hoist his glass in my direction. Straight off I heard him sing out —

"Below there, ahoy! Shake her up, shake her up! Heave on a hundred million billion tons of brimstone!"

"Ay—ay, sir!"

"Pipe the stabboard watch! All hands on deck!"

"Ay—ay, sir!"

"Send two hundred thousand million men aloft to shake out royals and sky-scrapers!"

"Ay—ay, sir!"

"Hand the stuns'ls! Hang out every rag you've got! Clothe her from stem to rudder-post!"

"Ay—ay, sir!"

In about a second I begun to see I'd woke up a pretty ugly customer, Peters. In less than ten seconds that comet was just a blazing cloud of red-hot canvas. It was piled up into the heavens clean out of sight—the old thing seemed to swell out and occupy all space; the sulphur smoke from the furnaces—oh, well, nobody can describe the way it rolled and tumbled up into the skies, and nobody can half describe the way it smelt. Neither can anybody begin to describe the way that monstrous craft begun to crash along. And such another powwow—thousands of bo's'n's whistles screaming at once, and a crew like the population of a hundred thousand worlds like ours all swearing at once. Well, I never heard the like of it before.

We roared and thundered along side by side, both doing our level best, because I'd never struck a comet before that could lay over me, and so I was bound to beat this one or break something. I judged I had some reputation in space, and I calculated to keep it. I noticed I wasn't gaining as fast, now, as I was before, but still I was gaining. There was a power of excitement on board the comet. Upwards of a hundred billion passengers swarmed up from below and rushed to the side and begun to bet on the race. Of course this careened her and damaged her speed. My, but wasn't the mate mad! He jumped at that crowd, with his trumpet in his hand, and sung out —

"Amidships! amidships, you——! or I'll brain the last idiot of you!"

Well, sir, I gained and gained, little by little, till at last I went skimming sweetly by the magnificent old conflagration's nose. By this time the captain of the comet had been rousted out, and he stood there in the red glare for'ard, by the mate, in his shirtsleeves and slippers, his hair all rats' nests and one suspender hanging, and how sick those two men did look! I just simply couldn't help putting my thumb to my nose as I glided away and singing out:

"Ta-ta! ta-ta! Any word to send to your family?"

Peters, it was a mistake. Yes, sir, I've often regretted that—it was a mistake. You see, the captain had given up the race, but that remark was too tedious for him—he couldn't stand it. He turned to the mate, and says he—

"Have we got brimstone enough of our own to make the trip?"

"Yes, sir."

"Sure?"

"Yes, sir—more than enough."

"How much have we got in cargo for Satan?"

"Eighteen hundred thousand billion quintillions of kazarks."

"Very well, then, let his boarders freeze till the next comet comes. Lighten ship! Lively, now, lively men! Heave the whole cargo overboard!"

Peters, look me in the eye, and be calm. I found out, over there, that a kazark is exactly the bulk of a *hundred and sixty-nine worlds like ours*! They hove all that load overboard. When it fell it wiped out a considerable raft of stars just as clean as if they'd been candles and somebody blowed them out. As for the race, that was at an end.

The minute she was lightened the comet swung along by me the same as if I was anchored. The captain stood on the stern, by the after-davits, and put his thumb to his nose and sung out—

"Ta-ta! ta-ta! Maybe *you've* got some message to send to your friends in the Everlasting Tropics!"

Then he hove up his other suspender and started for'ard, and inside of three-quarters of an hour his craft was only a pale torch again in the distance. Yes, it was a mistake, Peters—that remark of mine. I don't reckon I'll ever get over being sorry about it. I'd'a' beat the bully of the firmament if I'd kept my mouth shut.

But I've wandered a little off the track of my tale; I'll get back on my course again. Now you see what kind of speed I was making. So, as I said, when I had been tearing along this way about thirty years I begun to get uneasy. Oh, it was pleasant enough, with a good deal to find out, but then it was kind of lonesome, you know. Besides, I wanted to get somewhere. I hadn't shipped with the idea of cruising forever. First off, I liked the delay, because I judged I was going to fetch up in pretty warm quarters when I got through; but towards the last I begun to feel that I'd rather go to—well, most any place, so as to finish up the uncertainty.

Well, one night—it was always night, except when I was rushing by some star that was occupying the whole universe with its fire and its glare—light enough then, of course, but I necessarily left it behind in a minute or two and plunged into a solid week of darkness again. The stars ain't so close together as they look to be. Where was I? Oh yes; one night I was sailing along, when I discovered a tremendous long row of blinking lights away on the horizon ahead. As I approached, they begun to tower and swell and look like mighty furnaces. Says I to myself —

"By George, I've arrived at last—and at the wrong place, just as I expected!"

Then I fainted. I don't know how long I was insensible, but it must have been a good while, for, when I came to, the darkness was all gone and there was the loveliest sunshine and the balmiest, fragrantest air in its place. And there was such a marvelous world spread out before me—such a glowing, beautiful, bewitching country. The things I took for furnaces were gates, miles high, made all of flashing jewels, and they pierced a wall of solid gold that you couldn't see the top of, nor yet the end of, in either direction. I was pointed straight for one of these gates, and a-coming like a house afire. Now I noticed that the skies were black with millions of people, pointed for those gates. What a roar they made, rushing through the air! The ground was as thick as ants with people, too—billions of them, I judge.

I lit. I drifted up to a gate with a swarm of people, and when it was my turn the head clerk says, in a businesslike way —

"Well, quick! Where are you from?"

"San Francisco," says I.

"San Fran—what?" says he.

"San Francisco."

He scratched his head and looked puzzled, then he says —

"Is it a planet?"

By George, Peters, think of it! "Planet?" says I; "it's a city. And moreover, it's one of the biggest and finest and—"

"There, there!" says he, "no time here for conversation. We don't deal in cities here. Where are you from in a *general* way?"

"Oh," I says, "I beg your pardon. Put me down for California."

I had him *again*, Peters! He puzzled a second, then he says, sharp and irritable —

"I don't know any such planet—is it a constellation?"

"Oh, my goodness!" says I. "Constellation, says you? No—it's a State."

"Man, we don't deal in States here. *Will* you tell me where you are from *in general—at large*, don't you understand?"

"Oh, now I get your idea," I says. "I'm from America—the United States of America."

Peters, do you know I had him *again*? If I hadn't I'm a clam! His face was as blank as a target after a militia shooting-match.

He turned to an under clerk and says —

"Where is America? *What* is America?"

The under clerk answered up prompt and says —

"There ain't any such orb."

"*Orb?*" says I. "Why, what are you talking about, young man? It ain't an orb; it's country; it's a continent. Columbus discovered it; I reckon likely you've heard of *him*, anyway. America—why, sir, America—"

"Silence!" says the head clerk. "Once for all, where—are—you—*from?*"

"Well," says I, "I don't know anything more to say—unless I lump things, and just say I'm from the world."

"Ah," says he, brightening up, "now that's something like! *What* world?"

Peters, he had *me*, that time. I looked at him, puzzled, he looked at me, worried. Then he burst out —

"Come, come, what world?"

Says I, "Why, *the* world, of course."

"*The* world!" he says. "H'm! there's billions of them! . . . Next!"

That meant for me to stand aside. I done so, and a sky-blue man with seven heads and only one leg hopped into my place. I took a walk. It just occurred to me, then, that all the myriads I had seen swarming to that gate, up to this time, were just like that creature. I tried to run across somebody I was acquainted with, but they were out of acquaintances of mine just then. So I thought

On his arrival in Heaven, Captain Stormfield discovers that the myriads swarming up to its gates include many beings not of his own world.

the thing all over and finally sidled back there pretty meek and feeling rather stumped, as you may say.

"Well?" said the head clerk.

"Well, sir," I says, pretty humble, "I don't seem to make out which world it is I'm from. But you may know it from this—it's the one the Saviour saved."

He bent his head at the Name. Then he says, gently —

"The worlds He has saved are like the gates of heaven in number—none can count them. What astronomical system is your world in?—perhaps that may assist."

"It's the one that has the sun in it—and the moon—and Mars"—he shook his head at each name—hadn't ever heard of them, you see—"and Neptune—and Uranus—and Jupiter—"

"Hold on!" says he—"hold on a minute! Jupiter . . . Jupiter . . . Seems to me we had a man from there eight or nine hundred years ago—but people from that system very seldom enter by this gate." All of a sudden he begun to look me so straight in the eye that I thought he was going to bore through me. Then he says, very deliberate, "Did you come *straight here* from your system?"

"Yes, sir," I says—but I blushed the least little bit in the world when I said it.

He looked at me very stern, and says —

"That is not true; and this is not the place for prevarication. You wandered from your course. How did that happen?"

Says I, blushing again —

"I'm sorry, and I take back what I said, and confess. I raced a little with a comet one day—only just the least little bit—only the tiniest lit—"

"So—so," says he—and without any sugar in his voice to speak of.

I went on, and says—

"But I only fell off just a bare point, and I went right back on my course again the minute the race was over."

"No matter—that divergence has made all this trouble. It has brought you to a gate that is billions of leagues from the right one. If you had gone to your own gate they would have known all about your world at once and there would have been no delay. But we will try to accommodate you." He turned to an under clerk and says—

"What system is Jupiter in?"

"I don't remember, sir, but I think there is such a planet in one of the little new systems away out in one of the thinly worlded corners of the universe. I will see."

He got a balloon and sailed up and up and up, in front of a map that was as big as Rhode Island. He went on up till he was out of sight, and by and by he came down and got something to eat and went up again. To cut a long story short, he kept on doing this for a day or two, and finally he came down and said he thought he had found that solar system, but it might be fly-specks. So he got a microscope and went back. It turned out better than he feared. He had rousted out our system, sure enough. He got me to describe our planet and its distance from the sun, and then he says to his chief —

"Oh, I know the one he means, now, sir. It is on the map. It is called the Wart."

Says I to myself, "Young man, it wouldn't be wholesome for you to go down *there* and call it the Wart."

Well, they let me in, then, and told me I was safe forever and wouldn't have any more trouble.

Then they turned from me and went on with their work, the same as if they considered my case all complete and shipshape. I was a good deal surprised at this, but I was diffident about speaking up and reminding them. I did so hate to do it, you know; it seemed a pity to bother them, they had so much on their hands. Twice I thought I would give up and let the thing go; so twice I started to leave, but immediately I thought what a figure I should cut stepping out amongst the redeemed in such a rig, and that made me hang back and come to anchor again. People got to eyeing me—clerks, you know—wondering why I didn't get under way. I couldn't stand this long—it was too uncomfortable. So at last I plucked up courage and tipped the head clerk a signal. He says—

"What! you here yet? What's wanting?"

Says I, in a low voice and very confidential, making a trumpet with my hands at his ear—

"I beg pardon, and you mustn't mind my reminding you, and seeming to meddle, but hain't you forgot something?"

He studied a second, and says—

"Forgot something? . . . No, not that I know of."

"Think," says I.

He thought. Then he says—

"No, I can't seem to have forgot anything. What is it?"

"Look at me," says I, "look me all over."

He done it.

"Well?" says he.

"Well," says I, "you don't notice anything? If I branched out amongst the elect looking like this, wouldn't I attract considerable attention?—wouldn't I be a little conspicuous?"

"Well," he says, "I don't see anything the matter. What do you lack?"

"Lack! Why, I lack my harp, and my wreath, and my halo, and my hymn-book, and my palm branch—I lack everything that a body naturally requires up here, my friend."

Puzzled? Peters, he was the worst puzzled man you ever saw. Finally he says—

"Well, you seem to be a curiosity every way a body takes you. I never heard of these things before."

I looked at the man awhile in solid astonishment; then I says—

"Now, I hope you don't take it as an offence, for I don't mean any, but really, for a man that has been in the Kingdom as long as I reckon you have, you do seem to know powerful little about its customs."

"Its customs!" says he. "Heaven is a large place, good friend. Large empires have many and diverse customs. Even small dominions have, as you doubtless know by what you have seen of the matter on a small scale in the Wart. How can you imagine I could ever learn the varied customs of the countless kingdoms of heaven? It makes my head ache to think of it. I know the customs that prevail in those portions inhabited by peoples that are appointed to enter by my own gate—and hark ye, that is quite enough knowledge for one individual to try to pack into his head in the thirty-seven millions of years I have devoted night and day to that study. But the idea of learning the customs of the whole appalling expanse of heaven—O man, how insanely you talk! Now I don't doubt that this odd costume you talk about is the fashion in that district of heaven you belong to, but you won't be conspicuous in this section without it."

I felt all right, if that was the case, so I bade him good-day and left. All day I walked towards the far end of a prodigious hall of the office, hoping to come out into heaven any moment, but it was a mistake. That hall was built on the general heavenly plan—it naturally couldn't be small. At last I got so tired I couldn't go any farther; so I sat down to rest, and begun to tackle the queerest sort of strangers and ask for information, but I didn't get any; they couldn't understand my language, and I could not understand theirs. I got dreadfully lonesome. I was so downhearted and homesick I wished a hundred times I never had died. I turned back, of course. About noon next day, I got back at last and was on hand at the booking-office once more. Says I to the head clerk—

"I begin to see that a man's got to be in his own heaven to be happy."

"Perfectly correct," says he. "Did you imagine the same heaven would suit all sorts of men?"

"Well, I had that idea—but I see the foolishness of it. Which way am I to go to get to my district?"

He called the under clerk that had examined the map, and he gave me general directions. I thanked him and started; but he says—

"Wait a minute; it is millions of leagues from here. Go outside and stand on that red wishing-carpet; shut your eyes, hold your breath, and wish yourself there."

"I'm much obliged," says I; "why didn't you dart me through when I first arrived?"

"We have a good deal to think of here; it was your place to think of it and ask for it. Good-by; we probably sha'n't see you in this region for a thousand centuries or so."

"In that case, *o revoor*," says I.

I hopped onto the carpet and held my breath and shut my eyes and wished I was in the booking-office of my own section. The very next instant a voice I knew sung out in a business kind of a way—

"A harp and a hymn-book, pair of wings and a halo, size 13, for Cap'n Eli Stormfield, of San Francisco!—make him out a clean bill of health, and let him in."

I opened my eyes. Sure enough, it was a Pi Ute Injun I used to know in Tulare County; mighty good fellow—I remembered being at his funeral, which consisted of him being burnt and the other Injuns gauming their faces with his ashes and howling like wild-cats. He was powerful glad to see me, and you may make up your mind I was just as glad to see him, and felt that I was in the right kind of a heaven at last.

Finally settled in, Captain Stormfield sports all the requisite heavenly gear he has looked forward to having.

Just as far as your eye could reach, there was swarms of clerks, running and bustling around, tricking out thousands of Yanks and Mexicans and English and A-rabs, and all sorts of people in their new outfits; and when they gave me my kit and I put on my halo and I took a look in the glass, I could have jumped over a house for joy, I was so happy. "Now *this* is something like!" says I. "Now," says I, "I'm all right—show me a cloud."

Inside of fifteen minutes I was a mile on my way towards the cloud-banks and about a million people along with me. Most of us tried to fly, but some got crippled and nobody made a success of it. So we concluded to walk, for the present, till we had some wing practice.

We begun to meet swarms of folks who were coming back. Some had harps and nothing else; some had hymn-books and nothing else; some had nothing at all; all of them looked meek and uncomfortable; one young fellow hadn't any-thing left but his halo, and he was carrying that in his hand; all of a sudden he offered it to me and says—

"Will you hold it for me a minute?"

Then he disappeared in the crowd. I went on. A woman asked me to hold her palm branch, and then *she* disappeared. A girl got me to hold her harp for her, and by George, *she* disappeared; and so on and so on, till I was about loaded down to the guards. Then comes a smiling old gentleman and asked me to hold *his* things. I swabbed off the perspiration and says, pretty tart—

"I'll have to get you to excuse me, my friend—*I* ain't no hat-rack."

About this time I begun to run across piles of those traps, lying in the road. I just quietly dumped my extra cargo along with them. I looked around, and, Peters, that whole nation that was following me were loaded down the same as I'd been. The return crowd had got them to hold their things a minute, you see. They all dumped their loads, too, and we went on.

When I found myself perched on a cloud, with a million other people, I never felt so good in my life. Says I, "Now this is according to the promises; I've been having my doubts, but now I *am* in heaven, sure enough." I gave my palm branch a wave or two, for luck, and then I tautened up my harp-strings and struck in. Well, Peters, you can't imagine anything like the row we made. It was grand to listen to, and made a body thrill all over, but there was considerable many tunes going on at once, and that was a drawback to the harmony, you understand; and then there was a lot of Injun tribes, and they kept up such another war-whooping that they kind of took the tuck out of the music. By and by I quit performing, and judged I'd take a rest. There was quite a nice mild old gentleman sitting next to me, and I noticed he didn't take a hand; I encouraged him, but he said he was naturally bashful, and was afraid to try before so many people. By and by the old gentleman said he never could seem to enjoy music somehow. The fact was, I was beginning to feel the same way; but I didn't say anything. Him and I had a con-siderable long silence, then, but of course it warn't noticeable in that place. After about sixteen or seventeen hours, during which I played and sung a little, now and then—always the same tune, because I didn't know any other—I laid down my harp and begun to fan myself with my palm branch. Then we both got to sighing pretty regular. Finally, says he—

"Don't you know any tune but the one you've been pegging at all day?"

"Not another blessed one," says I.

"Don't you reckon you could learn another one?" says he.

"Never," says I; "I've tried to, but I couldn't manage it."

"It's a long time to hang to the one—eternity, you know."

"Don't break my heart," says I; "I'm getting low-spirited enough already."

After another long silence, says he —

"Are you glad to be here?"

Says I, "Old man, I'll be frank with you. This *ain't* just as near my idea of bliss as I thought it was going to be, when I used to go to church."

Says he, "What do you say to knocking off and calling it half a day?"

"That's me," says I. "I never wanted to get off watch so bad in my life."

So we started. Millions were coming to the cloud-bank all the time, happy and hosannahing; millions were leaving it all the time, looking mighty quiet, I tell you. We laid for the new-comers, and pretty soon I'd got them to hold all my things a minute, and then I was a free man again and most outrageously happy. Just then I ran across old Sam Bartlett, who had been dead a long time, and stopped to have a talk with him. Says I—

"Now tell me—is this to go on forever? Ain't there anything else for a change?"

Says he—

"I'll set you right on that point very quick. People take the figurative language of the Bible and the allegories for literal, and the first thing they ask for when they get here is a halo and a harp, and so on. Nothing that's harmless and reasonable is refused a body here, if he asks it in the right spirit. So they are outfitted with these things without a word. They go and sing and play just about one day, and that's the last you'll ever see them in the choir. They don't need anybody to tell them that that sort of thing wouldn't make a heaven—at least not a heaven that a sane man could stand a week and remain sane. That cloud-bank is placed where the noise can't disturb the old inhabitants, and so there ain't any harm in letting everybody get up there and cure himself as soon as he comes.

"Now you just remember this—heaven is as blissful and lovely as it can be; but it's just the busiest place you ever heard of. There ain't any idle people here after the first day. Singing hymns and waving palm branches through all eternity is pretty when you hear about it in the pulpit, but it's as poor a way to put in valuable time as a body could contrive. It would just make a heaven of warbling ignoramuses, don't you see? Eternal Rest sounds comforting in the pulpit, too. Well, you try it once, and see how heavy time will hang on your hands. Why, Stormfield, a man like you, that had been active and stirring all his life, would go mad in six months in a heaven where he hadn't anything to do. Heaven is the very last place to come to *rest* in—and don't you be afraid to bet on that!"

Says I—

"Sam, I'm as glad to hear it as I thought I'd be sorry. I'm glad I come, now."

Says he—

"Cap'n, ain't you pretty physically tired?"

Says I—

"Sam, it ain't any name for it! I'm dog-tired."

"Just so—just so. You've earned a good sleep, and you'll get it. You've earned a good appetite, and you'll enjoy your dinner. It's the same here as it is on earth—you've got to earn a thing, square and honest, before you enjoy it. You can't enjoy first and earn afterwards. But there's this difference, here: you can choose your own occupation, and all the powers of heaven will be put forth to help you make a success of it, if you do your level best. The shoemaker on earth that had the soul of a poet in him won't have to make shoes here."

"Now that's all reasonable and right," says I. "Plenty of work, and the kind you hanker after; no more pain, no more suffering—"

"Oh, hold on; there's plenty of pain here—but it don't kill. There's plenty of suffering here, but it don't last. You see, happiness ain't a *thing in itself*—it's only a *contrast* with something that ain't pleasant. That's all it is. There ain't a thing you can mention that is happiness in its own self—it's only so by contrast with the other thing. And so, as soon as the novelty is over and the force of the contrast dulled, it ain't happiness any longer, and you have to get something fresh. Well, there's plenty of pain and suffering in heaven—consequently there's plenty of contrasts, and just no end of happiness."

Says I, "It's the sensiblest heaven I've heard of yet, Sam, though it's about as different from the one I was brought up on as a live princess is different from her own wax figger."

—Extract from *Captain Stormfield's Visit to Heaven* (1909)

———————————

We'll leave the good captain now, but many surprises still await him. Heaven isn't the place he thought it would be, but it is indeed a large place . . . a very large place, and in it he will find almost everything a person could imagine—and the story's author could imagine a lot!

———————————

25.

"WELCOME TO THE SIXTH CENTURY!"

———————•——•——•———————

Mark Twain most fully expressed his fascination with early history in A Connecticut Yankee in King Arthur's Court, *his 1889 novel about a late nineteenth-century American factory foreman who unaccountably finds himself in early sixth-century England. What he tries to accomplish in that distant land is full of interest, but his visit there nearly meets an abrupt and painful end. On his arrival, he is taken before King Arthur, denounced as a "sky-monster," and sentenced to be burned at the stake. "Welcome," indeed! Fortunately, he happens to know the exact date of an eclipse, and is not above applying a little "Yankee ingenuity" to that knowledge. This excerpt begins after the Yankee has been captured, denounced, and thrown, naked, into a castle dungeon.*

———————•——•——•———————

I was so tired that even my fears were not able to keep me awake long.

When I next came to myself, I seemed to have been asleep a very long time. My first thought was, "Well, what an astonishing dream I've had! I reckon I've waked only just in time to keep from being hanged or drowned or burned or something. . . . I'll nap again till the whistle blows, and then I'll go down to the arms factory and have it out with Hercules."

But just then I heard the harsh music of rusty chains and bolts, a light flashed in my eyes, and that butterfly, Clarence, stood before me! I gasped with surprise; my breath almost got away from me.

"What!" I said, "you here yet? Go along with the rest of the dream! scatter!"

But he only laughed, in his light-hearted way, and fell to making fun of my sorry plight.

"All right," I said resignedly, "let the dream go on; I'm in no hurry."

"Prithee what dream?"

Immediately after mysteriously awakening in sixth-century England, the Connecticut arms factory foreman is captured by a knight, chained, and taken to Camelot to be imprisoned in King Arthur's castle.

"What dream? Why, the dream that I am in Arthur's court—a person who never existed; and that I am talking to you, who are nothing but a work of the imagination."

"Oh, la, indeed! and is it a dream that you're to be burned to-morrow? Ho-ho—answer me that!"

The shock that went through me was distressing. I now began to reason that my situation was in the last degree serious, dream or no dream; for I knew by past experience of the life-like intensity of dreams, that to be burned to death, even in a dream, would be very far from being a jest, and was a thing to be avoided, by any means, fair or foul, that I could contrive. So I said beseechingly:

"Ah, Clarence, good boy, only friend I've got—for you *are* my friend, aren't you?—don't fail me; help me to devise some way of escaping from this place!"

"Now do but hear thyself! Escape? Why, man, the corridors are in guard and keep of men-at-arms."

"No doubt, no doubt. But how many, Clarence? Not many, I hope?"

"Full a score. One may not hope to escape." After a pause—hesitatingly: "and there be other reasons—and weightier."

"Other ones? What are they?"

"Well, they say—oh, but I daren't, indeed daren't!"

"Why, poor lad, what is the matter? Why do you blench? Why do you tremble so?"

"Oh, in sooth, there is need! I do want to tell you, but—"

"Come, come, be brave, be a man—speak out, there's a good lad!"

He hesitated, pulled one way by desire, the other way by fear; then he stole to the door and peeped out, listening; and finally crept close to me and put his mouth to my ear and told me his fearful news in a whisper, and with all the cowering apprehension of one who was venturing upon awful ground and speaking of things whose very mention might be freighted with death.

"Merlin, in his malice, has woven a spell about this dungeon, and there bides not the man in these kingdoms that would be desperate enough to essay to cross its lines with you! Now God pity me, I have told it! Ah, be kind to me, be merciful to a poor boy who means thee well; for an thou betray me I am lost!"

I laughed the only really refreshing laugh I had had for some time; and shouted:

"Merlin has wrought a spell! *Merlin*, forsooth! That cheap old humbug, that maundering old ass? Bosh, pure bosh, the silliest bosh in the world! Why, it does seem to me that of all the childish, idiotic, chuckle-headed, chicken-livered superstitions that ev—oh, damn Merlin!"

But Clarence had slumped to his knees before I had half finished, and he was like to go out of his mind with fright.

"Oh, beware! These are awful words! Any moment these walls may crumble upon us if you say such things. Oh call them back before it is too late!"

Now this strange exhibition gave me a good idea and set me to thinking. If everybody about here was so honestly and sincerely afraid of Merlin's pretended magic as Clarence was, certainly a superior man like me ought to be shrewd enough to contrive some way to take advantage of such a state of things. I went on thinking, and worked out a plan. Then I said:

"Get up. Pull yourself together; look me in the eye. Do you know why I laughed?"

"No—but for our blessed Lady's sake, do it no more."

"Well, I'll tell you why I laughed. Because I'm a magician myself."

"Thou!" The boy recoiled a step, and caught his breath, for the thing hit him rather sudden; but the aspect which he took on was very, very respectful. I took quick note of that; it indicated that a humbug didn't need to have a reputation in this asylum; people stood ready to take him at his word, without that. I resumed.

"I've known Merlin seven hundred years, and he—"

"Seven hun—"

"Don't interrupt me. He has died and come alive again thirteen times, and traveled under a new name every time: Smith, Jones, Robinson, Jackson, Peters, Haskins, Merlin—a new alias every time he turns up. I knew him in Egypt three hundred years ago; I knew him in India five hundred years ago—he is always blethering around in my way, everywhere I go; he makes me tired. He don't amount to shucks, as a magician; knows some of the old common tricks, but has never got beyond the rudiments, and never will. He is well enough for the provinces—one-night stands and that sort of thing, you know—but dear me, *he* oughtn't to set up for an expert—anyway not where there's a real artist. Now look here, Clarence, I am going to stand your friend, right along, and in return you must be mine. I want you to do me a favor. I want you to get word to the king that I am a magician myself—and the Supreme Grand High-yu-Muckamuck and head of the tribe, at that; and I want him to be made to understand that I am just quietly arranging a little calamity here that will make the fur fly in these realms if Sir Kay's project is carried out and any harm comes to me. Will you get that to the king for me?"

The poor boy was in such a state that he could hardly answer me. It was pitiful to see a creature so terrified, so unnerved, so demoralized. But he promised everything; and on my side he made me promise over and over again that I would remain his friend, and never turn against him or cast any enchantments upon him. Then he worked his way out, staying himself with his hand along the wall, like a sick person.

Presently this thought occurred to me: how heedless I have been! When the boy gets calm, he will wonder why a great magician like me should have begged a boy like him to help me get out of this place; he will put this and that together, and will see that I am a humbug.

I worried over that heedless blunder for an hour, and called myself a great many hard names, meantime. But finally it occurred to me all of a sudden that these animals didn't reason; that *they* never put this and that together; that all their talk showed that they didn't know a discrepancy when they saw it. I was at rest, then.

But as soon as one is at rest, in this world, off he goes on something else to worry about. It occurred to me that I had made another blunder: I had sent the boy off to alarm his betters with a threat—I intending to invent a calamity at my leisure; now the people who are the readiest and eagerest and willingest to swallow miracles are the very ones who are hungriest to see you perform them;

suppose I should be called on for a sample? Suppose I should be asked to name my calamity? Yes, I had made a blunder; I ought to have invented my calamity first. "What shall I do? what can I say, to gain a little time?" I was in trouble again; in the deepest kind of trouble: . . . "There's a footstep!—they're coming. If I had only just a moment to think . . . Good, I've got it. I'm all right."

You see, it was the eclipse. It came into my mind in the nick of time, how Columbus, or Cortez, or one of those people, played an eclipse as a saving trump once, on some [islanders], and I saw my chance. I could play it myself, now, and it wouldn't be any plagiarism, either, because I should get it in nearly a thousand years ahead of those parties.

Clarence came in, subdued, distressed, and said:

"I hasted the message to our liege the king, and straightway he had me to his presence. He was frighted even to the marrow, and was minded to give order for your instant enlargement, and that you be clothed in fine raiment and lodged as befitted one so great; but then came Merlin and spoiled all; for he persuaded the king that you are mad, and know not whereof you speak; and said your threat is but foolishness and idle vaporing. They disputed long, but in the end, Merlin, scoffing, said, 'Wherefore hath he not *named* his brave calamity? Verily it is because he cannot.' This thrust did in a most sudden sort close the king's mouth, and he could offer naught to turn the argument; and so, reluctant, and full loth to do you the discourtesy, he yet prayeth you to consider his perplexed case, as noting how the matter stands, and name the calamity—if so be you have determined the nature of it and the time of its coming. Oh, prithee delay not; to delay at such a time were to double and treble the perils that already compass thee about. Oh, be thou wise—name the calamity!"

I allowed silence to accumulate while I got my impressiveness together, and then said:

"How long have I been shut up in this hole?"

"Ye were shut up when yesterday was well spent It is 9 of the morning now."

"No! Then I have slept well, sure enough. Nine in the morning now! And yet it is the very complexion of midnight, to a shade. This is the 20th, then?"

"The 20th—yes."

"And I am to be burned alive to-morrow." The boy shuddered.

"At what hour?"

"At high noon."

"Now then, I will tell you what to say." I paused, and stood over that cowering lad a whole minute in awful silence; then, in a voice deep, measured, charged with doom, I began, and rose by dramatically graded stages to my colossal climax, which I delivered in as sublime and noble a way as ever I did such a thing in my life: "Go back and tell the king that at that hour I will smother the whole world in the dead blackness of midnight; I will blot out the sun, and he shall never shine again; the fruits of the earth shall rot for lack of light and warmth, and the peoples of the earth shall famish and die, to the last man!"

I had to carry the boy out myself, he sunk into such a collapse. I handed him over to the soldiers, and went back.

★ ★ ★

In the stillness and the darkness, realization soon began to supplement knowledge. The mere knowledge of a fact is pale; but when you come to *realize* your fact, it takes on color. It is all the difference between hearing of a man being stabbed to the heart, and seeing it done. In the stillness and the darkness, the knowledge that I was in deadly danger took to itself deeper and deeper meaning all the time; a something which was realization crept inch by inch through my veins and turned me cold.

But it is a blessed provision of nature that at times like these, as soon as a man's mercury has got down to a certain point there comes a revulsion, and he rallies. Hope springs up, and cheerfulness along with it, and then he is in good shape to do something for himself, if anything can be done. When my rally came, it came with a bound. I said to myself that my eclipse would be sure to save me, and make me the greatest man in the kingdom besides; and straightway my mercury went up to the top of the tube, and my solicitudes all vanished. I was as happy a man as there was in the world. I was even impatient for tomorrow to come, I so wanted to gather in that great triumph and be the center of all the nation's wonder and reverence. Besides, in a business way it would be the making of me; I knew that.

Meantime there was one thing which had got pushed into the background of my mind. That was the half-conviction that when the nature of my proposed calamity should be reported to those superstitious people, it would have such an effect that they would want to compromise. So, by and by when I heard footsteps coming, that thought was recalled to me, and I said to myself, "As sure as anything, it's the compromise. Well, if it is good, all right, I will accept; but if it isn't, I mean to stand my ground and play my hand for all it is worth."

The door opened, and some men-at-arms appeared. The leader said:

"The stake is ready. Come!"

The stake! The strength went out of me, and I almost fell down. It is hard to get one's breath at such a time, such lumps come into one's throat, and such gaspings; but as soon as I could speak, I said:

"But this is a mistake—the execution is tomorrow."

"Order changed; been set forward a day. Haste thee!"

I was lost. There was no help for me. I was dazed, stupefied; I had no command over myself, I only wandered purposely about, like one out of his mind;

so the soldiers took hold of me, and pulled me along with them, out of the cell and along the maze of underground corridors, and finally into the fierce glare of daylight and the upper world. As we stepped into the vast enclosed court of the castle I got a shock; for the first thing I saw was the stake, standing in the center, and near it the piled fagots and a monk. On all four sides of the court the seated multitudes rose rank above rank, forming sloping terraces that were rich with color. The king and the queen sat in their thrones, the most conspicuous figures there, of course.

To note all this, occupied but a second. The next second Clarence had slipped from some place of concealment and was pouring news into my ear, his eyes beaming with triumph and gladness. He said:

"'Tis through *me* the change was wrought! And main hard have I worked to do it, too. But when I revealed to them the calamity in store, and saw how mighty was the terror it did engender, then saw I also that this was the time to strike! Wherefore I diligently pretended, unto this and that and the other one, that your power against the sun could not reach its full until the morrow; and so if any would save the sun and the world, you must be slain to-day, while your enchantments are but in the weaving and lack potency. Odsbodikins, it was but a dull lie, a most indifferent invention, but you should have seen them seize it and swallow it, in the frenzy of their fright, as it were salvation sent from heaven; and all the while was I laughing in my sleeve the one moment, to see them so cheaply deceived, and glorifying God the next, that He was content to let the meanest of His creatures be His instrument to the saving of thy life. Ah how happy has the matter sped! You will not need to do the sun a *real* hurt—ah, forget not that, on your soul forget it not! Only make a little darkness—only the littlest little darkness, mind, and cease with that. It will be sufficient. They will see that I spoke falsely—being ignorant, as they will fancy—and with the falling of the first shadow of that darkness you shall see them go mad with fear; and they will set you free and make you great! Go to thy triumph, now! But remember—ah, good friend, I implore thee remember my supplication, and do the blessed sun no hurt. For *my* sake, thy true friend."

I choked out some words through my grief and misery; as much as to say I would spare the sun; for which the lad's eyes paid me back with such deep and loving gratitude that I had not the heart to tell him his good-hearted foolishness had ruined me and sent me to my death.

As the soldiers assisted me across the court the stillness was so profound that if I had been blindfold I should have supposed I was in a solitude instead of walled in by four thousand people. There was not a movement perceptible in those masses of humanity; they were as rigid as stone images, and as pale; and dread sat upon every countenance. This hush continued while I was being chained to the stake;

it still continued while the fagots were carefully and tediously piled about my ankles, my knees, my thighs, my body. Then there was a pause, and a deeper hush, if possible, and a man knelt down at my feet with a blazing torch; the multitude strained forward, gazing, and parting slightly from their seats without knowing it; the monk raised his hands above my head, and his eyes toward the blue sky, and began some words in Latin; in this attitude he droned on and on, a little while, and then stopped. I waited two or three moments; then looked up; he was standing there petrified. With a common impulse the multitude rose slowly up and stared into the sky. I followed their eyes, as sure as guns, there was my eclipse beginning! The life went boiling through my veins; I was a new man! The rim of black spread slowly into the sun's disk, my heart beat higher and higher, and still the assemblage and the priest stared into the sky, motionless. I knew that this gaze would be turned upon me, next. When it was, l was ready. I was in one of the most grand attitudes I ever struck, with my arm stretched up pointing to the sun. It was a noble effect. You could *see* the shudder sweep the mass like a wave. Two shouts rang out, one close upon the heels of the other:

Stripped and set to be burned at the stake, the Yankee uses his knowledge that an eclipse is about to occur to cow the king and assembled knights and nobility by threatening to blot out the sun.

"Apply the torch!"

"I forbid it!"

The one was from Merlin, the other from the king. Merlin started from his place—to apply the torch himself, I judged. I said:

"Stay where you are. If any man moves—even the king—before I give him leave, I will blast him with thunder, I will consume him with lightnings!"

The multitude sank meekly into their seats, and I was just expecting they would. Merlin hesitated a moment or two, and I was on pins and needles during that little while. Then he sat down, and I took a good breath; for I knew I was master of the situation now. The king said:

"Be merciful, fair sir, and essay no further in this perilous matter, lest disaster follow. It was reported to us that your powers could not attain unto their full strength until the morrow; but—"

"Your Majesty thinks the report may have been a lie? It *was* a lie."

That made an immense effect; up went appealing hands everywhere, and the king was assailed with a storm of supplications that I might be bought off at any price, and the calamity stayed. The king was eager to comply. He said:

"Name any terms, reverend sir, even to the halving of my kingdom; but banish this calamity, spare the sun!"

My fortune was made. I would have taken him up in a minute, but I couldn't stop an eclipse; the thing was out of the question. So I asked time to consider. The king said:

"How long—ah, how long, good sir? Be merciful; look, it groweth darker, moment by moment. Prithee how long?"

"Not long. Half an hour—maybe an hour."

There were a thousand pathetic protests, but I couldn't shorten up any, for I couldn't remember how long a total eclipse lasts. I was in a puzzled condition, anyway, and wanted to think. Something was wrong about that eclipse, and the fact was very unsettling. If this wasn't the one I was after, how was I to tell whether this was the sixth century, or nothing but a dream? Dear me, if I could only prove it was the latter! Here was a glad new hope. If the boy was right about the date, and this was surely the 20th, it *wasn't* the sixth century. I reached for the monk's sleeve, in considerable excitement, and asked him what day of the month it was.

Hang him, he said it was the *twenty-first!* It made me turn cold to hear him. I begged him not to make any mistake about it; but he was sure; he knew it was the 21st. So, that feather-headed boy had botched things again! The time of the day was right for the eclipse; I had seen that for myself, in the beginning, by the dial that was near by. Yes, I was in King Arthur's court, and I might as well make the most out of it I could.

The darkness was steadily growing, the people becoming more and more distressed. I now said:

"I have reflected, Sir King. For a lesson, I will let this darkness proceed, and spread night in the world; but whether I blot out the sun for good, or restore it, shall rest with you. These are the terms, to wit: You shall remain king over all your dominions, and receive all the glories and honors that belong to the kingship; but you shall appoint me your perpetual minister and executive, and give me for my services one per cent. of such actual increase of revenue over and above its present amount as I may succeed in creating for the state. If I can't live on that, I sha'n't ask anybody to give me a lift. Is it satisfactory?"

There was a prodigious roar of applause, and out of the midst of it the king's voice rose, saying:

"Away with his bonds, and set him free! and do him homage, high and low, rich and poor, for he is become the king's right hand, is clothed with power and authority, and his seat is upon the highest step of the throne! Now sweep away this creeping night, and bring the light and cheer again, that all the world may bless thee."

But I said:

"That a common man should be shamed before the world, is nothing; but it were dishonor to the *king* if any that saw his minister naked should not also see him delivered from his shame. If I might ask that my clothes be brought again—"

"They are not meet," the king broke in. "Fetch raiment of another sort; clothe him like a prince!"

My idea worked. I wanted to keep things as they were till the eclipse was total, otherwise they would be trying again to get me to dismiss the darkness, and of course I couldn't do it. Sending for the clothes gained some delay, but not enough. So I had to make another excuse. I said it would be but natural if the king should change his mind and repent to some extent of what he had done under excitement; therefore I would let the darkness grow a while, and if at the end of a reasonable time the king had kept his mind the same, the darkness should be dismissed. Neither the king nor anybody else was satisfied with that arrangement, but I had to stick to my point.

It grew darker and darker and blacker and blacker, while I struggled with those awkward sixth-century clothes. It got to be pitch dark, at last, and the multitude groaned with horror to feel the cold uncanny night breezes fan through the place and see the stars come out and twinkle in the sky. At last the eclipse was total, and I was very glad of it, but everybody else was in misery; which was quite natural. I said:

"The king, by his silence, still stands to the terms." Then I lifted up my hands—stood just so a moment—then I said, with the most awful solemnity: "Let the enchantment dissolve and pass harmless away!"

There was no response, for a moment, in that deep darkness and that grave-yard hush. But when the silver rim of the sun pushed itself out, a moment or two later, the assemblage broke loose with a vast shout and came pouring down like a deluge to smother me with blessings and gratitude; and Clarence was not the last of the wash, to be sure.

—*A Connecticut Yankee in King Arthur's Court* (1889), chapters 5-6

————•——

Armed with considerable knowledge of nineteenth-century science and technology, the Yankee time-traveler is truly a "superior man" in the sixth century. He will go on to try transforming England into a modern civilization, but will he continue to pretend that everything he does is "magic"? One of the ironies of Connecticut Yankee *is that the Yankee uses real science to perform "miracles," but he always tells people he is performing magic.*

————•——

26.

"THE FRAGILITY OF FAME"

Like Tom Sawyer, Mark Twain's Connecticut Yankee, Hank Morgan, is a shameless show-off. He likes nothing better than putting on a show and piling on gaudy effects before a large audience. And who could be easier to dazzle than the primitive denizens of sixth-century England, who have never seen such nineteenth-century wonders as electricity, machinery, or even fireworks until Hank shows them? After spending several years modernizing England, Hank sees his reputation soar to new heights when he restarts the long-dormant waters of the sacred fountain in the Valley of Holiness. It does not take long, however, for his towering reputation to sink back to ground level!

Saturday noon I went to the well and looked on a while. Merlin was still burning smoke-powders, and pawing the air, and muttering gibberish as hard as ever, but looking pretty down-hearted, for of course he had not started even a perspiration in that well yet. Finally I said:

"How does the thing promise by this time, partner?"

"Behold, I am even now busied with trial of the powerfulest enchantment known to the princes of the occult arts in the lands of the East; an it fail me, naught can avail. Peace, until I finish."

He raised a smoke this time that darkened all the region, and must have made matters uncomfortable for the hermits, for the wind was their way, and it rolled down over their dens in a dense and billowy fog. He poured out volumes of speech to match, and contorted his body and sawed the air with his hands in a most extraordinary way. At the end of twenty minutes he dropped down panting, and about exhausted. Now arrived the abbot and several hundred monks and nuns, and behind them a multitude of pilgrims and a couple of acres of foundlings, all drawn by the prodigious smoke, and all in a grand state of excitement. The abbot inquired anxiously for results. Merlin said:

"If any labor of mortal might break the spell that binds these waters, this which I have but just essayed had done it. It has failed; whereby I do now know that that which I had feared is a truth established; the sign of this failure is, that the most potent spirit known to the magicians of the East, and whose name none may utter and live, has laid his spell upon this well. The mortal does not breathe, nor ever will, who can penetrate the secret of that spell, and without that secret none can break it. The water will flow no more forever, good Father. I have done what man could. Suffer me to go."

Of course this threw the abbot into a good deal of a consternation. He turned to me with the signs of it in his face, and said:

"Ye have heard him. Is it true?"

"Part of it is."

"Not all, then, not all! What part is true?"

"That that spirit with the Russian name has put his spell upon the well."

"God's wownds, then are we ruined!"

"Possibly."

"But not certainly? Ye mean, not certainly?"

"That is it."

"Wherefore, ye also mean that when he saith none can break the spell—"

"Yes, when he says that, he says what isn't necessarily true. There are conditions under which an effort to break it may have some chance—that is, some small, some trifling chance—of success."

"The conditions—"

"Oh, they are nothing difficult. Only these: I want the well and the surroundings for the space of half a mile, entirely to myself from sunset to-day until I remove the ban—and nobody allowed to cross the ground but by my authority."

"Are these all?"

"Yes."

"And you have no fear to try?"

"Oh, none. One may fail, of course; and one may also succeed. One can try, and I am ready to chance it. I have my conditions?"

"These and all others ye may name. I will issue commandment to that effect."

"Wait," said Merlin, with an evil smile. "Ye wit that he that would break this spell must know that spirit's name?"

"Yes, I know his name."

"And wit you also that to know it skills not of itself, but ye must likewise pronounce it? Ha-ha! Knew ye that?"

"Yes, I knew that, too."

"You had that knowledge! Art a fool? Are ye minded to utter that name and die?"

"Utter it? Why certainly. I would utter it if it was Welsh."

"Ye are even a dead man, then; and I go to tell Arthur."

"That's all right. Take your gripsack and get along. The thing for *you* to do is to go home and work the weather, John W. Merlin."

It was a home shot, and it made him wince; for he was the worst weather-failure in the kingdom. Whenever he ordered up the danger-signals along the coast there was a week's dead calm, sure, and every time he prophesied fair weather it rained brickbats. But I kept him in the weather bureau right along, to undermine his reputation. However, that shot raised his bile, and instead of starting home to report my death, he said he would remain and enjoy it.

My two experts arrived in the evening, and pretty well fagged, for they had traveled double tides. They had pack-mules along, and had brought everything I

Armed with modern tools and skills, the Yankee's assistants descend into the monastery's fountain to repair its ancient leak.

needed—tools, pump, lead pipe, Greek fire, sheaves of big rockets, roman candles, colored fire sprays, electric apparatus, and a lot of sundries—everything necessary for the stateliest kind of a miracle. They got their supper and a nap, and about midnight we sallied out through a solitude so wholly vacant and complete that it quite overpassed the required conditions. We took possession of the well and its surroundings. My boys were experts in all sorts of things, from the stoning up of a well to the constructing of a mathematical instrument. An hour before sunrise we had that leak mended in ship-shape fashion, and the water began to rise. Then we stowed our fireworks in the chapel, locked up the place, and went home to bed.

———————••••———————

The next day, the Yankee's men completed the work and placed a rope fence a hundred feet square around the platform to keep off spectators.

———————••••———————

My idea was, doors open at 10:30, performance to begin at 11:25 sharp. I wished I could charge admission, but of course that wouldn't answer. I instructed my boys to be in the chapel as early as 10, before anybody was around, and be ready to man the pumps at the proper time, and make the fur fly. Then we went home to supper.

The news of the disaster to the well had traveled far by this time; and now for two or three days a steady avalanche of people had been pouring into the valley. The lower end of the valley was become one huge camp; we should have a good house, no question about that. Criers went the rounds early in the evening and announced the coming attempt, which put every pulse up to fever heat. They gave notice that the abbot and his official suite would move in state and occupy the platform at 10:30, up to which time all the region which was under my ban must be clear; the bells would then cease from tolling, and this sign should be permission to the multitudes to close in and take their places.

I was at the platform and all ready to do the honors when the abbot's solemn procession hove in sight—which it did not do till it was nearly to the rope fence, because it was a starless black night and no torches permitted. With it came Merlin, and took a front seat on the platform; he was as good as his word for once. One could not see the multitudes banked together beyond the ban, but they were there, just the same. The moment the bells stopped, those banked masses broke and poured over the line like a vast black wave, and for as much as a half hour it continued to flow, and then it solidified itself, and you could have walked upon a pavement of human heads to—well, miles.

We had a solemn stage-wait, now, for about twenty minutes—a thing I had counted on for effect; it is always good to let your audience have a chance to work up its expectancy. At length, out of the silence a noble Latin chant—men's voices—broke and swelled up and rolled away into the night, a majestic tide of melody. I had put that up, too, and it was one of the best effects I ever invented. When it was finished I stood up on the platform and extended my hands abroad, for two minutes, with my face uplifted—that always produces a dead hush—and then slowly pronounced this ghastly word with a kind of awfulness which caused hundreds to tremble, and many women to faint:

"Constantinopolitanischerdudelsackspfeifenmachersgesellschafft!"

Just as I was moaning out the closing hunks of that word, I touched off one of my electric connections and all that murky world of people stood revealed in a hideous blue glare! It was immense—that effect! Lots of people shrieked, women curled up and quit in every direction, foundlings collapsed by platoons. The abbot and the monks crossed themselves nimbly and their lips fluttered with agitated prayers. Merlin held his grip, but he was astonished clear down to his corns; he had never seen anything to begin with that, before. Now was the time to pile in the effects. I lifted my hands and groaned out this word—as it were in agony—

"Nihilistendynamittheaterkaestchenssprengungsattentaetsversuchungen!"

—and turned on the red fire! You should have heard that Atlantic of people moan and howl when that crimson hell joined the blue! After sixty seconds I shouted—

"Transvaaltruppentropentransporttrampelthiertreibertrauungsthrae-
nentragoedie!"

—and lit up the green fire! After waiting only forty seconds this time, I spread my arms abroad and thundered out the devastating syllables of this word of words—

"Mekkamuselmannenmassenmenchenmoerdermohrenmuttermarmor-
monumentenmacherz!"

—and whirled on the purple glare! There they were, all going at once, red, blue, green, purple!—four furious volcanoes pouring vast clouds of radiant smoke aloft, and spreading a blinding rainbowed noonday to the furthest confines of that valley. In the distance one could see that fellow on the pillar standing rigid against the background of sky, his seesaw stopped for the first time in twenty years. I knew the boys were at the pump now and ready. So I said to the abbot:

"The time is come, Father. I am about to pronounce the dread name and command the spell to dissolve. You want to brace up, and take hold of something." Then I shouted to the people: "Behold, in another minute the spell will be broken, or no mortal can break it. If it break, all will know it, for you will see the sacred water gush from the chapel door!"

I stood a few moments, to let the hearers have a chance to spread my announcement to those who couldn't hear, and so convey it to the furthest ranks, then I made a grand exhibition of extra posturing and gesturing, and shouted:

"Lo, I command the fell spirit that possesses the holy fountain to now disgorge into the skies all the infernal fires that still remain in him, and straightway dissolve his spell and flee hence to the pit, there to lie bound a thousand years. By his own dread name I command it—**BGWJJILLIGKKK!**"

Then I touched off the hogshead of rockets, and a vast fountain of dazzling lances of fire vomited itself toward the zenith with a hissing rush, and burst in mid-sky into a storm of flashing jewels! One mighty groan of terror started up from the massed people—then suddenly broke into a wild hosannah of joy—for there, fair and plain in the uncanny glare, they saw the freed water leaping forth! The old abbot could not speak a word, for tears and the chokings in his throat; without utterance of any sort, he folded me in his arms and mashed me. It was more eloquent than speech. And harder to get over, too, in a country where there were really no doctors that were worth a damaged nickel.

You should have seen those acres of people throw themselves down in that water and kiss it; kiss it, and pet it, and fondle it, and talk to it as if it were alive, and welcome it back with the dear names they gave their darlings, just as if it had been a friend who was long gone away and lost, and was come home again. Yes, it was pretty to see, and made me think more of them than I had done before.

I sent Merlin home on a shutter. He had caved in and gone down like a landslide when I pronounced that fearful name, and had never come to since. He never had heard that name before—neither had I—but to him it was the right one. Any jumble would have been the right one. He admitted, afterward, that that spirit's own mother could not have pronounced that name better than I did. He never could understand how I survived it, and I didn't tell him. It is only young magicians that give away a secret like that. Merlin spent three months working enchantments to try to find out the deep trick of how to pronounce that name and outlive it. But he didn't arrive.

When I started to the chapel, the populace uncovered and fell back reverently to make a wide way for me, as if I had been some kind of a superior being—and I was. I was aware of that. I took along a night shift of monks, and taught them the mystery of the pump, and set them to work, for it was plain that a good part of the people out there were going to sit up with the water all night, consequently it was but right that they should have all they wanted of it. To those monks that pump was a good deal of a miracle itself, and they were full of wonder over it; and of admiration, too, of the exceeding effectiveness of its performance.

It was a great night, an immense night. There was reputation in it. I could hardly get to sleep for glorying over it.

★　★　★

My influence in the Valley of Holiness was something prodigious now. It seemed worth while to try to turn it to some valuable account. The thought came to me the next morning, and was suggested by my seeing one of my knights who was in the soap line come riding in. According to history, the monks of this place two centuries before had been worldly minded enough to want to wash. It might be that there was a leaven of this unrighteousness still remaining. So I sounded a Brother:

"Wouldn't you like a bath?"

He shuddered at the thought—the thought of the peril of it to the well—but he said with feeling:

"One needs not to ask that of a poor body who has not known that blessed refreshment sith that he was a boy. Would God I might wash me! but it may not be, fair sir, tempt me not; it is forbidden." And then he sighed in such a sorrowful way that I was resolved he should have at least one layer of his real estate removed, if it sized up my whole influence and bankrupted the pile. So I went to the abbot and asked for a permit for this Brother. He blenched at the idea—I don't mean that you could see him blench, for of course you couldn't see it without you scraped him, and I didn't care enough about it to scrape him, but I knew the blench was there, just the same, and within a book-cover's thickness of the surface, too—blenched, and trembled. He said:

"Ah, son, ask aught else thou wilt, and it is thine, and freely granted out of a grateful heart—but this, oh, this! Would you drive away the blessed water again?"

"No, Father, I will not drive it away. I have mysterious knowledge which teaches me that there was an error that other time when it was thought the institution of the bath banished the fountain." A large interest began to show up in the old man's face. "My knowledge informs me that the bath was innocent of that misfortune, which was caused by quite another sort of sin."

"These are brave words—but—but right welcome, if they be true."

"They are true, indeed. Let me build the bath again, Father. Let me build it again, and the fountain shall flow forever."

"You promise this?—you promise it? Say the word—say you promise it!"

"I do promise it."

"Then will I have the first bath myself! Go—get ye to your work. Tarry not, tarry not, but go."

I and my boys were at work, straight off. The ruins of the old bath were there yet in the basement of the monastery, not a stone missing. They had been left just so, all these lifetimes, and avoided with a pious fear, as things accursed. In two days we had it all done and the water in—a spacious pool of clear pure water that a body could swim in. It was running water, too. It came in, and went out, through the ancient pipes. The old abbot kept his word, and was the first to try it. He went down black and shaky, leaving the whole black community above troubled and worried and full of bodings; but he came back white and joyful, and the game was made! another triumph scored.

It was a good campaign that we made in that Valley of Holiness, and I was very well satisfied, and ready to move on now, but I struck a disappointment. I caught a heavy cold, and it started up an old lurking rheumatism of mine. Of course the rheumatism hunted up my weakest place and located itself there. This was the place where the abbot put his arms about me and mashed me, what time he was moved to testify his gratitude to me with an embrace.

When at last I got out, I was a shadow. But everybody was full of attentions and kindnesses, and these brought cheer back into my life, and were the right medicine to help a convalescent swiftly up toward health and strength again; so I gained fast.

Sandy was worn out with nursing; so I made up my mind to turn out and go a cruise alone, leaving her at the nunnery to rest up. My idea was to disguise myself as a freeman of peasant degree and wander through the country a week or two on foot. This would give me a chance to eat and lodge with the lowliest and poorest class of free citizens on equal terms. There was no other way to inform myself perfectly of their everyday life and the operation of the laws upon it. If I went among them as a gentleman, there would be restraints and conventionalities which would shut me out from their private joys and troubles, and I should get no further than the outside shell.

One morning I was out on a long walk to get up muscle for my trip, and had climbed the ridge which bordered the northern extremity of the valley, when I came upon an artificial opening in the face of a low precipice, and recognized it by its location as a hermitage which had often been pointed out to me from a distance as the den of a hermit of high renown for dirt and austerity. I knew he had lately been offered a situation in the Great Sahara, where lions and sandflies made the hermit-life peculiarly attractive and difficult, and had gone to Africa to take possession, so I thought I would look in and see how the atmosphere of this den agreed with its reputation.

My surprise was great: the place was newly swept and scoured. Then there was another surprise. Back in the gloom of the cavern I heard the clink of a little bell, and then this exclamation:

"*Hello Central! Is this you, Camelot?*——Behold, thou mayst glad thy heart an thou hast faith to believe the wonderful when that it cometh in unexpected guise and maketh itself manifest in impossible places—here standeth in the flesh his mightiness The Boss, and with thine own ears shall ye hear him speak!"

Now what a radical reversal of things this was; what a jumbling together of extravagant incongruities; what a fantastic conjunction of opposites and irreconcilables—the home of the bogus miracle become the home of a real one, the den of a mediaeval hermit turned into a telephone office!

The telephone clerk stepped into the light, and I recognized one of my young fellows. I said:

"How long has this office been established here, Ulfius?"

"But since midnight, fair Sir Boss, an it please you. We saw many lights in the valley, and so judged it well to make a station, for that where so many lights be needs must they indicate a town of goodly size."

"Quite right. It isn't a town in the customary sense, but it's a good stand, anyway. Do you know where you are?"

"Of that I have had no time to make inquiry; for whenas my comradeship moved hence upon their labors, leaving me in charge, I got me to needed rest, purposing to inquire when I waked, and report the place's name to Camelot for record."

"Well, this is the Valley of Holiness."

It didn't take; I mean, he didn't start at the name, as I had supposed he would. He merely said:

"I will so report it."

"Why, the surrounding regions are filled with the noise of late wonders that have happened here! You didn't hear of them?"

"Ah, ye will remember we move by night, and avoid speech with all. We learn naught but that we get by the telephone from Camelot."

"Why *they* know all about this thing. Haven't they told you anything about the great miracle of the restoration of a holy fountain?"

"Oh, *that?* Indeed yes. But the name of *this* valley doth woundily differ from the name of *that* one; indeed to differ wider were not pos—"

"What was that name, then?"

"The Valley of Hellishness."

"*That* explains it. Confound a telephone, anyway. It is the very demon for conveying similarities of sound that are miracles of divergence from similarity of sense. But no matter, you know the name of the place now. Call up Camelot."

He did it, and had Clarence sent for. It was good to hear my boy's voice again. It was like being home. After some affectionate interchanges, and some account of my late illness, I said:

"What is new?"

"The king and queen and many of the court do start even in this hour, to go to your valley to pay pious homage to the waters ye have restored, and cleanse themselves of sin, and see the place where the infernal spirit spouted true hell-flames to the clouds—an ye listen sharply ye may hear me wink and hear me likewise smile a smile, sith 'twas I that made selection of those flames from out our stock and sent them by your order."

"Does the king know the way to this place?"

"The king?—no, nor to any other in his realms, mayhap; but the lads that holp you with your miracle will be his guide and lead the way, and appoint the places for rests at noons and sleeps at night."

"This will bring them here—when?"

"Mid-afternoon, or later, the third day."

★   ★   ★

When I got back to the monastery, I found a thing of interest going on. The abbot and his monks were assembled in the great hall, observing with childish wonder and faith the performances of a new magician, a fresh arrival. His dress was the extreme of the fantastic; [like] the sort of thing an Indian medicine-man wears. He was mowing, and mumbling, and gesticulating, and drawing mystical figures in the air and on the floor—the regular thing, you know. He was a celebrity from Asia—so he said, and that was enough. That sort of evidence was as good as gold, and passed current everywhere.

How easy and cheap it was to be a great magician on this fellow's terms. His specialty was to tell you what any individual on the face of the globe was doing at the moment; and what he had done at any time in the past, and what he would do at any time in the future. He asked if any would like to know what the Emperor of the East was doing now? The sparkling eyes and the delighted rubbing of hands made eloquent answer—this reverend crowd *would* like to know what that monarch was at, just at this moment. The fraud went through some more mummery, and then made grave announcement:

"The high and mighty Emperor of the East doth at this moment put money in the palm of a holy begging friar—one, two, three pieces, and they be all of silver."

A buzz of admiring exclamations broke out, all around:

"It is marvelous!" "Wonderful!" "What study, what labor, to have acquired a so amazing power as this!"

Would they like to know what the Supreme Lord of Inde was doing? Yes. He told them what the Supreme Lord of Inde was doing. Then he told them what the Sultan of Egypt was at; also what the King of the Remote Seas was about. And so on and so on; and with each new marvel the astonishment at his accuracy rose

Back at the monastery, the Yankee finds the monks awed by the outlandish performance of a gaudily dressed magician.

higher and higher. They thought he must surely strike an uncertain place some time; but no, he never had to hesitate, he always knew, and always with unerring precision. I saw that if this thing went on I should lose my supremacy, this fellow would capture my following, I should be left out in the cold. I must put a cog in his wheel, and do it right away, too. I said:

"If I might ask, I should very greatly like to know what a certain person is doing."

"Speak, and freely. I will tell you."

"It will be difficult—perhaps impossible."

"My art knoweth not that word. The more difficult it is, the more certainly will I reveal it to you."

You see, I was working up the interest. It was getting pretty high, too; you could see that by the craning necks all around, and the half-suspended breathing. So now I climaxed it:

"If you make no mistake—if you tell me truly what I want to know—I will give you two hundred silver pennies."

"The fortune is mine! I will tell you what you would know."

"Then tell me what I am doing with my right hand."

"Ah-h!" There was a general gasp of surprise. It had not occurred to anybody in the crowd—that simple trick of inquiring about somebody who wasn't ten thousand miles away. The magician was hit hard; it was an emergency that had never happened in his experience before, and it corked him; he didn't know how to meet it. He looked stunned, confused; he couldn't say a word. "Come," I said, "what are you waiting for? Is it possible you can answer up, right off, and tell what anybody on the other side of the earth is doing, and yet can't tell what a person is doing who isn't three yards from you? Persons behind me know what I am doing with my right hand—they will indorse you if you tell correctly." He was still dumb. "Very well, I'll tell you why you don't speak up and tell; it is because you don't know. *You* a magician! Good friends, this tramp is a mere fraud and liar."

This distressed the monks and terrified them. They were not used to hearing these awful beings called names, and they did not know what might be the consequence. There was a dead silence now; superstitious bodings were in every mind. The magician began to pull his wits together, and when he presently smiled an easy, nonchalant smile, it spread a mighty relief around; for it indicated that his mood was not destructive. He said:

"It hath struck me speechless, the frivolity of this person's speech. Let all know, if perchance there be any who know it not, that enchanters of my degree deign not to concern themselves with the doings of any but kings, princes, emperors, them that be born in the purple and them only. Had ye asked me what Arthur the great king is doing, it were another matter, and I had told ye; but the doings of a subject interest me not."

"Oh, I misunderstood you. I thought you said 'anybody,' and so I supposed 'anybody' included—well, anybody; that is, everybody."

"It doth—anybody that is of lofty birth; and the better if he be royal."

"That, it meseemeth, might well be," said the abbot, who saw his opportunity to smooth things and avert disaster, "for it were not likely that so wonderful a gift as this would be conferred for the revelation of the concerns of lesser beings than such as be born near to the summits of greatness. Our Arthur the king—"

"Would you know of him?" broke in the enchanter.

"Most gladly, yea, and gratefully."

Everybody was full of awe and interest again right away, the incorrigible idiots. They watched the incantations absorbingly, and looked at me with a "There, now, what can you say to that?" air, when the announcement came:

"The king is weary with the chase, and lieth in his palace these two hours sleeping a dreamless sleep."

"God's benison upon him!" said the abbot, and crossed himself; "may that sleep be to the refreshment of his body and his soul."

"And so it might be, if he were sleeping," I said, "but the king is not sleeping, the king rides."

Here was trouble again—a conflict of authority. Nobody knew which of us to believe; I still had some reputation left. The magician's scorn was stirred, and he said:

"Lo, I have seen many wonderful soothsayers and prophets and magicians in my life days, but none before that could sit idle and see to the heart of things with never an incantation to help."

"You have lived in the woods, and lost much by it. I use incantations myself, as this good brotherhood are aware—but only on occasions of moment."

When it comes to sarcasming, I reckon I know how to keep my end up. That jab made this fellow squirm. The abbot inquired after the queen and the court, and got this information:

"They be all on sleep, being overcome by fatigue, like as to the king."

I said:

"That is merely another lie. Half of them are about their amusements, the queen and the other half are not sleeping, they ride. Now perhaps you can spread yourself a little, and tell us where the king and queen and all that are this moment riding with them are going?"

"They sleep now, as I said; but on the morrow they will ride, for they go a journey toward the sea."

"And where will they be the day after to-morrow at vespers?"

"Far to the north of Camelot, and half their journey will be done."

"That is another lie, by the space of a hundred and fifty miles. Their journey will not be merely half done, it will be all done, and they will be HERE, in this valley."

That was a noble shot! It set the abbot and the monks in a whirl of excitement, and it rocked the enchanter to his base. I followed the thing right up:

"If the king does not arrive, I will have myself ridden on a rail: if he does I will ride you on a rail instead."

Next day I went up to the telephone office and found that the king had passed through two towns that were on the line. I spotted his progress on the succeeding day in the same way. I kept these matters to myself. The third day's reports showed that if he kept up his gait he would arrive by four in the afternoon. There was still no sign anywhere of interest in his coming; there seemed to be no preparations making to receive him in state; a strange thing, truly. Only one thing could explain this: that other magician had been cutting under me, sure. This was true. I asked a friend of mine, a monk, about it, and he said, yes, the magician had tried some further enchantments and found out that the court had concluded to make no

The painful fate awaiting the phony magician.

journey at all, but stay at home. Think of that! Observe how much a reputation was worth in such a country. These people had seen me do the very showiest bit of magic in history, and the only one within their memory that had a positive value, and yet here they were, ready to take up with an adventurer who could offer no evidence of his powers but his mere unproven word.

—*A Connecticut Yankee in King Arthur's Court* (1889), chapters 23-24

Hank's mistake may lie in his pretending to be something he is not. He uses real science and technology to modernize sixth-century England, but instead of touting his achievements for what they really are, he claims to perform his "miracles" by magic. No one in the sixth century expects magic to make sense, so it's no wonder people believe the claims of any charlatan who happens to come along!

27.

"THE DEATH DISK"

War is a pitiless business in which blameless officers are sometimes executed to pay for the failings of their troops. Such is the premise of this uncharacteristically sentimental Mark Twain story. Its maudlin nature might be explained by the possibility that it is based on an incident that really happened during England's seventeenth-century civil war.

I

This was in Oliver Cromwell's time. Colonel Mayfair was the youngest officer of his rank in the armies of the Commonwealth, he being but thirty years old. But young as he was, he was a veteran soldier, and tanned and war-worn, for he had begun his military life at seventeen; he had fought in many battles, and had won his high place in the service and in the admiration of men, step by step, by valor in the field. But he was in deep trouble now; a shadow had fallen upon his fortunes.

The winter evening was come, and outside were storm and darkness; within, a melancholy silence; for the Colonel and his young wife had talked their sorrow out, had read the evening chapter and prayed the evening prayer, and there was nothing more to do but sit hand in hand and gaze into the fire, and think—and wait. They would not have to wait long; they knew that, and the wife shuddered at the thought.

They had one child—Abby, seven years old, their idol. She would be coming presently for the good-night kiss, and the Colonel spoke now, and said:

"Dry away the tears and let us seem happy, for her sake. We must forget, for the time, that which is to happen."

"I will. I will shut them up in my heart, which is breaking."

"And we will accept what is appointed for us, and bear it in patience, as knowing that whatsoever He doeth is done in righteousness and meant in kindness—"

"Saying, His will be done. Yes, I can say it with all my mind and soul—I would I could say it with my heart. Oh, if I could! if this dear hand which I press and kiss for the last time—"

"Sh! sweetheart, she is coming!"

A curly-headed little figure in night-clothes glided in at the door and ran to the father, and was gathered to his breast and fervently kissed once, twice, three times.

"Why, papa, you mustn't kiss me like that; you rumple my hair."

"Oh, I am so sorry—so sorry: do you forgive me, dear?"

"Why, of course, papa. But are you sorry?—not pretending, but real, right down sorry?"

"Well, you can judge for yourself, Abby," and he covered his face with his hands and made believe to sob. The child was filled with remorse to see this tragic thing which she had caused, and she began to cry herself, and to tug at the hands, and say:

"Oh, don't, papa, please don't cry; Abby didn't mean it; Abby wouldn't ever do it again. Please, papa!" Tugging and straining to separate the fingers, she got a fleeting glimpse of an eye behind them, and cried out: "Why, you naughty papa, you are not crying at all! You are only fooling! And Abby is going to mamma, now: you don't treat Abby right."

She was for climbing down, but her father wound his arms about her and said: "No, stay with me, dear: papa was naughty, and confesses it, and is sorry—there, let him kiss the tears away—and he begs Abby's forgiveness, and will do anything Abby says he must do, for a punishment; they're all kissed away now, and not a curl rumpled—and whatever Abby commands—"

And so it was made up; and all in a moment the sunshine was back again and burning brightly in the child's face, and she was patting her father's cheeks and naming the penalty—"A story! a story!"

Hark!

The elders stopped breathing and listened. Footsteps! faintly caught between the gusts of wind. They came nearer, nearer—louder, louder—then passed by and faded away. The elders drew deep breaths of relief, and the papa said: "A story, is it? A gay one?"

"No, papa: a dreadful one."

Papa wanted to shift to the gay kind, but the child stood by her rights—as per agreement, she was to have anything she commanded. He was a good Puritan soldier and had passed his word—he saw that he must make it good. She said:

"Papa, we mustn't always have gay ones. Nurse says people don't always have gay times. Is that true, papa? She *says* so."

The mamma sighed, and her thoughts drifted to her troubles again. The papa said, gently: "It is true, dear. Troubles have to come; it is a pity, but it is true."

"Oh, then tell a story about them, papa—a dreadful one, so that we'll shiver, and feel just as if it was *us*. Mamma, you snuggle up close, and hold one of Abby's hands, so that if it's too dreadful it'll be easier for us to bear it if we are all snuggled up together, you know. Now you can begin, papa."

"Well, once there were three Colonels—"

"Oh, goody! I know Colonels, just as easy! It's because you are one, and I know the clothes. Go on, papa."

"And in a battle they had committed a breach of discipline."

The large words struck the child's ear pleasantly, and she looked up, full of wonder and interest, and said:

"Is it something good to eat, papa?"

The parents almost smiled, and the father answered:

"No, quite another matter, dear. They exceeded their orders."

"Is *that* someth—"

"No; it's as uneatable as the other. They were ordered to feign an attack on a strong position in a losing fight, in order to draw the enemy about and give the Commonwealth's forces a chance to retreat; but in their enthusiasm they overstepped their orders, for they turned their feint into a fact, and carried the position by storm, and won the day and the battle. The Lord General was very angry at their disobedience, and praised them highly, and ordered them to London to be tried for their lives."

"Is it the great General Cromwell, papa?"

"Yes."

"Oh, I've seen *him*, papa! and when he goes by our house so grand on his big horse, with the soldiers, he looks so—so—well, I don't know just how, only he looks as if he isn't satisfied, and you can see the people are afraid of him; but *I'm* not afraid of him, because he didn't look like that at me."

"Oh, you dear prattler! Well, the Colonels came prisoners to London, and were put upon their honor, and allowed to go and see their families for the last—"

Hark!

They listened. Footsteps again; but again they passed by. The mamma leaned her head upon her husband's shoulder to hide her paleness.

"They arrived this morning."

The child's eyes opened wide.

"Why, papa! is it a *true* story?"

"Yes, dear."

"Oh, how good! Oh, it's ever so much better! Go on, papa. Why, mamma!—dear mamma, are you crying?"

"Never mind, dear—I was thinking of the—of the—poor families."

"But don't cry, mamma: it'll all come out right—you'll see; stories always do. Go on, papa, to where they lived happy ever after; then she won't cry any more. You'll see, mamma. Go on, papa."

"First, they took them to the Tower before they let them go home."

"Oh, I know the Tower! We can see it from here. Go on, papa."

"I am going on as well as I can, in the circumstances. In the Tower the military court tried them for an hour, and found them guilty, and condemned them to be shot."

"Killed, papa?"

"Yes."

"Oh, how naughty! Dear mamma, you are crying again. Don't, mamma; it'll soon come to the good place—you'll see. Hurry, papa, for mamma's sake; you don't go fast enough."

"I know I don't, but I suppose it is because I stop so much to reflect."

"But you mustn't do it, papa; you must go right on."

"Very well, then. The three Colonels—"

"Do you know them, papa?"

"Yes, dear."

"Oh, I wish I did! I love Colonels. Would they let me kiss them, do you think?" The Colonel's voice was a little unsteady when he answered:

"One of them would, my darling! There—kiss me for him."

"There, papa—and these two are for the others. I think they would let me kiss them, papa; for I would say, 'My papa is a Colonel, too, and brave, and he would do what you did; so it can't be wrong, no matter what those people say, and you needn't be the least bit ashamed'; then they would let me—wouldn't they, papa?"

"God knows they would, child!"

"Mamma!—oh, mamma, you mustn't. He's soon coming to the happy place; go on, papa."

"Then, some were sorry—they all were; that military court, I mean; and they went to the Lord General, and said they had done their duty—for it was their duty, you know—and now they begged that two of the Colonels might be spared, and only the other one shot. One would be sufficient for an example for the army, they thought. But the Lord General was very stern, and rebuked them forasmuch as, having done duty and cleared their consciences, they would beguile him to do less, and so smirch his soldierly honor. But they answered that they were asking nothing of him that they would not do themselves if they stood in his great place and held in their hands the noble prerogative of mercy. That stuck him, and he paused and stood thinking, some of the sternness passing out of his face. Presently he bid them wait, and he retired to his closet to seek counsel of God in prayer; and when he came again, he said: 'They shall cast lots. That shall decide it, and two of them shall live.'"

"And did they, papa, did they? And which one is to die?—ah, that poor man!"

"No. They refused."

"They wouldn't do it, papa?"

"No."

"Why?"

"They said that the one that got the fatal bean would be sentencing himself to death by his own voluntary act, and it would be but suicide, call it by what name one might. They said they were Christians, and the Bible forbade men to take their own lives. They sent back that word, and said they were ready—let the court's sentence be carried into effect."

"What does that mean, papa?"

"They—they will all be shot."

Hark!

The wind? No. Tramp—tramp—r-r-r-umble-dumdum, r-r-rumble-dumdum—

"Open—in the Lord General's name!"

"Oh, goody, papa, it's the soldiers!—I love the soldiers! Let *me* let them in, papa, let *me!*"

She jumped down, and scampered to the door and pulled it open, crying joyously: "Come in! come in! Here they are, papa! Grenadiers! I know the Grenadiers!"

The file marched in and straightened up in line at shoulder arms; its officer saluted, the doomed Colonel standing erect and returning the courtesy, the soldier wife standing at his side, white and with features drawn with inward pain, but giving no other sign of her misery, the child gazing on the show with dancing eyes. . . .

One long embrace, of father, mother, and child; then the order, "To the Tower—forward!" Then the Colonel marched forth from the house with military step and bearing, the file following; then the door closed.

"Oh, mamma, didn't it come out beautiful! I *told* you it would; and they're going to the Tower, and he'll *see* them! He—"

"Oh, come to my arms, you poor innocent thing!" . . .

Cromwell's Puritan soldiers march Colonel Mayfair to captivity.

II

The next morning the stricken mother was not able to leave her bed; doctors and nurses were watching by her, and whispering together now and then. Abby could not be allowed in the room, she was told to run and play—mamma was very ill. The child, muffled in winter wraps, went out and played in the street awhile; then it struck her as strange, and also wrong, that her papa should be allowed to stay at the Tower in ignorance at such a time as this. This must be remedied; she would attend to it in person.

An hour later the military court were ordered into the presence of the Lord General. He stood grim and erect, with his knuckles resting upon the table, and indicated that he was ready to listen. The spokesman said: "We have urged them to reconsider; we have implored them; but they persist. They will not cast lots. They are willing to die, but not to defile their religion."

The Protector's face darkened, but he said nothing. He remained a time in thought, then he said: "They shall not all die; the lots shall be cast *for* them." Gratitude shone in the faces of the court. "Send for them. Place them in that room there. Stand them side by side with their faces to the wall and their wrists crossed behind them. Let me have notice when they are there."

When he was alone he sat down, and promptly gave this order to an attendant: "Go, bring me the first little child that passes by."

The man was hardly out at the door before he was back again—leading Abby by the hand, her garments lightly powdered with snow. She went straight to the Head of the State, that formidable personage at the mention of whose name the principalities and powers of the earth trembled, and climbed up in his lap and said:

"I know *you*, sir; you are the Lord General; I have seen you; I have seen you when you went by my house. Everybody was afraid; but *I* wasn't afraid, because you didn't look cross at *me*; you remember, don't you? I had on my red frock—the one with the blue things on it down the front. Don't you remember that?"

A smile softened the austere lines of the Protector's face, and he began to struggle diplomatically with his answer:

"Why, let me see—I—"

"I was standing right by the house—*my* house, you know."

"Well, you dear little thing, I ought to be ashamed, but you know—"

The child interrupted, reproachfully.

"Now, you *don't* remember it. Why, I didn't forget *you*."

"Now I am ashamed, but I will never forget you again, dear; you have my word for it. You will forgive me now, won't you, and be good friends with me, always and forever?"

"Yes, indeed I will, though I don't know how you came to forget it; you must be forgetful; but I am too, sometimes. I can forgive you without any trouble, for I think you *mean* to be good and do right, and I think you are just as kind—but you must snuggle me better, the way papa does—it's cold."

"You shall be snuggled to your heart's content, little new friend of mine, always to be *old* friend of mine hereafter, isn't it? You mind me of my little girl—not little any more, now—but she was dear, and sweet, and daintily made, like you. And she had your charm, little witch—your all-conquering sweet confidence in friend and stranger alike, that wins to willing slavery any upon whom its precious compliment falls. She used to lie in my arms, just as you are doing now; and charm the weariness and care out of my heart and give it peace, just as you are doing now; and we were comrades, and equals, and playfellows together. Ages ago it was, since that pleasant heaven faded away and vanished, and you have brought it back again;—take a burdened man's blessing for it, you tiny creature, who are carrying the weight of England while I rest!"

"Did you love her very, very, *very* much?"

"Ah, you shall by this; she commanded and I obeyed!"

"I think you are lovely! Will you kiss me?"

"Thankfully—and hold it a privilege, too. There—this one is for you; and there—this one is for her. You made it a request; and you could have made it a command, for you are representing her, and what you command I must obey."

The child clapped her hands with delight at the idea of this grand promotion—then her ear caught an approaching sound; the measured tramp of marching men.

"Soldiers! —soldiers, Lord General! Abby wants to see them!"

"You shall, dear; but wait a moment, I have a commission for you."

An officer entered and bowed low, saying, "They are come, your Highness," bowed again, and retired.

The Head of the Nation gave Abby three little disks of sealing-wax; two white, and one of ruddy red—for this one's mission was to deliver death to the Colonel who should get it.

Young Abby Mayfair holding the fateful "death" disk.

"Oh, what a lovely red one! Are they for me?"

"No, dear; they are for others. Lift the corner of that curtain, there, which hides an open door; pass through, and you will see three men standing in a row, with their backs toward you and their hands behind their backs—so—each with one hand open, like a cup. Into each of the open hands drop one of those things, then come back to me."

Abby disappeared behind the curtain, and the Protector was alone. He said, reverently: "Of a surety that good thought came to me in my perplexity from Him who is an ever-present help to them that are in doubt and seek His aid. He knoweth where the choice should fall, and has sent His sinless messenger to do His will. Another would err, but He cannot err. Wonderful are His ways, and wise—blessed be His holy name!"

The small fairy dropped the curtain behind her and stood for a moment examining with alert curiosity the appointments of the chamber of doom, and the rigid figures of the soldiery and the prisoners; then her face lighted merrily, and she said to herself: "Why, one of them is papa! I know his back. He shall have the prettiest one!" She tripped gaily forward and dropped the disks into the open hands, then peeped around under her father's arm and lifted her laughing face and cried out:

"Papa! look what you've got. *I* gave it to you!"

He glanced at the fatal gift, then sunk to his knees and gathered his innocent little executioner to his breast in an agony of love and pity. Soldiers, officers, released prisoners, all stood paralyzed, for a moment, at the vastness of this tragedy, then the pitiful scene smote their hearts, their eyes filled, and they wept unashamed. There was deep and reverent silence during some minutes, then the officer of the guard moved reluctantly forward and touched his prisoner on the shoulder, saying, gently:

"It grieves me, sir, but my duty commands."

"Commands what?" said the child.

"I must take him away. I am so sorry."

"Take him away? Where?"

"To—to—God help me! —to another part of the fortress."

"Indeed you can't. My mamma is sick, and I am going to take him home." She released herself and climbed upon her father's back and put her arms around his neck. "Now Abby's ready, papa—come along."

"My poor child, I can't. I must go with them."

The child jumped to the ground and looked about her, wondering. Then she ran and stood before the officer and stamped her small foot indignantly and cried out:

"I told you my mamma is sick, and you might have listened. Let him go— you *must!*"

"Oh, poor child, would God I could, but indeed I must take him away. Attention, guard! . . . fall in! . . . shoulder arms!" . . .

Abby was gone—like a flash of light.

In a moment she was back, dragging the Lord Protector by the hand. At this formidable apparition all present straightened up, the officers saluting and the soldiers presenting arms.

"Stop them, sir! My mamma is sick and wants my papa, and I *told* them so, but they never listened to me and are taking him away."

The Lord General stood as one dazed.

"Your papa, child? Is he your papa?"

"Why, of course—he was *always* it. Would I give the pretty red one to any other, when I love him so? No!"

A shocked expression rose in the Protector's face, and he said:

"Ah, God help me! through Satan's wiles I have done the cruelest thing that ever man did—and there is no help, no help! What can I do?"

Abby cried out, distressed and impatient: "Why you can make them let him go," and she began to sob. "Tell them to do it! You told me to command, and now the very first time I tell you to do a thing you don't do it!"

A tender light dawned in the rugged old face, and the Lord General laid his hand upon the small tyrant's head and said: "God be thanked for the saving accident of that unthinking promise; and you inspired by Him, for reminding me of my forgotten pledge, O incomparable child! Officer, obey her command—she speaks by my mouth. The prisoner is pardoned; set him free!"

—"The Death Disk" (1901)

———————◆———————

It is difficult to imagine two men more different than Mark Twain and Oliver Cromwell. They did, however, share one compelling trait—their wholehearted devotion to their daughters. Filial love explains why the Lord General obeys Abby in this tale. It may also explain why the tale itself found its way into Mark Twain's writings.

———————◆———————

PART VI.

———•———

Ironic Twists & Clever Deceptions

Mark Twain loved stories with surprising twists, which he often worked into his writings. He wrote this section's first tale, "Lucretia's Man in the Cotton Mask," as a comic antidote to what he called the Civil War's romantic "sickly war stories." It starts off conventionally but toward the end takes a punch-in-the-face turn. The next story, "A Mysterious Gender-Bending Impasse" (originally titled "An Awful, Terrible Medieval Romance"), builds to what readers expect will be a similarly shocking ending, only to provide an entirely different kind of surprise. The next two pieces, excerpted from *Roughing It* (1872), are generously embellished reminiscences of people and events Mark Twain observed during his time in Nevada during the early 1860s. "Repentance & Reform" recalls his experience on an unsuccessful prospecting trip with two older men. He and his companions are all slaves to individual vices that they renounce when it appears they're certain to die after getting lost in a fierce blizzard. Each man couldn't be more sincere in his renunciation, but how will their reforms hold up if they survive the storm? The second excerpt, "A Visitation of God," should appeal to legally minded readers, as it is about an eastern attorney who can't wait to show up Nevada's frontier bumpkins with his legal brilliance. Without giving away what happens, we can say the attorney might have benefitted from a closer study of the case before opening his mouth in court. Finally, Mark Twain never contracted cholera himself, but his life was profoundly influenced by periodic epidemics of the bacterial disease. Indeed, it might be said he would not have been born in upstate Missouri but for an epidemic in St. Louis! He mentions the disease frequently in his writings, but nowhere more enthusiastically than in his posthumously published tale about an undertaker, included here as "Joy Cometh in the Mourning." Its title says all readers need to know about the undertaker's enthusiasm.

28.

"LUCRETIA'S MAN IN
THE COTTON MASK"

————— ⋯■◆■⋯ —————

The unnamed auditor of this old-fashioned "condensed novel" sets it up neatly. It is a simple love story, but one with a mysterious twist. Lucretia Borgia Smith is deeply in love with young Reginald de Whittaker, whom she ardently wants to enlist in the Union Army during the Civil War. Unfortunately, her excessively haughty demeanor causes her to spurn Reginald the night before he goes off to fight, not giving him a chance to tell her he has enlisted. Consequently, Lucretia never learns what becomes of him until she reads that a soldier named "R. D. Whittaker" is badly wounded. Happily, this Lucretia Borgia is not the kind of femme fatale her medieval Italian namesake was reputed to be! Bursting with love for her fallen hero, she rushes off to tend to her man.

————— ⋯■◆■⋯ —————

I am an ardent admirer of those nice, sickly war stories which have lately been so popular, and for the last three months I have been at work upon one of that character, which is now completed. It can be relied upon as true in every particular, inasmuch as the facts it contains were compiled from the official records in the War Department at Washington. It is but just, also, that I should confess that I have drawn largely on *Jomini's Art of War*, the *Message of the President and Accompanying Documents*, and sundry maps and military works, so necessary for reference in building a novel like this. To the accommodating Directors of the Overland Telegraph Company I take pleasure in returning my thanks for tendering me the use of their wires at the customary rates. And finally, to all those kind friends who have, by good deeds or encouraging words, assisted me in my labors upon this story of "Lucretia Smith's Soldier," during the past three months, and whose names are too numerous for special mention, I take this method of tendering my sincerest gratitude.

CHAPTER I

On a balmy May morning in 1861, the little village of Bluemass, in Massachusetts, lay wrapped in the splendor of the newly-risen sun. Reginald de Whittaker, confidential and only clerk in the house of Bushrod & Ferguson, general dry goods and grocery dealers and keepers of the Post-office, rose from his bunk under the counter and shook himself. After yawning and stretching comfortably, he sprinkled the floor and proceeded to sweep it. He had only half finished his task, however, when he sat down on a keg of nails and fell into a reverie. "This is my last day in this shanty," said he. "How it will surprise Lucretia when she hears I am going for a soldier! How proud she will be—the little darling!" He pictured himself in all manner of warlike situations; the hero of a thousand extraordinary adventures; the man of rising fame; the pet of Fortune at last; and beheld himself, finally, returning to his own home, a bronzed and scarred Brigadier-General, to cast his honors and his matured and perfect love at the feet of his Lucretia Borgia Smith.

At this point a thrill of joy and pride suffused his system; but he looked down and saw his broom, and blushed. He came toppling down from the clouds he had been soaring among, and was an obscure clerk again, on a salary of two dollars and a half a week.

CHAPTER II

At 8 o'clock that evening, with a heart palpitating with the proud news he had brought for his beloved, Reginald sat in Mr. Smith's parlor awaiting Lucretia's appearance. The moment she entered, he sprang to meet her, his face lighted by the torch of love that was blazing in his head somewhere and shining through, and ejaculated "Mine own!" as he opened his arms to receive her.

"Sir!" said she, and drew herself up like an offended queen.

Poor Reginald was stricken dumb with astonishment. This chilling demeanor, this angry rebuff where he had expected the old, tender welcome, banished the gladness from his heart as the cheerful brightness is swept from the landscape when a dark cloud drifts athwart the face of the sun. He stood bewildered a moment, with a sense of goneness on him like one who finds himself suddenly overboard upon a midnight sea, and beholds the ship pass into shrouding gloom, while the dreadful conviction falls upon his soul that he has not been missed. He tried to speak, but his pallid lips refused their office. At last he murmured:

"O, Lucretia! what have I done—what is the matter—why this cruel coldness? Don't you love your Reginald any more?"

Her lips curled in bitter scorn, and she replied, in mocking tones:

"Don't I love my Reginald any more? No, I *don't* love my Reginald any more! Go back to your pitiful junk shop and grab your pitiful yard-stick, and stuff cotton in your ears, so that you can't hear your country shout to you to fall in and shoulder arms! Go!" And then, unheeding the new light that flashed from his eyes, she fled from the room and slammed the door behind her.

Only a moment more! Only a single moment more, he thought, and he could have told her how he had already answered the summons and signed his name to the muster-roll, and all would have been well—his lost bride would have come back to his arms with words of praise and thanksgiving upon her lips. He made a step forward, once, to recall her, but he remembered that he was no longer an effeminate dry-goods student, and his warrior soul scorned to sue for quarter. He strode from the place with martial firmness, and never looked behind him.

CHAPTER III

When Lucretia awoke next morning, the faint music of a fife and the roll of a distant drum came floating upon the soft spring breeze, and as she listened the sounds grew more subdued, and finally passed out of hearing. She lay absorbed in thought for many minutes, and then she sighed and said, "Oh, if he were only with that band of fellows, how I could love him!"

Looking downhearted, Reginald de Whittaker (second from left) marches off to war with other young Bluemass recruits.

In the course of the day a neighbor dropped in, and when the conversation turned upon the soldiers, the visitor said:

"Reginald de Whittaker looked rather down-hearted, and didn't shout when he marched along with the other boys this morning. I expect it's owing to you, Miss Loo, though when I met him coming here yesterday evening to tell you he'd enlisted, he thought you'd like it and be proud of—Mercy! what in the nation's the matter with the girl?"

Nothing, only a sudden misery had fallen like a blight upon her heart, and a deadly pallor telegraphed it to her countenance. She rose up without a word and walked with a firm step out of the room, but once within the sacred seclusion of her own chamber, her strong will gave way and she burst into a flood of passionate tears. Bitterly she upbraided herself for her foolish haste of the night before, and her harsh treatment of her lover at the very moment that he had come to anticipate the proudest wish of her heart, and to tell her that he had enrolled himself under the battle-flag and was going forth to fight as *her* soldier. Alas! other maidens would have soldiers in those glorious fields, and be entitled to the sweet pain of feeling a tender solicitude for them, but she would be unrepresented. No soldier in all the vast armies would breathe her name as he breasted the crimson tide of war! She wept again—or, rather, she went on weeping where she left off a moment before. In her bitterness of spirit, she almost cursed the precipitancy that had brought all this sorrow upon her young life. "Drat it!" The words were in her bosom, but she locked them there, and closed her lips against their utterance.

For weeks she nursed her grief in silence, while the roses faded from her cheeks. And through it all she clung to the hope that some day the old love would bloom again in Reginald's heart, and he would write to her; but the long summer days dragged wearily along, and still no letter came. The newspapers teemed with stories of battle and carnage, and eagerly she read them, but always with the same result: the tears welled up and blurred the closing lines—the name she sought was looked for in vain, and the dull aching returned to her sinking heart. Letters to the other girls sometimes contained brief mention of him, and presented always the same picture of him—a morose, unsmiling, desperate man, always in the thickest of the fight, begrimed with powder, and moving calm and unscathed through tempests of shot and shell, as if he bore a charmed life.

But at last, in a long list of maimed and killed, poor Lucretia read these terrible words, and fell fainting to the floor: "R. D. Whittaker, private soldier, desperately wounded!"

CHAPTER IV

On a couch in one of the wards of a hospital at Washington lay a wounded soldier; his head was so profusely bandaged that his features were not visible, but there was no mistaking the happy face of the young girl who sat beside him—it was Lucretia Borgia Smith's. She had hunted him out several weeks before, and since that time she had patiently watched by him and nursed him, coming in the morning as soon as the surgeon had finished dressing his wounds, and never leaving him until relieved at nightfall. A ball had shattered his lower jaw, and he could not utter a syllable; through all her weary vigils she had never once been blessed with a grateful word from his dear lips; yet she stood to her post bravely and without a murmur, feeling that when he did get well again she would hear that which would more than reward her for all her devotion.

At the hour we have chosen for the opening of this chapter, Lucretia was in a tumult of happy excitement; for the surgeon had told her that at last her Whittaker had recovered sufficiently to admit of the removal of the bandages from his head, and she was now waiting with feverish impatience for the doctor to come

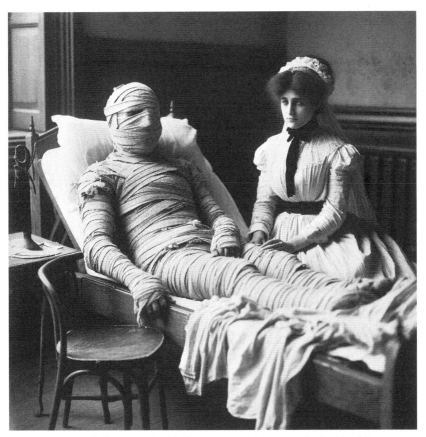

Consumed with love and admiration for her fallen hero, Lucretia gently caresses the bandaged leg of the mute R. D. Whittaker.

and disclose the loved features to her view. At last he came, and Lucretia, with beaming eyes and a fluttering heart, bent over the couch with anxious expectancy. One bandage was removed, then another and another, and lo! the poor wounded face was revealed to the light of day.

"O my own dar—"

What have we here! What is the matter! Alas! it was the face of a stranger!

Poor Lucretia! With one hand covering her upturned eyes, she staggered back with a moan of anguish. Then a spasm of fury distorted her countenance as she brought her fist down with a crash that made the medicine bottles on the table dance again, and exclaimed:

"O confound my cats if I haven't gone and fooled away three mortal weeks here, snuffling and slobbering over the wrong soldier!"

It was a sad, sad truth. The wretched, but innocent and unwitting impostor was R. D., or Richard Dilworthy Whittaker, of Wisconsin, the soldier of dear little Eugenie Le Mulligan, of that State, and utterly unknown to our unhappy Lucretia B. Smith.

Such is life, and the trail of the serpent is over us all. Let us draw the curtain over this melancholy history—for melancholy it must still remain, during a season at least, for the real Reginald de Whittaker has not turned up yet.

—"Lucretia Smith's Soldier" (1864)

———— •—— ————

The central mystery in this sickly story, obviously, is what became of Lucretia's soldier, the real Reginald de Whittaker. We'll never know, but if he was badly wounded, perhaps Eugenie Le Mulligan of Wisconsin has been taking care of him in another hospital. After all, it is possible that his mute face could be completely covered by another cotton mask!

———— •—— ————

29.

"A MYSTERIOUS
GENDER-BENDING IMPASSE"

———————•————

*In this next condensed novel the setting is an early thirteenth-century German princi-
pality—a time and place where concepts of "gender identity" did not yet exist. Gender
did matter, however, and, as in this tale, sometimes mattered a great deal. Throughout his long writing career, Mark Twain enjoyed toying with switched-identity and
cross-dressing themes. His 1885 novel* Huckleberry Finn *contains several examples
of both. The condensed novel following below is one of his earliest and most elaborate
attempts at a cross-dressing story. It has a bizarre story line, so perhaps it's not surprising that he writes himself into a corner!*

———————•————

CHAPTER I: THE SECRET REVEALED

It was night. Stillness reigned in the grand old feudal castle of Klugenstein. The
year 1222 was drawing to a close. Far away up in the tallest of the castle's towers
a single light glimmered. A secret council was being held there. The stern old lord
of Klugenstein sat in a chair of state meditating. Presently he said, with a tender
accent: "My daughter!"

A young man of noble presence, clad from head to heel in knightly mail,
answered: "Speak, father!"

"My daughter, the time is come for the revealing of the mystery that hath
puzzled all your young life. Know, then, that it had its birth in the matters which
I shall now unfold. My brother Ulrich is the great Duke of Brandenburgh. Our
father, on his deathbed, decreed that if no son were born to Ulrich the succession
should pass to my house, provided a son were born to me. And further, in case

no son were born to either, but only daughters, then the succession should pass to Ulrich's daughter if she proved stainless; if she did not, my daughter should succeed if she retained a blameless name. And so I and my old wife here prayed fervently for the good boon of a son, but the prayer was vain. You were born to us. I was in despair. I saw the mighty prize slipping from my grasp—the splendid dream vanishing away! And I had been so hopeful! Five years had Ulrich lived in wedlock, and yet his wife had borne no heir of either sex.

"'But hold,' I said, 'all is not lost.' A saving scheme had shot athwart my brain. You were born at midnight. Only the leech, the nurse, and six waiting-women knew your sex. I hanged them every one before an hour sped. Next morning all the barony went mad with rejoicing over the proclamation that a son was born to Klugenstein—an heir to mighty Brandenburgh! And well the secret has been kept. Your mother's own sister nursed your infancy, and from that time forward we feared nothing.

"When you were ten years old a daughter was born to Ulrich. We grieved, but hoped for good results from measles, or physicians, or other natural enemies of infancy, but were always disappointed. She lived, she throve—Heaven's malison upon her! But it is nothing. We are safe. For, ha! ha! have we not a son? And is not our son the future duke? Our well-beloved Conrad, is it not so?—for woman of eight-and-twenty years as you are, my child, none other name than that hath ever fallen to *you!*

"Now it hath come to pass that age hath laid its hand upon my brother, and he waxes feeble. The cares of state do tax him sore, therefore he wills that you shall come to him and be already duke in act, though not yet in name. Your servitors are ready—you journey forth to-night.

"Now listen well. Remember every word I say. There is a law as old as Germany, that if any woman sit for a single instant in the great ducal chair before she hath been absolutely crowned in presence of the people—She Shall Die! So heed my words. Pretend humility. Pronounce your judgments from the Premier's chair, which stands at the *foot* of the throne. Do this until you are crowned and safe. It is not likely that your sex will ever be discovered, but still it is the part of wisdom to make all things as safe as may be in this treacherous earthly life."

"Oh, my father! is it for this my life hath been a lie? Was it that I might cheat my unoffending cousin of her rights? Spare me, father, spare your child!"

"What, hussy! Is this my reward for the August fortune my brain has wrought for thee? By the bones of my father, this puling sentiment of thine but ill accords with my humor. Betake thee to the duke instantly, and beware how thou meddlest with my purpose!"

Let this suffice of the conversation. It is enough for us to know that the prayers, the entreaties, and the tears of the gentle-natured girl availed nothing.

Neither they nor anything could move the stout old lord of Klugenstein. And so, at last, with a heavy heart, the daughter saw the castle gates close behind her, and found herself riding away in the darkness surrounded by a knightly array of armed vassals and a brave following of servants.

The old baron sat silent for many minutes after his daughter's departure, and then he turned to his sad wife, and said—

"Dame, our matters seem speeding fairly. It is full three months since I sent the shrewd and handsome Count Detzin on his devilish mission to my brother's daughter Constance. If he fail we are not wholly safe, but if he do succeed no power can bar our girl from being duchess, e'en though ill fortune should decree she never should be duke!"

"My heart is full of bodings; yet all may still be well."

"Tush, woman! Leave the owls to croak. To bed with ye, and dream of Brandenburgh and grandeur!"

CHAPTER II: FESTIVITY AND TEARS

Six days after the occurrences related in the above chapter, the brilliant capital of the Duchy of Brandenburgh was resplendent with military pageantry and noisy with the rejoicings of loyal multitudes, for Conrad, the young heir to the crown, was come. The old duke's heart was full of happiness, for Conrad's handsome person and graceful bearing had won his love at once. The great halls of the palace were thronged with nobles, who welcomed Conrad bravely; and so bright and happy did all things seem that he felt his fears and sorrows passing away and giving place to a comforting contentment.

But in a remote apartment of the palace a scene of a different nature was transpiring. By a window stood the duke's only child, the Lady Constance. Her eyes were red and swollen and full of tears. She was alone. Presently she fell to weeping anew, and said aloud:

"The villain Detzin is gone—has fled the dukedom! I could not believe it at first, but, alas! it is too true. And I loved him so. I dared to love him though I knew the duke, my father, would never let me wed him. I loved him—but now I hate him! With all my soul I hate him! Oh, what is to become of me? I am lost, lost, lost! I shall go mad!"

CHAPTER III: THE PLOT THICKENS

A few months drifted by. All men published the praises of the young Conrad's government, and extolled the wisdom of his judgments, the mercifulness of his sentences, and the modesty with which he bore himself in his great office. The old duke soon gave everything into his hands, and sat apart and listened with proud satisfaction while his heir delivered the decrees of the crown from the seat of the Premier. It seemed plain that one so loved and praised and honored of all men as Conrad was could not be otherwise than happy. But, strangely enough, he was not. For he saw with dismay that the Princess Constance had begun to love him! The love of the rest of the world was happy fortune for him, but this was freighted with danger! And he saw, moreover, that the delighted duke had discovered his daughter's passion likewise, and was already dreaming of a marriage. Every day somewhat of the deep sadness that had been in the princess's face faded away; every day hope and animation beamed brighter from her eye; and by and by even vagrant smiles visited the face that had been so troubled.

Conrad was appalled. He bitterly cursed himself for having yielded to the instinct that had made him seek the companionship of one of his own sex when he was new and a stranger in the palace—when he was sorrowful and yearned for a sympathy such as only women can give or feel. He now began to avoid his cousin. But this only made matters worse, for, naturally enough, the more he

Conrad is dismayed to realize that her cousin, the Princess Constance, is beginning to love her, believing her to be a man.

avoided her the more she cast herself in his way. He marveled at this at first, and next it startled him. The girl haunted him; she hunted him; she happened upon him at all times and in all places, in the night as well as in the day. She seemed singularly anxious. There was surely a mystery somewhere.

This could not go on forever. All the world was talking about it. The duke was beginning to look perplexed. Poor Conrad was becoming a very ghost through dread and dire distress. One day as he was emerging from a private anteroom attached to the picture-gallery Constance confronted him, and seizing both his hands in hers, exclaimed—

"Oh, why do you avoid me? What have I done—what have I said, to lose your kind opinion of me—for surely I had it once? Conrad, do not despise me, but pity a tortured heart? I cannot, cannot hold the words unspoken longer, lest they kill me—I LOVE YOU, CONRAD! There, despise me if you must, but they would be uttered!"

Conrad was speechless. Constance hesitated a moment, and then, misinterpreting his silence, a wild gladness flamed in her eyes, and she flung her arms about his neck and said—

"You relent! you relent! You *can* love me—you *will* love me! Oh, say you will, my own, my worshiped Conrad!"

Conrad groaned aloud. A sickly pallor overspread his countenance, and he trembled like an aspen. Presently, in desperation, he thrust the poor girl from him, and cried—

"You know not what you ask! It is forever and ever impossible!" And then he fled like a criminal, and left the princess stupefied with amazement. A minute afterward she was crying and sobbing there, and Conrad was crying and sobbing in his chamber. Both were in despair. Both saw ruin staring them in the face.

By and by Constance rose slowly to her feet and moved away, saying—

"To think that he was despising my love at the very moment that I thought it was melting his cruel heart! I hate him! He spurned me—did this man—he spurned me from him like a dog!"

CHAPTER IV: THE AWFUL REVELATION

Time passed on. A settled sadness rested once more upon the countenance of the good duke's daughter. She and Conrad were seen together no more now. The duke grieved at this. But as the weeks wore away Conrad's color came back to his cheeks, and his old-time vivacity to his eye, and he administered the government with a clear and steadily ripening wisdom.

Presently a strange whisper began to be heard about the palace. It grew louder; it spread farther. The gossips of the city got hold of it. It swept the dukedom. And this is what the whisper said—

"The Lady Constance hath given birth to a child!"

When the lord of Klugenstein heard it he swung his plumed helmet thrice around his head and shouted—

"Long live Duke Conrad!—for lo, his crown is sure from this day forward! Detzin has done his errand well, and the good scoundrel shall be rewarded!"

And he spread the tidings far and wide, and for eight-and-forty hours no soul in all the barony but did dance and sing, carouse and illuminate, to celebrate the great event, and all proud and happy at old Klugenstein's expense.

CHAPTER V: THE FRIGHTFUL CATASTROPHE

The trial was at hand. All the great lords and barons of Brandenburgh were assembled in the Hall of Justice in the ducal palace. No space was left unoccupied where there was room for a spectator to stand or sit. Conrad, clad in purple and ermine, sat in the Premier's chair, and on either side sat the great judges of the realm. The old duke had sternly commanded that the trial of his daughter should proceed without favor, and then had taken to his bed broken-hearted. His days were numbered. Poor Conrad had begged, as for his very life, that he might be spared the misery of sitting in judgment upon his cousin's crime, but it did not avail.

The saddest heart in all that great assemblage was in Conrad's breast.

The gladdest was in his father's, for, unknown to his daughter "Conrad," the old Baron Klugenstein was come, and was among the crowd of nobles triumphant in the swelling fortunes of his house.

After the heralds had made due proclamation and the other preliminaries had followed, the venerable Lord Chief Justice said: "Prisoner, stand forth!"

The unhappy princess rose, and stood unveiled before the vast multitude. The Lord Chief Justice continued—

"Most noble lady, before the great judges of this realm it hath been charged and proven that out of holy wedlock your Grace hath given birth unto a child, and by our ancient law the penalty is death excepting in one sole contingency, whereof his Grace the acting duke, our good Lord Conrad, will advertise you in his solemn sentence now; wherefore give heed."

Conrad stretched forth his reluctant scepter, and in the selfsame moment the womanly heart beneath his robe yearned pityingly toward the doomed prisoner, and the tears came into his eyes. He opened his lips to speak, but the Lord Chief Justice said quickly—

"Not there, your Grace, not there! It is not lawful to pronounce judgment upon any of the ducal line SAVE FROM THE DUCAL THRONE!"

A shudder went to the heart of poor Conrad, and a tremor shook the iron frame of his old father likewise. CONRAD HAD NOT BEEN CROWNED—dared he profane the throne? He hesitated and turned pale with fear. But it must be done. Wondering eyes were already upon him. They would be suspicious eyes if he hesitated longer. He ascended the throne. Presently he stretched forth the scepter again, and said:

"Prisoner, in the name of our sovereign Lord Ulrich, Duke of Brandenburgh, I proceed to the solemn duty that hath devolved upon me. Give heed to my words. By the ancient law of the land, except you produce the partner of your guilt and deliver him up to the executioner you must surely die. Embrace this opportunity—save yourself while yet you may. Name the father of your child!"

A solemn hush fell upon the great court—a silence so profound that men could hear their own hearts beat. Then the princess slowly turned, with eyes gleaming with hate, and, pointing her finger straight at Conrad, said—

"Thou art the man!"

An appalling conviction of his helpless, hopeless peril struck a chill to Conrad's heart like the chill of death itself. What power on earth could save him! To disprove the charge he must reveal that he was a woman, and for an uncrowned woman to sit in the ducal chair was death! At one and the same moment he and his grim old father swooned and fell to the ground.

The remainder of this thrilling and eventful story will not be found in this or any other publication, either now or at any future time.

—"A Medieval Romance" (1870)

Mark Twain was not above playing jokes on his readers, and he certainly does so in this unresolved story. "The truth is," he admitted, "I have got my hero (or heroine) into such a particularly close place that I do not see how I am ever going to get him (or her) out of it again, and therefore I will wash my hands of the whole business, and leave that person to get out the best way that offers—or else stay there. I thought it was going to be easy enough to straighten out that little difficulty, but it looks different now." Readers must, therefore, supply their own ending to this mysterious tale—which may be one of the reasons it was originally published under the title "The Awful, Terrible Medieval Romance." It really is kind of awful!

30.

"REPENTANCE & REFORM"

———————·———————

Three weary prospectors are fleeing a Nevada mountain lodge that is surrounded by flood waters during a storm. Their dreams of mineral riches now faded away, they are struggling to get back to Carson City. Mr. Ballou is a grizzled blacksmith addicted to card-playing who has a knack for remarkable malapropisms. Mr. Ollendorff is a hard-drinking Prussian military veteran whose own special knack is making bad situations worse. The young narrator is an optimistic greenhorn whose greatest vice is smoking. All three men are about to face a life-and-death struggle that moves them to repent their sins.

———————·———————

By the fifth or sixth morning the waters had subsided from the land, but the stream in the old river bed was still high and swift and there was no possibility of crossing it. On the eighth it was still too high for an entirely safe passage, but life in the inn had become next to insupportable by reason of the dirt, drunkenness, fighting, etc., and so we made an effort to get away. In the midst of a heavy snow-storm we embarked in a canoe, taking our saddles aboard and towing our horses after us by their halters. The Prussian, Ollendorff, was in the bow, with a paddle, Ballou paddled in the middle, and I sat in the stern holding the halters. When the horses lost their footing and began to swim, Ollendorff got frightened, for there was great danger that the horses would make our aim uncertain, and it was plain that if we failed to land at a certain spot the current would throw us off and almost surely cast us into the main Carson [River], which was a boiling torrent, now. Such a catastrophe would be death, in all probability, for we would be swept to sea in the "Sink" or overturned and drowned. We warned Ollendorff to keep his wits about him and handle himself carefully, but it was useless; the moment the bow touched the bank, he made a spring and the canoe whirled upside down in ten-foot water. Ollendorff seized some brush and dragged himself ashore, but Ballou and I had to swim for it, encumbered with our overcoats. But we held on to the canoe, and although we were washed down nearly to the Carson, we managed to push the boat ashore and make a safe landing. We were cold and water-soaked, but safe. The horses made a landing, too, but our saddles were gone, of course. We tied the animals in the sage-brush and there they had to stay for twenty-four hours. We baled out the canoe and ferried over some food and blankets for them, but we slept one more night in the inn before making another venture on our journey.

The next morning it was still snowing furiously when we got away with our new stock of saddles and accoutrements. We mounted and started. The snow lay so deep on the ground that there was no sign of a road perceptible, and the snow-fall was so thick that we could not see more than a hundred yards ahead, else we could have guided our course by the mountain ranges. The case looked dubious, but Ollendorff said his instinct was as sensitive as any compass, and that he could "strike a bee-line" for Carson city and never diverge from it. He said that if he were to straggle a single point out of the true line his instinct would assail him like an outraged conscience. Consequently we dropped into his wake happy and content. For half an hour we poked along warily enough, but at the end of that time we came upon a fresh trail, and Ollendorff shouted proudly:

"I knew I was as dead certain as a compass, boys! Here we are, right in somebody's tracks that will hunt the way for us without any trouble. Let's hurry up and join company with the party."

So we put the horses into as much of a trot as the deep snow would allow, and before long it was evident that we were gaining on our predecessors, for the tracks grew more distinct. We hurried along, and at the end of an hour the tracks looked still newer and fresher—but what surprised us was, that the number of travelers in advance of us seemed to steadily increase. We wondered how so large a party came to be traveling at such a time and in such a solitude. Somebody suggested that it must be a company of soldiers from the fort, and so we accepted that solution and jogged along a little faster still, for they could not be far off now. But the tracks still multiplied, and we began to think the platoon of soldiers was miraculously expanding into a regiment—Ballou said they had already increased to five hundred! Presently he stopped his horse and said:

"Boys, these are our own tracks, and we've actually been circussing round and round in a circle for more than two hours, out here in this blind desert! By George this is perfectly hydraulic!"

Then the old man waxed wroth and abusive. He called Ollendorff all manner of hard names—said he never saw such a lurid fool as he was, and ended with the peculiarly venomous opinion that he "did not know as much as a logarythm!"

We certainly had been following our own tracks. Ollendorff and his "mental compass" were in disgrace from that moment. After all our hard travel, here we were on the bank of the stream again, with the inn beyond dimly outlined through the driving snow-fall. While we were considering what to do, the young Swede landed from the canoe and took his pedestrian way Carson-wards, singing his same tiresome song about his "sister and his brother" and "the child in the grave with its mother," and in a short minute faded and disappeared in the white oblivion. He was never heard of again. He no doubt got bewildered and lost, and Fatigue delivered him over to Sleep and Sleep betrayed him to Death. Possibly he followed our treacherous tracks till he became exhausted and dropped.

Presently the Overland stage forded the now fast receding stream and started toward Carson on its first trip since the flood came. We hesitated no longer, now, but took up our march in its wake, and trotted merrily along, for we had good confidence in the driver's bump of locality. But our horses were no match for the fresh stage team. We were soon left out of sight; but it was no matter, for we had the deep ruts the wheels made for a guide. By this time it was three in the afternoon, and consequently it was not very long before night came—and not with a lingering twilight, but with a sudden shutting down like a cellar door, as is its habit in that country. The snow-fall was still as thick as ever, and of course we could not see fifteen steps before us; but all about us the white glare of the snow-bed enabled us to discern the smooth sugar-loaf mounds made by the covered sage-bushes, and just in front of us the two faint grooves which we knew were the steadily filling and slowly disappearing wheel-tracks.

Now those sage-bushes were all about the same height—three or four feet; they stood just about seven feet apart, all over the vast desert; each of them was a mere snow-mound, now; in any direction that you proceeded (the same as in a well laid out orchard) you would find yourself moving down a distinctly defined avenue, with a row of these snow-mounds on either side of it—an avenue the customary width of a road, nice and level in its breadth, and rising at the sides in the most natural way, by reason of the mounds. But we had not thought of this. Then imagine the chilly thrill that shot through us when it finally occurred to us, far in the night, that since the last faint trace of the wheel-tracks had long ago been buried from sight, we might now be wandering down a mere sage-brush avenue, miles away from the road and diverging further and further away from it all the time. Having a cake of ice slipped down one's back is placid comfort compared to it. There was a sudden leap and stir of blood that had been asleep for an hour, and as sudden a rousing of all the drowsing activities in our minds and bodies. We were alive and awake at once—and shaking and quaking with consternation, too. There was an instant halting and dismounting, a bending low and an anxious scanning of the road-bed. Useless, of course; for if a faint depression could not be discerned from an altitude of four or five feet above it, it certainly could not with one's nose nearly against it.

★　★　★

We seemed to be in a road, but that was no proof. We tested this by walking off in various directions—the regular snow-mounds and the regular avenues between them convinced each man that *he* had found the true road, and that the others had found only false ones. Plainly the situation was desperate. We were cold and stiff and the horses were tired. We decided to build a sage-brush fire and camp out till morning. This was wise, because if we were wandering from the right road and the snow-storm continued another day our case would be the next thing to hopeless if we kept on.

All agreed that a camp fire was what would come nearest to saving us, now, and so we set about building it. We could find no matches, and so we tried to

After realizing they have been riding in circles, the three prospectors recognize they have become hopelessly lost in the blizzard.

make shift with the pistols. Not a man in the party had ever tried to do such a thing before, but not a man in the party doubted that it *could* be done, and without any trouble—because every man in the party had read about it in books many a time and had naturally come to believe it, with trusting simplicity, just as he had long ago accepted and believed *that other* common book-fraud about Indians and lost hunters making a fire by rubbing two dry sticks together.

We huddled together on our knees in the deep snow, and the horses put their noses together and bowed their patient heads over us; and while the feathery flakes eddied down and turned us into a group of white statuary, we proceeded with the momentous experiment. We broke twigs from a sage bush and piled them on a little cleared place in the shelter of our bodies. In the course of ten or fifteen minutes all was ready, and then, while conversation ceased and our pulses beat low with anxious suspense, Ollendorff applied his revolver, pulled the trigger and blew the pile clear out of the county! It was the flattest failure that ever was.

This was distressing, but it paled before a greater horror—the horses were gone! I had been appointed to hold the bridles, but in my absorbing anxiety over the pistol experiment I had unconsciously dropped them and the released animals had walked off in the storm. It was useless to try to follow them, for their footfalls could make no sound, and one could pass within two yards of the creatures and never see them. We gave them up without an effort at recovering them, and cursed the lying books that said horses would stay by their masters for protection and companionship in a distressful time like ours.

We were miserable enough, before; we felt still more forlorn, now. Patiently, but with blighted hope, we broke more sticks and piled them, and once more the Prussian shot them into annihilation. Plainly, to light a fire with a pistol was an art requiring practice and experience, and the middle of a desert at midnight in a snow-storm was not a good place or time for the acquiring of the accomplishment. We gave it up and tried the other. Each man took a couple of sticks and fell to chafing them together. At the end of half an hour we were thoroughly chilled, and so were the sticks. We bitterly execrated the Indians, the hunters and the books that had betrayed us with the silly device, and wondered dismally what was next to be done. At this critical moment Mr. Ballou fished out four matches from the rubbish of an overlooked pocket. To have found four gold bars would have seemed poor and cheap good luck compared to this. One cannot think how good a match looks under such circumstances—or how lovable and precious, and sacredly beautiful to the eye. This time we gathered sticks with high hopes; and when Mr. Ballou prepared to light the first match, there was an amount of interest centred upon him that pages of writing could not describe. The match burned hopefully a moment, and then went out. It could not have carried more regret with it if it had been a human life. The next match simply flashed and died. The wind puffed the third one out just as it was on the imminent verge of success. We gathered together closer than ever, and developed a solicitude that was rapt and painful, as Mr. Ballou scratched our last hope on his leg. It lit, burned blue and sickly, and then budded into a robust flame. Shading it with his hands, the old gentleman bent gradually down and every heart went with him—everybody, too, for that matter—and blood and breath stood still. The flame touched the sticks at last, took gradual hold upon them—hesitated—took a stronger hold—hesitated again—held its breath five heart-breaking seconds, then gave a sort of human gasp and went out.

Nobody said a word for several minutes. It was a solemn sort of silence; even the wind put on a stealthy, sinister quiet, and made no more noise than the falling flakes of snow. Finally a sad-voiced conversation began, and it was soon apparent that in each of our hearts lay the conviction that this was our last night with the living. I had so hoped that I was the only one who felt so. When the others calmly acknowledged their conviction, it sounded like the summons itself. Ollendorff said:

"Brothers, let us die together. And let us go without one hard feeling towards each other. Let us forget and forgive bygones. I know that you have felt hard towards me for turning over the canoe, and for knowing too much and leading you round and round in the snow—but I meant well; forgive me. I acknowledge freely that I have had hard feelings against Mr. Ballou for abusing me and calling me a logarythm, which is a thing I do not know what, but no doubt a thing considered disgraceful and unbecoming in America, and it has scarcely been out of my mind and has hurt me a great deal—but let it go; I forgive Mr. Ballou with all my heart, and—"

Poor Ollendorff broke down and the tears came. He was not alone, for I was crying too, and so was Mr. Ballou. Ollendorff got his voice again and forgave me for things I had done and said. Then he got out his bottle of whisky and said that whether he lived or died he would never touch another drop. He said he had given up all hope of life, and although ill-prepared, was ready to submit humbly to his fate; that he wished he could be spared a little longer, not for any selfish reason, but to make a thorough reform in his character, and by devoting himself to helping the poor, nursing the sick, and pleading with the people to guard themselves against the evils of intemperance, make his life a beneficent example to the young, and lay it down at last with the precious reflection that it had not been lived in vain. He ended by saying that his reform should begin at this moment, even here in the presence of death, since no longer time was to be vouchsafed wherein to prosecute it to men's help and benefit—and with that he threw away the bottle of whisky.

Mr. Ballou made remarks of similar purport, and began the reform he could not live to continue, by throwing away the ancient pack of cards that had solaced our captivity during the flood and made it bearable. He said he never gambled, but still was satisfied that the meddling with cards in any way was immoral and injurious, and no man could be wholly pure and blemishless without eschewing them. "And therefore," continued he, "in doing this act I already feel more in sympathy with that spiritual saturnalia necessary to entire and obsolete reform." These rolling syllables touched him as no intelligible eloquence could have done, and the old man sobbed with a mournfulness not unmingled with satisfaction.

My own remarks were of the same tenor as those of my comrades, and I know that the feelings that prompted them were heartfelt and sincere. We were all sincere, and all deeply moved and earnest, for we were in the presence of death and without hope. I threw away my pipe, in doing it felt that at last I was free of a hated vice and one that had ridden me like a tyrant all my days. While I yet talked, the thought of the good I might have done in the world and the still greater good I might *now* do, with these new incentives and higher and better aims to guide me if I could only be spared a few years longer, overcame me and the tears came again. We put our arms about each other's necks and awaited the warning drowsiness that precedes death by freezing.

It came stealing over us presently, and then we bade each other a last farewell. A delicious dreaminess wrought its web about my yielding senses, while the snow-flakes wove a winding sheet about my conquered body. Oblivion came. The battle of life was done.

★　　★　　★

I do not know how long I was in a state of forgetfulness, but it seemed an age. A vague consciousness grew upon me by degrees, and then came a gathering anguish of pain in my limbs and through all my body. I shuddered. The thought flitted through my brain, "this is death—this is the here-after."

Then came a white upheaval at my side, and a voice said, with bitterness:

"Will some gentleman be so good as to kick me behind?"

It was Ballou—at least it was a towzled snow image in a sitting posture, with Ballou's voice.

I rose up, and there in the gray dawn, not fifteen steps from us, were the frame buildings of a stage station, and under a shed stood our still saddled and bridled horses!

An arched snow-drift broke up, now, and Ollendorff emerged from it, and the three of us sat and stared at the horses without speaking a word. We really had nothing to say. We were like the profane man who could not "do the subject justice," the whole situation was so painfully ridiculous and humiliating that words were tame and we did not know where to commence anyhow.

The joy in our hearts at our deliverance was poisoned; well-nigh dissipated, indeed. We presently began to grow pettish by degrees, and sullen; and then, angry at each other, angry at ourselves, angry at everything in general, we moodily dusted the snow from our clothing and in unsociable single file plowed our way to the horses, unsaddled them, and sought shelter in the station.

I have scarcely exaggerated a detail of this curious and absurd adventure. It occurred almost exactly as I have stated it. We actually went into camp in a snow-drift in a desert, at midnight in a storm, forlorn and hopeless, within fifteen steps of a comfortable inn.

For two hours we sat apart in the station and ruminated in disgust. The mystery was gone, now, and it was plain enough why the horses had deserted us. Without a doubt they were under that shed a quarter of a minute after they had left us, and they must have overheard and enjoyed all our confessions and lamentations.

After breakfast we felt better, and the zest of life soon came back. The world looked bright again, and existence was as dear to us as ever. Presently an uneasiness came over me—grew upon me—assailed me without ceasing. Alas, my regeneration was not complete—I wanted to smoke! I resisted with all my strength, but the flesh was weak. I wandered away alone and wrestled with myself an hour. I recalled my promises of reform and preached to myself persuasively, upbraidingly, exhaustively. But it was all vain; I shortly found myself sneaking among the snow-drifts hunting for my pipe. I discovered it after a considerable search, and crept away to hide myself and enjoy it. I remained behind the barn a good while, asking myself how I would feel if my braver, stronger, truer comrades should catch me in my degradation. At last I lit the pipe, and no human being can feel meaner and baser than I did then. I was ashamed of being in my own pitiful company. Still dreading discovery, I felt that perhaps the further side of the barn would be somewhat safer, and so I turned the corner. As I turned the one corner, smoking, Ollendorff turned the other with his bottle to his lips, and between us sat unconscious Ballou deep in a game of "solitaire" with the old greasy cards!

Absurdity could go no farther. We shook hands and agreed to say no more about "reform" and "examples to the rising generation." . . .

—*Roughing It* (1872), chapters 31-33

As dawn breaks and finds the recently repentant sinners still alive, all three men immediately return to their recently renounced vices.

———————— ••• • ◆ •• ————————

It is easy to see where Mark Twain got his inspiration for this tale. In his autobiography he wrote, "My repentances were very real, very earnest; and after each tragedy they happened every night for a long time. But as a rule they could not stand the daylight. They faded out and shredded away and disappeared in the glad splendor of the sun. They were the creatures of fear and darkness, and they could not live out of their own place."

———————— ••• • ◆ •• ————————

31.

"A VISITATION OF GOD"

———————•———————

The period is the early 1860s, when the newly formed Nevada Territory is greeting its freshly appointed attorney general, a man named General Buncombe. Buncombe has come out west with a poor opinion of frontier settlers and is anxious to impress them with his brilliance as a lawyer. He soon gets his big chance, but he fails to factor in how resentful westerners are of eastern pomposity and how clever they can be in Mark Twain's writings!

———————•———————

The mountains are very high and steep about Carson, Eagle and Washoe Valleys—very high and very steep, and so when the snow gets to melting off fast in the Spring and the warm surface-earth begins to moisten and soften, the disastrous land-slides commence. The reader cannot know what a land-slide is, unless he has lived in that country and seen the whole side of a mountain taken off some fine morning and deposited down in the valley, leaving a vast, treeless, unsightly scar upon the mountain's front to keep the circumstance fresh in his memory all the years that he may go on living within seventy miles of that place.

General Buncombe was shipped out to Nevada in the invoice of Territorial officers, to be United States Attorney. He considered himself a lawyer of parts, and he very much wanted an opportunity to manifest it—partly for the pure gratification of it and partly because his salary was Territorially meagre (which is a strong expression). Now the older citizens of a new territory look down upon the rest of the world with a calm, benevolent compassion, as long as it keeps out of the way—when it gets in the way they snub it. Sometimes this latter takes the shape of a practical joke.

When heavy snowfalls get to melting and warm earth begins to soften in the high mountains of western Nevada, disastrous land-slides often occur.

One morning Dick Hyde rode furiously up to General Buncombe's door in Carson city and rushed into his presence without stopping to tie his horse. He seemed much excited. He told the General that he wanted him to conduct a suit for him and would pay him five hundred dollars if he achieved a victory. And then, with violent gestures and a world of profanity, he poured out his griefs. He said it was pretty well known that for some years he had been farming (or ranching as the more customary term is) in Washoe District, and making a successful thing of it, and furthermore it was known that his ranch was situated just in the edge of the valley, and that Tom Morgan owned a ranch immediately above it on the mountain side. And now the trouble was, that one of those hated and dreaded land-slides had come and slid Morgan's ranch, fences, cabins, cattle, barns and everything down on top of *his* ranch and exactly covered up every single vestige of his property, to a depth of about thirty-eight feet. Morgan was in possession and refused to vacate the premises—said he was occupying his own cabin and not interfering with anybody else's—and said the cabin was standing on the same dirt and same ranch it had always stood on, and he would like to see anybody make him vacate.

"And when I reminded him," said Hyde, weeping, "that it was on top of my ranch and that he was trespassing, he had the infernal meanness to ask me why didn't I *stay* on my ranch and hold possession when I see him a-coming! Why didn't I *stay* on it, the blathering lunatic—by George, when I heard that racket and looked up that hill it was just like the whole world was a-ripping and a-tearing down that mountain side—splinters, and cord-wood, thunder and lightning, hail and snow, odds and ends of hay stacks, and awful clouds of dust!—trees going end over end in the air, rocks as big as a house jumping 'bout a thousand feet high and busting into ten million pieces, cattle turned inside out and a-coming head on with their tails hanging out between their teeth!—and in the midst of all that wrack and destruction sot that cussed Morgan on his gate-post, a-wondering why I didn't *stay and hold possession!* Laws bless me, I just took one glimpse, General, and lit out'n the county in three jumps exactly.

"But what grinds me is that that Morgan hangs on there and won't move off'n that ranch—says it's his'n and he's going to keep it—likes it better'n he did when it was higher up the hill. Mad! Well, I've been so mad for two days I couldn't find my way to town—been wandering around in the brush in a starving condition—got anything here to drink, General? But I'm here now, and I'm a-going to law. You hear *me!*"

Never in all the world, perhaps, were a man's feelings so outraged as were the General's. He said he had never heard of such high-handed conduct in all his life as this Morgan's. And he said there was no use in going to law—Morgan had no shadow of a right to remain where he was—nobody in the wide world would uphold him in it, and no lawyer would take his case and no judge would listen to it. Hyde said that right there was where he was mistaken—everybody in town sustained Morgan; Hal Brayton, a very smart lawyer, had taken his case; the courts being in vacation, it was to be tried before a referee, and ex-Governor [Isaac] Roop had already been appointed to that office and would open his court in a large public hall near the hotel at two that afternoon

The General was amazed. He said he had suspected before that the people of that Territory were fools, and now he knew it. But he said rest easy, rest easy and collect the witnesses, for the victory was just as certain as if the conflict were already over. Hyde wiped away his tears and left.

At two in the afternoon referee Roop's Court opened, and Roop appeared throned among his sheriffs, the witnesses, and spectators, and wearing upon his face a solemnity so awe-inspiring that some of his fellow-conspirators had misgivings that maybe he had not comprehended, after all, that this was merely a joke. An unearthly stillness prevailed, for at the slightest noise the judge uttered sternly the command:

"Order in the Court!"

And the sheriffs promptly echoed it. Presently the General elbowed his way through the crowd of spectators, with his arms full of law-books, and on his ears fell an order from the judge which was the first respectful recognition of his high official dignity that had ever saluted them, and it trickled pleasantly through his whole system:

"Way for the United States Attorney!"

The witnesses were called—legislators, high government officers, ranchmen, miners, Indians, [Chinese], negroes. Three fourths of them were called by the defendant Morgan, but no matter, their testimony invariably went in favor of the plaintiff Hyde. Each new witness only added new testimony to the absurdity of a man's claiming to own another man's property because his farm had slid down on top of it. Then the Morgan lawyers made their speeches, and seemed to make singularly weak ones—they did really nothing to help the Morgan cause. And now the General, with exultation in his face, got up and made an impassioned effort; he pounded the table, he banged the law-books, he shouted, and roared, and howled, he quoted from everything and everybody, poetry, sarcasm, statistics, history, pathos, bathos, blasphemy, and wound up with a grand war-whoop for free speech, freedom of the press, free schools, the Glorious Bird of America and the principles of eternal justice! [Applause.]

When the General sat down, he did it with the conviction that if there was anything in good strong testimony, a great speech and believing and admiring countenances all around, Mr. Morgan's case was killed. Ex-Governor Roop leant his head upon his hand for some minutes, thinking, and the still audience waited for his decision. Then he got up and stood erect, with bended head, and thought again. Then he walked the floor with long, deliberate strides, his chin in his hand, and still the audience waited. At last he returned to his throne, seated himself, and began, impressively:

"Gentlemen, I feel the great responsibility that rests upon me this day. This is no ordinary case. On the contrary it is plain that it is the most solemn and awful that ever man was called upon to decide. Gentlemen, I have listened attentively to the evidence, and have perceived that the weight of it, the overwhelming weight of it, is in favor of the plaintiff Hyde. I have listened also to the remarks of counsel, with high interest—and especially will I commend the masterly and irrefutable logic of the distinguished gentleman who represents the plaintiff. But gentlemen, let us beware how we allow mere human testimony, human ingenuity in argument and human ideas of equity, to influence us at a moment so

Finally having his opportunity in court, General Buncombe pounds the table, shouts, roars, and quotes from every-thing and everybody.

solemn as this. Gentlemen, it ill becomes us, worms as we are, to meddle with the decrees of Heaven. It is plain to me that Heaven, in its inscrutable wisdom, has seen fit to move this defendant's ranch for a purpose. We are but creatures, and we must submit. If Heaven has chosen to favor the defendant Morgan in this marked and wonderful manner; and if Heaven, dissatisfied with the position of the Morgan ranch upon the mountain side, has chosen to remove it to a position more eligible and more advantageous for its owner, it ill becomes us, insects as we are, to question the legality of the act or inquire into the reasons that prompted it. No—Heaven created the ranches and it is Heaven's prerogative to rearrange them, to experiment with them, to shift them around at its pleasure. It is for us to submit, without repining. I warn you that this thing which has happened is a thing with which the sacrilegious hands and brains and tongues of men must not meddle. Gentlemen, it is the verdict of this court that the plaintiff,

Richard Hyde, has been deprived of his ranch by the visitation of God! And from this decision there is no appeal."

Buncombe seized his cargo of law-books and plunged out of the court-room frantic with indignation. He pronounced Roop to be a miraculous fool, an inspired idiot. In all good faith he returned at night and remonstrated with Roop upon his extravagant decision, and implored him to walk the floor and think for half an hour, and see if he could not figure out some sort of modification of the verdict. Roop yielded at last and got up to walk. He walked two hours and a half, and at last his face lit up happily and he told Buncombe it had occurred to him that the ranch underneath the new Morgan ranch still belonged to Hyde, that his title to the ground was just as good as it had ever been, and therefore he was of opinion that Hyde had a right to dig it out from under there and—

The General never waited to hear the end of it. He was always an impatient and irascible man, that way. At the end of two months the fact that he had been played upon with a joke had managed to bore itself, like another Hoosac Tunnel, through the solid adamant of his understanding.

—*Roughing It* (1872), chapter 34

The general may have fared better had he personally inspected the landslide before taking on Hyde's case. Unfortunately for him, he didn't have time to do that, but it may not have mattered. Mark Twain had a prejudice against lawyers, so any case Buncombe could have fought, including a landslide case, would have been a steeply uphill battle.

32.

"JOY COMETH IN THE MOURNING"

---·—•—·---

In Pudd'nhead Wilson's Calendar, Mark Twain offers this advice: "Let us endeavor so to live that when we come to die even the undertaker will be sorry." Good advice that, but that is not what this tale suggests. Its lesson, if any, is joyfully to accept whatever good fortune falls one's way and not to examine too closely whence it comes.

---·—•—·---

W e did not drop suddenly upon the subject, but wandered into it in a natural way—I and my pleasant new acquaintance. He said it "was about this way"—and began:

Toward nightfall on 14th January, 18—, I trudged into the poor little village of Hydesburg. I had walked far, that day; at least it seemed far for a half-starved boy of fifteen to have come. I had lain in the barn the night before, and been discovered and roughly driven away early in the morning. I had begged for food and shelter at three farm houses during the day, but had been refused. At the last place the children set the dogs on me and I was glad to get away with some loss of flesh and a part of my rags. I was very hungry, now, and very tired. The wounds made by the dogs were stiff and painful, but I had been an outcast for a month and had fared harshly all the time. I was hopeless, now, and afraid to supplicate at any door.

The darkness drew on, the outlines of the village houses grew vague, the lights began to twinkle in the windows. The wind swept the street in furious gust, driving a storm of snow and sleet before it. I stopped in front of a small house and leaned on the low fence, for there was a pleasant picture, for an outcast, visible through one of the windows. It was a family at supper. There was a roaring wood fire burning on the hearth; there was a cat curled up in a chair, asleep; there were some books on a what-not, some pictures on the wall; but mainly there with the smoking supper; a benevolent looking man of middle-age sat at the foot of the table; a motherly dame at its head, a little boy and girl at one side. It was like looking into paradise.

I never once thought of knocking at that door. I had had enough of cuffs and curses. I no longer believed that there were men in the world who would pity me, or any other miserable creature.

It was very dark, now. A man who was running by behind an umbrella, struck against me with such a shock that both of us fell. He cursed me roundly as he gathered himself up, and gave me a good-bye kick as he left. It caught me on one of my dog-bites and made me cry out with the pain. Then he was lost in the darkness in the driving storm. But a sweet, girlish voice said, "Poor thing, are you hurt?" And I saw a dim figure bending over me. I said—

"I only stopped just a minute. I was not meaning any harm, please. I'm going away, now."

The girl said—

"Going away? Where? Do you live in the village?"

"No, please."

"Then where are you going, such a night as this?"

"I don't know."

"What! Haven't you any place to stay?"

"No."

"Nor any friends?"

"No."

"Yes, you have!"

"Where?"

"There—in the house—my father's house. We are your friends. Come."

She helped me up, and tried to lead me toward the door, whereat I was very glad for a moment, but then straightway, afraid again. So I said—

"Please let me go away, and I will not come anymore. Honest, I will not."

But it was no use. The girl dragged me into the house, I expecting nothing else but to be hustled out again the next moment. But it was not so. The whole family gathered about me, took me to the fire, and more warmed me with their pitying wounds words than the fire did.

I carried a full stomach to a good bed that night. And I worshipped those people, knowing no gods but these, nor desiring any other.

II

When two weeks had gone by, from that time, my former life had dimmed to a dream. It seemed to me as if I had always been a part of this dear good loving family. I called Mr. Cadaver father and his wife mother. Jimmy and Mary and Grace were brother and sisters to me. Grace was the one that saved me. She was eighteen years old, and so fair and shapely, and so sweet and so unapproachably beautiful that it was heaven to me to look at her face and listen to her voice.

Business was prosperous, and we were all as blithe and happy as birds. I became useful in many ways and felt the gratification of knowing that I was earning the bread I ate. I learned to assist Grace in decorating the insides of the coffins with pleated cambrics or costlier stuffs, according to the requirements of the customers. We talked and sang by the hour while we made crosses of flowers or wreathed immortelles. Sometimes, as she wrought with her nimble needle upon a shroud, she would tell me the simple history of the person who was to wear it; for it was but a little village, and she knew all about everybody. All day long the music of her father's plane was heard in the back shop, and we lived in an atmosphere of deep peace and contentment. I learned to arrange the coffins in the front shop so as to get the best effects, gracing the neat rows with festoons of crape depending from immortelles fastened against the walls, with here and there a soft white shroud and in the intervals finely polished coffin plates that reflected the sunlight almost like mirrors. I took care of the horse, and was often allowed to drive the hearse. There was no rival in our business in the village. We had it all.

But by and by there came an evil day. I will tell about this. Gracie had a sweetheart whom she dearly loved and had promised to marry. This was a most excellent young man named Joseph Parker, who had commenced life in the humblest circumstances, but had risen by honest endeavor till he was now sexton to the village church, and grave digger. The graveyard was owned by several citizens, who presently wished to sell it. It was pleasantly located on a hill side and very desirable. Young Parker conceived the idea of buying it. It was a great chance, but the price was a vast one, being six hundred dollars, and he had no money. Mr. Cadaver loved Joseph, and he could not bear to see this opportunity lost; he looked from Grace's beseeching eyes to Joseph's and his heart was touched. He said—

"You shall have the graveyard, my children; take yourselves off, now, and be happy."

You should have seen Gracie throw her arms around his neck, and pat his cheek and cry for joy.

So Mr. Cadaver mortgaged his house for the six hundred dollars, borrowed the money of old Marlow the skinflint, and the beautiful graveyard was Joseph's. That was a happy night. We all sat around the fire, Joseph with Gracie's little hand in his, and all the talk was of how good and sweet was life. Joseph said—

"If we have a good season, I can pay off the debt in six months."

"That will be a pleasant thing," said the old man; "and I think the signs are in favor of a good season. It is a very changeable winter, with much wet and much cold."

"Yes," said Mrs. Cadaver, "it is just such a winter as the one before Jimmy was born. There was ever so much croup and pneumonia in the spring."

"I remember it," said Gracie. "Here was ever so much sickness, and very few got well. I remember father's saying he had never seen business so brisk."

Mr. Cadaver drew a long sigh. He said:

"Those were great days—great days. They don't often come. However, it is not for us to complain; that would be ungrateful indeed."

Grace smiled sweetly and said—

"Dear old father, to hear him talk, one would think he was afraid somebody might think him capable of being ungrateful. Why father, adversity only brings out your gentleness and patience. Do you remember the time that not one person died in this village during twenty-eight days? Were you downcast? Did you show any bitterness? No—not one angry word escaped your lips. You hardly even betrayed annoyance."

Mr. Cadaver kissed her cheek lovingly and patted her on the head. He said—

"There—there's your punishment, little flatterer!"

He beamed on her with fatherly pride, and there was moisture in his eyes. Gracie turned her pretty mouth toward Joseph, and said—

"How can you see me so cruelly punished and not protect me?"

"Because you deserved it, poor child—you deserved double what you got—and there 'tis!"

He kissed the rosy lips, and got a pretty little love-box on his ear for his pains. Everybody laughed, and we all fell to joking and chaffing and had such a good time. By and by Mr. Cadaver took down the old family Bible, put on his spectacles and reverently read a chapter, and then prayed. We always had family worship, morning and evening.

But as I said before, trouble was to come. Business began to grow dull while the winter was still upon us. It steadily slackened. Presently it had so dwindled that there was no trade but in chronic consumptions, and it is hardly worth while to mention that there is never much doing in cases of that sort in little country villages. The joy in the faces of the family gradually gave way to anxious looks, and we had but little pleasant talk, evenings. Things only grew worse as time went on. The spring opened gloomily. We had day after day of brilliant sunshine, clamor of warbling birds, balmy, healing, vivifying atmosphere—there was everything to make us dismal, heartsick, hopeless. The spring dragged its disastrous length along and left a memorable record behind it—three months and a half with scarcely a demise.

We got ready for the summer trade. There came news that the cholera had appeared in the seaports, and for the first time in months we had an old-time evening of innocent gaiety in place of bowed heads and heavy sighs. The disease spread from village to village, till it reached within five miles of us—then it split apart and wandered far away on either side, leaving our town untouched!

Mr. Cadaver frets as the town's declining death rate slackens his mortuary trade.

"It is very hard," said Mr. Cadaver, and we saw the tears trickle through his fingers as he sat with his hands clasped over his face, rocking to and fro and softly moaning.

Once it had been our happiness on peaceful Sabbath afternoons, to stroll to Joseph's graveyard and count the new mounds and talk of the prospects. But this had long ceased. There were no new mounds any more; the turf had grown old upon all; there was no longer anything about the graveyard that could cheer our hearts, but much to sadden them.

There came a time, at last, when we all realized that imminent disaster was hovering over us. Nothing had been paid on the graveyard and the six hundred dollars would soon fall due. Old Marlow got to haunting the place with his evil eye. He would intrude in the most unexpected way and remind Mr. Cadaver to get ready to move out of the house if the money was not forthcoming on the appointed day.

How the days flew! Once Mr. Cadaver appealed to him for a little time.

"Time!" cried old Marlow. "What on!"

"Business, Mr. Marlow."

"Business! Tush! You have none. What are your assets? Come—show them up, man."

Mr. Cadaver showed him his list of coffins and other stock, and also a list of neighbors who were very low. These latter Mr. Marlow derided—laughed over the list brutally. Said he—

"You call these people assets? There ain't one in the lot but will outlast this generation!"

"But sir, the doctor said this morning that old Mrs. Hale and Mr. Samson—"

"Bother what the doctor said! Mrs. Hale has been dying for ten years, and old Samson for fifteen. Call such stock as that assets! The idea!"

"I have heard that George Simpson had a very bad night last night, and there is every hope—I mean every prospect that he—"

"Drop your hopes of George Simpson, my friend. He sat up in bed this morning and ate a fricasseed chicken."

Mr. Cadaver murmured with a sigh, "This is indeed an unexpected blow." He tried once more to throw a favorable aspect upon some of his assets, but Marlow scouted every name and said there was neither man, woman nor child in the list but would get well. He finally said:

"Hark ye! You have neglected your business till ruin stares you in the face and it serves you right."

"I, sir? I cannot bury people if they will not die. Please have pity—think of my poor family—do not be hard with me, Mr. Marlow. I am sure my assets are lower than you think them to be, and if you would only give me a little time to realize on them—"

"Not another word!" cried Marlow. "You will pay the last cent day after tomorrow or out of this house you go!"

He banged the door and went.

III

That next day was a day never to be forgotten. All day long the family sat grouped together, saying little, now and then looking into each other's stony eyes, now and then clasping each other in a long embrace, and many were the smothered sobs that were heard, many the tears that fell. I could not bear this sight long at a time. I fitted restlessly from house to house where we had hopes, but gained no comfort. One client was "better to-day;" another "about the same;" another had a "stronger pulse;" another had had "an easier night than usual." Always these dismal refrains. Whenever I entered our stricken home, I had to meet the mute inquiry of those pathetic eyes, but I never had to speak—my own looks conveyed my heavy tidings and the hopeless heads were bowed once more.

I was up all night, wandering about the village. The fatal day came, the sun rose and still I wandered from house to house—but not to inquire—had no heart to do that any longer. I only took friends of mine to these houses, and told them to wait, and if they got any news, to bring it to me with all speed.

Two hours later there was a scene in our home. Old Marlow was there, gloating over his victims. He paced the floor banging upon it with his stick and talking like this:

"Come, the sooner you clear out of this, the better you'll suit me. A pack of paupers, that is what you are! Fine assets, truly! Coffins rotting away without sale, a graveyard that's become a grazing ground, a gang of convalescents that the lightning couldn't make marketable!"

So he raved on, enjoying himself. One after another my friends came softly to the door, whispered their tidings to me and glided away. I let the old man storm on. At last my poor old Cadaver rose feebly up, gathered his weeping wife to his side, and said—

"Go, my little children, and you, my poor daughter and my poor Joseph, go forth from the old home; it has no shelter, more, for our breaking hearts. Out into the bleak world we will go together, and together will we starve and die."

And so, with bended heads and streaming eyes, they moved slow and sadly toward the door. Marlow waved his hand and said—

"Farewell, a long farewell! My house is well rid—"

"Hold!" I shouted. "Stay where you are!"

Everybody stared with inquiring astonishment. Old Marlow grew red with rage. "What means this?" he cried.

"It means this!" said I. "Samson is no more! old Mrs. Hale is at peace! Philip Martin has fallen with apoplexy! William Thompson is drowned! George Simpson has had a relapse and the rattle is in his throat! And hark ye, wretch, the cholera is at our very doors and in its most malignant form!"

With a wild joy Mr. Cadaver threw his arms around my neck and murmured—

"O, precious, precious tidings!—blest be the tongue that has uttered them!"

Joseph and Gracie embraced with tears of gratitude, and then astounded me by embracing me, too. In an instant misery was gone and tumultuous happiness had taken its place. I turned upon old Marlow and said—

"There, sir, is the door, be gone! You will be paid, never fear. And if you should want to borrow any money," I said, with bitter sarcasm, "do not hesitate to say so, for we can procure all we want, with our present business prospects."

He went away raging, and we went gaily to work dusting stock and getting ready for the most lucrative day's work our little shop had ever known.

Little remains to be told. Our prosperity moved straight along without a halt. Everything seemed to conspire to help us. No village in all the region was so ravaged by the pestilence as was ours, the doctors were the first to go, and those

Radiating new confidence, Mr. Cadaver contemplates how the cholera epidemic will restore prosperity to his mortuary and cemetery businesses.

who supplied their places passed through our hands and Joseph's without halt or delay. The graveyard grew in grace and beauty day by day till there was not a grass-patch visible in it, not a level spot to trouble the eye. All in good time Joseph and Gracie were married, and there was a great and costly wedding. As if to make everything complete and leave nothing to be desired, the commerce of the wedding day paid the entire expense of the occasion, and Mr. Marlow himself headed the procession in a sixty-dollar casket.

—"The Undertaker's Tale" (n.d.)

"Undertaking," a New Orleans man of that profession once told Mark Twain, is "the dead-surest business in Christendom, and the nobbiest." Nobby the business may be, but as this tale shows, it isn't necessarily dead-sure.

APPENDIX

———————•———————

Given the present volume's emphasis on macabre themes, it seems appropriate to conclude the book by summing up Mark Twain's life with this appreciative brief biography written by Z. Pfennig, the obituary editor of the Cork Center Gazette.

———————•———————

OBITUARY

Mark Twain, AT LAST, is dead. These simple words will be read with but one feeling by all our subscribers from Baffin's Bay to the Gulf of Mexico, and from the Atlantic to the Pacific. In comparison with this announcement the views of Mr. Mitchell on the ethics of the coal strike sink into insignificance. To this traveler who has just passed over the Divide into the Great Beyond the question of coal supply is no longer open. He is apparently at rest. "After life's fitful fever he sleeps well," a privilege memory denied him for many years. We bespeak for him on the other side a tolerance not accorded him here.

The subject of this notice was born near a small hamlet on the trail to Thunder Mountain in the State of Idaho, soon after the appearance of the great comet which preceded the war of 1812. It was commonly predicted at the time that the comet would be followed by disaster. Mr. Twain's boyhood days were passed upon a raft in the Mississippi River where he acquired a liberal education and a knowledge of navigation. While engaged in this pursuit he was a constant reader of the editorials in this paper and was inspired by them to adopt literature as a profession. Many of his best efforts have appeared anonymously in these columns, and will be soon offered in book form as premiums to new subscribers who pay in advance our regular price of two dollars if paid in money, or three dollars if paid in produce.

In addition to his contributions to this paper Mr. Twain found time to write several books, notably, "Roughing it," "Paradise Lost," "Innocents Abroad," "The Vicar of Wakefield," "Huckleberry Finn," "Barriers Burned Away," and a poem entitled "Beautiful Snow." From a cipher recently discovered in the latter work it is suspected that Mr. Twain wrote the Mormon Bible and a work on games commonly accredited to one Hoyle. But undoubtedly the best and most finished production of this author was his Scrap Book. We have sat for hours with our eye glued to the pages of that book and wondered at the hold its columns had upon us.

As a writer Mark Twain was a success. And yet he knew nothing of the Scotch dialect, and could not report a base ball game or a prize fight in the ordinary style of a sporting editor. He was remarkably sincere in all his statements and painfully accurate in all his descriptions. Naturally serious and inclined to melancholy his writings partake of these characteristics to a marked degree. Some have classed him with Baxter, others with Bunyan, and still others with Watts. We class him with Jeremiah. Upon the whole we almost regret his death.

— Letter from Edwin Baylies to Mark Twain, November 25, 1902 (Mark Twain Papers, the Bancroft Library, University of California at Berkeley)

This obituary was composed in November 1902—almost seven and one-half years before Mark Twain died. A distinguished Johnstown, New York, attorney named Edwin Baylies wrote it in response to an open letter Mark Twain had published in Harper's Weekly *under the title "Amended Obituaries." Mark Twain's letter appealed to newspapers and magazines to publish whatever standing obituaries of him they had on file, so he could check them for accuracy. "For the best Obituary—one suitable for me to read in public, and calculated to inspire regret," he offered as a prize a self-portrait he had drawn. Widely reprinted, his letter elicited many obituary notices. The winner of his prize is not known, but Baylies's entry, which he signed "Z. Pfennig," may be the best.*

In the interest of full disclosure, it should be explained that the Cork Center Gazette *did not exist. A Cork Creek runs through Johnstown, but most of the statements in the obituary are as bogus as the name "Z. Pfennig." The important thing, however, is that the obituary succeeds in inspiring regret—and we know that Mark Twain liked it!*

The self-portrait Mark Twain offered as a prize (Harper's Weekly, November 15, 1902).

ACKNOWLEDGMENTS

My first thanks must go to my aptly named Mark Twain buddy, Mark Dawidziak. His brilliant book *Everything I Need to Know I Learned in the Twilight Zone* gave me the idea of assembling a collection of Mark Twain's writings that might work as *Twilight Zone* episodes. My resultant book has taken a different course, obviously, but Mark has continued to help with his always wise advice and unflagging encouragement. Another of my stalwart Mark Twain pals, Barbara Schmidt, the administrator of the twainquotes.com website, has stood by constantly with helpful suggestions. I must not forget to thank my agent, Charlotte Gusay, for her enthusiastic help and encouragement, and Rowman & Littlefield's editorial director, Rick Rinehart, for his help and encouragement. Finally, I must acknowledge another of my Mark Twain friends, Linda Morris. She does not yet know about this book, but after I wrote that Mark Twain "writes himself into a corner" in my introduction to "A Mysterious Gender-Bending Impasse," I discovered that Linda had said *exactly* the same thing in her book *Gender Play in Mark Twain: Cross-Dressing and Transgression* (2007; page 27). Is this an example of deliberate or unconscious plagiarism? I'm not sure which it is, but I want Linda to know that when I steal ideas from her, I usually try to be less obvious about it.

ABOUT THE EDITOR

R. Kent Rasmussen holds a doctorate in history from UCLA and is a retired reference-book editor. He has long been recognized as a leading world authority on Mark Twain, about whom he has published thirteen books. Those volumes include such now-standard reference works as *Mark Twain A to Z*; its expanded revision, *Critical Companion to Mark Twain*; and *The Quotable Mark Twain*. Mark Twain books that he has edited include four volumes of critical essays; several collections of Mark Twain's own writings, including *Autobiographical Writings* (Penguin Classics edition); and *Mark Twain for Dog Lovers*, a Lyons Press publication. He lives in Thousand Oaks, California.